LIFEBLOOD

Also by N. J. Cooper

No Escape

LIFEBLOOD

N J Cooper

SIMON &
SCHUSTER

London · New York · Sydney · Toronto

A CBS COMPANY

First published in Great Britain by Simon & Schuster UK Ltd, 2010
A CBS Company

1 3 5 7 9 10 8 6 4 2

Simon & Schuster UK Ltd
1st Floor
222 Gray's Inn Road
London WC1X 8HB

www.simonandschuster.co.uk

Simon & Schuster Australia
Sydney

A CIP catalogue record for this book is available from the British Library

ISBN 978-1-84737-415-8

Typeset by Hewer Text UK Ltd, Edinburgh
Printed and bound in the UK by
CPI Mackays, Chatham ME5 8TD

For
Octavia, Robin, Phoebe and William Chave

Acknowledgments

As usual, I've been lucky enough to have great help, advice and consolation from a whole army of friends and colleagues. I'd like to thank them all, in particular, Elizabeth Atkinson, Suzanne Baboneau, Mary Carter, Stephanie Glencross, Jane Gregory, Isabelle Grey, Simon and Joanna Jeans, Professor Henry Mayr-Harting, Ayo Onatade, Florence Partridge, David Roberts, James Turner QC; Sheila Turner and Libby Yevtushenko.

Lifeblood 1. the blood, considered as vital to sustain life. 2. the essential or animating force.

Collins English Dictionary, 1979

Prologue

Tuesday, 23 December 2003

Pain has its uses, Lizzie thinks. It scares you into doing what you're told. It lets you know you're alive in spite of everything. But it keeps waking you up, and when they see your eyes open, they think they own you.

'Tell us what he did and we'll get him,' the cop said the last time she made that mistake. 'You must tell us. What did he call himself? What does he look like? Who is he? You knew him, didn't you? You know who he is. You must tell us. Fucking *talk* to me.'

Lizzie knows the cop's here again today because she can recognize the smell of his smoky breath and clothes, but he's not the one speaking now.

'It's definitely the same m.o., Sarge.' This is a woman's voice, sensible and quiet. 'Although the damage is *much* worse this time. Even so, I'm sure it's Randall Gyre again.'

It is, thinks Lizzie. He told me so himself.

She got to the pub soon after nine, shaking after yet another fight with her mother, looking for her dad. The Eagle and Dumpling in Cowes was his pub. It had always been his refuge from the wars at home. But he wasn't here tonight. Lizzie stood just inside the doorway, looking round, wanting him.

A tall, good-looking bloke leaning against the bar caught her eye and raised his glass to her. Lizzie smiled and watched his face soften into the kind of welcome that almost made her forget the stuff her mother had shouted at her. He pushed himself upright and strolled towards her.

'Hi, I'm Randall Gyre. Can I get you a drink?'

'Thanks. I'm Lizzie – Lizzie Fane. Vodka and tonic would be great.'

'Coming up.'

More pain comes, different and even more frightening, as one of the doctors sticks another needle in her arm and joggles her body. Bits feel so loosely attached they might come away in the doctors' hands, like the mushy legs of the chicken she once left in the fridge too long.

Lizzie feels bruised and rotten all over. Everything holding her together has been ripped and torn, just like her connection to Before.

She doesn't even know when that was. Each time she comes round, she has no idea if it's the same day or tomorrow, or even yesterday.

She knows it's still hospital, though, from the squeaks and rattles of the trolleys. And from the smells: disinfectant and alcohol. But clean, medical alcohol, not like the sweet stuff Randall bought her. That coated her mouth and slid down her throat and screwed up her sense of danger.

All the misery had gone and she wasn't shaking any more. Even the disappointment of not finding her dad was OK now. She felt like her whole body was smiling at Randall. The pub's hard benches had become awesomely comfortable. His laughing voice was like dark-blue silk, soft but intense, and beautiful and very strong.

'You're fantastic, Lizzie. Why haven't we met before? If you live on the Island, someone must've been hiding you away from

me. I've been coming over for holidays all my life. It isn't fair: I could've seen you playing in the sand, and kicked a football with you, and teased you about your dolls, and watched you turn beautiful and take on the world. Now here you are complete, and I've wasted half my life without you.'

'I wouldn't have liked you if you'd hurt my dolls.' She smiled up at him. 'I loved them more than anyone real. It's much better to meet as grown-ups. Can I get you another beer?'

'Later. Why don't we go outside for a bit? Somewhere more private. There are too many people here, Lizzie.'

Outside, he flung his arm round her shoulders and pulled her closer so he could kiss her. She loved it, and she loved his after-shave: expensive, citrus but somehow peppery too.

'God, you're gorgeous! Come here.'

She's choking as the smell fills up her nostrils and closes her throat and burns in her lungs and makes her head swim and the bed whirl around her. Someone's fiddling with her drips again. A hard weight presses down on her neck. She opens her eyes, sees Randall's face, and screams. But no sound comes out.

Seconds later, or hours or days, more feet are running towards her.

Voices come at her through the hot smelly fog. One is firm and female, the other young and male, but safe because it's wobbling with worry, not shouting or slick with fake charm.

'Her temperature shouldn't be this high. I don't understand it. The cuts have all been cleaned and stitched. They're healing, even the internal ones. The infection's been under control for days now. Her temperature should be down.'

'But—'

'Ice,' says the man. His voice is so high now it's nearly a scream. 'Get some ice packs, Nurse. No – a fan first. Yes, that's right. Start with a fan. Hurry. What are you waiting for? Hurry! I *told* you!'

'Call the consultant.' The quiet words are firm and, for Lizzie, nearly as good as having her hand held. 'You can't deal with this on your own.'

'I can manage. We'll get her temperature down and Doctor Franklin can see her in the morning. Fetch a fan.'

'It's not enough. She's got septicaemia.' The nurse's voice is still respectful, but only just.

Lizzie feels the sheet lifted at the bottom of the bed. Then comes the nurse's voice again, more forceful now.

'Look. Her feet are as pale as her hands. Septicaemia.'

The sheet is tucked in again, too tightly so that Lizzie's toes are bent under.

'It can't be. She's been on i/v antibiotics for five days.'

'Look at the drip, Doctor.' Now even the nurse's voice is rising in panic. 'Someone's turned it off.'

They start tugging at her again. Lizzie's mind screams, *No, no, no, no, no!*

She was fighting, hitting, kicking, biting. But Randall was so strong nothing could get him off her. The more she fought, the harder he cut down into her. The blood from the first cuts was already sticky as the new stuff flooded out.

In the end, his voice was cold and hard, like the broken glass itself. 'If you talk about this, if you ever identify me to anyone, I'll find you and kill you. Wherever you are, I'll find you. And I will kill you. Remember this.'

Then came the extra sharp pain, ripping right through her vagina and, up, deep inside her.

'It's not just the drip. Something's been missed,' says the nurse. 'You've got to do another internal, Doctor.'

The smell of powdered rubber gloves mixes with the sound of them snapping against his fingers. Lizzie knows what's coming. The sheet is torn away again, this time pulling her big toe as it catches in one of the ripped patches. His hands push her tight knees apart.

Screams fill her head. The coldness of the steel speculum against her torn and sewn skin warns her to beware, just before the pain begins again.

She has to pull her mind away from them. She can't stop them, any more than she could stop him.

'Glass,' says the doctor. 'Christ Almighty! There's another piece of glass, right up by the cervix.'

'Call Doctor Franklin.'

'I can't.' Now the doctor sounds even more frightened. 'She doesn't like me waking her. She thinks I should be able to cope, that I get hysterical over nothing.'

'Not this time,' says the nurse grimly. 'She needs to be here. Get her. *Now.* I'll phone the parents. They need to be here, too.'

Much later, Lizzie hears her mother's voice, urgent and angry, and the woman doctor's, explaining why they're moving her to the intensive care unit. The bed swings as it's pulled away from the wall. Lizzie feels sick and keeps her eyes tightly closed.

The change of air temperature tells her they're away from the ward. The bed's still again. No one says anything. She lets her heavy lids rise and sees a porter looking up over her head, waiting. Swivelling her eyes to the side, she sees her mother sobbing as she leans against the torso of a tall man in a white coat. Is this the one who was panicking? Lizzie raises her lids even higher. There's no name-badge on his lapel. She looks further up so she can see his face. The scream builds in her throat, choking her, but she still can't make any sound.

Randall sees her recognizing him. His eyes glisten, his lips widen, then part in a smile of pure, triumphant satisfaction. His lips frame the silent words:

'You're dying, Lizzie. You shouldn't have talked.'

Chapter 1

Four years later – Friday morning, 26 September 2008

Karen arrived at the probation office in west London a few minutes early, hoping she looked invulnerable. And in charge. Her height usually helped – she was five foot nine – and this morning in her flat in Southampton she'd spent ages picking the right stuff to wear.

She loved clothes and was slim enough to carry off almost anything, but when she was dealing with violent male criminals she had to hide her real self. Today she'd tied back her shoulder-length blonde hair and was wearing roomy black bootleg trousers with a copper-coloured jacket hanging open over a loose cream shirt.

Taking a careful breath and settling her shoulders, she rang the bell. A short, plump man in his early forties opened the door, bringing with him a gust of instant coffee, dust and a confusion of smells from flowery scent to bleach. His chinos were creased and baggy, and his striped shirt was stretched tight over his beer gut. As he inspected her, she wondered why he looked as if he hated her.

He took several steps back, as though to make sure he didn't have to tilt his head too far to meet her eyes.

'Karen Taylor?' he said, without even a hint of welcome. 'Hi. I'm Dave Pickney. Come in. Your interviewee's late. He just phoned – should be here within fifteen minutes. Tea while you wait? Or coffee?'

'Thanks. Tea would be great. Milk, no sugar,' Karen said, not prepared to risk instant coffee but pleased at the prospect of something that might ease her dry throat. Nerves always made her feel as though she'd swallowed a lump of blotting paper that mopped up all available saliva. 'Do your clients usually phone if they're going to be late?'

Dave's belated smile drove deep lines into his plump cheeks. 'Not often. But this is one smooth operator. You'll see. Have a seat and I'll get the tea.'

Karen took one of the four dark-brown bucket chairs and put her briefcase on the floor beside it. At her own request, she'd been told nothing about the man she was about to meet or what his crime had been. All she knew was that he would be a major offender, who had either killed or seriously assaulted at least one other person and was now out of prison on licence.

She wasn't physically frightened. Quite apart from Dave and the staff she could hear phoning and typing in the background, there'd be a camera recording everything that happened. No offender, however vicious or stupid, would risk attacking her in a place like this. But she still had plenty to worry about, and some of the men she'd already interviewed had been so verbally violent she'd had a hard time pretending to be cool.

Her job was to decide whether prison had rehabilitated these men or left them with all their brutality intact. The old system of working out which criminals could be safely let back into the community had failed so often that the government needed to find a better way.

Karen was only one of a whole group of experts chosen by the Ministry of Justice to help in the search. She'd been given twenty-five men to assess and was due to report in eight months' time, after which she'd have to wait – perhaps for years – to find out whether her conclusions were right or not. Some criminals re-offended as soon as they got out; others spent years behaving perfectly, then killed again, sometimes in exactly the same way as the first time, often picking a new victim who could have been a twin of the original.

'Here we are,' said Dave, coming back with a thick earth-coloured mug in each pudgy hand. He put one on the low table in front of Karen and raised the other in a kind of toast, adding in a voice spiky with malice, 'I saw your conclusions about John Clarence.'

She took a cautious sip of the mahogany-coloured liquid before looking up at him.

'I didn't know you were on the circulation list,' she said, sounding more polite than she felt.

At the start of the project, she'd been made to sign a fero-cious confidentiality document, which meant she wasn't allowed to talk about it to anyone, even to ask university colleagues for advice or support. Now it looked as though the civil servants felt free to share her work with anyone they chose.

'I'm part of the team overseeing the whole project,' Dave said, still looking at her as if she was his enemy. It made her twitchy. 'I'm impressed by your courage, I must say.'

'Courage is a scary word to use in that tone of voice,' Karen said, hiding her suspicion of him. She took another sip of the strong tea, nearly flinching as the tannin hit her palate, along with a few bobbles of undissolved dried milk. 'Don't you mean stupidity?'

'Not exactly,' he said, putting his head on one side and offering a creepy smirk. 'More foolhardiness. Maybe it comes of being an academic with no practical experience on the ground.'

Karen wasn't going to give him the satisfaction of a protest. If he was as resentful as he sounded, he'd love to know he'd got to her.

'You take a man who beat his wife to a pulp,' he went on, clearly enjoying himself, 'slamming her against the wall again and again until the back of her head's the texture of a rotten tomato, and decide he's no danger to anyone? Aren't you pushing it a bit?'

'Maybe. But I'm not going to fudge my results,' Karen said, as all her hidden anxieties lurched to the surface of her mind. She put her tea on the table.

Dave came even closer, perching on the edge of the table and only just missing her mug. He looked ready for a treat. As he settled himself, she watched his thighs squish upwards and outwards. She thought they looked like the filling in a lumpy old duvet as they spread inside his crumpled chinos.

'Here's a textbook case of poor impulse control and inability to manage anger,' he said, as though lecturing a first-year student, 'leading to unpredictable violence. Men like John Clarence *always* re-offend. Anyone involved in the real world could've told you that.'

'If you're right,' Karen said with a smile, thinking that if she had to work with the man she might as well try to make him like her, 'my report will be lining cat-litter trays in no time, and I'll be on the streets.'

'It'll be a lot worse than that.' Dave laughed, and the patronising note set her teeth on edge. 'You'll have a starring role as the latest media monster. You'll get filthy hate mail. You'll probably be sacked, and any good work you've done in the past will be ignored. You'll definitely understand how witches felt in the sixteenth century.'

He'd described all Karen's worst waking nightmares. But she wasn't going to let him see it.

'No one in this business is right a hundred per cent of the time,' he went on with glee. 'I just hope you don't make a cockup with today's subject.'

'Why today's particularly?' Karen said.

Dave pretended to hesitate, looking her up and down before adding with fake kindness, 'I'd better not say too much. But he's got powerful supporters. Whichever way you go, you'll be taking one hell of a risk. And if you're wrong, you'll be pilloried in the press. Don't think your youth and legs and hair and eyes will help you then.'

'Youth?' Karen laughed artistically.

She'd come to academic forensic psychology much later than most people, having married at eighteen, right out of school. Widowed five years later, she'd had to set about getting herself an education just as everyone else was being promoted at work.

'I'm thirty-five,' she added, still trying to keep the conversation polite.

'You don't look it.' Now Dave sounded sour. 'The press'll hate you even more than if you were a bristly hag.'

The door bell rang, which helped Karen use her own impulse control to stop herself picking up her mug to throw at him.

Dave headed off to unlock the door, saying over his shoulder, 'You can go into that first office and I'll bring him in. Don't let any of his smoothness fool you: he's one of the worst you'll ever meet, however long you stay in this business.'

Chapter 2

The 23-year-old who'd once been Lizzie Fane leaned forwards, her knife loaded with blood-coloured paint, to fill the narrow serpentine gap between the great basalt cliffs that filled her giant canvas. If she got this right, she should be able to see the painting as either a gory chasm or a flame-topped mountain range.

When the red had been laid on the canvas with all the jagged rage she'd wanted, she stepped back, wiping the knife on a rag. All around her were the good familiar smells of paint, canvas, turpentine, woodshavings and size. Her studio was little more than a glorified shed in the garden of the small white farmhouse she rented in the obscure and tiny Somerset village of Hoaxley, but it was all she needed.

What she saw on the easel made her nod in satisfaction. The red could be either blood or fire. You could be at the top or the bottom of the mountains of hell.

She let out a tiny breath of relief no one else would have heard, and loaded a thin brush with the pale grey she always used for her secret pseudonym: Lee Wills.

When the painting was dry enough, she would pack it up and send it to the dealer she'd found on the internet, who'd been doing amazingly well for her ever since she'd submitted the first Lee Wills painting. She'd called it *Light Out of Dark*, even

though the light then was only the tiniest speck in a furious sea
of threatening darkness.

Once this one had gone, she would revert to the sweet undis-
turbing landscapes she was becoming known for in the village,
where everyone believed her name was Lisa Raithe and where
for most of the time she could feel herself to be Lisa: an untroubled, comfortable kind of young woman, without the slightest
knowledge of violence – or interest in it.

Although Anton, the dealer, was always asking for more information about 'Lee Wills' and begging for face-to-face meetings,
she'd held him off so far. They communicated only through her
solicitor, who was the one person she'd trusted with the truth.
He received the cheques Anton sent, organized her accounts,
paid her bills and taxes, and did everything she needed to keep
her hiding place and her real identity safe from everyone, even
her father.

Neither her mind nor her scarred body would ever let her
forget Randall's threat: 'Wherever you are, I'll find you. And I
will kill you.'

She looked at the painting she'd just finished, slashed through
with the pure red river of her hate, and was proud of the way she
was fighting back.

For quite a lot of the time now, she could enjoy being Lisa,
who was straightforward as well as comfortable – mostly – and
nearly normal. Lee wasn't normal at all, but it was Lee who
could fend off the nightmares when they came, and who would
one day get justice for what had happened to Lizzie. And justice,
she'd discovered, was lifeblood.

She wasn't mad. The three sides of her personality were only
that. She let herself think of them as separate people, because
that was easier, but all the time she knew they were really her.
Just a way of making it possible to live with the memory of what
Randall had done.

The phone rang, shocking her back into the present. After a

moment, she picked it up and heard the expected voice, quiet, gentle, and softly burred with the local accent:

'Lisa. It's me. You coming to the pub tonight?'

Outside the studio window, the sun blazed along the narrow river like the red version in her painting. The light would be gone by eight. She still didn't like walking home in the dark, even here, even though the pub was only about five hundred yards from her cottage. But she *was* fighting back.

'Yes,' she said firmly into the phone. 'I could be there by seven. You coming, Jed?'

'Yeah. And I want to buy your tea,' he said. 'We'd be celebrating. That new restaurant in Hope Street's going to be organic and I'm to supply their veg and herbs. Don't turn me down again, Lisa. You know I get family rates at the pub.'

She still didn't like letting anyone else pay for anything. She couldn't forget what it had been like to stand by a bar and take drinks from Randall.

Not that Jed was anything like Randall.

'OK. Great,' she said into the phone. 'Thanks. See you later.'

She pressed the red button to silence the phone, then had to work on the voices in her head. They clanged around, some whispering, others yelling at her about the risks she was taking.

'I can trust Jed,' she said aloud, determined to make the voices stop. 'I can. So shut up.'

'Why?' whispered one. 'You were wrong before. Why d'you think you're not wrong now? Just because Jed's not smooth and rich like Randall, that doesn't mean he won't turn on you. How naïve are you? Were they right, all those people who said you were asking for it last time? Do you *want* to be raped again?'

Something out in the garden caught in her peripheral vision. Her head whipped round to the left so she could look directly at it.

Everything seemed normal, but she had seen something bigger

than an animal, just for a second. She reached for the heavy bunch of keys and let herself out into the garden.

No footprints could be seen in the soft fertile earth or on the damp grass. She moved on to the river. A swan slid along the surface, looking stately and contemptuous as it turned its head towards her. The sound of oars, or a canoe paddle, splashing on the water came from further up the river, past the bend. Someone was working hard to get his boat out of view fast.

Lisa wrapped her arms around her shuddering body and thought about putting barbed wire across the top of the six stone steps that led down from her garden to the river.

Chapter 3

Friday, 26 September, 10.30 a.m.

'Doctor Taylor, I *am* sorry to have kept you waiting. It's good of you to see me.'

The man who strolled into the small light office ahead of Dave was at least six foot tall, dark-haired and dressed in clean black jeans that looked new, with a round-necked grey T-shirt and a beautifully cut jacket of grey-flecked black cashmere. His eyes were the colour of fresh conkers and they twinkled at Karen with good humour and intelligent appreciation. He smelled of Penhaligon's Blenheim Bouquet, the peppery-citrus aftershave her husband had always used because someone had told him it was what rich successful bankers wore.

Even so, Karen found herself smiling back at him and knew she had to get a grip on the meeting fast.

'Have a seat and we'll get cracking,' she said. 'I hope they've explained how I want you to answer a set of questions as quickly as you can, and without bothering to try to work out what they mean or what you think I want you to write. OK?'

'Yeah. Sounds just like a Myers-Briggs.'

'You've taken a psychometric test before?'

'I had to for work.' He sat obediently, crossing his legs and offering an image of total relaxation. 'In the old days, of course. Since I was convicted of—'

'I have to stop you there,' Karen said very quickly. 'It's important for the study that I know nothing of your life, sentence or
crime.' She laughed a little: 'Alleged or otherwise.'

'I suppose it would muddle the scientific purity of your investigation,' he said, laughing back at her, as though they were at
a party and flirting. 'But God! It's refreshing. You can't imagine
what it's been like these f— these few years. Everyone thinks
they know what I'm like because of what they've been told I did.'

Hold on, Karen told herself. Don't respond. Just because he
speaks your language and looks as though he understands and
likes you, don't get involved. He's a subject like any other.

She handed him a basic ballpoint and the first of her sheets of
questions. This section had no particular significance and was
unlikely to tell her anything useful about the respondents. She
used it as a way of easing them into their tests – and stopping
them working out what the questions were designed to show, if
they were sophisticated enough to think of it or want to control
the way they answered.

This one's definitely sophisticated enough, Karen thought.

'As I said,' she added aloud, with an easy smile, 'the quicker
you can answer, the better.' Something about the knowing way
he looked up at her made her offer a tiny challenge. 'Some of my
subjects find reading and writing so hard they take hours. You'll
do better than that. But there'll be things even you won't understand. Don't hesitate to say. I won't judge you.'

Karen got back a fast, harsh flash of anger that interested
her. Forcing her mind to stop working out what it might mean,
she pulled a batch of unrelated papers out of her briefcase and
pretended to concentrate on them. The camera was recording the
session, so she didn't have to watch his reactions as he dealt with
her questions. She could play and replay the films later, when she
was analysing the answers.

'Done,' he said, pushing the sheet back across the table in
record time.

Karen didn't even look at his answers as she gave him the next set of questions, all of which dealt with situations likely to generate frustration: at a bus stop; in hospital; driving a car stuck behind four caravans; discussing football with an enemy supporter; being harassed by someone else's child; and so on. For each imaginary scene, he had to tick the box that most appropriately described his natural response.

This time he finished the sheet even more quickly than before. She gave him the third without a word.

'You know, Doctor Taylor, it might be easier if you gave me the whole bunch in one go. It would save you trouble.'

'It's no trouble,' she said, still not letting him take control. 'Quick as you can now.'

When he'd finished all her sets of questions, she locked his sheets away in her briefcase and thanked him.

'Pleasure,' he said, well back into his charming mode. 'What happens now?'

'I take these back to my office, enter the data into my computer model, analyse them, find out whether I need to know more, then have a proper interview with you, during which we will talk about your time in prison and the offence that sent you there, whatever it was.'

'Alleged offence,' he said with an air of languid correction, as though it didn't really matter to him.

'Of course,' she said. Something about him chilled her, in spite of his intelligent responsiveness. 'Have you got a flat yet, or are you in a hostel? How are you finding the transition to life outside?'

He gestured towards his immaculate jacket. 'Can you really see me in a hostel with drunken, drug-addled, illiterate, aggressive scum?'

Ah, she thought, unable to keep her mind completely dumb, so he's an arrogant shit as well as a professional charmer with anger-management issues. She smiled again, still trying to make herself look admiring.

'I'm staying at my mother's, on Campden Hill,' he added in the drawling tones of a man at ease all over the world, 'putting everything back together as quickly as possible. I have several interviews lined up, thank God, with people who remember me from life before prison.'

'Right,' Karen said, knowing that even the tiniest of cottages on Campden Hill in west London cost well over a million pounds. 'Aren't you lucky?'

'Lucky?' He almost spat out the word.

'Yes,' she said, not allowing herself to flinch at the hatred in the sound. 'Very lucky.'

He moved so fast she didn't have time to react before she felt his right hand around her left wrist, squeezing so hard the bones shifted painfully. She glanced towards the camera. Dave or one of his staff should be here any minute. She sat as patiently as she could, not pulling away. No one came. The man held on and squeezed hard. Karen's breathing shortened and her throat grew tighter and tighter.

'Now you know how I've felt all these years,' he said, letting her go at last. 'Tethered. Humiliated. Afraid. There's been no luck of any kind.'

Karen looked down at her wrist and saw the deep, pale-yellow indentations in her pink skin, showing where his fingers had been. There'd be bruises later.

'That wasn't very sensible,' she said, meeting his gaze with her own eyes absolutely steady, 'for a man out of prison on parole.'

'I didn't hurt you.' He laughed, and the sound made her feel as though someone had wiped an ice cube up and down her warm spine. 'Not enough, anyway.'

She glanced towards the camera again and a second later the door opened and Dave put his head round it.

'Everything OK?' he asked in the most casual of voices.

Karen looked at him for long enough, she hoped, to tell him she knew he'd let her sweat for longer than he had to, then she said, 'Fine, thanks. We're done here.'

She glanced at her paroled offender, adding, 'I'll see you in seven days' time.'

'So I gather.' He got to his feet and held out his right hand, as though he expected her to shake it.

'You may go,' Karen said, not moving from her chair. 'Mr Pickney will refund the cost of your journey here.'

When they'd gone, she sat back, trying not to see quite how much the man she'd interviewed had in common with her dead husband. It wasn't just the eye-wateringly expensive aftershave they both liked. Peter had had just the same kind of superficial charm, as well as the subterranean rage that had emerged whenever he'd been challenged or shown anything that even hinted at disrespect.

How much else did the two of them share? Peter had been a conman, using his seductiveness to entice his victims into believing in his mythical financial skills, then take them for everything they had. Since his death Karen had often wondered whether it had actually been the money that had driven him or the pleasure he'd taken in ruining other people's lives.

'Nasty piece of work, isn't he?' Dave said, coming back with the earth-coloured mugs in his hand. 'You'd never have thought he was a successful property dealer before he went down, would you? More tea?'

'Thanks, but I'd better be off.' Karen glanced at the big clock over the door. 'I could just catch the 13.20 back to Southampton if I go now, then have the whole afternoon to work. I'll see you next week when I come back to interview him.'

'I'd give it a minute or two more,' Dave said, coming to peer out of the window over her shoulder. 'Gyre's still down there, hanging about. You don't want him following you home, now do you? You're just his type: tall and blonde. His victims are usually a bit younger, but, like I say, you don't look thirty-five.'

*　　*　　*

Karen took the later train. When she eventually made her way to Waterloo Station, she couldn't stop thinking of the tall blonde victims of the man Dave had called Gyre. How many had there been? And what – exactly – had he done to them? Were they all dead?

Every time a car backfired or a grimy London pigeon flew too close, she flinched and rubbed her still-aching wrist against her thigh. When someone touched her arm as he rushed past, she nearly yelled at him. And every street seemed to be full of tall dark-haired men, loitering on corners, watching her. Each time she noticed one, she had to check he was a stranger.

You've got to stop this, she thought. You'll scare yourself even more efficiently than Dave just tried to. Get a grip.

The frustration of battling through the crowds at Waterloo and listening to the braying loudspeakers soon stopped her thinking of anything else. She found her platform in the end and made her way towards the barrier. A black cat strolled just in front of her, brushing against her leg. She dropped her ticket. Bending down to pick it up, she found herself staring at a pair of perfectly clean new black jeans. She took her time reaching for the ticket so she had a moment to prepare, then straightened up ready to face Gyre.

She saw a lanky teenager with his mum and little sister, all three of them staring at her as though she was a freak. Karen smiled and held out her ticket with a rueful expression designed to show them what a fool she'd been. It didn't make them look any less surprised by her tension, or the slowness of her movements. Giving up, she turned and stuffed the ticket in the automatic reader, before walking along the outside of the train until she found her compartment.

If she'd been paying for herself, it would have been a standard one, but the Ministry of Justice had her on a similar expenses regime to Members of Parliament, who always travelled first class so that they could work discreetly on the train, undisturbed by curious passengers. Karen had no idea whether they did any work, but she always did. She had too many projects on the go to waste an uninterrupted hour and a half. Today, she opened her laptop at once and started inputting the answers Gyre had given about the minutiae of his responses to everyday life.

Building them into a net that covered almost every aspect of a man's existence could, Karen believed, give a clear indication of how he would respond to much more dangerous stimuli. Every individual was different and every offender motivated by different stresses and memories, but there were enough common factors to be useful.

The train pulled out of Waterloo at last, into a haze of muddy rain that splattered the window beside her, sounding like handfuls of gravel being thrown at the toughened glass. By the time they'd flashed, unstopping, through Woking, twenty-nine miles away, her skin was prickling with adrenaline and her mind was charged up like a nuclear-powered generator.

Today's completed tests showed a tendency to re-offend that was almost off the scale. Karen had never seen a clearer example of someone untroubled by conscience, a controlling, angry man, who was determined to display his power over other people at every possible opportunity. Even more alarming was the repeated revelation of his intense pleasure in hurting women, physically and emotionally. He was excited by the very idea.

Karen examined her wrist and saw that dark-grey bruises were already forming in the oval spaces where his fingers had gripped her flesh.

Now she had no problem seeing what his offence had been. All the facts would be waiting for her in her office at the university in Southampton, along with details of his identity, background and sentence. But she was clear enough in her own mind that he had to be a rapist, and exceptionally violent.

The securely couriered package was waiting on Karen's desk, signed for by the departmental assistant. There had been so many

recent losses of supposedly secure data on disks or memory sticks
– or even old-fashioned files – that Al Marks and his bosses had
been determined that they were not going to have any embarrassing mishaps with revelations about dangerous offenders out
on licence in the community.

Inside the padded envelope was the usual password-protected
computer disk. Karen laid it ready on her desk, before hanging
her jacket on the hook behind the door and switching on the
kettle she kept in her office. Ever since she'd worked out the
High Street price of her caffeine habit, she'd brewed her own and
saved a fortune.

The kettle boiled and she tipped the water onto the grounds
in the filter paper before inserting the disk into the side of her
laptop. Today's choice of coffee was a beautifully fruity, lightly
acidic Kenya peaberry.

All the usual security boxes popped up on her screen and she
typed in her password and her security-check number and waited,
pouring her coffee black. The rich smell she loved even more
than the taste rose from the surface. Outside the window someone was drilling into the road and traffic clanked and coughed its
way through the latest jam. Down the hall phones were ringing
and doors slamming.

Karen was used to shutting out all distractions when she was
working and barely heard the cacophony as Randall Gyre's
history rose line by line on her screen.

He had been convicted only once, of grievous bodily harm,
for which he had served four years of a nine-year sentence. The
length of his punishment alone told Karen that the injuries he'd
inflicted must have been very bad indeed.

The Senior Investigating Officer's name caught Karen's eye
and made her smile.

Charlie Trench.

They'd met last year, when she'd been doing some research on
the Isle of Wight and found herself involved in more drama than

she ever wanted to face again. Charlie had been a crucial part of it, and she'd liked him a lot. If she hadn't already been committed to Will, she might have . . .

Karen shut down the thought at once, just as firmly as she'd stopped herself phoning Charlie during the long winter evenings when Will had been on call in Brighton, all her mates had been too busy to play, and even the charms of Mozart and coffee or good wine had palled.

For the first few weeks after the Island dramas had ended, Karen had waited for Charlie to phone her. She'd been so sure he would she'd even practised what she might say if the odd casual meeting for drinks or a meal had got out of hand: something on the lines of, 'I've loved working with you, Charlie, and I think you're great, but as you know I'm involved with Will. I don't think it'd be fair to . . .'

Her face bunched up into a grimace of self-disgust. Charlie hadn't given her the opportunity to say any of it. There hadn't been any drinks or meals; not even a friendly text.

The trouble with being a psychologist, she told herself, is that it forces you to face your own subconscious. You fancied the hell out of Charlie and wanted him to try to break down your resistance so you could enjoy being chased and yet *still* feel all virtuous because you managed to stay faithful to Will.

Needing to get back to work, she ordered herself to forget Charlie's wickedly gleaming dark eyes and concentrate on the files.

His team had quickly identified the attacker, and Randall Gyre had been tried for both rape and GBH. The double charge obviously meant the Crown Prosecution Service hadn't been confident of getting a rape conviction, in spite of the victim's injuries. Having seen the way Randall presented himself, and having had a taste of his charm, Karen wasn't surprised.

Even if he hadn't been so plausible and appealing, he might have got away with it if he hadn't been so violent. Frighteningly few alleged rapists received guilty verdicts in the English courts. The latest figures suggested that fewer than 6 per cent of reported rapes ended in conviction.

Some of those allegations could have been false, but in Karen's view the few malicious accusers were more than balanced by the number of women who never went anywhere near the police, thinking they wouldn't be believed, or not wanting to put themselves through the added trauma of investigation and possibly hostile lawyers in court. Forty per cent of raped women were thought never to tell anyone what happened to them.

Colleagues had warned Karen that you didn't stand much chance of seeing a rapist convicted unless he was a total stranger to his entirely sober – and modestly dressed – victim and jumped her in front of a working security camera that recorded his facial features as well as all his actions while he was leaving plenty of DNA evidence at the scene and on his victim's body.

Randall's past history was even more illuminating. He had been in court twice before the current case, both times on charges of rape that had resulted in not-guilty verdicts. The victim in the second of those had been injured more severely than the first, though less badly than Lizzie Fane. The progression was clear, and alarming.

Karen reached for the phone and punched in the number for Al's direct line at the Ministry of Justice.

While she waited for him to answer, she examined the photographs of the three victims. As Dave had hinted, all the women were tall and slender and blonde, just as she was herself. But these pictures showed another progression: each of the victims was more beautiful than the one before, as though Randall had been testing himself with a more enticing – and probably more difficult – target every time.

Karen wondered how many others there'd been, who had not reported what he'd done to them. She'd walked down enough dark streets on her own to have some idea of how they must have felt at the moment when they realized what was going to happen. What must it do to them all to know that he still hadn't been properly punished?

'Marks,' said the cool efficient voice in her ear, once the ringing tone had stopped.

'Al? It's Karen here – Karen Taylor. I've got my preliminary results from Subject Eleven's tests and I've been reading up his past history.'

'Oh, yes? Are you going to tell me he's another John Clarence, who should be protected from any vigilante violence at all costs because he, himself, is not really a violent man, in spite of all the evidence everyone else has?'

'Absolutely not.' Karen's voice was hard.

She had to forget she could have been one of Randall's victims if she'd had the bad luck to come up against him when he was hunting. Her job now was to do everything in her power to protect any other woman who might catch his eye.

'I'm phoning to warn you that Randall's a serious danger to the public.' Her voice was at its driest and most authoritative because she knew Al responded better to that than any overt emotion. 'The tests I'm analysing here make it look highly likely that he'll do it again. And next time he may kill.'

Chapter 4

'So?' Down the phone Al's voice sounded casual in the extreme.

'So you've got to get him back in custody,' Karen said, managing not to shout insults at him. 'And *fast*, Al, before he finds the next woman he wants to rape.'

'Come on. You know that's impossible.'

The blood pounded in her head as it always did when she was on the point of losing her temper.

'You've *got* to do something.'

'Don't shout at me, Doctor Taylor.'

Karen said nothing. All she wanted to do was swear at him. And that would be fatal.

After a moment Al started again in a slightly friendlier voice: 'Come on, Karen, you know how these things work. I'll minute your call, and you can write it up in your report. If your prediction comes true, you'll get the credit. If it doesn't, you can console yourself with the knowledge of all those young women who have not been killed as you thought they would be.'

'And if another woman *is* raped and murdered, how are you going to feel then?' In response to the softening of his tone, she'd managed to quieten her own again. 'Come on, Al, will you at least *warn* someone?'

'Who – every chief constable in the country? What'll they do? What *can* they do?'

'You passed on my views of John Clarence.'

'Only to MAPPA, the tracking group that deals with the most serious offenders out on licence.'

'And to Dave Pickney,' Karen said, letting out some of the outrage she felt.

'Well, members of the working party, yes. But they're bound by rules of confidentiality, just like you.'

'So everyone on the panel will be told what I think about Randall?'

'I'd have thought it likely,' Al said airily.

'Then maybe one of *them* will do something to stop the next rape.'

'Now, Karen,' Al's clever young voice had taken on a patronising note she didn't like at all. 'You're getting emotional again. Don't let your feelings get in the way of all the good your report could do if it's not tainted. We have to take the long view. However you may be tempted to talk about your assessment of Gyre, don't give in to it. You're bound – absolutely – by the confidentiality document you signed. If you break it, all your work will be for nothing. I must go. My other phone's ringing. Keep me informed. Goodbye.'

Karen slammed the receiver back on the phone, hating him, and muttering, 'Long view. Bloody long view. How can I?'

Al was right, of course. She knew that, just as she knew she couldn't do anything to mess up her study. If she broke her contract, they could throw her off the project. All her reports so far would be binned, she'd never know how far to trust the tests she'd designed, and she wouldn't have done anything to stop Randall raping – and maybe killing – his next victim.

But the idea of what he had done and would do again ate into her mind. She couldn't leave it like this. After a minute or two, she pulled his test sheets forwards again to re-check her conclusions, hoping to find that she'd got them wrong.

She hadn't. When she was sure, she opened her email and typed a short note to Al:

> We spoke. I informed you of my conclusion that Randall Gyre is a serious danger to the public and should not be living unsupervised in the community.

Someone knocked on the door of her office. She pressed 'send' and called out, 'Come in.'

The door opened and from outside it a bubbly voice called, 'Karen, darling?'

'Dillie!' Karen said as she stood up. It was a quarter of a century since she'd called her mother anything else.

Dillie swept in, bringing with her a cloud of lily-of-the-valley scent from her favourite Diorissimo. She was dressed with unusual conservatism in a plain black pencil skirt and emerald linen jacket, with no more than an exotically coloured bird-of-paradise brooch in her lapel to show she was more exciting than anyone else in the world. Mainly enamel, the brooch had real feathers for the bird's tail and must have been a good four inches tall, which was a lot for someone who could manage only five foot three herself, even on tiptoes.

'What on earth are you doing here?' Karen said.

'I had a meeting.' Dillie reached up to kiss her cheek. 'Are you going to let me sit down?'

Karen hastily cleared a heap of undergraduate essays off the only spare chair. They were the first of the academic year, and they'd have to be marked soon. Research into the minds and habits of men like Randall might get her blood running in a way her students never could, but teaching them was her first responsibility and she couldn't shirk it. Not for long, anyway.

Dillie brushed dust off the chair, then sat down, looking critically at her daughter.

'I thought your newfound fame might have brought some money with it. But you look ghastly. Can you really not afford anything better cut than those awful trousers?'

Karen thought of explaining the need for camouflage when dealing with sadistic sex offenders, then shrugged. There was no point. Her appearance was an old battleground between them. She'd inherited the blonde hair Dillie now had to fake, and the pretty button of a face that looked so charming on someone as small as Dillie and so absurd on Karen, and she'd never been allowed to forget it.

She had her height from her father, but she'd missed out on his long face and chiselled cheekbones, which seemed unfair.

'There's no money in academia, as you know. Not like advertising.' Karen didn't mean to wind-up her mother, but Dillie flushed, which suggested the business might be in crisis again. That would explain her relatively sober outfit, too. 'What's up?'

'Nothing.' Dillie's tone was casual, as though she was completely untroubled by anything. 'Why should it be?'

Karen waited, knowing it wouldn't be long before she got the story.

'Oh, all right, darling. We are having the tiniest little financial difficulty. Nothing important. Cash-flow hiccup. Temporary, of course.' Dillie paused, as though expecting a response. Karen did her best.

'Of course,' she repeated. 'How does that bring you to Southampton? You're surely far too glamorous to have clients in a city like this one.'

Dillie laughed, the delicate sound rising into an artfully musical declaration of amusement, which ratcheted up Karen's suspicions at once.

'Come on, Dillie. Out with it. What do you want me to do for you?'

'Since you ask, buy that horrid little hut you love so much on the Pile of Shite,' said Dillie.

Karen had no difficulty translating her mother's request for her to buy the Isle of Wight holiday chalet that Dillie had inherited from *her* mother. Karen manufactured her own tone of light amusement.

'No one would ever suspect that you were one of the world's great advertising geniuses,' she said. 'I've never heard a less enticing proposition.'

Dillie's mask of cheerful insouciance slipped a little. 'That's because I don't want to diddle you. But one good thing is that that weird neighbour – you know, the Elephant Man – has died, so you wouldn't have a dotty stalker with a passion for shotguns living on your doorstep in the middle of those spooky woods.'

Karen felt all kinds of emotions stirring in the least protected parts of her mind. Nostalgia mixed with fear and irritation and longing. She struggled to contain them.

'How much d'you expect to get?'

'I was over there having it valued this morning.' Dillie looked at her daughter, over the edge of her coffee mug, as though checking how far she could go. Then she shrugged, saying, 'The agent thinks on the open market we could probably get about half a million. For you, darling, we'd let it go for fifty thousand less.'

Karen thought of her last stay on the Island, trying to dredge up memories of all the chalet's disadvantages so she wouldn't rush into a decision she might regret. She'd had to cook in its wholly inadequate kitchen, put out enamel bowls all over the kitchen floor to catch rain from leaks in the roof and generally endure the under-furnished, under-equipped musty squalor that had developed over the years of her mother's neglect.

Even with that list in mind, Karen couldn't forget the rest. As a child, she'd thought the chalet was like something out of a fairytale. If she'd been offered three wishes, she'd have asked all three times to live there for ever with her grandmother and her beloved brother, Aidan, and nobody else at all.

Summer holidays had been the best, full of amazing walks over the chalk downs, surrounded by the sweetness of wild flowers and clouds of colour from the butterflies: Common Blues and speckled Skippers and others whose names Karen couldn't remember now. Painted Admirals or Red Ladies or something. If she had a chance to spend more time there, they'd become second nature again.

She thought of long hot afternoons on the Island's emptier beaches, with Aidan burying her in the sand up to her neck, or shrimping with him in weedy pools among the rocks and watching for porpoises out at sea, while Granny kept an eye on them as she did her knitting, so expert she never had to look down at her stitches or the pattern. Once or twice they'd even built driftwood fires on the shingle and roasted potatoes and sausages wrapped in banana skins to stop them scorching in the flames.

Karen had learned all her cooking on the Island, just as she'd learned to swim and to ride a bike without stabilisers. She'd had her first kiss there, her first period, her first hangover. More or less everything important in her life before she'd married had happened on the Island. It would always feel like home.

The house doesn't have to be musty and neglected, she told herself, thinking of all kinds of ways to make the ramshackle chalet truly light and airy. Even gorgeous. Maybe.

'Come on, Karen.' Dillie was wheedling now. 'The land itself must be worth four hundred and fifty grand on its own. It does go all the way to the sea, you know. You could make something of it. Open it up. Get rid of those ghastly trees. You could probably turn a tidy profit on it. In the end.'

'I'll have to think.' Karen probably had enough saved to pay for a deposit, but she had no idea whether anyone would give her a mortgage for the rest. She already owed a lot on her penthouse flat here in Southampton. There was no way she could commit herself until she'd talked to her bank.

'Don't take too long. It's urgent. Really urgent.' Dillie shook her body, like someone emerging from a sauna, found her cheerful smile again from somewhere, and bounced up from the hard chair to kiss Karen. 'So do your best. And think about a facial. A better haircut wouldn't hurt either. Presentation is all. No one listens to you if you look a mess – least of all banks. Bye now.'

She blew out of the room, banging the door behind her.

Karen was left to wonder what it would have been like to have a mother who cared more about her children than her business affairs. Without her grandmother and the Island, Karen would have been lost.

Maybe she should nip over this evening and prowl around the chalet to see how much she'd mind if it were sold to a stranger.

If she did, she could also grab the opportunity to warn Charlie discreetly about Randall. As Senior Investigating Officer in the Lizzie Fane case, surely he had a right to know the man was out and probably heading his way.

Karen twizzled her Rolodex for the right card, then faced the fact that she'd never actually deleted Charlie's number from her mobile. She hesitated with her thumb on the keypad, aware of all sorts of things she'd rather not have known about herself. She also remembered that Will was due at her flat later.

He often had to cancel at the last minute, so it would be a pity to miss the opportunity of going to the Island and then find herself hanging about alone in the flat, short-changed and probably cross. Just to be sure, she checked her emails and saw one was indeed from Will.

The sight of his name on her screen brought with it an instant mental picture of the man himself: not much taller than she was, very fit and strong in spite of his slight build, with blond hair and intent blue eyes, and the steadiest hands she'd ever seen in anyone. But then he had to have steady hands – he was a neurosurgeon.

Karen had come to have a kind of mesmerised awe for the work he did, even when the discipline that was essential to it morphed into the kind of control-freakery that drove her mad. But then how could you dig into the organ that provided life and self and sensation and emotion and absolutely everything if you doubted yourself in any way at all?

Knowing she couldn't have done his kind of work in a million years, even if she'd had the technical skill, Karen opened his email. As usual he hadn't wasted a second on getting down the essentials. He didn't quite use text-speak in his emails, but nearly.

> Can't come tonight after all. Operating on a child. Tricky meningioma. Should arrive first thing Sat and stay till Sun pm. Hpe OK. If not, email. Wx.

With guilt punishing her for the momentary spurt of satisfaction, Karen pressed down on the phone's keys with her thumb.

'Charlie Trench,' said an energetic voice in her ear a second later. Karen could have picked his Geordie accent out of a dozen others, even after all this time.

'Hi. This is Karen Taylor. I don't know if—'

'Karen.' His voice sounded full of suspicion. 'Where are you?'

'Southampton. But it looks as if I've got to come to the Island later on today. I wondered if you . . . if you were around. Can I buy you a drink?'

There was only the briefest hesitation before he said: 'Sure. You going to that chalet of yours?'

'In the end. But I thought I'd come in on a Red Jet and maybe meet you in Cowes. How would that be?'

'So I could give you a lift out there?' Now his voice had a reassuring laugh in it. 'Taxis are cheaper than buying drinks for thirsty coppers.'

'Ah, but then I wouldn't get to see you.' Karen laughed too, glad at the evidence that he remembered her well enough to tease, even though he'd never phoned her all through the long winter

months, and then the summer too. 'And these days I can afford
taxis *and* drinks. You don't have to drive me.'

'We'll see. What time'll you land?'

'Six?'

'I'll be on Fountain Quay, Karen. Bye.'

Impossible not to smile. Impossible not to remember the
mixture of warmth and rage, the passion for justice, and the
undercurrent of danger that ran through him. You always felt
with Charlie as though he could have gone either way. He'd
chosen the police, but if things in his life had been only slightly
different, he might have been running a boxing gym full of other
ex-cons in some tough housing estate by now.

Karen caught sight of her distorted reflection in the shining
kettle. Her baggy clothes wouldn't do for this. If she were meeting Charlie she'd want something that fitted instead of hanging
like a sack all round her.

As she mentally went through her wardrobe, she remembered the confidentiality clause in her contract with the Minstry
of Justice. Charlie might have the moral right to know about
Randall, but that wouldn't help if the Ministry got to hear that
she'd told him their secrets. Could she trust him?

Chapter 5

Charlie still looked like a rougher, tougher, taller version of Robert Downey Jr., with his spiky dark hair, high forehead, round dark eyes and strong chin. Last year Karen had never seen him dressed in anything but black. Now he was transformed by a collarless natural linen shirt, which he wore hanging loose over the top of faded blue jeans. The warm beige of the linen suited his dark good looks better than shabby black leather ever had. He'd shaved carefully too.

'Karen,' he said, straightening up and opening the passenger door of his absurdly staid dark-blue Ford. 'Good to see you again.'

He sounded as though he meant it, so she leaned forwards to kiss his cheek and caught a strong whiff of toothpaste. Drawing back, she saw his lips twist into a familiar smile and felt as though they'd met only a week ago, not almost a year.

'And you. Where would you like to go?' she said, then remembered the pub he'd introduced her to last year, with its ravishingly beautiful pregnant landlady, Peg. 'The Goose Inn?'

'Still the best pub on the Island,' he said with an easy grin.

Karen wondered if he'd noticed her new skinny indigo jeans or the incredibly soft black leather jacket with the draped front that looked ten times more expensive than it actually had been.

'And Peg's still running the bar,' he went on, apparently oblivious to all the efforts she'd made for him. 'Her kid's almost crawling already.'

'Does she talk to you these days?'

He nodded and put the car in gear. 'She knows I only go there now because I like the place; not for intel. The menu's grown, too. We can eat before I take you out to the chalet. Or do you want to do it the other way round?'

Karen considered for a moment. There wouldn't be enough light after even an early dinner to see anything very much, and as far as she knew the electricity at the chalet was switched off still. She had a torch with her, but it wouldn't be the same.

'If we did it the other way round, we could relax and not rush our food,' she said casually.

'Fine.' Charlie glanced in the mirror, then over his shoulder, then performed a tight, fast U-turn and speeded up towards the north-western end of the Island. 'You got a problem at the chalet?'

'No. My ditsy parents want to flog it and have been kind enough to give me first refusal. I don't . . .'

'You don't what?'

She shrugged. 'I'm not sure I can afford it. And my life's geographically complicated enough as it is, with me working in Southampton and Will in Brighton.'

'You're tempted, though, aren't you?' Charlie still had the sound of laughter in his voice.

'Yeah. Well. Maybe,' she said, glad to have put Will's name into the open between them so quickly. 'No, you're right: I am tempted, but that's not the only reason I came here this time. Now we're in the car with no one to overhear, there's something I need to say to you.'

'You're pregnant,' Charlie said in a voice of horror. 'And it's mine.'

Karen gaped at him for a moment, then laughed. 'As far as I can remember, you and I were never on those kind of terms. And I haven't seen you for eleven months: I'm not an elephant.'

'True,' he said, sounding as though he was enjoying himself, 'but that's the kind of voice women use for that sort of announcement.'

'Is it? The story of your past must be pretty interesting. But this is serious.'

'Sorry,' he said, without any apology in his voice at all. 'Carry on.'

'What d'you remember of Randall Gyre?'

The cheerful atmosphere in the car froze at once, as though a film of water had been sprayed across a skating rink. Karen could almost hear the crackle.

'Why d'you ask?' Charlie's voice was as brittle as the atmosphere.

'I'm not supposed to say this to anyone, but I . . .' Karen hesitated, then added, 'You told me once that you know how to keep secrets. Do you still?'

'Depends what they are and why they're secret.'

'I'm doing some confidential work for the Ministry of Justice,' she began, before outlining her project in the vaguest possible terms.

'And you've come across Gyre?' Charlie said at the end. 'He's part of your study? I heard they'd let him out, the stupid bastards.'

'I *know* he's going to do it again. Next time he won't stop at rape and GBH.'

'You don't have to tell me that.' Now Charlie sounded as bitter as a burnt onion. 'I may not have three fancy degrees and God-knows-how-many psychology prizes, but I could've told them that for free.'

'I also think he's likely to revisit the scene of his last crime in order to do it better this time – in his terms, I mean – to get it right, to win, after losing to you last time round.'

'Now that is a new idea.' Charlie dragged his attention from the road and glanced at her for a second. 'Why?'

'He hates being beaten by anyone over anything. And you beat him.'

'If only.'

'I don't mean physically.' Karen wished Charlie wouldn't play games. He must have known what she meant. 'You arrested, interviewed and charged him. Humiliated him. And he went down.'

'But not for rape.' Charlie didn't sound impatient, but anger hardened his voice, a deep visceral kind of anger that made her shiver.

'Why does that bother you so much after all this time?' she asked, with real curiosity.

Charlie signalled right to turn off down the narrow muddy road that led to the chalet. They were halfway down it before he spoke again.

'If Lizzie, his victim, could've known the jury believed her, she'd have had a better chance of getting over it. She wouldn't have had to run.'

'Run? I don't understand.'

'Doesn't your project include anything about victims? They're supposed to be at the heart of the justice system these days. Or so the last course I had to go on said.'

'Could be,' Karen said. 'But my report'll be a tiny part of the whole project, and it doesn't go as far as victims. Where did Lizzie run? And when?'

'Right after the trial. No one knows where. She was nineteen by then, and in pieces. She'd waived anonymity in court because some arsehole persuaded her it'd help get Gyre convicted. If I could get my hands on whoever it was . . . Fuck it.'

They'd arrived. Charlie grabbed the handbrake as though it was the neck of the person who'd advised Lizzie so badly.

The last of the light had gone in Hoaxley, Somerset when Lisa Raithe said she had to go home because she had work to finish. Jed got to his feet at once, smiling at her in the usual way, as if he was the kindest man on the planet and she his special charge.

His skin had a reddish tan from all the hours spent out of doors, and his eyes were a soft brown, set behind lids that drooped with a sleepy kindness. Lisa knew he worked incredibly hard, but she'd never seen him rushed, and whenever she turned to him he always had time for whatever she wanted. She couldn't imagine him in any kind of fight or even an argument. At the very worst, he'd smile and walk away. In all her time here, she had never heard him shout or seen him frown.

'Stay there,' he said, resting one of his big scarred hands lightly on her shoulder. 'I'll pay, then walk you back.'

'You don't have to. It's less than half a mile, down a tiny safe tarmac road. I'll be fine.' She thought of whoever had been on the river this afternoon, first watching her then hurrying to get out of sight.

'I know.' Jed tightened his hand for a second, then let her go. 'But I like to see you safely in. Won't be long.'

Lisa nodded and patted the pocket of her jeans to make sure she had her keys. Obedient to their deal, she hadn't brought any money, and she never carried a phone. The old one hadn't helped her in the shitty alley on the Island, so why take the risk of having something to be mugged for if you didn't have to? Not that anyone ever got mugged out here. But she always felt safer when she showed herself lacking everything anyone else could want.

Someone moved between her and the bar, giving her a good view of the long low table in front of the empty fireplace, where newspapers were stacked for any customer who didn't want to talk. Lisa looked away at once. It was four years since she'd read a paper, or listened to the news on the radio or watched it on television. She didn't want anything infecting the safe life she'd made here.

'Thank you, Jed,' she said when he came back. 'That fish pie was great. I really liked it.'

'Fred's got the food better'n it was. In the old days you'd think it was rook pie or stewed mice you were eating.' He laughed with the slow rumbling sound that always made Lisa think of fresh potatoes falling from a sack.

Jed waved to his brother, a big bald man, behind the bar and called out, 'Bye, Fred! See you tomorrow.'

'Righty-ho. Bye, Lisa. Go carefully, girl. You want to watch my big brother on nights like this. Full moon soon. He'll be getting frisky again. Can't help it, a child of nature like him.'

Fred laughed, and the sound wasn't like anything homely, or even pleasant. His leering eyes sent goose bumps all down Lisa's arms. Impossible not to think of *Macbeth*, which had been one of her A-level set books, and the witches who'd said, 'By the pricking of my thumbs, something wicked this way comes.'

'Don't listen to him,' Jed said, pushing open the pub's heavy door for her. 'Get him fishing or walking, and he's fine. He's only like this in here.'

Lisa touched his arm in apology for her shiver. 'I know.'

As he shut the pub door behind them, she looked to left and right. There was no one waiting for her. Nothing moved. Jed took her arm and she liked feeling the warmth of his big body against hers.

They walked back along the road, hearing the slosh of the river and the flap of the geese flying overhead.

'I saw the kingfisher today,' Lisa said, when they were almost back at her little white cottage. 'A first for me. I was on the bank today, painting the orchard, and there he was. A flash of orange, then the greeny-blue. I felt . . .' She paused.

'What?' Jed asked, looking puzzled. 'What did you feel, Lisa?'

'Properly part of the place at last.'

He put an arm around her shoulders and pulled her nearer him. She resisted and looked away, over her shoulder. A shadow moved nearer the hedge. She peered more closely and a large bird rose up off the top of it. Was the bird big enough to have made the shadow?

'You *are* part of the place,' Jed said into her hair.

'I've only been here four years. The rest of you were born here.' Lisa laughed a little to hide her longing to go back and search the hedge. She felt as though she was always playing Grandmother's Footsteps now, with someone creeping up behind her every time she looked straight ahead, then hiding when she looked back.

Jed held her closer, unaware of all the instincts that were screaming at her, and said, 'Doesn't matter. You're part of us. Even if you're not much more'n a baby.'

'I'm twenty-three,' she said, pretending to be offended so she could extract herself from his arm and take a proper backwards look without being too obvious.

He laughed, which was what she'd hoped would happen, and didn't seem to mind her moving away.

She couldn't see anything wrong. No shadows. No watchers. She'd been making it up again.

'That makes you a baby t'me,' he said, noticing nothing. 'Though you sound older when you talk these days than when you first came. Must be mixing with us. I c'd be your dad.' He put both hands on her shoulders and turned her to face him again. 'I'll be thirty-nine next January.'

Over his shoulder, she could see the faint outline of the huge moon through the waving leaves of one of the willows. He bent his head. He was going to kiss her.

Lisa smelled the beer he'd been drinking. She told herself all over again that he was the kindest and safest of men. She'd often watched him pricking out vegetable seedlings or thinning the exotic salad leaves he grew, his big, scarred fingers amazingly delicate as he parted one leaf from the rest. Even when he was propagating the shrubbier herbs and had to slice into one with a scalpel, he did it with the kind of care you'd use if the twig had nerve-endings like a human.

She kissed him back. His lips were soft. He didn't force anything, just waited for her. He *was* safe.

'Nice,' she said, standing back after only a few seconds. 'Really nice, Jed. But I have to work. If I don't, I'll get weird. You don't want to be anywhere near me then.'

'I always want to be near you.'

She didn't answer. He'd kept one hand on her shoulder and now she could feel the force in it. She made herself stand absolutely still, waiting.

'Lisa, what is it? You're happy when you're with me, I c'n tell. You know I . . . well, you know what I want. Do we have to carry on like this?' His voice was still delivered slowly but the tone was hardening in a way she'd never heard from him. 'You're not a nun. And I'm no monk. I can't wait for ever.'

Lisa longed for him to laugh his warm, rumbling laugh, but he didn't. And his hand was still heavy on her shoulder. She stood as if she was paralysed. Kissing him was nearly always fine, and once or twice she'd thought about letting things go further. But each time her body had stopped her, seizing up so tightly that everything hurt too much. She couldn't have touched herself, let alone had anyone else near her.

'Please don't be angry,' she said at last, hearing her voice shake. She watched him fight for control over his spurt of temper and produce a small, tight version of his usual wide open smile.

'What's the matter, Lisa? You don't think I'm going to . . . well, hurt you, do you?'

'No.' She tried to laugh for him but her tongue swelled painfully. 'I'm sure you wouldn't. But I'm not very good at this. Jed, I don't . . . I can't . . . I don't want everyone knowing.'

'You think I'd talk in the village about you?' He still sounded angry and she knew she was going to have to tell him something, if only to bring him back to gentleness.

'I had a bad experience once,' she said, trying to pull her courage together.

'I may be only a farmer, an' a dunce at school, but I'm not blind.' Jed took four steps backwards as though it was now he who didn't want to be touched.

'Physically bad. I know you're not the same as . . . well, as him. Nothing like him. But I'm still not . . . I'm not ready to try again. Not yet. I'm sorry. I would if I could. It'd be you if it was anyone. I just . . .'

'It's OK.' Jed was clearly fighting to keep the smile on his face. She tried to see past the effort and the small vein she could see pumping madly at the left side of his forehead.

'I can see it isn't OK, Jed. Dear Jed. I'll try to . . . I'm sorry. I'd better go in. Thanks for supper.'

She moved forwards across the space he'd driven between them, so she could stroke his face. Her palm prickled against his stubble. He grabbed her wrist and pulled her arm away.

'Don't!' he said sharply. 'If I can't . . . it's not fair.'

He let her go then, turned away and tramped heavily off towards the field path to his house across the river. Lisa watched him in the moonlight for several minutes, listening in the cool darkness and hearing only the few familiar rustlings of small nocturnal creatures. At last she shrugged and let herself into the house.

Inside, she double-locked the door. Then came the nightly routine: she checked all the window locks, then the back door. All the bolts were shot. All the keys removed from their locks so that no one could break a window and reach in to turn the key.

She went upstairs to run herself a bath, stripped and, as usual, ignored the long mirror screwed to the wall beside the basin. No reflection was necessary to remember or assess her hideous body. She knew too well how each of her breasts looked: like a ball of soft raw pork in a darker-pink net. Randall had left the scars of long cuts up the inside of both her thighs, too.

How could she let anyone else see it all?

As she turned off the taps, she thought about the thick lines in her skin that were still easily visible whenever she squinted down at them, even though they were pink now rather than the dark purple they'd once been. The puckering along the knitted edges was smoothing out with time. So were the other scars, the internal ones. One day she'd be in a state to look in the mirror; even share herself again. One day. But not yet.

The scars would never go completely. Which was good. If they did, there'd probably be no more Lee Wills. And without Lee, she'd be defenceless again.

An image began to build itself in her mind, an image of the pure blazing streak of self overtaken by darkness.

Forgetting the bath, she pulled on her clothes again and hurried downstairs to pick up her keys. When she'd unlocked the back door, she grabbed the heavy torch and swung it right round the garden to make sure no one was there, watching, waiting. Everything was still.

She locked the door behind her and ran to the studio so she could rough out the basics of her idea, just brushing charcoal lines on to the stretched canvas to get the main point down before it escaped into the great swill of memory and opportunities ignored.

This one'll be half-dark and half-light, she thought, not yet knowing whether there would be a bridge across the chasm.

If there was, it would have to look like a tunnel through the mountains too. Everything in a Lee Wills painting had to be seen both ways.

She was back in the alley now, with Randall . . .

'So what're you going to do about the chalet?' Charlie asked when he and Karen were sitting opposite each other in the Goose Inn, waiting for Peg, the licensee, to bring their chicken-and-olive pies.

Charlie was nursing a half-pint of Peg's Special home brew, and Karen was sipping a glass of chilled Sauvignon Blanc. Peg had opened a fresh bottle for her. The wine wasn't anything like as good as the latest case Will had sent her from a new vineyard he'd discovered in France, but it was more than drinkable.

'I'm still not sure. It's got possibilities, but it would need a hell of a lot of work,' Karen said. 'The garden too. As you saw, it's a total jungle. I've a mate in the Architecture Department at Southampton University, Stella Atkins. I might ask her what she thinks I could do with the place.'

'If you moved over here, we—' Charlie began, just as Peg appeared with a loaded tray. 'Ah. Those look great, pet. Thanks.'

Peg put their plates on the table, asked if they wanted any more to drink, then left them alone. The three drinkers perched on stools by the bar watched her all the way back, clearly resentful of anyone who took her away from them.

'Look at them,' Karen said, amused. 'They're like starving cats faced with a pint of cream.'

Charlie glanced over her shoulder at Peg.

'Why not? She's gorgeous. Got the most kissable mouth I've ever seen on a woman.'

Karen took a big swig of wine and found it much more acid than before. Charlie let his gaze focus on her again.

'Although,' he went on, as though there had been no digression, 'I guess you're only here now because you want information about Gyre.'

'Not so much that,' Karen said. 'I wanted to warn you he's likely to come back so you can make plans to protect the public.'

'Not a lot I can do,' Charlie said. 'Think about it: we get thousands of visitors, even at this time in the year. We can't check 'em all. If we had face-recognition software, it'd be different.'

'Can you tell me *why* he didn't go down for rape?'

Little bumps appeared on the side of Charlie's jaw and all the blood was driven from around his lips as he clamped them together. Karen was surprised but pleased to see how much he cared.

'All the usual. Plus the pub's CCTV.' He scowled at his beer.

'CCTV?' Karen said, amazed. 'In an obscure pub on the Island?'

'Yeah. They had some trouble in Cowes Week one year and the brewery insisted. Lizzie's bad luck. *More* bad luck.'

He glanced up at Karen and she saw dark misery in his eyes.

'The tapes show her flirting with Gyre,' he went on. 'Laughing at his jokes, stroking his arm, leaning in towards him and gazing up at him.'

'Poor girl.' Karen thought of several casual encounters she'd had after Peter's death, any of which could have ended like Lizzie's. It was Karen's great good luck that none of the men she'd met had been a rapist. But it was only luck.

'She even bought him a drink,' Charlie said. 'They left the place hand-in-hand. The jury took the view that any reasonable man in his position would've thought she wanted sex.'

'But not the injuries.'

'No. Not them. Which is why they convicted him of GBH.' There were notes in Charlie's voice Karen didn't understand.

The rage she could hear so clearly was easy to accept. Anyone who'd had to watch a violent rapist he'd arrested declared not guilty would be angry. And the unhappiness was fair, too. But there was some kind of shame, as well, and altogether much more emotion than she'd have expected of a man like him. She decided to probe a little.

'Had you known her before?'

'Lizzie? No.'

'D'you see her now?'

'Christ, no. I told you: she ran away from the Island right after the trial. I suppose I spoke to her five times in all.'

'So what was it about her that makes you so . . . so wound up by her story?'

Charlie stared down at his toffee-coloured beer, then swallowed most of it in one great gulp.

'We let her down.'

'More, please,' Karen said, and watched him pushing himself to his feet. She quickly corrected herself. 'I meant more information, not wine. I've still got lots. And you're ignoring your pie. It'll get cold.'

He picked up his fork, then let it drop again. 'Puts you off your grub. A couple of my junior officers— Shit! What the fuck's going on?'

Karen looked up to see Peg fighting off the last of the drinkers at the bar. Before she could move, Charlie leapt out of his chair, leaving it to clatter over on to its side on the floor, and ran to the bar to grab a handful of the drinker's shirt in his right hand. Charlie used his grip on the fabric to drag the man off Peg. Even from the table Karen could hear the shirt rip.

'Fuck off, arsehole,' the drinker gasped, as though he was being severely choked.

Karen reached the bar and saw the deep red marks of his fingers on Peg's neck. She was coughing, hard, and her eyes were wet. Leaving Charlie to deal with the attacker, Karen pulled up the bar's flap so she could get behind it to hold Peg's shoulders.

'You're OK,' Karen said, feeling Peg's light-boned body trembling under her hands. 'Charlie's got him. He can't hurt you now. Hold on. I'll get you some water in a minute.'

'Stop it!' Peg gasped. 'Charlie! Stop it. For God's sake! You'll kill him.'

Chapter 6

Karen looked behind her to see the man who'd attacked Peg flat on his face on the floor. Charlie had one knee planted into his back and was pulling his left arm so high up his back his hand was almost touching his neck.

'Charlie, don't!' Peg shouted. 'Don't.'

He looked up at her. Karen saw the skin on his face was greyish-white and stretched, like elastic under ferocious tension. His eyes were on fire with determination and his mouth twisted into a grimace that made her swallow hard.

Peg had got her breath back now and had most of the trembling under control.

'Let him go!' she said more quietly. 'He's only a drunk.'

'He was strangling you,' Charlie said through clenched teeth, but he relaxed his grip a little, which allowed the man to pull his arm free. He also managed to turn his face to one side so he could speak.

'I wasn't strangling her, arsehole.' He coughed twice and spat on the floor. 'I was only trying to kiss the silly cunt. She shouldn't of pulled away. All she had to say was "no".'

'Shut the fuck up,' Charlie said, putting more weight on his knee.

Karen was terrified she'd hear the man's spine snap. Charlie wasn't looking at her. All his attention was on Peg.

'He hurt you?'

'Not much,' Peg said. 'I'm glad you got him off me. But that's enough now. Come on, let him go.'

Peg hurried round from behind the bar and leaned down to tug at Charlie's shoulder. He sighed, then moved his knee and allowed her to help him up. For an instant Charlie hung on to her shoulders, then let her go. Bending over the drunken attacker, Peg told him, 'Get up and get out. I don't want to see you in here again.'

'What about him?' said the man, straightening his clothes and rubbing his breastbone. 'He's a fucking maniac.'

'But not a drunk,' Charlie said, running his fingers through his spiky hair. 'Now get out, like the lady says. And don't come back. People don't do this kind of thing on the Island.'

The three of them watched the man grab his fleece from one of the bar stools and leave, lurching into the side of the door on his way out. Moments later, they heard a car door slam, then an engine cough, before starting up and revving hard.

Charlie peered out of the window and wrote something on a pad, before pulling out his phone and making a call. He came back to the two women, looking more like his usual cheerful self.

'That'll fix him. Traffic will pick him up and breathalyse him. Not likely to be the first time, so with luck he'll lose his licence. You OK, Peg?'

'Fine,' she said, sounding dryer than usual. 'But he's right, Charlie. You *are* a maniac. You're a DCI, for God's sake. What would've happened if I hadn't stopped you and he'd reported you? You can't face another disciplinary, you really can't.'

Karen was surprised to see a faint flush creeping up Charlie's stubbly cheeks. Just as she was surprised to understand how much he must have been confiding in Peg.

'Wouldn't have come to that,' he said. 'You need a drink, Peg. What'll you have? I know you don't take drinks from punters, but I'm not that kind of punter, and this is a one-off. You should have something.'

'OK then. Brandy and ginger,' she said, smiling at him in a way that made Karen take herself to task even more savagely than usual for all the imaginary conversations she'd had with him throughout last winter. 'Thanks, love.'

Peg dragged her gaze away from Charlie's face and smiled a much cooler, politer sort of smile in Karen's direction.

'I'll be fine now. You go back and finish your dinner. Go on, the pair of you.'

Karen watched Charlie debating with himself. After a moment he shrugged and led the way back to their table.

'So,' he said, picking up his beer. 'Where were we?'

'You were telling me how Lizzie was short-changed,' Karen said, still reeling mentally from what she'd just seen him do, 'but you probably don't want to go on talking about that old case now, with Peg in such a state.'

'It's fine,' he said, but he leaned sideways so he could look round her to make sure the other woman was still safe behind her bar.

Facing Karen again, he went on: 'Yeah. Right. I had a couple of young officers who ignored an emergency call from an old bloke who heard a woman scream somewhere near the pub – the Eagle and Dumpling in Cowes. He was on two sticks, he said when he phoned, so he couldn't do anything himself, but he wanted it investigated.'

'That makes sense,' Karen said, ignoring her now-warm white wine.

'He was thanked for his report and told we'd see to it. He was to get himself home and not to worry.' Charlie sounded more bitter by the moment. 'A call went out. The two wankers who should've responded were near the end of their shift. Did a bit of private prioritizing.'

'On what?' Karen said when he paused. He looked murderous.

'Rescuing a red squirrel stuck up a chimney.' Charlie swallowed hard, as though something was stuck in his throat.

'A *squirrel*?' Karen said, not surprised he was angry. She'd have lost it completely. 'Rat with a tail?'

'Red squirrels are one of the Island's best things,' he said, mastering his temper. 'And protected by law. But it's no excuse. Fuck it! A woman was screaming. They *should've* gone to help. No one else was within easy reach of the pub. By the time the only other car got there, all they found was Lizzie, bleeding from everywhere. More or less unconscious.'

'What happened to the two young officers?' Karen asked, making mental notes all the time.

Charlie stared at her. She'd never seen eyes that bleak. After a moment, he shook himself.

'I told them how their lives were going to be if I had anything to do with it. Funnily enough the pair of them decided to leave. Job and Island.' He stopped, looking sick.

Karen wondered whether he was thinking how lucky he was they hadn't taken him to an industrial tribunal.

'But they weren't the only ones,' he went on, still full of fury. 'Everybody involved screwed up: the first of my blokes to question Lizzie in hospital before the specialist team arrived; the doctors; the lawyers. Even the poor little bitch's mother.'

'What?' Karen had had enough trouble with Dillie to be instantly sympathetic to any other mistreated daughter. 'What did her mother do to her?'

Charlie drained his beer, checked on Peg again, then concentrated on Karen. His expression was changing into something warmer, less scary.

'Not her fault, and she's never stopped hating herself for it. There was more CCTV, from the hospital this time. Nearly as bad as the stuff from the pub. The defence used this lot in the trial too.'

'Showing what?' Karen asked, too impatient to wait for all Charlie's details without prompting him.

He sighed. 'Her mother, Sally, leaning against Gyre as they waited for a lift to arrive, with him more or less mopping her tears, only inches from the bed where her daughter was fighting for her life. Literally inches.'

Charlie's hands tightened around his empty glass so hard Karen thought of the drunk's spine all over again.

'You can guess what the lawyers made of it,' he added. 'Though to be fair, he had nicked a white coat, so she'd every reason to believe he was a doctor.'

Karen nodded. Putting on a pompous, drawling voice, she said: 'Can you imagine, members of the jury, a man who had raped a young woman bothering to visit her in hospital, showing himself to be on such affectionate terms with her mother? Of course not. My client had nothing to do with Ms Fane's injuries and he certainly did not rape her. Indeed, he went to the trouble – at some risk to himself – of posing as a doctor so that he could see for himself that she was all right.' Reverting to her own voice, Karen added: 'Something like that?'

'More or less,' Charlie said in an unhappy growl. 'Except that they claimed he'd "borrowed" the white coat to ensure that he didn't bring in any infection that could make her condition worse. Bastard. Sally doesn't think Lizzie'll ever forgive her.'

'"A mother's place is in the wrong",' Karen quoted.

'She tried to make up for it,' Charlie said. 'Complained to everyone about everything, especially the hospital. Campaigned for a public apology. When it didn't happen, she tried to make Lizzie sue Doctor Franklin, the consultant, who fucked up by not ensuring she'd been properly examined and all the infective matter removed from her body, and then failing to spot that septicaemia was developing.'

'*Did* Lizzie sue?' Karen asked.

Charlie shook his head. He shovelled a large forkful of pie into his mouth and then swallowed it without much chewing, like a python ingesting a goat.

'Lizzie'd had enough. Couldn't take any more, even when it

was meant to help her. She lost it, told her mother she hated her and left the Island for good.'

'How old was she then?' Karen asked.

'Nineteen. She'd been a few weeks short of her birthday when the rape happened. Blonde. Pretty. Naïve as fuck. Back on the Island after her first term at art school in London.'

Karen remembered how vulnerable she'd felt at that age, already married and already unhappily discovering that neither husband nor life was anything like she'd expected. She'd felt lost and desperate. What must it have been like for Lizzie? Physically healing after the attack but discovering that all the people she should have been able to trust had made her ordeal worse than it had to be. No wonder she'd run away. But where? And how?

'Did she have any money?' Karen asked.

'She got something from the Criminal Injuries Compensation Board, and her dad gave her everything he could afford. Sally didn't like it at all, thought he was making everything worse. "Enabling" her to go. But he said Lizzie was tough enough to cope – "had a core of steel" were his words – and that she'd find it easier to get over it if the rest of us left her alone.'

'You can see his point,' Karen said. 'But it must've been hard. What a man!'

'Yeah.' Charlie pushed his plate away, with most of the food still smeared across it. 'I hope to God she's OK now, all on her own Christ-knows-where.'

The finality of his comment made Karen hold back on the rest of her questions.

'I was quite surprised to find you still here on the Island,' she said instead. 'I thought you'd have been tempted back to the Met by now.'

Charlie laughed, but he looked a little shamefaced. 'I did get an offer, but I like it here now. I'm buying a flat on the edge of East Cowes. Great view over the Solent.'

Nice and convenient for this place, Karen thought, looking around the cosy pub and working out that it would be only about fifteen minutes' drive, if that. Last year Peg had talked a fair bit about her husband. Karen rather wished she could see evidence of him now.

'I'd better get back,' she said. 'Thanks for filling me in about the case. I'll ask Peg to call me a cab. Maybe her husband's.'

'No need,' Charlie said. 'I'll run you back to Fountain Quay. It's not far out of my way.'

They said goodnight to Peg and went out into soft autumn darkness. Karen tilted back her head, enjoying the sight of the stars. Tonight they looked tightly packed and diamond-sharp in the hugeness of the black sky. In Southampton there was always far too much light pollution to see anything smaller than the moon.

She felt Charlie's hand closing around her elbow, warm and firm but without any of the roughness he'd shown so clearly tonight.

'Amazing, innit?' he said quietly, waving his free hand over his head in an expansive gesture she'd never seen from him before. 'Makes me want to be in a boat miles out to sea, where there'd be no distraction from all this.'

Karen moved towards his parked car. She wanted to say something affectionate but didn't know how. He unlocked the car from ten feet away. Then he stopped in front of her so she couldn't move any further from him.

'Karen?'

'Yes?' she said softly. 'What is it, Charlie?'

'You said Gyre's likely to come back here to the Island to re-stage the crime with a new victim he may even kill.'

Karen pulled on her professional mask with difficulty.

'That's right,' she said crisply.

'Are you sure it isn't more likely that he'll try to find where Lizzie's gone so he can kill *her*? It's what he said he'd do.'

Chapter 7

Lisa unlocked the studio door and stumbled out into the pearly dawn light. She'd been painting for five hours and her shoulders and neck were stiff as cardboard. Rolling her head back, she looked up first into the pale pinkish sky, where the birds were already clustering about the trees, then straight ahead over the river towards the orchard and the Tor beyond. In winter, thick white mist would settle as far as the horizon, sometimes hovering a foot above the grass, but today the air was absolutely clear and tingling with the first hint of autumn.

No one was about yet, and it was still cold. Lisa went back into the studio to grab the old khaki cagoule that had once been her father's and pulled it round her body. Sometimes she thought she could catch a faint hint of his smell from the fabric: Boots shaving soap, oil from the old Morgan that was his pride and joy, and the rich blue cheeses that were his favourite food.

She missed him more than she could ever let herself admit, and she often thought of the day when she'd left the Island. When he'd stood in front of her, with tears oozing out of his eyes, just before she'd boarded the ferry, the last thing he'd said was: 'I'm going to find it tough waiting for the day when you're ready to come home, but I know you've got to go, and I know why. I won't come looking for you, I promise, but when you need something, phone me. Whatever it is you want – more dosh, a chat, to be picked up from John o' Groats or Land's End. Anything.'

Hugging his cagoule around herself, Lisa thought she might be nearly ready to phone him. She'd always known she'd have to wait until she could be sure she was whole again. If not, she'd let him look after her and she'd never become strong enough.

Soon, she promised herself. I'll pick up the phone soon.

Her feet made deep indentations in the long, dew-laden grass, as she walked towards the rickety bridge over the river into the orchard her landlords had made when they'd bought the field opposite their garden. She was concentrating on the safety of Now.

The birds were singing so loudly she could only just hear the river and the whirring of next door's small wind turbine. She liked being alone with the friendly sounds. Then one of their horses snorted, as though he'd been disturbed. Keeping as quiet as she could, Lisa hurried over the bridge and towards the hedge so she could look over it.

All she could see were the footprints.

Someone had made deep, shoe-shaped marks in the damp grass, and they were heading from the far edge of the field towards the boundary with her orchard, where they stopped and turned back. Her neighbours never came in that direction. Their prints always started and ended at the house. And these couldn't be Jed's, either. They were far too small. Lisa backed away and turned, as though by ignoring the evidence of a prowler she could forget it. And then she saw a gap in the hedge, as though he'd been pushing a way through and been disturbed.

She sank down until she was squatting on the ground, well below the level of the hedge. A small toad emerged from under a heap of longer grass at the side and sat watching her, its black eyes looking beady and its loose throat pulsing. So fragile, she thought. So easy to kill by mistake, or on purpose. She reached forward, as though to touch it, then held back.

It didn't move away, but its breathing changed, as she could see from the way the paler skin of its throat puffed out and sank back faster and faster. Fear did that to you, she thought, and hated herself. There was only one living thing she wanted to feel fear of her.

Karen woke to the sound of Will's key in her lock soon after seven. She ran her tongue round the inside of her mouth and pushed the duvet aside to move quickly and quietly to the bathroom. He was the cleanest man she had ever met. Tangled hair would be fine, but she needed to brush her teeth.

They'd developed a routine during the fourteen months they'd been seeing each other. If he couldn't make it by Friday night, he would let himself in first thing on Saturday, make coffee and cook something – bacon sandwiches, an omelette, or coddled eggs – and bring a loaded tray to her room. It amused them both to pretend she would still be asleep when he came in and be surprised by the feast.

Today was different. He reached her bedroom door before she was back from the bathroom and she emerged, still wiping sticky toothpaste from her lips. He looked taut on the outside, as though he was trying to hide some internal collapse.

'The patient died,' she said, remembering it had been a child. 'I'm sorry, Will.'

He didn't speak, but she could see from a minute release in the tense muscles around his blue eyes that she'd been right. She dropped the towel on the floor so she could put her arms around him.

His strong, narrow body felt as stiff as a frozen leg of lamb, and he smelled of unscented soap, medicated shampoo, and the rosemary shaving oil he always used.

Breathing in, she waited for him to mend. Eventually, his neck softened and he let his fair head droop until it lay on her shoulder. He would never admit to the weakness of misery or a sense of failure, and he'd hated any attempt she'd ever made to try to talk through his feelings; however, she had learned that he could be comforted in silence like this when something really bad had happened.

They stood there for long enough to give her cramp in her arms, but she wasn't going to move until he did. When he did, it was to raise his head, kiss her cheek briefly, and say, 'I'll get breakfast on the go. In here? Or do you want to get up?'

'I'll dress,' she said, taking her cue from the question itself.

Normally he would never ask it. There were times when she wondered why she played such a subservient role in their relationship.

This is one of them, she thought, as she went to choose her clothes.

Apart from last week's thunderstorms, the whole of September had been hot, and the way the sunlight was already dancing over the waves beyond her window told her today would be much the same, so she chose a pair of white linen crops that would show off her smoothly tanned legs, and a red-and-white striped T-shirt with red buttons along one shoulder. Her toenails were much the same colour, so she could go without shoes.

Unlocking the French doors to the narrow balcony over the sea, she rearranged the round zinc table and matching chairs so that both she and Will would be able to look out across the steel wire barrier towards the Island, then returned to the living room for seat cushions.

By the time she had everything ready, he was back with his tray. He was wearing his usual weekend uniform of newly washed blue jeans, slung very low on his narrow hips, with a pristine pink cotton shirt tucked in. His cheekbones were almost as chiselled as her father's, although his face wasn't as long. In fact, Will's was almost square but because he carried not one single ounce of spare flesh, it never looked heavy.

He put the tray down on the table. Karen saw small rounds of French toast neatly piled on the big serving plate, dusted with icing sugar and partnered by crushed raspberries and cream.

'Wow!' she said.

'It's a recipe called Poor Knights of Windsor,' he said. 'I'd bought the ingredients before yesterday's débâcle and didn't want to waste them, so it's a rather inappropriately celebratory breakfast.'

'Looks wonderful. And we have got something to celebrate,' she said, scooping a generous quantity of the crisp and fragrant bread on to her own plate. There was a scent of sherry somewhere and cinnamon too.

She often wondered whether he starved himself when he was alone. Even for a man as scrupulous about his workouts as Will, it was amazing for a thirty-eight-year-old to be able to eat this kind of thing and still keep a shape any man of twenty would envy.

'Really?' His deep voice was slower than usual. 'Good. I could do with hearing something cheerful.'

'I'm about to acquire a holiday property,' Karen said lightly. 'At least, I think I am. Unless you've got any violent objections.'

'Why would I?' he said, with an expression of detached interest. 'Your money, your house – your decision. Where? Tuscany? Greece?'

She laughed. 'Too exotic for me. No, the Island.' She waved across the Solent towards the wooded mass that rose on the far side, only twelve miles away. 'Maybe I should put up a flagpole in the garden and sort out a series of signals. You'd be able to see them from here, if not from Brighton.'

'You're not thinking of buying your parents out of their hideous wooden bungalow, are you?' he said in a tone of voice that expressed absolute disbelief rather than the kind of criticism she hated from anyone, but particularly from him because when it came from him it mattered too much. 'Why on earth?'

Karen repeated the story of her mother's urgent need of cash and her own happy memories of the chalet. Will glanced over his shoulder towards the immaculate, very modern, very gleaming rooms behind him.

'Wouldn't it be like going backwards?' he said.

'No.' Karen felt defensive and accused. She tried not to let it affect her voice. 'Why?'

'You hated your childhood, and you've moved on. You're a successful and respected forensic psychologist now,' Will said. 'The flat suits you: elegant, spare, stylish. Why go back into those horrible muddy woods to live in a dingy little hut?'

'I'm planning to make it *un*dingy. Cut a swathe through the trees for a sea view. You know, it could be quite comfortable.' Karen paused, then spoke without thinking too much, letting the words bubble up from somewhere far below the surface of her mind. 'I thought it might be a refuge for us both, right away from work. Somewhere we could . . . kind of be our real selves.'

Will raised one fair eyebrow, looking as absurdly young as usual.

'That sounds as if you're unhappy, Karen. What have I done?'

'Nothing,' she said as fast she could. 'Of course I'm not unhappy. I just think it could be . . . good, if we had somewhere away from work, where no one could get at us, where we wouldn't have to worry about looking professional all the time. D'you see what I mean?'

His face relaxed a little. 'I get the drift. Although I'm not sure I'd have chosen the Island for our playground.'

'Think how easy it is for us both to get to. Unlike abroad.' Karen shuddered as she thought of their last trip to the French vineyards and the delays they'd endured getting there. 'No airport queues and hanging around for delayed flights and security crises. Summers are supposed to be getting hotter, after all. In which case the Island's woods won't be muddy for ever. It could work.'

Will stretched his arm across the table, turning his hand palm upwards. 'I'm not sure either of us will be any different, even if we're not worrying about our public image all the time.'

She took his hand. 'I'm not sure either, but I can't help feeling that if we could just mess about for a bit, we might – oh, I don't know.'

Will poured himself more coffee. He'd chosen espresso beans for this morning, so it was very black and very strong. He raised his cup to his lips, inhaling the rich scent.

'What we've got now works,' he said with a lightness she didn't find convincing. 'Doesn't it? Why risk it by looking for something else?'

Because it's not *quite* enough, Karen thought, but she couldn't say it because she didn't want to hurt him.

Two days later, Karen was lying on a long white chair in her best friend's local health club. Stella was more or less her own age but had got going on her career much sooner than Karen and was now a senior figure in the Architecture Department at the university.

After a long swim and a good stint in the steam room, Karen felt wonderful, full of exhausted cleanliness. The sensation was nearly enough to make her stop chewing over her two biggest anxieties: whether she had hurt Will by showing she wanted more from their relationship, and how she was going to handle her impending full-on interview with Randall. Now she knew the details of his conviction – and had some knowledge of at least three of his victims – she was more than reluctant to come face to face with him again.

Killing was one thing. She could cope with murderers and the stories they told themselves to justify what they'd done. But she really did not want to hear Randall talk about why he chose tall, slender, blonde women to rape and hack up with filthy chunks of broken glass, or tell her about the pleasure he got from it.

'Anyone in there?'

At the sound of Stella's voice, Karen looked sideways and smiled at her friend, glad to be dragged away from her uncomfortable thoughts.

'Sorry. I was in a dream,' she said.

'I was just saying I can't offer your chalet-transformation as an undergraduate assignment – too far off the syllabus – but I like the idea of running it as a competition,' Stella said, pulling up a corner of her towelling dressing-gown to mop some chlorine from her eye.

She wasn't as tall as Karen, and her basic shape was much more curvy, but she kept herself in trim with regular trips to the pool. The twenty lengths they'd just achieved hadn't even made her breathless, unlike Karen who hadn't done any serious swimming since school, and not a lot then. Splashing in the shallows on a beach was much more her bag. Although that could never block out thought in the way real, hard swimming had just done.

'Private commissions are rare these days, so we might get quite a few entries,' Stella went on, pushing her fingers through the tangles in her damp red hair. 'There are lots of internet chat rooms used by architects and designers. Artists too, who might come up with more imaginative solutions than someone used to building constraints. Why don't I put out the word through some of them? See who bites.'

'Is that safe?' Karen felt so protective of the chalet she didn't want mad strangers having anything to do with it. 'You never know who's really who in a chat room.'

'We can get round that.' Stella was one of the most competent people Karen had ever met and she'd always been able to weed every anxiety out of her mind before it had a chance to take root. Karen envied her and wondered if the three or four years that separated them might bring her the same skill.

'But there is one problem,' Stella added. 'What if all the entries were crap? Would we have to give a prize, whatever? You don't want some useless con-artist getting his hands on your house.'

'I don't know,' Karen said. 'I hadn't even thought about it. We'd better check out the law of lotteries and competitions. I think they're all lumped in together.'

'You can do that,' Stella said, 'while I work out the terms of the brief. Have you got any photos of the site?'

'No, but I can get some. And somewhere there must be a map showing the boundaries of the property.'

'Property sounds very grand,' Stella said, laughing. 'I thought you said it was a bit of a shit heap. How big *is* it?'

'A couple of acres or a little more. The chalet itself isn't up to much. If you were an estate agent, you might say it was a summerhouse.' Karen paused for second, thinking of Dillie's description of the place, then she added with a short giggle: 'But you'd be lying.'

'Like most estate agents,' Stella said cheerfully. 'OK, you get the photographs. I'll nip over to the Island as soon as I can, have a look round and let you know what I think.'

Karen felt like kissing her. 'Fantastic! Now, what about a drink?'

'Good idea.'

As they passed a huge mirror on the way to their changing rooms, Karen stopped and peered at her small round face.

'What's up?' Stella said. 'Got a spot or something?'

'No. Luckily. But my mother told me I need a facial.'

'Bollocks!' Stella's voice was even warmer than usual. 'You look great. It's only jealousy. They all do it. Mine's always banging on about getting my hair coloured so I'm not a coppernob any more.'

'Coppernob! What a cow!'

'Yeah. She keeps telling me that's why Danny left me and why all my other relationships go tits up.' Stella laughed with a sound that made Karen think of breaking glass. Then she linked her arm into Karen's and towed her away from the mirror.

'Thank God for mates,' Stella said. 'What would we do without each other? Come on, let's get that drink and forget about our bloody mothers. And everyone else.'

*   *   *

On Friday the marks of Randall's fingers were still visible on Karen's wrist, which amazed her. She felt as though it was months since their first meeting.

But she'd had a lot to do in the intervening days, battling with her mortgage company and her bank, both of which had been reluctant to lend more than half the money her mother wanted for the chalet. Eventually, in desperation, Karen had phoned Aidan in the States, knowing that as a successful lawyer in Boston he would have a far better credit rating than she would ever achieve and hoping he would be able to offer her bank some kind of supporting guarantee. In fact, he'd done far more. He'd listened to what she wanted and asked no questions. Instead he'd told her he would wire the money as soon as she wanted it. She wondered what it would be like to have earned so much you could pay out a quarter of a million pounds just like that.

She and Dillie had exchanged contracts two days ago, with completion set for a quick but just feasible three weeks' time. With exchange, Dillie had been able to relax, safe in the knowledge that her cherished business had once again escaped bankruptcy by moments. And Karen had been able to get back to work on Randall's case, researching other serial rapists who'd shown the same kind of escalating violence and going over and over the answers he'd given her at their first meeting. Nothing she'd found had reassured her. He *was* extremely dangerous.

But not to me, she kept telling herself as the still-green trees flashed past the train windows, and she stroked her wrist. Provided I keep my professional face on and don't let him see he's getting to me, I can keep absolute control.

After a moment her own thoughts made her laugh. All she had to do was be like Will. He *never* lost control.

The ticket inspector was making his way down the corridor of the train. Karen scuffled in her briefcase for her tickets. As usual when she was nervous, she couldn't remember where she'd put them.

*   *   *

'So, Doctor Taylor,' Randall said, crossing one long leg over the other. 'You said by now you'd know all about my alleged offence and the trial.' He sounded quite as languid and confident as last week. 'Where do we go from here?'

'I ask you for your account of what happened that night,' Karen said with a coolness she didn't feel. The start of this bit always made her uncomfortable, even when she was dealing with a bog-standard killer rather than the kind of vicious sadist he was.

Randall gave a small, sexy chuckle, as though he'd been offered a longed-for treat, and re-crossed his legs.

'I'll admit I was on the pull. Stuck on the Island for Christmas, escorting my mother for our traditional visit to my godmother and her family. You can see why I needed a buzz. That Island gets bloody dull. Fine in grilling sun for Cowes Week or something, but hell in midwinter when the only people you see are geriatrics, eking out their last few months on earth as best they can.'

'So you were on the pull. Carry on from there,' Karen said pleasantly, resisting the urge to draw her sleeve down over her wrist. 'Any luck?'

'Absolutely. I was in this pub, looking around, you know, and thinking I was on a hiding to nothing when in walks this leggy blonde, looking pissed off.'

He broke off to let his gaze rake up and down what he could see of Karen's body. She kept her face stony.

'On her own, too,' Randall went on. 'No boyfriend to get in the way. And looking like she could take on the world, pissed off or not, in the way those very young girls sometimes do. You know, before they've any idea of the risks they're taking.'

'I know what you mean,' Karen said, when he paused again.

'Great. I buy her a drink, and we're away. I couldn't believe my luck. She was practically unzipping my jeans before we were halfway through the first glass.'

'Then it all went wrong.' Karen needed Randall to think she was on his side, but the words were hard to say with the necessary air of carefree humour. Still, she had to try. 'Why? Was she just a silly little cock-tease?'

'D'you know,' he said, clasping his hands around his knee and leaning forwards as though they were the oldest closest friends, 'I don't think she was. Not the classic kind, anyway. She was egging me on, you see – panting, groaning, grabbing my dick, squeaking.'

'In the pub?' Karen allowed amazement to sound in her voice.

'No.' He looked as though he was enjoying a particularly juicy memory. 'We found a quiet corner outside. But not far away. She was too desperate to wait.'

'I see. What then?'

'More of the same,' Randall said. 'Until she shrieked in my ear that she wanted me to hurt her.'

Karen blinked. 'Is that usual – in your experience?'

'Damned unique.' Randall sat back and laughed again. 'I did my best. I'm well brought up like that. Always try to do what a woman I'm fucking asks. Then Lizzie started to say I was getting it wrong and screamed louder and louder about what she wanted. D'you know? In the end, what she wanted made me feel sick.'

'Did you actually vomit?' Karen was interested in this part of the story, which didn't fit with anything in his record or the tests he'd completed for her.

'Christ, no! I told her I wasn't going any further. If she wanted to be fucked by a psychopath she'd have to find someone else. I gave her a few bruises, maybe a scrape or two. No more than that. She must have found someone more amenable after me and got him to do the rest. Cut her up with a bottle, or so I heard.'

How long had he worked on that story? Karen imagined him lying on his bunk in the cell, reliving every moment of what he'd done, telling it first one way then another until he arrived at the perfect exonerating narrative. Probably enjoying every moment of it too.

'Got more than she bargained for.' Randall offered a different smile this time – sweeter, gentler. 'In fact, I feel sorry for the poor kid. I'm going to tell her so as soon as I find her. D'you know where she is now? I hear she's left the Island.'

'I have no contact with any victim,' Karen said, planning to warn Charlie and Al at the Ministry of Justice that Randall had just shown the first sign that he really was planning to go after Lizzie.

'That's a pity,' he said in a voice that was horribly at odds with his smile, harder and sharper and more determined. 'But I'm sure you can put me on to someone who can tell me where she is, Doctor Taylor.'

'I'm puzzled,' Karen said, completely ignoring his comment.

'A brilliant psychologist like you?' He laughed, almost visibly pulling himself back into his charming mode. 'Hard to believe.'

'At your trial . . .' Karen broke off to explain. 'You see, I've been reading the trial transcripts. In court, you admitted to hurting her and being carried away and going further than you'd meant. That doesn't exactly square with what you've just told me.'

'That was the lawyers.' Randall still sounded relaxed as he leaned back more comfortably in his chair. 'They felt we were more likely to get the jury on side if I didn't rub it in about what a little freak she was.'

He rearranged his features so that he could produce the expression of an honest confider.

'*I* didn't like the idea of lying in court, of course. But apparently not many jurors would believe in a young and beautiful woman actually asking to be hurt. In a way, I can see what they meant. I mean, it surprised me. So I went along with them. Jurors aren't exactly known for their sophistication.' He paused again, as though waiting for a comment.

Karen nodded, which seemed to be enough.

'But I never said anything about cutting her up,' he went on, sounding injured. 'That should be clear in the transcripts.'

'It is,' Karen said, adding casually enough to bounce him into an important admission: 'You just said she was unique, but you have met other masochistic women, haven't you?'

'A few. None as bad as Lizzie. I can see it's tough for them, you know.' Randall could have been discussing the difficulties of shoppers who can't find their favourite brand of lipstick for all the emotion he was showing. 'The respectable ones anyway. The other kind can go on the streets, where they know they'll be hurt sooner or later. But middle-class ones have to trick violence out of blokes like me.'

'It does seem to happen to you rather often.' Karen kept everything but sympathy out of her voice.

'How do you mean?' He'd seen where she was going now and managed to make himself look puzzled.

'Well, you had been in court a couple of times before this case, hadn't you?'

'Not for hurting anyone.' Randall was really good at this, sounding nicely offended by Karen's suggestion. He made his eyebrows meet over his beautiful eyes, as though frowning over a confusing problem. 'Didn't they give you the full story, Doctor Taylor? Both times it was a girl who'd got a bit over-excited at a party. Woke up next morning feeling ashamed of herself for shagging a stranger and thought she'd get out of it by blaming me. Neither of *those* juries had any problem seeing through their silly stories.'

'But both of them had cuts on their thighs, didn't they?' Karen kept her voice calm. 'Not as bad as Lizzie's, but unmistakably recent cuts.'

'Coincidence. Nothing to do with me.' Randall's beautifully shaped lips were pinched now. And his eyes were hard.

'OK. So on those occasions your lawyers didn't suggest that you should lie to the court to get a more . . . appropriate verdict?'

Karen's mouth was aching with the effort of keeping her expression friendly when in fact she longed to grab him and force him to admit he knew precisely what he'd done, exactly how badly he'd hurt Lizzie and all his other victims.

More than anything else she wanted to make him grovel to them. Each one in turn. In full public view.

Something of her real feelings must have shown because Randall uncrossed his legs and said in ludicrously hurt tones, 'You're like those prosecution lawyers, twisting everything I say. I didn't lie; I merely refrained from explaining the full depths of Lizzie's depravity. And I said I was sad she'd been hurt so badly after I left her.'

'That *was* chivalrous of you,' Karen said with full sarcasm, unable to hold herself back.

'I have to be here, Doctor Taylor, but I don't have to put up with that kind of insult. Have you got any other questions? If not, I'd like to end this interview. Now.'

'I can't let you go yet,' she said, holding his gaze with her own and letting him see her power over him.

In return she got a flash of vicious hatred. It was gone in a second, masked by a patronizing patience. But the hatred had been there. And she knew exactly what it meant. She took a moment to collect herself, remembered Will and his total self-control, and at last smiled at Randall again.

'As you say,' she said, 'you have to be here. It is a condition of your licence. I'm now going to ask you about some of the answers you gave on your tests. You may not remember them, so if necessary I can show you the sheets you filled in for me. Are you ready?'

He produced another of his languid, seductive smiles.

'My dear Doctor Taylor, I'm ready for anything. The question is: are you?'

Bloody cheek! ran the subject line of an email from Anton, Lisa's dealer, forwarded by her solicitor. Within the message, she saw that Anton had written:

Thought you should see this. Have a look at the website and
let me know if you'd like me to protest at the way they've
stolen the title of your first exhibition. A noisy argument could
be good – generate publicity for the new show. Hope you're
working hard. Can't wait to see the last canvas.

Anton

Lisa clicked on the link he'd included, to see a well-designed
page headed: *Light out of Darkness*. Below the title was an easily
recognizable roughly diamond-shaped outline that made Lisa's
whole body stiffen, as though someone was inserting steel rods
into her arms and legs.

No one who knew the Isle of Wight could miss this. Perfectly
in proportion, looking like a pair of pursed lips with the twin
points of West and East Cowes divided by the Medina River
providing the philtrum at the top, it showed her home of
eighteen years – and the scene of everything Randall had done
to her.

Who had made the link between the Island and her Lee Wills
paintings?

She searched the web page for clues. Below the lip-shaped
sketch was a box, made up of two T-squares. Inside the box
were the words: *Calling all imaginative architects, designers and
artists. Click here.*

With one finger on her mouse, Lisa hesitated. Having all the
necessary firewall and virus protection in place to make sure
no malware could get into her system must mean she'd still
be safe, even if this was an attempt to winkle her out into the
open.

The URL simply said: *www.isleofwightcomp.com/details*

Tempted to click on the left-hand button of her mouse, she
held back. Wasn't there too much at stake to take any risks at
all?

But she had to know what was going on. Moving the cursor across the screen was hard, but she forced herself to do it, double-clicked on her browser icon and went into Google. Even then she hesitated.

Her fingers felt huge and clumsy, slipping over the keys. She pulled her hands back and laid them on her lap, one inside the other, looking at the screen, trying to deal with the fear that was choking her, bringing back the scent of Randall's aftershave, all citrus and pepper, mixed with the sweet copperiness of her own blood.

Could typing his name hurt her?

Even if he had no access to the internet in prison, he would have visitors and letters. He was easily rich enough to be paying people to look for her, to track her down. One of them might have inserted some kind of spyware into her computer, a keylogger or something like that, which would alert him to the moment when she cracked and risked showing herself to him. She thought of the shadows that followed her everywhere, and the footsteps, and the mysterious person on the river who was always just out of sight when she followed the sounds to try to identify him.

Her right forefinger was stroking the mouse button now as she remembered Randall's triumph when he thought he was watching her die in hospital.

She *couldn't* let him win.

A moment later, she'd typed his name into the search box: *Randall Gyre.*

Hundreds of hits showed up on the screen instantly. Scrolling through the list, she found one that said: *Parole board decisions.*

Amazed that the authorities should publish this kind of material on line, Lisa clicked on the link, trying to stop her heart banging so painfully in her chest.

The site had nothing to do with the government. It turned

out to belong to a group campaigning to keep violent offenders in prison for the full length of their sentences – something which, they said, hardly ever happened. And it gave a list of serious offenders who had been released early. Right at the top was Randall's name.

He was out and running free.

Lisa felt as though the house was cracking around her.

Visions of her mother cosying up to him in the hospital at the end of the bed, where she was lying ripped up and infected, joined a soundtrack of his threats, running round and round her mind on a loop. '*I will kill you. I will kill you.*'

Her right hand lay across her left breast. Even through the fabric of her shirt, her fingertips could feel the scars, raised and hard and now burning all over again.

She *had* to know. No way could she sit here, waiting for him, wondering if he had made the link between her and Lee Wills, trying to guess who else could be involved, whether he was paying Anton to report on her movements, who else he was manipulating into helping him now. She had to find out for sure.

Moving the screen back to the address for the Island site, Lisa hovered her cursor over the instruction *Click here* and pressed hard on the mouse button. A creaking pause was followed by a new page unfolding on the screen.

Are you the person to transform a tatty 1930s wooden holiday chalet into a thing of beauty?

Lisa read on, resisting the temptation to feel safer. This didn't sound anything like Randall, but he had known she was going to be an artist. Could this be his way of enticing her out of her hiding place?

She looked carefully at the hideous little 1930s wooden chalet. It didn't look like anywhere Randall would know anything about. He'd been so full of himself and his background and his money when they were chatting in the pub. And he'd talked a lot about the big old sixteenth-century farmhouse above Bembridge, where he'd been staying over Christmas. This little shack couldn't be less like that. Wouldn't he be ashamed even to know about it? Or would he guess that's what she'd think?

She read on, determined to find something to tell her who was doing this.

If you are that person, apply now for an information pack, entry form and competition rules. Although the organizers reserve the right to withhold the prize if entries are not up to standard, you could win the chance to redesign the entire site, including the house, and oversee the project, subject to all necessary permissions.

Clever solutions and vision are more important than experience. Practical professional help may be available to the right person, qualified architect or not. There are no competition fees and no expenses will be repaid, except to the winner – so keep your receipts in case that's you. Any hard-copy material will be submitted at your own risk and will not be returned.

No addresses were given, nor the names of any of the judges, which seemed odd.

Hoping she wasn't making a terrible mistake, Lisa applied for an on-line information pack. It promised photographs, site measurements, planning constraints, and a budget. That way, she'd have to get something that would lead her to the competition's backers.

Over the top of her screen, she saw the familiar figure of Jed, talking to himself as he slowly crossed his nearest field, carrying a bucket towards the newly ploughed field where he planned to over-winter his spring cabbages. She wondered about him all over again. He seemed as perfectly safe as the organic vegetables he grew, and he'd recovered from his short spurt of temper the other night. She'd come nearer trusting him than anyone else. But even Jed might be one of Randall's creatures.

Chapter 8

Karen was in her office early on Tuesday morning, analysing the results from her first meeting with Subject Twelve, who wasn't nearly as alarming as Randall. The door was flung back so hard it hit the wall and almost bounced shut again. Looking round, she saw the squat figure and outraged face of Max Pitton, the head of her department.

'Hi, Prof,' she said. 'What's up? Coffee?'

'No.' He kicked the door shut behind him with a casual jerk of one foot, then stood in front of her desk, planting both hands on it and glowering at her. 'What are you playing at, Karen?'

'What d'you mean?' Karen wasn't scared of Max, even in a mood like this. Behind his gravelly voice and often furious sarcasm, he was one of her biggest supporters, and a great friend.

'One of your second-year students has been wasting my time and energy, whingeing on about how you've had his essay for ten days and he hasn't heard a thing from you. He's pidged you, too, and you still haven't answered. Forgetting what we pay you for, Karen?'

Conscience made her throat tighten, which meant her voice sounded cold instead of lightly teasing.

'But Max, it was you who told me I must broaden my horizons, expand my life, take on work outside the university and create a public profile for myself.'

'Don't pretend to be stupid,' he snapped. 'Of course you must take on public work, and get it right so you don't screw up *all* our futures. But—'

'Your future, Max? You're impregnable.'

'But not at the expense of your students,' he said severely, ignoring her attempt to lighten the atmosphere. 'You need a solid teaching base for all the rest. Shape up, Karen. If I get any more complaints, I'll have to make this official instead of dishing out a friendly warning.'

Laughter bubbled up and she found herself snorting with amusement. 'Oh, Max! You are wonderful. If this is a friendly warning, God save me from serious criticism.'

Light flickered in his brown eyes for a second, but he fought his response and kept his full lips tucked tightly together in a supposedly harsh frown.

'OK. OK.' She looked at the pile of essays, of which she'd now managed to comment on about half, and thought about her unchecked pigeonhole downstairs, and the meeting she had to fix with a post-graduate student working for his Masters. 'I'll get to it as soon as I can.'

'You better had!' Max hooked a foot round the leg of the only free chair in the untidy room and pulled it forward so that he could sit down. 'So, where's my coffee?'

Her left eyebrow flew up. 'Have I got time to go making coffee for professors when I'm supposed to be marking students' essays?'

Max laughed at last. 'You win. So what about dinner tonight? I want to hear about this Island project of yours and why you haven't told me you're buying up property over there.'

Who's told him? she wondered, feeling cross. The gossip in this place!

'Fine,' she said aloud. 'I'll meet you at Mario's. Seven-thirty? If you get there first, order my *spaghetti puttanesca*, will you?'

'Will do.'

Both of them always chose the same things in their favourite everyday restaurant, an unshowy small Italian place, where
they'd eaten so often over the past five or six years that they
practically had their own napkins.

'Don't be late. And make sure those bloody essays are back
with their owners by then – OK?'

'I'll do my best. Bye, Max.'

'In a minute,' he said, glaring at her all over again. 'How's it
going with Will?'

'I don't know what you mean.' She meant to sound dignified
but her voice came out defensive.

'Don't be silly. Of course you do.'

'Even if I do, it's none of your business.' She'd always been
well aware that she'd have to fight to keep her life with Will safe
from Max's professional curiosity.

'Any relationship with a man as withheld as he is will be tricky,
particularly for a woman with a marriage like yours behind her,'
Max said. He smiled, showing off his long yellow teeth. 'I take a
fatherly interest.'

'Well, I wish you wouldn't.' Karen was serious now. 'Just
because you introduced us doesn't give you the right to treat us
like lab animals. I love the man.'

'And love is . . . ?' Max waited, with a theatrical air of expecta-
tion, with both hands and eyebrows raised, mouth slightly open,
and bright black eyes as round as oranges.

'Bugger off, Prof.'

He laughed. Karen watched him prepare to leave, flinging one
final mocking glance at her over his shoulder. She felt a mixture
of relief at being let off the hook and pleasure at the prospect of
picking up the conversation again at dinner. Max's monstrosities
had a bizarre and contradictory appeal.

When the sound of his heavy trampling footsteps had faded,
Karen finished her own work. She had too much self-respect to
drop everything just because Max had given his orders. Then she

reached for the top essay on the pile and plunged back into the student's views on the aetiology of offending behaviour, ready to give more consideration than usual to her comments to make up for the delay.

She'd finished three essays before she was distracted by the phone.

'Doctor Taylor,' she said into the receiver, pushing away the next with relief.

'Hi, Karen. Alastair Marks here.' He sounded more tentative than usual, much less the untouchable, unemotional Ministry of Justice civil servant who had reprimanded her for hysteria and emotionalism only last week.

'Hi, Al. What can I do for you?'

He coughed. 'Erm. It's not quite like that. Erm. This is rather difficult, in view of the conclusions you came to about your Subject Eleven.'

'Randall, you mean,' Karen said, impatient with his continuing insistence on scientific detachment. 'What's happened? Has he done it again already?'

'Erm. Not as far as we know. But he has . . . erm, well . . .' Al swallowed, then began again. 'He's disappeared, Karen. In view of something he said to Pickney after your last encounter, and your own conclusions about the risk he offers to women in general, my line manager and I felt you had to be informed.'

'Let me get this right,' Karen said with what felt like impressive moderation, while hot fury surged up into her brain. 'Randall has broken the terms of his licence and made some kind of threat in relation to me, which has not previously been passed on to me. Is that what you're saying?'

'More or less. Thank you for being so sensible about it.'

'Sensible?' Karen heard her voice rising to a most unprofessional shriek. She breathed deeply to make herself sound serious and confident. 'I'm not feeling remotely sensible about it. I'm furious. *What* did he say about me?'

Al coughed to give himself time to think.

'Come on! Come on!' Karen knew she sounded like a hectoring broadcaster. 'You can't stop here.'

This time Al sighed, as though showing that he took no responsibility for what she was about to hear. 'Well, Doctor Taylor, according to Dave, Gyre said: "I'm not the only one, am I? You'd like to pin her down, too, wouldn't you? Force her legs apart with your knee, see her squirm and hear her squeal. Snotty cow, isn't she?"'

Karen said nothing. Al's sigh was even heavier: 'Very properly Dave reported it.'

'Without commenting on his own views of my – what was it Randall called it? – snottiness?'

'Of course, Karen. Dave's on your side. We all are.'

'Oh, yeah? You should have passed this on at once. As soon as I told you how dangerous Randall is.'

Al coughed again.

'Why didn't you have him watched?' Karen demanded. 'How *could* you let this happen? When was he last seen? What're the police doing now? Checking "known associates", I hope.'

'Hardly. He's nearly forty. Before he went down, he'd socialized all over this country and most of Europe and the States. He's got friends everywhere.'

'Unlikely,' Karen said, thinking of the personality revealed in his tests. She didn't think he had many friends at all. 'What about his mother's place on Campden Hill?'

'What about it?'

'Have you been there? Questioned her?'

'That leads very neatly, Karen, on to my next request.'

'Oh, yeah?' she said again, full of suspicion.

'I've been authorized to find out whether we – that is, my department – could retain your professional services to assess the various possible avenues we should now be exploring in relation

to his return. It would be highly embarrassing for the government if . . . if a man like Gyre, released early, should be found
to—' Al broke off, before saying much more naturally: 'Will you
help us, Karen?'

'I suppose so, but it's a pity you didn't listen to me in the
beginning.'

'Don't rub it in,' he said, sounding almost boyish with relief.
'How soon can you start?'

She looked at the pile of boring essays, then at the clock. 'If
you could set up an appointment for me to talk to his mother this
afternoon, I could be in Kensington by . . . oh, by about half-past
twelve. Better say one o'clock.'

She hoped she'd get her marking finished on the train so that
she could face Max at Mario's at half-past seven. The fast train
service between Southampton and London had always been
useful; never more so than now. Which was why she could never
actually live on the Island. However gorgeous she made the
chalet, it could only ever be for weekends and holidays. If she
made it good enough, she might be able to let it and earn enough
to start paying Aidan back.

'Done,' Al said at once, sounding even more cheerful. 'If there's
a problem, I'll phone you. When you've come to some conclusions about the best places to look, we can get the police on it,
but until then we can't start squandering their budgets. He could
be anywhere by now.'

'Even so, you should alert the Isle of Wight police *at once*.
Randall has unfinished business there.'

'I'll get something put in train. Would you be prepared to talk
to the local plods there?'

'Of course,' Karen said, suppressing a smile. Then she had to
cut Al off so she could phone Charlie and beg him to pretend
he knew nothing about her involvement with Randall when the
Ministry of Justice contacted him.

*   *   *

'OK,' Charlie said at once when Karen had told him what she wanted. 'When'll you be back here?'

'Fairly soon, I should think. Now I have an official interest in Randall's whereabouts, I'll need to talk to the people he was staying with when he raped Lizzie, as well as to her family.' Karen considered her options for a moment, then added: 'Her family first, I think. Did you say they're still on the Island?'

'Her mother is – Sally. I can set up a meeting if you like.'

'Great. Thanks. I have to go to London more or less now, but I'll be back tonight. Let me know when you manage to fix it and I'll come straight over to the Island. It's urgent. Bye, Charlie.'

The 'place on Campden Hill,' turned out not to be a house, but a large flat in one of the huge dark-red brick buildings that lined the middle part of the expensive road, which led up from Kensington High Street to Notting Hill Gate. A uniformed porter admitted Karen to the block and pointed out the lift, telling her to go up to the second floor.

Beneath her feet, the carpet felt astonishingly squidgy, like thick moss. There was no sound from anywhere, except for the faint whine of the lift's mechanism. She pressed the shining brass button for the second floor and emerged only moments later, to see a heavy, polished, mahogany door silently opening at the far end of the hall, which was carpeted in the same luxurious way as the main foyer.

'Doctor Taylor?' said a surprisingly tall woman with a voice so confident it sounded as though she was used to giving orders. 'Do come in.'

For some subconscious reason she hadn't time to examine, Karen had expected Randall's mother to be a papery, elderly victim, not a vigorous, elegant woman, barely older than Dillie and a lot more restrained. Mrs Gyre had perfectly streaked and well-cut short hair, and she was wearing a charcoal suit. Its unobtrusive perfection shouted Giorgio Armani at Karen.

Not even Emporio Armani, she thought: it's Collezione at least.

Karen straightened her own natural linen jacket and wished she'd picked something more imposingly glamorous this morning.

Mrs Gyre took her into a sparsely furnished room that looked as though it had been designed as a formal dining room, now converted into an office. The décor was as coolly modern as the foyer's had been traditional. Neatly placed in the centre of the polished glass table was a tray containing two perfect, dark grey porcelain cups, a matching tea pot and jug, a bottle of mineral water, two tumblers and a plate of crustless sandwiches.

'Do sit down, Doctor Taylor.'

'You do know who I am, don't you?' Karen was surprised by the welcome and the courtesy.

'You're a Ministry of Justice psychologist, who was the first person to treat my son with decency and intelligence since his outrageous arrest nearly five years ago,' she said, sitting opposite Karen and picking up the tea pot. 'He told me he liked and respected you. Would you like a cup of tea? Or would you prefer water?'

'Tea, please. I am glad your son felt I was treating him properly,' Karen began. 'But my job is to assess his future behaviour, and now that he—'

'I do understand that,' Mrs Gyre said, revealing the first sign of tension. Karen couldn't believe anyone as controlled and conventional as she was would normally interrupt a visitor in mid-sentence. 'As does he, Doctor Taylor. Do help yourself to sandwiches: smoked salmon or Brie and rocket.'

'Thank you. I was worried about what he might do next, even before he disappeared.'

'"Disappeared" is rather a loaded word.' Mrs Gyre pushed the filled tea cup towards Karen. 'All that's happened is that he has gone away for a few days to get his head straight after the shock

– the good, but nonetheless destabilizing, shock – of his release, and has forgotten to inform his probation officer.'

'Are you sure about that?'

'I can't say that I blame him.' Mrs Gyre clearly wasn't going to waste time dealing with questions she found intrusive. 'Of all the indignities Randall's had to suffer, this perpetual checking in and humiliating himself in front of small-time functionaries . . .'

The strong voice dwindled and Mrs Gyre shrugged, as though words simply failed her. She poured her own tea, adding a slice of lemon with her fingers.

'Did he warn *you* he was going away?' Karen said.

'Certainly not. He may be living here until he gets a flat of his own again, but he's not a child. I don't explain myself to him, nor he to me. Neither of us has to ask permission for an exeat.'

'What about his phone? Have you tried to ring him?'

Mrs Gyre looked a little self-conscious. 'I have – which was probably a mistake. I left a voicemail, but I'm not surprised he hasn't answered. It would have driven me mad, at his age, if my mother had tried to track me down.'

'Would he have the phone with him?' Karen asked and watched the other woman once again shrug her magnificent shoulders. 'So you have no idea where he might have gone?'

'I'm afraid not.'

'Might his father know?'

Mrs Gyre looked at Karen as though she were a delinquent employee. 'Quite impossible. Randall has never known his father.'

Interested, Karen prepared to ask the first of a whole series of questions, but the other woman cut them off before she could start.

'Doctor Taylor, you should know that Randall's father and I divorced when my son was two. None of us has ever had any contact since the divorce went through.'

'Fine. I see. Then I'd like to ask something completely different, Mrs Gyre: have you ever talked to your son about the coincidence of his being ... unjustly accused of such similar crimes three times?'

Mrs Gyre sipped her tea, then put the cup carefully down on its saucer before raising her eyes to meet Karen's. She looked intelligent and sincere.

'Only once.'

'May I ask what happened?' Karen felt herself becoming more formal with every question, as though there were standards here in this large and expensive flat that would infect anyone who breathed its rarefied air.

'Very little. He agreed it was odd, but pointed out that members of the police, like everyone else, see what they think they're looking at. Once you've been accused of something like that, your name will crop up every time a similar accusation has to be made. You become a convenient first suspect.'

'That doesn't quite work,' Karen said, putting down her cup, too. She wished Mrs Gyre wouldn't talk as though giving a well-rehearsed lecture.

'These aren't cases of burglary or mistaken identity,' Karen went on. 'Randall's been involved with three completely separate women, and his story of what happened was different from theirs each time. Haven't you ever wondered about it?'

'Of course I have.' This time Mrs Gyre had waited without interruption, as though she was not at all worried by the questions. 'I am not a fool. But when you read the court transcripts, as I did each time, and hear what those young women did and said to encourage him, you see that he had every reason to believe that what he was doing was not only acceptable to them but actually desired by them.'

Karen opened her mouth to ask another question, but Mrs Gyre raised a hand like a traffic cop.

'My terror was that four years in a variety of our prisons would transform him from the son I loved into someone vengeful or degraded. These last three weeks have been of such reassurance to me. Please don't be afraid, Doctor Taylor.'

'Afraid?' Karen wondered who had warned this woman of her son's threats. 'Afraid of what?'

'That he's hiding somewhere, planning to commit a real rape out of fury at what he's suffered. He won't. My son is not capable of forcing a woman against her will. Or hurting her. You'll see.'

If confidence and determination could make anything happen, Karen thought, this woman had enough to ensure the whole world would remain crime-free for ever. Remembering everything she'd read and heard about Randall, as well as the bruises on her own wrist, Karen felt sorry for his mother.

Mrs Gyre half-turned in her chair and reached for a small leather-bound album, which she offered to Karen. She looked but didn't touch.

'Take it, Doctor Taylor. Look for anything in my son that points to the kind of depravity you're suggesting. If you can find something, you'll be the only one who ever has. Well, have a look and tell me what you see.'

Reluctant, but unable to think of any reasonable excuse, Karen took the album and turned its thick charcoal-coloured pages, staring down at a lifetime's photographs of the happy, dimpled baby who had become Randall Gyre, rapist and potential killer. As she saw the way his mother had smiled down at the baby she cradled in her arms, Karen felt her eyes dampen. Pity flooded her mind. But she had to put it right away while she did her job.

The baby was replaced by a toddler, who clearly took extreme delight in splashing through deep puddles in his red wellies, and who was in turn displaced by a serious-looking teenager, and then the beautifully dressed adult with the charming smile that hid so much arrogance and rage. Having reached him, Karen felt better, and closed the album.

'So you really cannot give me any pointers to his where-abouts?' she said, looking Mrs Gyre in the eye.

'None, I'm afraid.' The other woman smiled suddenly, reveal-ing a warmth that surprised Karen. She took the album back and held it down on her lap with both hands. 'You know, I assumed that, as a psychologist, you'd want me to talk about his childhood.'

'Why? Was there something about it that you feel could have explained the way he has been . . .' Karen hesitated, hoping Mrs Gyre would fill the gap. She didn't.

'Abuse isn't necessarily a factor in crime, you know,' Karen went on.

'You'd never believe that, reading the press, would you?' Mrs Gyre said, with a hint of a smile in her eyes. 'Every violent crimi-nal seems to have been abused by one or other parent.'

'There are plenty of other reasons why people resort to violence. Still, we haven't time to go into them now. Can you tell me what took Randall to the Island that Christmas?'

'His godmother lives there with her family,' said Mrs Gyre. 'Chloe Hemming.'

'Could I have her address?'

The fine dark eyebrows over Mrs Gyre's conker-brown eyes contracted. 'She was worried to death by the police at the time of the crime. Is it really necessary for her to be disturbed again? Randall isn't with her now.'

'How do you know?'

There was no warmth left in Mrs Gyre's face. Her expression was one of complete withdrawal. She flicked a glance towards the landline phone that stood on her sideboard.

'I asked her,' she said with a voice as dry as any desert. She glanced at her watch, a no-nonsense neat steel affair on a plain black leather strap. 'Is there anything else before you go?'

'Something he said to me suggested that he was going to try to find the victim from the Isle of Wight case, who's gone into hiding.' Karen felt pride at the way she'd managed not to say 'Randall's last victim'. 'Did he say anything about her to you?'

'Not a thing.' Mrs Gyre's face was hard now as well as cold. 'If there's nothing else, I ought to get on.'

'What about Randall's girlfriends?' Karen said quickly, registering the fact that she'd been more or less dismissed. 'A man of nearly forty must've had a few.'

'Indeed, yes.' Mrs Gyre re-crossed her legs and looked a little less impatient, as though this was an easier question to answer. 'There have been one or two I've thought he might marry, but it's never come to that yet. Don't forget he was only thirty-six when he went to prison. That's no age these days.'

'What were they like?' Karen waited to hear that the girlfriends had all been tall and slim and blonde, like his victims.

'Most have been of a similar type,' Mrs Gyre said. 'Dark brown hair, pale skin and rich brown eyes. All quite different from the women who've made up these unspeakable allegations about him. His girlfriends have all been more or less his own age, and professionals: lawyers, bankers, that kind of thing.'

'And what usually caused the break-up?' Karen wasn't sure she'd get anything useful from this line of questioning, but she wasn't going to waste any opportunity to find out more about both mother and son.

'Their overriding interest in their work.' Mrs Gyre frowned, then forced a smile. 'I told him that if he will fall for these successful women, he's going to come up against the same problem every time.'

'Which is?'

Mrs Gyre laughed. 'They'll always be more interested in their next promotion than arriving on time for dinner.'

Karen thought for a moment, remembering the quick temper and easily triggered frustration Randall had revealed in his test questions. 'Did their lateness make him angry?'

'Angry?' Mrs Gyre's voice stuck in her throat. She coughed. 'Randall does not get angry with women. At worst you could say he was irritated. They could get away with it once, but if they left him on his own in a restaurant twice, that was it. They were toast.'

Surprised by the phrase, Karen glanced at the two tall brushed steel and glass bookcases on either side of the empty fireplace. Behind their glass doors, she saw row upon row of files. Mrs Gyre's gaze followed hers.

'That's much too trite an observation,' Mrs Gyre said. When Karen waited for an explanation, the other woman added: 'Just because I have always worked hard, that does not mean my son has been picking women like me and trying to make them show him that they will always put him first because he feels that I did not.'

'Trite?' Karen said, thinking it was a more or less credible suggestion. 'Why would that be trite?'

'Because it's stereotypical and boring. Wrong, too. When Randall was very young, I took two years away from work to be with him, and later I ensured that I was home every evening in time to eat with him, bath him and read to him, and I never worked at weekends.'

'May I ask what work you did – do?'

'I am a fund manager,' Mrs Gyre said briefly. 'The one City job which ensures you can be home at the same time every night. Now, is there anything else?'

'Not at the moment.' Karen picked up her cup to finish the now cold tea. She put it back in its saucer. 'May I phone if something else comes up?'

'If necessary.' Mrs Gyre's smile returned. 'I'm out a lot, so you may have to leave a message with my cleaner. Please speak very clearly and slowly. Teresa's English isn't very good and her dignity is far too great to allow her to ask for either repetition or explanation.'

'I'll keep it simple,' Karen promised. 'Thank you for seeing me.'

Karen found herself outside the locked front door and standing alone on the thick carpet in only a few seconds. Wishing she knew a lot more about both Gyres, she pressed the button to call the lift.

A wheezing sound heralded its return but just as it slid to a stop, Karen's phone vibrated against her side. She pulled it from her pocket and saw her Ministry of Justice contact's name on the screen.

'Al,' she said into it. 'Hi.'

'Hi, Karen. Where are you?'

'Leaving Mrs Gyre's flat. Why?'

'That's Kensington, right? Can you drop into my office before you head back to Southampton? You should be able to get here to Victoria Street in half an hour. I've someone you need to meet, and he can't stay long.'

Karen looked at her watch. With at least one train every hour and an open ticket, she had no real excuse to refuse.

'OK.' There was no point asking who Al wanted her to talk to. He was so reluctant to give out even the most basic of information over the phone or email that she occasionally wondered whether he'd been transferred to the Ministry of Justice because one of the spying departments had found him too secretive.

A number 52 bus swayed towards the nearest stop as Karen reached it. She climbed on board, wishing the designers had actually sat in the kind of seats they imposed on travellers. Either there was no leg room at all or the seat was too narrow for comfort.

For once the traffic wasn't too bad and Karen relaxed as the bus trundled past the grand Edwardian buildings of Kensington and the formal green spaces of the park in front of the palace. The graceless red-brick facade of the 1960s Knightsbridge Barracks came as a jolt after the palace's perfect seventeenth-century symmetry, but Karen was soon distracted from architecture as her bus became snarled in a jam at what must have been the worst junction in London, with vast building works as well as three major routes colluding to stop anyone moving anywhere.

Increasingly impatient, Karen glanced down at her watch, then up again at the traffic lights, which seemed more or less stuck on red. Even when there was a short burst of green, the interval allowed only one or two cars out from her road.

At last her bus began to move again, and things gradually improved. They swept up towards Hyde Park Corner without another stop and round towards Victoria. As it happened, the last part of the journey was so easy she reached Victoria Street ahead of Al's estimate by a couple of minutes.

Making her way to the anonymous-looking modern block halfway between Victoria Station and Westminster Abbey, she gave her name at reception and was quickly taken upstairs to his office.

The room itself was plain and plainly decorated, with cheap-looking grey carpet tiles and white walls. His pale wooden desk had metal legs and took up most of the window wall, with bookshelves down either side. In front of the desk was a tiny conference table with four grey chairs around it.

Al got up from one, revealing himself to be quite a bit taller than Karen and very thin. Something about his badly cut hair, flakey skin and close-set dark eyes always made her think of the young mathematicians she encountered at the university.

Beside him was a broader watchful man in his early fifties. He, too, got to his feet and waited to be introduced.

'Detective Chief Superintendent Daniel Stokes,' Al said, 'from Winchester. Dan, this is Doctor Karen Taylor, who is advising us on Gyre.'

Karen waited, too experienced by now to rush into any situation she didn't yet understand.

'Karen, there's been a—'

'Why don't I do the talking?' The Winchester cop spoke in a tightly reined voice that told Karen how angry he must be.

She smiled at him and sat down on one of the free chairs. He dropped back into his own, but his spine was rigid and there was no friendliness in his expression.

'You've assessed Gyre as likely to be violent towards women,' he barked at her.

'That's right,' she said, feeling a nasty mixture of professional satisfaction and nausea. 'Who's he hurt this time?'

'Only to women?' Stokes said, ignoring her question.

'Not necessarily,' Karen said, fighting the queasiness. 'Who *has* he hurt now?'

'In what circumstances would he attack a man?'

One look at his obstinate face told her there was no point asking her question a third time.

'It would have to be a man who had humiliated him,' she said as patiently as she could, 'in his eyes at least; possibly a man he saw as having beaten him to some target they were both aiming for, or one who had held him up to public ridicule. Something like that. Taken something he hugely valued.'

'Which would be what?' Stokes was still banging out his questions as though she was a deliberately obstructive recruit.

'The likeliest would be his image of himself as all-powerful. I don't yet know him well enough to say more.' Karen tried to smile through the anxiety that was building as she thought of Randall's likeliest target. 'My tests were aimed at uncovering his tendency to re-offend. Nothing else.'

'Take a police officer instrumental in having him convicted by a jury and quite heavily sentenced by a judge,' said DCS Stokes. 'Would *he* count as a likely target?'

Karen bit down hard on her lower lip. Charlie. He'd arrested Randall, seen him charged, convicted and imprisoned. For Randall, Charlie must be a symbol of everyone who had to pay for what had been done to him. She kept silent until she could

be sure her voice wouldn't wobble, fighting to stay as well in
control as Will would have been. When she unclamped her teeth,
the blood rushed painfully back into her bitten lip.

'I think a man like that could definitely strike Randall as deserv-
ing punishment,' she said at last. 'I would expect the victim's
injuries to be highly visible, symbolic almost, and the body to be
placed somewhere it would easily be found. Does . . . does that
fit your case?'

'No,' Stokes said. 'One of my officers was found dead at home
in Winchester. Nothing public about it.'

Winchester. His home in Winchester.

Karen didn't repeat the words aloud, but they ran round
and round in her mind, generating relief like the sparks from a
Catherine wheel. Not far from the Island, but *not* the Island. She
barely heard DCS Stokes's voice as he offered more details:

'Throat cut from behind as he watched TV. There're no obvious personal motives involved, so we checked all his past cases.
Gyre's name came up, with a flag referring to this department.
When I got no joy on the phone or email, I had to come in person
to get the necessary information.'

No wonder he's so angry, Karen thought, glancing at Al.

He looked completely bland, as though he felt no guilt at all
for wasting the time of a man in charge of a serious murder
investigation.

'Why?' Karen said, amazed to hear her own voice sounding
absolutely normal. 'What's the connection?'

'Tod Williams, the dead man, gave evidence against Gyre in
court,' Al said, butting in and clearly irritating Stokes even more.

'More importantly,' Stokes said, trying to quell him with a
filthy look, 'he carried out the first interview with the victim; got
from her one crucial piece of evidence the prosecution managed
to persuade her to repeat in court, which made Gyre react
strongly enough to show a little of his true colours behind the
mask of smooth charm.'

He knows a lot about Randall, Karen thought, for a man who first sounded as though he'd only just heard the name.

'What evidence?' Al said, as though determined to show he had power here too.

DCS Stokes snorted. 'The first thing he said to her as he ripped off her shirt was "You have beautiful breasts. That's what I like. There's no point ruining saggy wrinkled titbags".'

Al looked as though he might be ill. Karen, still dizzy with the relief of knowing Charlie was alive, controlled her feelings better.

'That's what came through his test results most clearly,' she said. 'He likes overcoming resistance, and destroying, but he also likes the pain he creates. What did he do in court when the victim quoted him like that?'

Stokes looked at her as though she'd just put an enormous obstacle in his way.

'Nothing. It was the expression on his face,' Stokes snapped. 'Plain as anything. Even the jury could see it. He was excited. Licked his lips. Looked at her as if he was enjoying her humiliation. But that's water under the bridge. I need to know: *could* he have slit my officer's throat? There was no audience. His girlfriend was expected home, but no one else.'

'There's no reason to say Randall couldn't have done it,' Karen said, 'but unless there are other injuries that show sadistic enjoyment, it doesn't sound convincing.' She felt the atmosphere tighten and couldn't understand it. After a moment she added: 'I'd have to see details of the crime scene before I could say more.'

'The only other injuries were a few clumps of hair wrenched out of his scalp, as though his hair was grabbed at the very last minute before he died.' Stokes managed a small smile. 'If you want to see the scene, come back with me now.'

'Fine.' Karen knew there were plenty of trains from Winchester to Southampton, so she should still get back in time to meet Max at Mario's by half-past seven. 'If that's OK with you, Al?'

'Yes, of course,' Al said, but he held her back when Stokes had marched out of the room.

'Karen, he wants Gyre to be guilty. Try not to go along with it unless you have to,' he said in an urgent whisper. 'If there's any doubt at all, focus on it.'

'If Randall was there at the scene, there'll be DNA, won't there? He must be an easy match. The police'll have plenty of samples from all the earlier cases.'

'DNA traces aren't always picked up,' Al said, reverting to his normal pitch, 'whatever you might think from the press. I don't want any speculation of yours to muddy the waters if they don't get clear scientific evidence. Do you understand?'

'Perfectly,' she said. 'But I won't lie for you.'

'I didn't ask you to.'

Karen hoped her expression would signal her disdain. As far as she could tell from his face, he hadn't noticed anything. She wished she could read Stokes as easily as she understood Al.

'But if you could point us in the way of a likely suspect, that'd help,' Al went on. 'Somehow I don't think DCS Stokes is going to cooperate. I need a heads-up to manage expectations here.'

Karen wasn't going to promise anything.

The police driver got them to Winchester in only an hour and a half. Stokes opened a briefcase of papers, making it clear he didn't want to talk, but Karen could never read in a car without feeling sick, so she whiled away some of the time dreaming of having a professional chauffeur always available. No more parking hassles, she thought, no more anxiety about Gatso speed cameras; no more route-finding.

'Drop us off at Tod's place, will you,' DCS Stokes said to the driver, speaking in much less abrupt tones than he'd used with Al. He slapped the papers back in his briefcase and banged down the lid. 'I'll make my own way back.'

As the car slid to a halt by the kerb in a narrow road lined on both sides with small grey stone houses, Karen saw the expected blue-and-white police tape blocking off the pavement in front of one with a large brass 7 on its door. A uniformed constable was standing outside it. He nodded to the Chief Superintendent and held the tape aside to admit him and Karen.

The smell hit her in the face as soon as she stepped over the threshold.

Chapter 9

Lisa stood on the river bank, staring after the canoe that had just shot past her. She'd been working in the studio and had caught sight of a grey triangle edging out from under the huge willow that marked the boundary of her garden. At first she'd thought it was just a piece of litter, the kind of thing the river brought down every day. But she couldn't stop looking and eventually she'd had to come out to see for herself.

As soon as she'd stepped out of the studio, the grey triangle had grown larger and revealed itself to be the prow of a long plastic canoe, being paddled very fast by a man – she was sure it was a man – wearing a sunhat and glasses.

Either he'd just paused under the willow to rest or he'd been watching her. She thought of the splashes the other day, before she'd known Randall was out of prison, and the shadows that followed her wherever she went.

This wasn't Randall. The canoeist was much too squat to be him. But he could belong to Randall, be paid by Randall, be reporting to Randall.

Had he been sent to watch her, to find out whether she was going to take the bait of the Island competition?

Or was she letting paranoia destroy her?

Shivering, she turned back to the studio to stare miserably at her painting, knowing she wouldn't be able to concentrate on it now.

She pulled down the tent-like cover that always concealed her work in progress from any possible spy, cleaned her brushes and thought about how she might track down the competition's sponsors. If there was any possibility that Randall could be involved, she'd back off right away.

They'd already sent her an electronic application pack, which had a little more information in it, including the fact that one of the judges, Stella Atkins, was a lecturer in Architecture at the University of Southampton. It had also given her a map reference for the site. Lisa hadn't yet searched for that on GoogleEarth, but it would be easy enough. First she needed to find out who owned it – and if they had any connection to Randall.

Clicking through various sites, she found her way to the Land Registry's, which produced the answer straight away. The chalet and its surrounding acres were owned by someone called Dillys Taylor.

Clicking back on to Google, Lisa followed the first of nearly ten thousand links and found that Dillys Taylor, more usually known as Dillie, was one of two owners of an advertising agency. Nothing anywhere in the first hundred hits even suggested a link with Randall or anyone who had any connection to him. That didn't mean there wasn't one, of course. He could manipulate anyone into doing anything for him. Lisa would have to go on looking through all the thousands and thousands of links before she could be sure, but . . .

A new shadow fell over her shoulder, much too big to be one of the birds that found sanctuary in her cat-less, dog-less garden. She watched the shadow grow into the shape of a man, crossing the big window behind her. She wrapped her arms around her body, squeezing hard.

Someone knocked on the window. She relaxed her arms so she could reach for her phone in case she had to summon help and turned to face him.

Jed was peering through the glass, shading his eyes to avoid the reflection. With her heart-rate returning to something like normal, Lisa waved her free hand, then gestured towards the sink in the corner. He nodded and stepped back, so she put down the phone and went to rinse her hands at the sink. Typically, Jed waited outside in total patience until she'd finished, dried her hands, collected the padlock that secured the studio door, and let herself out.

'Hi,' she said, smiling without really seeing him. She pushed the hoop down into the lock. It was stiff, but her hands were very strong now.

'What about a drink?' she added. 'I've got a bottle of wine in the fridge. We could have it by the river – unless you think it's too early?'

She turned to look at Jed properly. His reddish face was stiffer than she'd ever seen it, even on the night when he'd so nearly lost his temper with her.

Her muscles tightened, and her mind braced itself for whatever was coming.

'Sorry to keep you waiting,' she said, making her voice far more welcoming than she felt.

'I want . . .' Jed stopped, then started again. 'I need . . . I *have* to know what he did to you. Now. You've got to tell me.'

'Who?'

'Don't.' His voice was getting angrier with every word. 'Don't make fun of me. You told me about the man who hurt you. I need to know what he did. I can't go on like this, not knowing. You've got to tell me.'

She stood in her garden, with the birds singing overhead and the river shushing as it rushed under the bridge, thinking, hating his bullying words but understanding them, too. He'd been so patient for so long. She couldn't keep him hanging on any more. At last she took his hand and led him towards the house.

Through the conservatory, kicking away the loose grapes that had dropped from the overhead vine, through the kitchen, upstairs to her bedroom. There, she closed the curtains, switched on the light, and pointed to the chair in the corner.

Jed sat in it, his eyes full of an unreadable expression, and his mouth stretched into a thin, hard line that made him look completely different from the gentle, kindly man she'd come to know.

Lisa stood in front of him and unbuttoned her shirt. She never wore a bra any more. At first it had been too painful as the scars healed, then she'd lost so much weight there was no point. She pulled aside the unbuttoned flaps of her shirt and looked at him as he saw her breasts for the first time.

He said nothing. But he didn't turn away. There was none of the disgust she'd expected, anywhere in his face. Slowly tears formed in his eyes and fell down his face.

Lisa did up her buttons again and walked across the room to hold his head against her. He swivelled in the chair and clutched his hands around her back and sobbed. She stroked his rough, wiry brown hair.

At last he raised his head.

'Am I hurting you?' he asked, his voice choked.

'No. The pain's long gone. I'm sorry you had to see it.'

'I asked. You could've told me to mind my own business.' He moved away from her, feeling in his pockets, as though for a handkerchief.

Lisa had never seen him with any such thing, so she went into the bathroom to tear off about two feet of loo paper for him.

He blew his nose, then wiped his eyes.

'I see. Now I know why ... You ... I ... Don't worry any more, Lisa. I'm sorry I shouted. I promise I won't – you know.'

'Hush, Jed,' she said. 'Hush. Now you've seen this bit, nothing will be so bad.'

'Is there . . . did he do other things?'

She looked over his head, unable now to meet his eyes. But her voice still worked.

'Oh, yes,' she said. 'There's plenty more.'

'You know I won't ever hurt you. Don't be frightened of me. I couldn't bear that.'

She took his face between her hands and kissed him. At this moment she felt certain that he could never be part of any conspiracy of Randall's. Jed was too simple, too straight, to get involved with a man like Gyre. Jed would run a mile rather than sit down with anyone like him. So smooth. So urban. Such a snob.

When she kissed him again, she let her lips part and her tongue emerge between them. Just for a second. Jed's arms tightened round her waist. She leaned against him and liked every sensation she could feel.

Later, she said, 'You won't tell anyone, will you? I don't want people to know, or – or pity me.' She shuddered. 'Or ask questions.'

'I can keep my mouth shut,' Jed said. 'And I won't ask anything. But if you want to talk, I'll listen. Always.'

Karen stood looking at the enormous brown patches of dried blood on the sofa where the dead man had been sitting and on the floor around his feet.

'The splatters show his assailant was stood behind him and made a single right-handed cut from the victim's left ear round to the right,' said the CSI, sounding bored, as though he hoped to impress DCS Stokes with his experience.

Karen studied the great spray of blood across the television and the chair beside it, with splashes that, on closer examination, looked like horizontal exclamation marks, with a long tapering mark followed by a small gap, then a dot.

'Here's where the blood spurted from the arteries,' said the CSI, a man in his late thirties, 'and here, here and here are where the assailant shook the knife, with the blood dropping directly downwards here and here and then, here, spraying through the air and landing obliquely. Get the picture?'

'I do. Thank you. Can you say from the spatters what the knife was like?'

'Small, with a thin short blade. Sharp.'

'Like a scalpel?' Karen said.

'Yeah.'

'If so, the killer must've had access to surgical supplies,' she began, but the CSI cut in before she could finish.

'Nope. Craftsmen and model-makers use them – designers, artists of all sorts. You can buy 'em anywhere.'

Karen examined the small room, focusing on the place from where the body had been removed, then looking up again. Thick net curtains covered the single window, which meant no one outside would have seen the moment when the blood spurted from Tod's severed neck.

The domesticity of the small space somehow made the killing even more horrifying than it would have been as part of the kind of public performance Randall would have given. Karen tried not to think how warm the blood must have felt to Tod as he died, or the totality of the pain he suffered. Some people said shock from this kind of wound would block the pain, but she'd never believed that.

'How're you getting on?' said DCS Stokes from behind her, as abrupt and impatient as ever. 'You going to need much longer?'

'Did any of the neighbours see anything?' Karen asked, turning away from the horror to look at Stokes over her shoulder, impatiently pushing away the blonde hair that stung her eyes.

'Not a thing. We've already done house-to-house. Everyone in the street works office hours. Whoever this was, he timed it just right. No one hanging around and plenty of people hurrying to get home, heads down. No one stopped to ask anyone anything and no one noticed anyone waiting on Tod's doorstep.'

'Is there a back way in?' Karen asked, glad to need such practical information. It helped control her imagination.

'Through the kitchen and the side passage by the bins, yeah. No signs of forced entry there either.'

'So, given Tod was watching TV when he was killed, he must have known his attacker and sat happily with his back to whoever it was, trusting him – or her, I suppose,' Karen said. 'This can't have needed much upper-body strength, so it could've been a woman. Anyway, it doesn't sound like Randall to me.'

'They weren't strangers.' DCS Stokes sounded as though he resented Karen wasting his time with the kind of trivial questions and comments the most junior detective on his force would have produced.

Karen waited, silently asking for more.

'They'd both been involved in the trial, hadn't they?' Stokes said sharply. 'They knew each other.'

'Not as friends.' Karen fought her own impatience because she knew it could only bug him. 'The victim would never have trusted *him*. If Randall had been here – for any reason – Tod would've been on his feet, facing him. Whatever.'

'But . . .' Stokes began. Karen interrupted before he could get any further:

'Lolling about watching TV while a violent ex-con prowled behind him with a scalpel in his hand? Give me a break, Superintendent!'

'Nowt so queer as folk,' said the CSI, trying to contain his laughter.

'Right.' After the single word, Karen ignored him as she filled the small room with imaginary people to work out how it could possibly have happened. 'I suppose it could've worked if the two of them are watching something *together*.' She turned back to Stokes to add: 'What was on?'

'*Six O'clock News*. Probably. It was set for BBC1, anyway. And time of death suggests somewhere round then.'

'OK,' Karen went on, still directing the scene in her mind. 'So, the killer gets up on some excuse – taking a piss, something like that – puts on protective gear, gets out the scalpel and slashes Tod's throat before he has any idea a matey evening is turning nasty. Then the killer packs away the bloody clothes and legs it.'

Karen wheeled round to face Stokes, wondering why someone so obviously busy – and so senior – was involved on the ground like this. The death of any copper merited more top-brass involvement than an ordinary killing, and there was the Ministry of Justice involvement, but this was still excessive. She tried to feel her way towards a reason for it.

'Tell me about the girlfriend,' she said, wondering why the woman hadn't been the first suspect. They usually were: wives, husbands, lovers were always thought more likely to have killed their partner than any stranger.

Stokes shrugged, but his face snapped into a deep frown that told Karen she might have touched a nerve.

'Fellow officer,' he said. 'Good record. No blood on her. No sign of any weapon or protective clothing, and a clear path where she'd come in from the street with dusty shoes. Couldn't have got back in time to do it, clean herself up *and* get rid of the evidence. We've been through all this, Doctor Taylor. If you haven't any more to offer, I've got to get back.'

Karen stared at him, still trying to understand the shifting impulses that drove his harsh voice and angry body language.

'Who is she?' she asked.

'Annie Colvin,' he said, as if it hurt to say the words. 'A DS.'

'And?'

'And nothing.'

'Come on, Superintendent,' Karen said, trying a friendly smile. 'Something about her makes you uncomfortable. I accept everything you've said about how she couldn't have done it. But if you don't tell me the problem, I can't help.'

He looked down at the CSI, who took the hint, if that's what it was, and muttered something about checking out the back door again. When he'd gone, DCS Stokes faced Karen.

'She has an involvement with Gyre.'

'What kind of involvement?' Karen asked, instantly suspicious.

'Professional,' Stokes said, back to his customary brusqueness. 'It was her told us all about him when we found the flag in the files. She's been chasing him most of her career.'

And that worries you, Karen thought. *Why?* Once again, she knew there was no point asking the question aloud. His expression was full of threat.

'I'd like to meet her,' she said.

'Can you leave it a day or two? Give her time to get her head together?'

Karen waited, sure something else was about to emerge, but Stokes didn't speak.

'Very well,' she said at last, hoping he hadn't asked for time in order to coach his protégée into what she should say to protect herself from a murder charge.

'Great. I'll fix it if you phone me to say where and when. Go carefully now. Whoever this bastard is, he's calculating and efficient. He could be watching the place. Anyone involved is at risk. Don't do anything stupid.'

'I won't. Thanks.' Karen noticed the way he insisted on using the male pronoun for his killer, when a unisex 'they' would have done fine. She turned back to face all the blood. Could a woman have done it?

Chapter 10

Karen lay on her sofa, listening to Mozart's Horn Concerto in E flat and wishing she could get the Winchester crime scene out of her mind, along with the powerful impression of a man trusting his visitor absolutely until the moment the scalpel entered his throat. Even dinner with Max last night hadn't helped.

In the old days she'd never been musical and rarely listened to anything classical until she'd read that Mozart had a discernible effect on the brain, making it work faster and better. She'd started to listen out of curiosity and soon found herself addicted. The oddest effect for her was the way the music could rinse her mind. Arriving home fraught and anxious, or irritable, she'd listen for half an hour and find herself free of all the frets, as though she'd been renewed in some way. This morning it wasn't working. And she had stuff to do.

She reached for the phone and pushed the button to speed dial Charlie's number.

'Karen! Great to hear from you.' His voice was bouncy with energy. 'I was going to phone in any case to say Eve Clarke's been round to the Hemmings' – you know, Gyre's friends here – to find out whether they've heard from him.'

'And?'

'Nothing. They've got no idea where he is. So you don't have to bother with them.'

'Right,' Karen said, not certain she had as much confidence in DS Clarke's judgement as Charlie had.

When they'd met last year, Karen had found Eve uncooperative and generally difficult, as well as possessive of Charlie.

'And Lizzie Fane's mother Sally is prepared to see you,' he went on. 'She'll meet us for coffee in Cowes tomorrow morning at ten-thirty. I know you wanted today, but she can't. Tomorrow OK?'

'Fine. Thanks, Charlie.'

'I'll pick you up at Fountain Quay at ten-fifteen. Be gentle. Sally needs all the support she can get. Meeting a shrink from the Ministry of Justice'll help, but she'll need more.'

'Don't promise her anything, will you?' Karen began, alarmed at the idea that he might suggest that she could do something official to help the woman.

'I'm not stupid, Karen.'

'I know. Listen, before you go . . .'

'You want *another* favour? What is it this time: a hitman to take out your bullying professor?' Charlie's voice had lightened.

'Idiot!' Karen had to laugh, but it didn't take her long to get over it. 'D'you remember a bloke involved in the rape case called Tod Williams?'

'Of course.' Charlie's voice had sobered again, too.

Karen waited.

'But he can't do you any good now,' Charlie added at last, sounding much further away. 'He's dead.'

'I wasn't sure you'd heard. I know you and he were friends. Anyway, I'm sorry, Charlie. When did they tell you?'

'It's all over the nick here, along with some wild ideas about who could've killed him.'

'I got involved because someone thinks it could be Randall, but I don't think it's anything to do with him.' Karen hesitated, then decided she'd be a fool if she didn't ask every question in her mind. 'Have you ever had anything to do with his girlfriend, DS Annie Colvin?'

'Not since she moved in with him.'

'When did you last see her?' Karen wished he'd tell her everything without any prompts.

'Months ago. Comes to the Island once in a while, and I see her then. First time was when she heard about Lizzie,' he said, as though he'd read Karen's mind. 'Helped us with unrecorded info on Gyre's history that's never come to court. All of which we passed on to the CPS, who couldn't use it.'

'Is that how she and Tod met in the first place?'

'Why d'you want to know, Karen?'

'She found Tod's body. Didn't they tell you that? I'm due to meet her to talk about it. I've been told in no uncertain terms that she couldn't have killed him, but I'd have said there are questions to be asked.'

'Not by you.' Charlie's comment was sharp enough to worry Karen. 'And not that kind of question. Unless she's had a total personality transplant, she's one of the good guys, although she—' He stopped.

Karen's landline rang again, but she ignored it, waiting for whatever it was Charlie hadn't wanted to say.

'Take your phone with you,' he went on with an unconvincing lightness of tone, 'and call me if you need anything. OK? And don't fucking well ask her if she did it. See you tomorrow.' He clicked off, without saying goodbye.

Karen's landline was still ringing. It could have been Stella, wanting to confirm the arrangement they'd made to meet on the Island. But there wasn't time to deal with it now. Karen left the phone ringing and ran.

Tod's partner looked as tired as though she'd just finished a marathon, with skin slack and eyes swollen in their baggy sockets. Her hair was well washed and brushed, but it hung close to her face, lank and immobile. And her shoulders were tilted forwards, as though she carried a great weight on her back. Karen, whose swindler husband had died nearly eleven years ago, knew all about that kind of exhaustion, and the guilt that made it so much worse.

'I am sorry about your partner's death,' Karen said, which was as good a way as any into what she wanted to discuss.

Annie nodded and popped a piece of nicotine chewing gum out of its dimple in the packet, carefully peeling off the foil covering.

'Don't talk about it,' she said in a tight, hoarse voice. 'My DCS said you wanted to know about Gyre. That's fine. I can talk about *him* for ever.'

'Great. But let me get us coffee first.' Karen looked at the nicotine gum and the way the fingers that held it were twitching. 'Unless you'd like a drink? There's a wine bar next door.'

Annie looked straight at Karen, then, perhaps recognizing friendliness in her expression, she nodded, saying, 'Let's go.'

'We could get something to eat, too,' Karen suggested, remembering too late the destructive effect alcohol had had on her defences in the first days after Peter's death.

'I can't eat at the moment,' Annie said. 'I feel sick all the time. But wine helps. Blunts things. You know.'

'I do. OK.' Karen didn't sense any violence in the other woman, but she was experienced enough to know that almost anyone could flip under the right provocation and then slot back into her usual self without showing any traces of what it hid. 'Lead on. I'll collect my stuff and follow you.'

Five minutes later, they were sitting at a table for four at the back of the otherwise empty wine bar, scanning the lists for wines served by the glass.

'Why don't we just get a bottle?' Annie said, waving to the waiter. 'We'll have the Rioja. Red. Please. And my friend wants to order some food.'

'Caesar salad,' Karen said, guessing they had one and too keen to start asking questions to waste any time looking at a menu. 'Thanks.'

As soon as the waiter had brought their wine, poured it and left again, Annie said, 'What do you want to know about that bastard Gyre?'

'Mostly where he could be now.'

'I wish I knew,' Annie said in a hopeless voice.

'How did you come across him in the first place?' Karen asked. 'Were you working on the Island when he raped Lizzie?'

Annie shook her head, releasing a cloud of dandruff. Karen could remember that symptom of grief and guilt too.

'I was in the Met. He raped a young woman there, too. Years ago. Medical student he met at a party. I was part of the team that interviewed her. It was right at the start of my career – in the mid-nineties. Before the days of Operation Sapphire and its new focus on sex offences. Gyre got off.' Annie grimaced and scratched her head. 'Like most of them still do.'

'I'm sorry.' Karen realized there was a lot more to this than just a frustrating piece of work that had gone wrong. 'It didn't end there for you, though, did it?'

'Nope. I got to know the victim afterwards and heard all about how he threatened to kill her if she ever talked. We became mates for a while – so I saw what happens, how women like her can't forget.' Annie rubbed both hands over her swollen eyes, then added with a bitterness that scraped across Karen's mind: 'I've wanted to get him ever since. *And* all the other bastards who help him wriggle out each time he's pulled in.'

'Charlie's much the same,' Karen said. 'He told me you helped him with information on cases that had never come to court. Weren't you worried at all about Data Protection?'

'Stuff that! What about victim protection? Charlie's the only one who ever had the guts to try and use what I told them. But then he can never stand seeing a woman hurt.' Annie sniffed away some tears. 'Not that it helped. Even Charlie couldn't get Gyre for rape; only GBH.'

She looked directly at Karen and said with enough deliberation to show she really meant it, 'I could bloody kill those women jurors.'

'Why only the women?' Karen asked, distracted from her main questions.

'They're always the worst – more prejudiced than any bloke. You could see what they were thinking, the evil bitches: "She was asking for it, that Lizzie was – leading him on. Drunk as a skunk, she looked on that CCTV film. Not a virgin, was she? Flirting." And on and on. Poor cow.'

Karen thought back to the files she'd read about Randall's past and the progression of violence from one to the next.

'I know he did serious physical damage to Lizzie. Was it the same with the medical student?'

Annie took a huge swallow of the vanilla-scented red wine, apparently not worrying about the nicotine gum already in her mouth. The wine didn't bring any more colour to her cheeks or light to her dark-grey eyes.

'Physically he wasn't quite so vicious – not that it helps. Being raped's bad enough, and then the threats to kill her. It's been years and she isn't over it yet.'

'What's happened to her?' Karen asked. 'Has she ever had any kind of approach from him? A message – anything like that?'

'Not that she's ever told me. She picked herself up after the pointless trial, re-took her exams.' Annie pushed the glass away, as though these memories were too strong to be soothed with wine. 'Qualified. She's got real guts, you know. Works herself into the ground still. Gives her an excuse not to have a life.'

'Any partner?'

'Not now. There're about four broken relationships behind her – men and women. Doesn't even try with either any more. Doesn't go out, doesn't have holidays; fights off depression with work.'

'Why did her relationships fail? Is it that she couldn't trust anyone after what Randall did?'

Annie neatly extracted the wine-stained nicotine gum she'd been chewing and stowed it carefully in its packet for later use, before grabbing her glass again and putting her face right into it to take another, even bigger, gulp of Rioja.

'My guess is she's so needy she terrifies herself,' she said, when the wine had gone down. It had left a small curving dark-red mark on either side of her mouth, like little horns. 'Can't say anything about what she wants or let it show, so she never gets it. That's hell for anyone with her. We . . . *they* get angry. Which makes her miserable. Like a vicious cycle. Getting worse all the time.'

'That sounds psychologically convincing,' Karen said, meaning it. 'You must have come to know her very well.'

A faint pink colour at last spread up into Annie's grey cheeks.

'Breaks my heart, you know. She was still more or less a child when that bastard attacked her. Oh, fuck it!' Annie's eyes filled with tears. 'Her face is like granite these days. So's her character. Bloody difficult to live with.'

Which sounded to Karen like an admission that one of the victim's failed relationships could have been with Annie herself. Was this what made Stokes and Charlie so uncomfortable? Were they worried about Annie's motives for moving in with a man in the first place?

Annie sucked up more wine. When she raised her head, Karen saw the horns were bigger and darker on either side of her mouth. 'I can't do this. Ask me about something else. Please.'

'Where could Randall be now?'

Annie rubbed the back of her hand under her dripping nose.

'I don't fucking know. If you find him, tell me. I need to keep tabs on him. And this time I've lost him.' She got to her feet and left the table so fast her shoulder bag caught on the back of an unoccupied chair, making it rock as she wrenched the strap away.

Karen watched her go, speculating about why her escape had had to be so abrupt. Was Annie too angry to stay? Too scared of what she might reveal if she said any more?

Panic hovered all round Lisa, like a swarm of hornets ready to sting. She couldn't paint any longer; everything she did to the canvas made it look prettier and sillier than ever. She saw shadows and phantom canoeists and stalkers every time she raised her head from her work. Like when she left the house and heard footsteps and heavy breathing behind her.

Each time she woke in the night now she could sense her watcher outside, but if she got up to swing a torch around the garden, she could never see anything. Except – sometimes – the same footprints in the drenched grass.

Worst of all, she'd lost the ability to be Lee. She was defenceless all over again, like a snail without its shell.

Was it because she'd told Jed the truth? Because she'd let him see her scars and allowed herself to care about him? Depend on him?

After she'd dressed again that day, he'd stroked her face with all the delicacy of touch he used on his smallest plants and said, 'You're safe now. I'll look after you, Lisa. You don't have to worry any more. He can't get you now. You're safe with me.'

She'd loved hearing it then. But now? Now she was terrified that she'd re-opened herself to all the old terrors.

One day she'd actually asked Jed if he'd ever seen anyone hanging about – or anyone new to the village on the river. He hadn't. The only people he'd ever seen rowing or canoeing were the usual three villagers. None of them had a grey canoe.

Lisa knew she was cracking up. She *had* to get Lee back.

Not knowing what else to do, she pulled down the cover over the hated canvas and sat on her stool, swivelling round on it as she held off the hornets, trying not to think about how much she needed Lee.

Turning round and round on the stool, pushing off with her feet whenever the movement slowed, she saw the roll of clean canvas and the stock of stretchers she kept under the work bench, her messy pile of pocket sketchbooks, the watercolours, the oils, the brushes in their jars, the untouched pack of rules and site plans for the Isle of Wight competition, then the roll of canvas again, the stretchers, the books, colours, brushes, stretchers, canvases. Round and round and round until she was so dizzy she almost fell off on to the floor.

Jamming her feet down to stop the stool, thinking of herself lying on the hard concrete, smelling the paints and the turps she used to clean her brushes before she washed them, she remembered the alley where she'd nearly died. Lee had been born there in that moment. Would she find the rage and strength and power again if she went back?

What would happen to her if she didn't?

Chapter 11

'Good to know you don't think Gyre did it. Any idea who could have?' Al said briskly.

Karen held the phone to her ear as she watched the wooded slopes of the Island approach through the splashed window of the catamaran that zoomed across the Solent, and thought about him sitting in his neat blue-and-grey office at the Ministry of Justice.

'The cops are worried it's his girlfriend, a DS,' she said. 'I don't have enough evidence either way. But it could be.'

'We need a lot more than speculation,' Al went on. 'What're you up to now?'

'On my way to meet Randall's last victim's mother, in case she has any new insights to offer about where he could be now,' Karen said, yet again envying Al's detachment as much as she disliked it. 'If only I could talk to Lizzie herself!'

'Why can't you?'

'She disappeared right after the trial. Didn't you know?'

'Nope. My responsibilities don't go as far as victims. Doesn't anyone know where she is?'

'Lizzie hasn't had any contact with anyone else involved since,' Karen said slowly. 'She could be in Australia for all anyone knows.'

'Not a bad idea, Australia. Gyre's not likely to follow her there, however vengeful he feels. Good luck with the mother,' Al said, still sounding cheerful. 'Let me know as soon as you get anything. We need to be ready to control this if it gets into the press. But don't let it distract you from the rest of the subjects. You've got fourteen to go, haven't you?'

'That's right.'

'And your full report's still due in March.'

'I haven't forgotten.' Karen thought of all her other work and Max's increasingly serious chasing.

'Great. By the way did you hear? John Clarence has got himself in trouble with the law again.'

Oh shit! Karen thought, remembering the unhappy man she'd interviewed, and anticipating the probation officer Dave's likely *Schadenfreude*. She waited for more.

'Assaulted a traffic warden apparently,' Al said.

'How bad's the damage?' Karen's stomach lurched as she remembered the account of Clarence's wife's head, beaten to the colour and texture of a rotten tomato.

'One smashed camera and a few scratches,' Al added cheerfully.

'Camera?' Some of Karen's dread dissolved.

'They carry them these days to prove they didn't invent the parking infringement. This warden was photographing Clarence's hired car when he saw her, lost his temper, grabbed the camera and flung it on the ground.'

'Doesn't sound too bad to me.' Karen leaned back in her seat and crossed her legs, noticing a chip in the cherry-red varnish on her toenails. 'Was he on a yellow line or something?'

'No.' Al dragged out the short word to far longer than it should have been. 'No. Part of one wheel was outside the white lines of his parking space.'

'And she was writing him a ticket for that?' Karen said, feeling better at once. She was peering through the window at the quay, but she couldn't see any sign of Charlie. 'I'm not surprised he lost it. Anybody could've done. Don't give me heart failure like that again. We're landing. I must go.'

Karen flipped the cover over her phone and made her way to the entrance. A small crowd filled the quay. She looked this way and that, searching for the familiar dark head and laughing face.

At last she saw him, running fast down Fountain Quay towards her, and felt a surge of pleasure she didn't want to analyse. She waved.

'Karen,' he called, beckoning. He was breathless, as though the run had started a long way away. Now they were closer, she could see he looked stressed out.

When she reached his side, she leaned towards him to kiss his cheek and felt his hands grip her elbows for a second. Then he let her go, much too soon.

'How'd you get on with Annie?' he said. 'Anything useful?'

'Not a lot. I liked her.'

He grinned and looked less worried.

'But I can't stop myself thinking about how Tod must have trusted whoever it was who killed him.' Karen stood close enough for her elbow just to touch Charlie's, but he quickly moved away. 'She has to be a likelier candidate than Randall. He'd have made more of a drama, probably getting excitement from the knowledge that he might be discovered at any moment.'

'Christ! I'd love to be a free-floating expert,' Charlie said with unusual savagery. 'You can make up anything you want, and never have to take responsibility for it.'

He strode ahead, then turned to look at her, trying to smile and not making a very good job of it. 'If I have hunches I have to back them up with DNA or fingerprints, or look like a twat.'

Karen knew better than to comment, so instead she hurried to catch up and asked whether his colleagues in Winchester had come up with any formal suspects yet.

'Not so far as I know. You're not the only person who thinks it's Annie.'

'Who—?'

'She's got plenty of scumbag colleagues, who suspect her just because she's a dyke,' Charlie said, not interested in anything Karen had been going to say. 'Well, bisexual, but usually a dyke.'

'As I understand it,' she said, wanting him to know she wasn't a scumbag, 'the theory is she wouldn't have had time to do it *and* get rid of the weapon and whatever protective clothes she had on before she called it in. Is that right?'

She paused, aware of something going on in his mind, and squinted sideways. He was looking dead ahead, scowling.

'Although I suppose there's no reason why she shouldn't have had an accomplice,' Karen said slowly. 'I mean, someone else could've been waiting outside to take away the knife and—'

'We'll be late. Come on.' Charlie turned without another word, walking up towards the centre of town so fast that Karen had to work to keep up, in spite of her long legs. When they reached the deli she'd planned to use for her picnic with Stella, she forced him to wait outside for her. The second she emerged with her backpack full of food and wine, he rushed her off again.

After a muscle-pumping, lung-aching eight minutes, he pushed open the door of an old-fashioned café and pointed to a plump woman, wearing a loose, low-cut dress made of Indian printed cotton. She was sitting at one of the tables near the window, with a much younger man beside her. He looked very tidy and rather damp, while she had artfully messy dyed blonde hair, good make-up, and a necklace of dark wooden beads supporting a massive silver pendant that hung between her full breasts.

'Charlie,' she said warmly before they were even halfway across the room. 'I thought you weren't coming. This must be Doctor Taylor.'

'Yup. Karen. Sally Fane.' He turned to shake hands with the younger man. 'And this is James Fullwell. He's a *real* doctor.'

'My biggest support apart from Charlie,' Sally said, clinging to the young man's free hand with both of hers. Karen caught a waft of warm spicy patchouli from her cleavage. 'He cut short his usual swim so he could be here now – even though it's his day off.'

James Fullwell made the greatest possible contrast to Sally, being tall and thin, with a prominent Adam's apple and, Karen noticed, deeply bitten fingernails. He was dressed in jeans and sweatshirt, but both were pressed into starchy perfection, and there was nothing casual in the way he wore them. A faint scent of chlorine hung about him, and a sports bag sagged at his feet, like a well-trained dog.

'I don't know what I'd have done without him all these years,' Sally said, leaning sideways so that her shoulder touched his arm. 'He looked after my Lizzie, you see, when he was only just qualified, and did better than all the senior doctors put together. Without him, she'd have died.'

Fullwell patted her hand, looking at Karen with a pleasant, modest expression that said with absolute clarity: Don't believe everything you hear.

She smiled at him, liking both his kindness and his self-deprecation.

'I'll get the coffees in,' he said, smiling back. 'They're short-handed here. It saves a good half-hour's wait to collect them. What can I get you, Doctor Taylor?'

'Karen, please. Double espresso. Thanks.'

'Me too,' Charlie said. 'Now, Sally, like I told you, Karen's advising us on Gyre's likely movements now he's broken his licence, and—'

'They should never have let him out.' Sally's voice throbbed. '*Never*. He should be dead by now. Nine years for what he did to Lizzie? Pathetic! Then they let him out after only four. It's disgusting. But what can you expect? Everyone failed my Lizzie except these two and Sergeant Williams.'

She wiped her eyes, then added spitefully, 'Not that I ever liked *him* after what he put her through at the start.'

Karen looked questioningly at Charlie, who shook his head, as though saying he hadn't passed on the news of Tod's death.

'Mrs Fane,' she began, 'I know Randall spent a lot of time on the Island, from when he was really quite young. Are you sure Lizzie'd never met him before?'

Sally nodded, then shrugged as though muddled about which gesture would express what she meant.

'It's only a tiny place,' she said, breathless, 'but like they said at his trial, there are sixty thousand men here and more women. There's no reason for us to know everyone. We never met him; none of us. He used to stay near Bembridge, with a family who've—'

'The Hemmings,' Karen said, interrupting only to show she knew exactly what Sally was talking about.

'That's right. We've always lived here in Cowes, in a flat over my boutique. Only me, now that Lizzie's father has gone and left me.' Tears spilled over Sally's lower lids, carrying mascara with them to make grey streaks down her face. She was quite unaware of them.

Charlie took a clean handkerchief from his pocket and handed it over, as though performing a familiar function. Karen realized he must have come prepared for exactly this.

'There's still big differences on the Island,' he was explaining to her. 'Kind of tribal. Sally's mates are the urban sophisticated sailing lot. Cosmopolitan. The Hemmings are old-style farmers. They'd look down on Sally as a "shopkeeper". Her daughter'd never be allowed to play with their kids.'

'If I'd been host to a rapist as violent and notorious as Randall, I'd be a bit more humble than that,' Karen said, meaning it. 'Move away, too, probably.'

'Not them.' Sally's eyes sharpened with hatred. A blob of spit appeared in the corner of her reddened mouth. She licked it away, then wiped her mouth on the handkerchief. 'Charlie's right. They're snobs. Posh snobs. They kept saying my Lizzie'd asked for it. Got drunk and asked for it. But she didn't.'

'Of course not,' Karen said, earning herself a grateful smile.

'I may not mix with that lot socially, but I hear all the gossip. The story their crowd still believe is that Lizzie led him on and got no more than what she deserved. They're probably planning a champagne thrash to celebrate him getting out.'

'Is he back here, then?' Karen asked, wondering whether her quest could be as easy to achieve as this.

The espresso machine hissed in the distance and she caught a wave of rich delectable coffee.

'Not so far as I've heard,' Sally said, disappointing her. 'Everyone's gone quiet. Why? You think he'd dare show his face again?'

'I think he might.' Karen glanced at Charlie, who was sitting expressionless, then back at Sally.

Her bravado had shrivelled to nothing. She was clutching both arms around herself and began to rock to and fro.

'He said he'd come back and kill my Lizzie,' she said, keening in every pause between words. 'That's why she ran away. He said he'd do anything to find her wherever she is. He's a devil. They should've kept him in for life. If you'd seen her body when he'd finished with it then . . .' She gasped and choked, whooping like a child with croup, fighting for breath.

Dr Fullwell came back with a tray of coffee cups. Seeing her state, he put down the tray at once, placed his hand in the middle of her back, and held it there, without moving.

'Breathe, Sally,' he said. 'Breathe. Come on, you can do it. These panic attacks are controllable. You don't have to give in to them.'

'See what I mean?' she gasped when her breathing was more or less normal. She looked up at Karen. 'He keeps me going. Thanks, Jamie. I'll be OK. She thinks Randall's coming back.'

'Gyre?' he said, looking amazed. He glanced at Karen, as though to check her sanity. '*Here*? After what he did? He wouldn't dare.'

'Karen thinks he has unfinished business with us,' Charlie said.

'I couldn't tell him anything about where Lizzie is. But he won't know that.' Sally was hyperventilating again, which at least stopped the keening. 'She's never been in touch. I still want to find her, of course I do. But I can't. I've even stopped Googling. But what if he thinks I know and he—?'

'Googling?' Karen said, so surprised she interrupted.

'On the computer. You know, looking for her name.' Sally looked puzzled that anyone could be so thick. 'There's nothing there. All I got were sites full of filth about rape and why it's such fun to torture women. That's what he'll do to me if he thinks I know where my Lizzie is.'

Her whole body was shaken now by deep rigors.

'Breathe, Sally,' said the doctor. 'Breathe.'

'Do you really believe Randall might think you'd tell him where Lizzie is?' Karen said, looking from Sally to the doctor and back again.

Tears welled in Sally's eyes.

James intervened. 'Not if he listens to Chloe Hemming,' he said, smiling at Sally, then at Karen. 'She'll get all the Island gossip and everybody here knows Lizzie's gone for good, and you can't find her. Don't be afraid, Sally. No one could think you could ever tell anyone where she is.'

Sally used Charlie's handkerchief to mop her face again, then emerged from behind it swollen-eyed and little flushed. 'What that bastard did to Lizzie was cruel, but what he did to me was worse.'

Karen sat up straighter, ready with her questions, but she wasn't given time to ask any of them.

'He wrecked my marriage, you know. My husband couldn't deal with losing her like that. He said it was my fault.'

'Where is he now?' Karen managed to ask as Sally paused for breath.

'God knows. I've never heard from him since the divorce. That's down to Randall Bloody Gyre, too.'

Charlie glanced at Karen with a questioning look in his eyes. She slightly shook her head, wishing she could talk to the doctor alone and get his take on it all. His hazel eyes were so watchful and his whole pose so attentive, she thought he probably picked up a great deal missed by everyone else. But it was easy to see that Sally wouldn't be shaken off. Karen knew she'd have to make a whole separate appointment with him, somewhere well away from everyone else.

She handed one of her cards to each of them, saying, 'Thank you for seeing me, Mrs Fane. If you hear anything on your Island grapevine about Randall's whereabouts, will you tell me?'

'I hate the way you call him Randall,' Sally said suddenly, sounding much more real and present. 'It makes him sound like a friend.'

'Sorry. I didn't mean to upset you. It's just a kind of shorthand.'

'You should be like Charlie and use his surname, like with any other villain. You're not going to help me get justice for my Lizzie, are you?'

'There's nothing I can do,' Karen said, 'except pass on your concerns to my contact at the ministry. I can promise you that.'

Sally looked at her with a grimace that suggested the offer wasn't any good to her.

'It'll have to do. Right – I've got to get back,' she said aloud. 'The boutique's the only thing I've got left. I can't lose it or I'll have nothing.' She clutched at the doctor's arm again and raised her sodden face towards his. 'Come on, Jamie. You'll take me back, won't you?'

He looked over his shoulder at the other two, as though he'd have preferred to stay with them, but he held up Karen's card, perhaps promising her he'd be in touch, then put it in the pocket of his jeans. Sally towed him through the café and out into the street, releasing a whole fresh burst of chlorine and patchouli scent.

'Wow,' Karen said when they'd gone. 'I'd never have had you down as a man who'd put up with that kind of free-flowing emotion. How often do you see her?'

'Sally? Every couple of weeks or so.'

'Why?' Karen thought of Annie's comment about how Charlie couldn't bear to see a woman hurt and hoped he might let her see further into that side of him.

'What do you mean?' He was glaring down at the dregs of his coffee as though he hated them. 'Why not?'

Karen saw he wasn't going to let down his guard. She tried to control her disappointment and waited. After a moment, he shrugged his big shoulders.

'Sally's had a hard time and she's a decent woman, who's deserved better from all of us,' he said. 'You can't blame her for finding it tough to get it together again.'

'Sally's a drama queen, milking her daughter's tragedy for every last drop of excitement she can squeeze out of it,' Karen said, knowing she sounded cold and not caring who heard her. 'I'm not surprised Lizzie ran away. The husband too. Have you got any idea where he is?'

'Nope.' Charlie shrugged. 'He buggered off. I've no reason to keep tabs on him.'

'I suppose not. They must have had a hell of a time with Sally. Listening to her, you'd think she was the main victim here.'

'Bollocks. You heard her say Gyre was a devil for what he did to Lizzie. Like I say, she's had a fuck of a lot to put up with.'

'Well, I think you and that doctor are saints to go on support-ing her.'

'James says helping Sally makes him feel less bad about taking so long to see what was really wrong with Lizzie,' Charlie said, without adding anything about his own motives.

'So he's getting all the traditional rewards of doing penance. Makes sense.' Karen thought again of Annie's comment and

longed to ask why Charlie was such a passionate defender of
hurt women.

But she knew he'd hate her questions, and probably refuse to
answer them. Just now Karen knew she wouldn't be able to cope
with that.

'Anyway, thanks for setting up the meeting,' she said brightly.
'I'd better be off. I'm due to meet an architect at the chalet.'

'And I've got someone to see in . . .' he checked his ancient
watch '. . . eight minutes.'

His phone rang. Karen watched him answer and saw the blood
surge into his cheeks, turning his already tanned skin even darker.

'When?' His voice practically exploded. 'Secure the scene, Eve.
We'll have to call in the Major Crime Team from the mainland,
but I'll be there asap.'

He turned towards Karen. 'Sonia Franklin's been found dead
now.'

'Who?'

'The consultant in charge of Lizzie's case,' Charlie said, so
impatient that it was clear he thought Karen should have known
about everything that was in his mind. 'Gave evidence against
Gyre at the trial, like Tod did. Come *on*! Didn't you even read
the fucking transcript? I must go. I'll phone.'

Karen watched his tough powerful figure disappearing down
the street and tried not to feel anything but professional curiosity. But she couldn't. She considered the idea of Randall's
keeping a list of everyone he wanted to punish, picking them off
one by one. If it was he who'd killed this consultant, then he was
probably still here on the Island, watching and waiting to get
everyone else on his list.

Karen sat down again, trying not to think beyond the obvious,
and ordered more coffee. She needed the caffeine hit badly.

Before the espresso was ready, Charlie was back and grabbing
her wrist. She felt the strength of his hand making her bones
creak. It reminded her horribly of Randall.

'You better come,' Charlie said.

'I've got to pay first,' she said, pointing to the counter, where they were making her espresso. Charlie wrenched a five-pound note from his pocket, waved it at the café's owner, who was working behind the red Formica counter. 'OK, Rosa?'

'Course, Charlie. Fine. See you.'

He dragged Karen towards the door. '*Come on.*'

She bent to pick up the rucksack that contained her notes, keys, phone and money, as well as the picnic she'd brought for Stella.

'I'm coming. Hang on. And tell me: who found the body? How was she killed? And *when?*'

Charlie scowled at her and didn't offer any kind of answer.

Chapter 12

Lisa pushed her way through the woods towards where the sea must be, fighting ivy and brambles and mud. She could smell the salt and the seaweed, as well as the fresh greenery she was crushing beneath her feet. For a horrible instant it reminded her of Randall's aftershave.

She forced herself to stand still, breathing in the air, testing it against her memory, feeling around for the strength the Lee persona gave her. It wasn't working yet. Lee was nowhere in her mind. Maybe that was because the smell *wasn't* Randall's. Maybe this place had nothing to do with him. Maybe the competition was real.

Whether it was or it wasn't, she was going to have to do some work on it in case anyone ever tracked her down and asked her why she'd come to the Island today.

The bungalow behind her was hideous, and all the window frames were rotten. It would have to be pulled down. Most of the trees would have to go with it if the site was to be rescued from dingy messiness. But if the planners cooperated, the place had possibilities.

At last Lisa found herself at the edge of the long drop to the sea, looking over the top of the trees down to the waves. Across the narrow stretch of water that divided the Island from the mainland, she saw the low green edge of Hampshire with its cosy red-brick cottages and small white farmhouses.

As views went it could have had more thrills.

She wheeled round, looking back towards the shack-like house, hidden now behind the trees. The land sloped up towards it. With a clearing made in the wood, in a kind of teardrop shape, and a new single-storey house built in a curve at the top of the tear . . .

Her mind was sharpening as ideas expanded within it. Maybe if she let it rip, worked seriously on this project, she could learn to feel like a survivor here. As an independent and successful painter, no longer the brutalized victim everyone remembered as Lizzie, maybe she'd be able to come back and face her old friends and family one day. She had a pocket sketchpad with her, as usual, and whipped it out, along with a 4B pencil, while she looked around for a perch.

She hadn't been working for five minutes before footsteps sounded in the trees ahead of her. She uncoiled her legs and stood wincing as the blood rushed back into her cramped muscles, sending the tingling pain of pins and needles all through them. Her right foot felt heavy and dead, hanging off the joint like a lump of cold lead.

The footsteps were coming closer. Lisa stuffed the book in her backpack and forced herself to walk sideways, out of the way, hoping she hadn't left footprints in the mud. Her foot started to work properly, and she trod lightly to avoid being heard.

'Whoever did this enjoyed it,' Karen said as she stood beside Charlie and DS Eve Clarke.

All three of them were now dressed in the white scene suits Eve had brought with her, with the hoods pulled up to prevent any loose hairs dropping into the crime scene, staring at the body of Dr Franklin.

Her dressing-gown, a vibrant silk kimono with a pattern of cranes and flying clouds, had been wrenched away from her body. The slash marks of a knife could be clearly seen in her skin, beneath and between the smears of blood from the huge wound in her neck.

Fresh blood smelled quite different from the day-old dried kind Karen had encountered at the Winchester crime scene.

'Looks as if the wounds on her breasts were made post-mortem,' Eve said in the small, tight, nasal voice Karen remembered from last year.

Eve still looked the same, too: skinny, freckled and resentful. Her tight skirt was too short and must have been the most impractical garment any working officer ever had. But her legs were very good, and her chic shoes suggested she knew it and wanted to show them off.

'It's no wonder the cleaner screamed when she saw it,' Eve went on, turning towards Karen with a patronizing expression clearly designed to show she didn't belong here. 'I don't know if DCI Trench told you, but we were called in by the gardener working next door. He came round to investigate the noise, found the cleaner screaming and pointing at the body, unable to speak.'

Karen nodded her thanks for the information, thinking it was merciful that Dr Franklin's body was still seated, propped against the high back of a Charles Rennie Mackintosh chair, so that gravity kept the wound in her neck more or less closed. Rigor mortis hadn't yet set in. You could see the softness of the muscle. The sweetish, coppery scent of the blood mixed with everything the body had expelled in the moment of death and made breathing difficult.

A cup of white coffee in front of the dead woman was splattered now and discoloured with the blood that had spurted from her arteries. A bagel, half-eaten, lay on a blue plate. Her teeth-marks could be clearly seen in the cream cheese she'd spread on it. Beyond that a glass plate held neat slices of orange interleaved with mint leaves.

'Did he know the cleaner?' Karen asked, concentrating on anything except the smell and sight of the slashed, stained body propped against the chair back.

'No. He's a casual, working for the agency that provides next-door's help. Why?' Eve's voice was heavy now with sarcasm. 'You suggesting the killer got away by posing as a cleaner?'

'You never know.' Karen shrugged off the suggestion that she was being absurd. 'Why was the victim breakfasting so late if she was a consultant at the hospital?' She was pleased to find that her voice betrayed none of the nausea that was churning away in her stomach.

'According to the information I've got so far, she'd been working extra hard and was taking a week's leave to recover,' Eve snapped, as though Karen had no right to ask any of these questions.

Eve turned to Charlie, who was standing in silence, looking at the floor.

'Sir, the team from Major Crimes won't be here for another hour at least and we shouldn't risk contaminating the scene. The cleaner's already trampled all over the ground floor.'

When he didn't answer or move, Eve turned to Karen: 'Haven't you seen enough yet? You shouldn't be here anyway.'

'I've seen almost enough.' Karen made herself look closely at the wounds, divorcing herself from the mind and feelings of the woman who had once lived in the mutilated body.

'Come on, Karen. Give me something I can use,' Charlie said, raising his head at last and looking straight at her. She thought she could see appalling sadness in his dark eyes, but none of the anger she'd expected from someone who so hated seeing a woman hurt. 'If the killer enjoyed this, *couldn't* it be Gyre?'

'Could be,' Karen began, 'but—'

'Sir! It's not our problem,' Eve said. 'Major Crimes will deal.'

'I'll wait outside,' Karen said, not wanting to be part of their fight, or to make Eve's resentment worse.

Charlie grabbed Karen's wrist again. Luckily this time he got
the other one so her bones had a chance to complete their recov-
ery. 'Now you're here you need to see the rest of the cottage.
You may spot things pointing to Gyre that Major Crimes'll miss.
None of them'll know anything about him. Not like you.'

'Sir, it's perfectly clear what happened. The victim's french
windows were open. She'd been out in the garden in her bare
feet.' Eve pointed towards Sonia's dark pink feet, both of which
had dry soil clinging to the edges.

Karen retched and tasted hot acid bile in her throat. She could
see that Eve despised her for the weakness. Karen knew the dark
pink colour in Sonia's feet came only from the pooling of blood
that could no longer be pumped around her body, but it didn't
stop them looking freaky.

Eve swung round to stare out through the open glass doors into
the small cottage garden that overlooked Carisbrooke Pond. A
neat brick terrace divided the cottage from the lawn and flower-
beds beyond, and a row of cobalt-blue glazed pots held a variety
of healthily growing herbs. Insects buzzed round and over them,
but nothing else moved.

'You can see where she went,' Eve insisted. 'She must have just
had a shower and still had damp feet when she went out to pick
the mint to go with her oranges. Some psycho saw her, followed
her in – and did this.'

The evidence of the dead woman's foray into her garden was
still there all around, from the soil marks on her feet and the
floor to the mint itself on the glass plate and on the draining
board, too, where the discarded stalks lay, still with a little damp
soil clinging to their roots.

'It must've happened very recently,' Karen said, staring first at
them, then at the faint footmarks that could still be seen in the
garden, 'if none of it's quite dry yet.'

'Not necessarily,' Eve said, clearly glad to be able to correct
Karen. 'Can't you feel the damp in the air? With this much

humidity, they're not going to dry any time soon. Like the blood. Major Crimes will get an expert to give us something more precise, but experience says it could've been anything up to – maybe – a couple of hours ago.'

Eve turned to her boss and went on: 'She was giving herself a leisurely morning treat, with the perfect breakfast in the sun, when some bastard came in and killed her. Major Crimes'll find him – so long as we don't screw up the scene and destroy the evidence. We must get out of here. Now. All of us.'

Charlie was staring at the corpse now, paying no attention to Eve, which clearly pissed her off.

'Sir!' she shouted.

'What?' He turned slowly.

'There's nothing we can do here,' Eve said, more quietly. 'We should get out now.'

'Not till Karen's looked round the house,' he said, as stubborn as ever.

'Where d'you want me to start?' Karen asked, still not wanting to get in the way of their fight.

'At the top and move down. Yes, I know, Eve. I heard: Major Crimes will deal. I don't care. I want an expert opinion now. On your way, Karen.'

She walked up the plain wooden treads of the open staircase to the top floor, keen to pick up any clues to the minds of the people who had been here, however tiny, however ambiguous.

From the outside, the building had looked like a traditional stone and red-brick Isle of Wight cottage, with a deep thatched roof, but inside everything was as modern as it could possibly be and immaculately kept.

Two bedrooms were obviously spares. Both had plump beds made up with pristine white cotton sheets and duvets. Neither showed any sign of recent occupation. The only bathroom had clearly been used. There was condensation still on the inside of the glass around the shower, and the scent of some sharply aromatic gel or soap. But there were no signs of anything relating to Randall.

Karen moved on into the main bedroom, to see that Dr Franklin had made her bed before breakfast, which seemed surprisingly obsessive, particularly for a woman who hadn't bothered to dress and had left muddy mint roots still lying on the draining board. In her place, Karen would have dressed and binned the mess left by the mint long before bothering to make her bed.

One of the wardrobe doors was open. Inside it, the clothes were perfectly pressed and hung with a military precision Will would have admired; colour coordinated, too. The contrast with the chaos, mess and pain evident downstairs in the kitchen was unspeakable.

Karen's eye was caught by a red plastic square on the wall, just as her phone began to ring again. Looking closer, she recognized a panic button and had to stop her imagination putting her in Sonia's mind. She turned away to answer the phone.

'Karen? It's Stella. You were supposed to be here by now. Are you stuck somewhere? Do you need me to pick you up? I did come with the car so I could drive over and get you.'

'You're a star. Sorry I'm late. I am a bit stuck. It'd be great if you could pick me up.' Karen gave her the address of the cottage in the old village of Carisbrooke, which was now more or less a suburb of Newport, adding: 'It's a crime scene, and there's a cop outside guarding it, so you probably won't be allowed near the house itself. D'you want to phone again when you're in the area? I'll come out and find you.'

'OK,' Stella said, always the easiest of companions.

'Maybe it's only women he likes to slash,' Charlie was saying as Karen came down the stairs.

She assumed she'd see Eve listening to him, but it turned out Charlie was alone and on the phone. After a moment, he said: 'Yeah. Right. Fine. Pool all info. Sensible. Right. Yeah, I agree.

Gyre has to be the major suspect in both, whatever the shrink says. If you come up with anything . . . Yeah, right. Bye.'

He stuffed the phone back in his pocket.

'DCS Stokes from Winchester,' he told Karen. 'You've met him, I hear. See anything upstairs?'

'Nothing but evidence that she was in control, cared about cleanliness and order and would've been terrified when her killer stuck a knife in her neck.'

Charlie's face was impassive, which worried Karen. Normally it was one of the most expressive she'd ever met.

'There's the same anomaly here that I saw in Tod's house in Winchester.'

'What?' Charlie's voice was hard and sharp, like the bark of a guard dog.

Was this out of loyalty to Annie Colvin? Karen had seen how much time he had for her. Whatever he and Stokes said, Annie had to be the obvious suspect for Tod's murder. In Karen's view, Annie was angry enough with everyone involved in all the rape cases to have gone after any of them. And, as a police officer and a woman, she was just the kind of visitor whose unexpected appearance would have been so unthreatening that Dr Franklin wouldn't have been scared for a second – until the knife appeared.

'Why's she still in her chair?' Karen said. 'Why, if it was Randall, would she sit waiting when a man she knew to be *so* dangerous walks through her french windows? Doesn't make sense.'

'Maybe she just didn't recognize him,' Eve said, coming back into the room from the garden. Her expression was as aggressive as her voice. 'People look different in real life than in the dock. It's nearly five years since she saw Gyre in court.'

'Yes, but—'

'And she's a doctor – sees hundreds of people every day at the hospital. Why would she recognize Gyre? She never had to identify him; hadn't even met him. All she did was give evidence on the damage done to her patient.'

'One reason why I wanted you to look upstairs, Karen,' Charlie said, paying no attention to Eve, which made her scowl even worse. 'Was there any sign of a bloke up there last night?'

'You think she could have *slept* with Gyre?' Eve said. 'That's mad, sir.'

'Covering all bases. You could be right and she didn't recognize him. He's a good-looking fucker. What's to stop him trying to pick her up so he could get her somewhere quiet to kill her in private? Easier than at the hospital with all those cameras. Was there anyone here with her last night, Karen?'

'It didn't look like it. The bed was made, so there was nothing to see there, but only one towel had been used and there was only one toothbrush in the holder.' Karen looked at the plain beautiful crockery on the white table. 'And no breakfast things for anyone else. Nothing in the sink.'

A dishwasher stood under the drainer. She gestured to it. 'May I?'

'I'll do it,' Charlie said, pulling the machine open, still wearing his protective gloves.

She leaned down and saw a single dinner plate, with marks of food, cutlery for one, and a lone wineglass.

'Unless her killer cleared up after himself, she *was* alone last night,' Karen said, stating the obvious.

Charlie didn't comment.

'Told you so,' Eve said, with satisfaction. 'Someone's going to have to go through all the CCTV from all the entry points on the Island. If it was Gyre, he'll be there on one of the films. We shouldn't wait for Major Crimes to start looking for that.'

'So get it under way, for Christ's sake!' Charlie spoke at last, but he sounded as though Eve was driving him mad. She didn't like it at all.

After a moment of heavy silence from all of them, he went on again: 'OK, Karen, that's it for now. I'll phone you when I need you.'

'I'm not accredited to deal with murder investigations,' she said. 'Of course I'll help in any way I can, but you're not allowed to use me in—'

'Fuck rules. The Ministry of Justice is using you to help find Gyre. That's good enough for me. How're you getting back?'

'A friend's picking me up. She should be here soon.'

'Sir, I—'

'In a minute, Eve. Karen, I'll walk you out.'

They stripped off their scene suits and bundled them into a heap outside the front door. On the pavement in front of the charming ancient cottage, Charlie had a word with his uniformed constable, then moved away to say to Karen in a voice so tense it showed her how much the question mattered, 'How serious are you about it not being Gyre?'

'Serious. As I said, I simply cannot see the victims sitting passively waiting to be killed by him. Can you?' Karen looked into Charlie's treacle-toffee eyes, and saw nothing in them: no light; no movement. After a painful pause, she added, 'But if it *is* Randall on a revenge kick, then someone needs to find Lizzie and get her some protection.'

'She doesn't want to be found,' he said dully. 'We've all tried.'

'No one can disappear for ever. She needs help.'

'You think I don't know that?' he burst out, with an urgency that made Karen's heart jolt. 'You think I'm not doing everything I can?'

'So what's the problem? People just don't dematerialize.'

'Budgets,' he snapped. 'Fucking budgets. I had to give up when I got told "There isn't any money. She chose to go. We told her we could only help if she kept in contact".'

'You know you're at risk, too, don't you?' Karen said, having no difficulty believing him. 'You and anyone else involved. You must be careful.'

'Karen,' he said, then stopped and turned his head away for a moment, as though he was searching the quiet village street for help. Then he looked back, grinning unconvincingly. 'I can take care of myself. I won't leave my patio doors open, or admit any lanky good-looking posh bloke who comes knocking. That your friend over there?'

Karen turned to look and saw Stella patiently waiting by her sleek, low-slung Toyota. Today she was wearing floppy indigo linen trousers and a fuchsia-coloured top that sizzled against her red hair.

'It is. I'd better go in a minute. But look around you, Charlie.' Karen gestured to the charming quiet village street. 'Someone must've seen something. If next-door's gardener heard the cleaner scream, someone must've seen a stranger, and they'll tell us.'

Charlie grabbed her hands for an instant and held on tight. 'I know. Don't worry. Once Major Crimes are here, house-to-house will happen. They're good enough at their job. It'll all be OK.'

'Great,' she said, wishing she knew just exactly what he was reassuring her about. 'Thanks. Bye.'

Karen hurried towards Stella, who was gazing past her at Charlie.

'He's tasty,' Stella said, popping her eyes at Karen. '*I* wouldn't mind being stuck out in the sticks with him. Who is he?'

'Hi,' Karen said, before slinging the rucksack on the back shelf of the car. 'He's a cop, running a murder investigation I'm kind of involved in. Sorry to be late.'

'Murder? Bloody hell. Can you really get away to picnic with me?'

'For the moment. Let's go. Did you come the back way or through Newport?'

'Through Newport,' Stella said, taking one more long look at Charlie, who was talking urgently into his phone again and paying no attention to anyone else.

Stella dragged her gaze back to Karen's face and smiled. 'If there's a prettier route, let's take it.'

Finding their way out of Carisbrooke was easy. They passed the mediaeval castle, where Charles I had spent the last night before his execution. Perched on its grassy hill, the grey stone keep provided a helpful landmark. But minutes later they'd taken a wrong turn and were in the middle of Newport after all.

None of the traffic or crowds were anything like Southampton's, which Karen hated, but they still got in the way of the gentle easy roads she'd planned to show Stella, some so narrow between the overarching trees that going down them on a sunny day like this was like rolling through a bright green tunnel.

Soon they found themselves passing the hospital, well on the way back to Cowes.

'Shit,' Karen said. Her head was aching, and her brain seemed to have stopped working. 'I've got us completely wrong. Sorry. Have you got a map?'

'In the pocket behind you,' Stella said, patiently pulling into a free parking space outside the hospital.

Karen stared down at the map, barely seeing it through the memories of Charlie's deadened eyes. Eventually, she retraced their route.

'Oh, I see. Look.' She planted her forefinger on the map and held it up to Stella. 'Here's where we should've turned. Sorry. And now it'll be quicker to take the main road after all. Turn right out of the hospital and go back to the roundabout.'

Stella was soon speeding along the main road towards Yarmouth, looking out for the junction that would take them to the lane down to the chalet.

'By the way,' she said, slowing down to make way for the oncoming traffic, 'we'll be getting at least one competition entry.'

'Yes?' Karen was glad of anything that could stop her thinking of Sonia's body, with the horrific slash masks only half-covered by the dressing-gown that was the one flamboyant piece of

colour in the whole restrained interior. Rigor must be setting in
now, stiffening the joints, as more blood pooled in her feet and
her buttocks.

'Yes,' Stella said, completely unaware of everything in Karen's
head. 'There was a woman there when I arrived first thing this
morning. I don't know who she thought I was because I found
her hiding in the woods, as though she was terrified, but we got
chatting and she soon calmed down. After a bit she said she was
definitely going to have a crack at the project.'

Stella glanced sideways at Karen, before adding slyly, 'I know
you said the surroundings are damp and gloomy, and I can see
what you meant, but this woman saw a lot of potential in the site.'

'Have you ever come across her before?'

'No. She's not an architect. A painter apparently – Lisa Raithe.
I've never seen anything she's done, but I'll look her up now
because she has interesting ideas. More interesting really than
the sort produced by most baby architects. I'm glad we opened
the competition up to artists and designers too.'

'You liked her.' Karen wasn't asking a question. And she was
glad to be faced with evidence of human beings who wanted to
cooperate, to build things together, not to rip each other apart.

'I did,' Stella said, with a warm smile. 'There was something
very appealing about her. She looked as if she might be weird
– quite tall, and immensely thin, anorexic even, and with that
elfin dark look of the Picts.' She paused, as though checking her
memory with the picture she'd just created, then added: 'Though,
of course, Picts are usually titchy.'

'Fingers crossed she produces something as good as her talk.'

'We'll see. I'm hungry,' Stella said. 'I don't suppose you remembered the picnic in the middle of your murder?'

'I got it first.' Karen wasn't sure she'd be able to eat anything.
The memory of Sonia's teethmarks in her half-eaten bagel would
put anyone off all thought of food. 'Let's have it by the sea.'

*   *   *

Later, as they were walking down the rough track towards the narrow beach, Karen suddenly stopped.

'Sorry, Stella,' she said. 'I've had a thought. Hang on a minute.'

She dug her phone out of her pocket, speed-dialled Charlie and, when he picked up the call, she said, 'was Tod hard of hearing?'

'What, you mean deaf? No idea. Why?'

'Just a thought: if he was watching telly and Randall had managed to spring the lock on the front door, with a credit card or whatever it is they use, and Tod had the sound turned up high, he might not've heard anything. That could be why he didn't turn to find out who was behind him, or struggle before the knife hit his neck.' She hoped it could be true; she'd liked Annie. But she had to add, 'although it doesn't explain Sonia.'

'Good point, though. I'll get on to Tod's colleagues and find out.'

'Try Annie. It's not the kind of thing a bloke would admit to mates if he could get away with it. People hate being accused of being deaf. But, living with him, she'd know. Bye. Oh, no – before you go, I meant to ask if Sonia was raped.'

'Don't know yet. The pathologist'll be doing the p.m. tomorrow morning. D'you want to be there? I could get you in.'

Karen had never attended a post-mortem, although she'd seen plenty of fictional versions on the screen, and she'd read enough of the Y-incision, the shriek of bone saws and the smells from distended stomachs, to know she didn't want to witness one. And she couldn't see what it could possibly add to her assessment of where Randall might be now and how to get him back in the control of the Ministry of Justice – or at least his probation officer.

'I don't think my being there would help you,' she said. 'But, Charlie, you will tell me if she had been sexually assaulted, won't you?'

'Sure. And if she'd had consensual sex last night. Bye, Karen.'

There was a lot more she wanted to say to him, but it couldn't be said yet, or with Stella eavesdropping. 'Bye, Charlie.'

She clicked off the phone and apologized to Stella, who was looking at her with unusually critical eyes. Karen braced herself for questions about knives and rape and bodies.

'Have you and Will broken up then?' Stella said, still frowning.

'What? No, of course not. Why?'

'The way you were talking on the phone just now – presumably to the tasty cop who was holding your hands in Carisbrooke . . .' Stella broke off, but she'd said more than enough for Karen to catch her meaning.

'I'm not *seeing* him,' she said.

'But you'd like to, wouldn't you?' Stella's green eyes narrowed as she laughed. 'Oh, come on, Karen. I'm not blind. I've always been able to see when you fancy someone. I'll never forget the way you were with Will at the beginning. Don't try to fake it.'

Karen laughed in spite of herself and everything that was churning around in her mind and making her feel so ill. 'OK, so Charlie's fit and I like flirting. So what? I'm with Will. I don't two-time people. I hate that. You just shortchange both of them. Yourself, too.'

'The tasty cop know that?'

'His name's Charlie.' Karen's impulse to laugh disappeared. She didn't like the way the conversation was going. 'It hasn't come up.'

'You'd better make plans then, because it's going to. I've never seen a man more . . .'

As Stella broke off, Karen promised herself she wouldn't ask for more, but she couldn't help it. The words escaped despite her resolutions: 'More what, Stella?'

The other woman laughed, with a sound full of mockery and no amusement at all. 'Come on, Karen! The way he looked at you when he was clinging to your hands. All you'd have to do is squeeze back and you'd be away.'

Karen turned and walked the last few yards down the track, relieved to emerge into the open space of the narrow beach. Huge grey stones made walking hard in her thin-soled sandals. She felt sorry for the gladiators who'd inspired them. But she ploughed on until she was right at the edge of the water.

The tide was high and for once the sea looked clear, not at all soupy, with the sun blazing down on it. Sails floated by further out to sea and gulls swooped and hovered above her, shrieking. Inhaling the scents of seaweed and salt, she listened to Stella's footsteps, then felt a hand on her back.

'It was only a tease,' Stella said, sounding more apologetic than usual. 'I didn't realize it was so serious.'

Karen turned at once and said: 'It isn't. It's just . . . oh, I don't know. I'm all over the place.' She stared out across the narrow stretch of water towards the Hampshire mainland. Then she swung back to face Stella.

'I don't know what to do.'

'About Will?'

Karen shrugged and kicked a huge stone, stubbing her toe on it when it didn't move.

'Shit!' She rubbed the bruised toe against her other calf. 'You see, Stella, I love Will. I *do*. He's amazing. I've never known anyone like him.'

'But?' Stella said. 'Come on, Karen, be honest. There's a but in there.'

'Everything's a bit, well, bloodless and – and, you know: polite.' Karen heard the start of a childish whine in her voice and tried to get rid of it with a little humour. 'Honestly, sometimes I feel like a pensioner when I'm with him. There's nothing we do or say that we couldn't do if we were about eighty.'

'Eighty's going a bit far. Come on, lighten up, Karen. Isn't this just because you got married so young the first time? You missed out on all the binge-drinking and irresponsible shagging the rest of us grew out of. Now, you want some of it too. Which is presumably why you've never moved in with Will. Too much commitment?'

'No. Practicality.' Karen tried not to feel offended. 'I work in Southampton and need to be there. He has to be within twenty miles or something of Brighton Hospital. Lewes suits him, but it'd kill me – far too staid.'

'Have it your own way.' Stella grinned. 'Anyway, who could blame you for wanting a bit of irresponsible shagging with Charlie? Any woman with working hormones would.'

'I don't know why we're even talking about it,' Karen said, trying not to care and failing.

'If you don't want him, I might have a crack at him myself,' Stella said, ignoring her completely. 'I've always liked a bit of rough. And your Charlie looks deliciously capable of quite a lot of rough.'

Karen bit back a protest. She reminded herself that Stella's sense of humour led her into a lot of jokes that were not always as funny as she thought.

Chapter 13

Friday, 10 October, noon

'You're absolutely right, Ian,' Karen said to her Masters student, who was making her work hard for forgiveness after ignoring him for too long. 'Statistics *are* dangerous things. But in a court, statistics are a forensic psychologist's main tool.'

'Like how?'

'An opinion, however expert the giver of it may be, will always be just that: an opinion; a suggestion; intuition; a matter of experience and judgement – a possibility. Statistics are *real*.'

'They can't prove anything,' Ian said, looking as though he enjoyed challenging her.

There were times when she wondered why he wanted to pursue a career in psychology, even within the legal system, rather than becoming a litigator, which would give his argumentativeness much more scope. He was broad-shouldered and burly and always dressed like a building-site labourer, but that did nothing to disguise his determination never to let anyone get away with anything he could challenge.

'They're only a suggestion too,' he went on. 'Look, if you stand up in the witness box and go, "statistics show eight out of ten men with this blood type and this kind of childhood experience, and this genetic malformation will commit the following crimes in adulthood", you're only telling the court that lots of men like the bloke in the dock will commit the crime, but two out of every ten won't. So how're statistics helping? He could be one of the twenty per cent who'll never commit any kind of crime. Statistics are, like, pointless.'

'Better than nothing,' Karen said, stifling her impatience and noticing that she was old enough to detest the way her juniors used 'like' as a kind of punctuation. 'So long as you understand them, and never misrepresent the results, they will always give the jury useful information on which to base their assessment of the evidence.'

'But—'

'Ian, you're almost never, as a psychologist, going to be able to say – hand on heart – such and such a proposition is absolutely true. You can only ever offer your conclusions and the facts on which you've based them. Accurate statistics are a better guide than most, which is why anyone planning any kind of forensic career needs to understand them well enough to be able to defend the way he or she uses them in court.'

Her landline rang, and she looked longingly at it. But this was Ian's time. She owed him an uninterrupted hour at least. Whatever news her caller wanted to give her, it had to wait. After four rings the answering machine cut in and silenced it. She smiled at Ian, wondering whether she could offer him a rapist based on Randall to analyse. Ian might come up with some insights that could help her now. And maybe Charlie too.

Better not, she thought, picking up the latest draft of Ian's dissertation to tell him about the parts of it which worried her far more than the possible inadequacies of statistical evidence.

At last he went, and she could listen to her messages. The final one was from Charlie. All he said was: 'You were right. Gyre *is* back here on the Island.'

'I knew it,' Karen said aloud. 'I bloody knew it.'

But was he there to kill all the people responsible for sending him to prison? Or to find Lizzie? Or to re-stage the rape with a new victim and, this time, get away with it?

Karen still didn't see how he could have murdered Sonia.

Charlie's recorded voice was pouring into her ear. 'We've spotted him for sure on CCTV on three separate occasions. Otherwise the man we think is him avoids showing his face to the cameras. But these three are clear. Can't have known there were cameras there. Still no idea where he's staying. The Hemmings haven't seen him. But he knows the Island so well, he could be anywhere. Camping even.'

Needing to talk to Charlie, Karen rang his mobile, but there was no answer. Frowning at her own phone, as though it had deliberately obstructed her, she looked up the number for his office and rang that. The switchboard said he was unavailable, so she asked instead for Eve.

'I'm trying to get Charlie,' Karen said abruptly as soon as the other woman gave her name. 'But he's not answering his mobile.'

'He's helping Major Crimes with a murder investigation,' Eve said, snippy as ever. 'He doesn't have time for idle chat. I can take a message. He'll get it when he's free.'

'He left a message on my phone. I have to reach him. D'you know where he is?'

'At work.'

'Eve, *please*. I'm worried.' Karen knew she couldn't put words to her worst anxieties, but she had to do something to get the information she needed. 'If Randall's killing people involved in getting him convicted for what he did to Lizzie, Charlie has to be at risk. I had a message from him only about fifteen minutes ago. Now he's not picking up.'

Karen found she had her free hand pressed to her chest, to hold down the banging of her heart.

'I'm worried,' she said again.

'I thought you said Gyre didn't kill Doctor Franklin.' Eve's voice was sugary with satisfaction at nailing the inconsistency.

'Eve, please.' Karen realized she was repeating herself. 'Please tell Charlie I rang back, and I'll answer my phone from now on. I couldn't before because I had a student.'

Something of her urgency must have broken through because Eve gave up the necessary information after all.

'He's meeting DS Colvin. They must be in a mobile black spot.'

'Meeting Annie? Why? Where?' Karen got hold of herself and calmed her voice. 'On the Island?'

'You sound like his mother, Karen. How do I know?'

'Did he take anyone with him?'

'To meet a fellow officer?' Eve sounded more contemptuous than ever. 'Don't be stupid. Why would he? A minute ago you had your knickers in a twist about Gyre. Now it's DS Colvin. Are you telling me you think she's in a conspiracy with Gyre, planning to see DCI Trench in his coffin?'

'Of course not,' Karen said, cutting off the call. That wasn't what worried her. But she couldn't explain herself to Eve so there was no point saying any more. She pressed in the number Annie had given her.

'Hi,' she said as soon as Annie answered. 'It's Karen Taylor here. Have you got Charlie with you? His mobile's on the blink.'

'He left about fifteen minutes ago,' Annie said, as though it didn't matter.

'Shit. Left where?'

'A pub outside East Cowes. I'm on my way to my car now. Stayed on for another coffee after he'd gone.' She sniffed, as though to tell Karen she'd wanted time alone to deal with her bereavement.

'The Goose Inn?' Even with everything else going on, Karen couldn't help a moment's outrage that Charlie had taken some-one else there.

'That's right,' Annie said. 'Nice place.'

'What did Charlie want? Can you say?'

'Don't see why not.' Annie's voice was getting stronger by the minute. 'He asked if Tod ever had any threats from Gyre, and then if he had any hearing problems.'

'Did he?' Karen said.

'No threats. Some hearing problems. Whatever.'

Something in Annie's curt replies made Karen say: 'Was that all Charlie wanted?'

'Nope. He talked about the fuck-up Tod made of the first Lizzie Fane interview.'

'Why would he do that?' Karen was genuinely curious.

'Don't be thick.' Annie snorted. 'He knows I hate blokes who mess with rape victims' minds. He was sounding me out in case I'd killed Tod because of what he put Lizzie through. I told him straight: why would I have waited four years?'

Karen could think of several reasons why someone would have taken this long to start killing all of Lizzie's tormentors, from the slow-burn of provocation taking time to build to the effect of Randall's release acting like a lit fuse on an unexploded bomb. But it wasn't going to help anyone if she put her ideas into words. Particularly not Annie. After all, slow-burn provocation was much more commonly seen in women than in men, whose testosterone-charged drives usually meant they reacted instantly.

'Didn't you mind coming over to the Island to answer questions like that?' Karen said instead. 'Couldn't Charlie have phoned?'

'I knew I'd be able to talk to him about Tod.' Annie sniffed heavily again and her voice trembled. 'I need that, you see. Everyone in Winchester's too embarrassed. Or angry, as if it's my fault. But Charlie was always nice to me when we were in the Met. You know, when he was having all that angst with Eve's sister. We kind of bonded. Look – I must go.'

Karen didn't have time to ask her anything else, such as when – exactly – she'd landed on the Island and where she'd been since. And how much of Charlie she'd actually seen. And whether she'd tried to stop him leaving the Goose Inn – if he had ever been there with her.

The phone had gone dead, leaving Karen to think how she could best track him down. Or whether he was deliberately lying low. Everyone knew there was no phone blackspot at the Goose Inn. As Eve had said, he was in the middle of a murder enquiry, even if it was being run by a team from the mainland. Normally he would have been answering his phone. Who was he hiding from? Or was someone else keeping him out of contact?

Karen rang his number again. There was still no answer, so she tried Eve once more.

'Sorry to bother you,' Karen said quickly. 'Charlie told me he'd let me know if Sonia had been raped. Has any news come through yet from the p.m.?'

'*I* don't hand out information to civilians.'

Eve put down the phone so quickly that even if Karen had been brave enough to ask for more information about her sister, there'd have been no time.

Lisa stood in the alleyway behind the pub, smelling the same acrid stench that had surrounded her when Randall had set out to destroy her life five years ago, and tried to find the strength she needed.

The smell was the only thing she recognized so far. She wondered whether lying on the ground might make the rest seem more familiar, as she tried to recreate in her mind what she'd seen over Randall's shoulder. But she couldn't. And she wasn't about to let any part of her body touch anything here unless she absolutely had to. Even her trainers would have to be binned as soon as possible. The place was disgusting.

No one was about. And there was no noise, except a thin rustle of waste paper as a mangy-looking cat sidled through the alley's rubbish. The cat scuttled past her, just brushing her foot with its tail. She felt the sensation even through the thick canvas of the trainer.

The tiny, unaggressive touch sent her memory into freefall and everything roared back: the powerlessness; the pain; the smell of her rapist's peppery-citrus aftershave. She was back in the horror.

When she had felt it and absorbed it and sensed the lifesaving courage seeping slowly back into her mind, she looked around again, breathing with care, dealing with the fallout.

Lee *was* back in her mind.

She could survive. She could do anything now.

The filthy cat had disappeared, as though it had picked up some of her hatred. She followed the direction it had taken and found that, behind a tall pile of old mattresses and spare fencing posts, the alley had an extension round the windowless back of a building. Here, everything was even more familiar. This must be where he'd brought her. She saw a pile of old foam rubber and a lot of broken glass.

In spite of Lee stiffening her, making her brave, making her know she'd be all right, her guts clenched, shooting pain right up through her, as far as her head. Saliva poured into her mouth. She bent over and vomited.

Later, when she'd wiped her mouth with a tissue and made sure she was more or less respectable, she staggered into the virtually empty pub and ordered a double vodka with Slimline tonic. She needed something to take away the filthy taste.

Karen sat at her computer, re-reading all the answers Randall had given her at their first meeting, in case anything offered an insight into his current activities. She wondered if Ian, her Masters student, would draw the same conclusions she had – and she decided to find out. She would present him with the data from both John Clarence and Randall, without telling him what either had done or what her conclusions had been, and see how he judged them. Reaching for the phone, she called his mobile and put her proposition to him.

'Great. Yeah. I'd like to have a look,' he said. 'What's this for?'

'Just some research,' she said, remembering all her undertakings of secrecy. 'I'll be interested to hear what you make of the tests and their responses. Shall I email the stuff?'

'Fine. I'll get back to you asap.'

He sounded just like Charlie when he said 'asap' in that brisk, waste-no-time-on-real-words kind of way. She tried to ring Charlie again and failed to get a response.

'Where the hell are you?' she said aloud as she clicked off her phone. 'And why the fuck aren't you answering your phone?'

She played her landline voicemail again and heard his familiar Geordie voice, sounding urgent and almost excited: 'Gyre *is* back here on the Island.'

Karen's laptop pinged as an email came through. She dragged her attention back from what might be happening to Charlie and saw Will's name in her in-box. Clicking the email open, she saw his usual clipped, almost text-like, style:

Just out of theatre. Wanted to phone but both yr lines busy. One clamped to each ear? Will x.

She heard the ring tone of his phone in her ear before she was even aware she'd called him.

'Hi! Will. It's me. Sorry about the phones.'

'No problem. I'm just out of theatre. A child. We got the tumour out, without any peripheral damage, I think.'

'That's great.' Karen tried to fill her voice with all the warmth and congratulation and reassurance he must have wanted when he phoned. 'I'm *so* pleased.'

'You sound all shaky. What's the problem?'

'Nothing.' Karen breathed deeply. 'I mean nothing to do with us. Work. A killer's on the loose and I've been asked to advise on finding him. I'm worried about what happens if I don't and he goes for someone else.'

'That won't do anyone any good,' Will said at once. 'You need to control that kind of anxiety, or you'll be no use to anyone.'

Karen didn't comment.

'Anyway, darling, I'm off for the rest of the day and have a late start tomorrow. Can I persuade you to come here to Lewes tonight? You haven't been here for weeks, and we haven't had nearly enough time together. I miss you.'

I don't want to go without knowing what's happening on the Island, she thought instantly, and knew she had to suppress it if she really meant to carry on her relationship with Will. Which she did.

'I'd love to come,' she said, again pouring warmth into her voice and this time hoping she wasn't overdoing it. 'There's a quick call I must make to a student, but then I'll set off. Should be with you – oh, in about two hours.'

'Don't rush it. I'd rather you took three than had an accident.'

'I have been driving for eighteen years, you know,' Karen said.

She always disliked the moments when Will took this kind of schoolmasterly tone with her. His assumption of authority made her tetchy and rebellious and do stupid things to prove she wasn't answerable to him. This time it made her want to take out her car and roar up a one-way street, the wrong way, at 90 miles an hour.

'I know, Karen, I know. And you've never had an accident. But if you're fretting about your runaway killer, you may get distracted . . .' Will broke off, then started again. 'If you'd seen the bits of smashed skull slicing into brain matter that I've seen from road traffic accidents, you'd take it more seriously.'

And if you'd seen me sit beside my husband in the front seat of his smashed Ferrari, holding his hand while he died, you'd know I didn't need reminding, she thought.

'Oh, God! I'm sorry. I forgot,' he said at once, almost as though he'd heard her thinking.

'No problem. See you when I see you,' she said aloud and put down the phone.

Five minutes later, her call made, she shut down her computer, shoved it into its bag, put her phone in her pocket and left

the office, locking it behind her. There was no need to go home
to pack: she kept a spare set of everything at Will's, and the car
was in the university car park, eight minutes' walk from her
building.

She wasn't surprised he was due to operate tomorrow, even
though it was a Saturday. He took every fourth weekend on call
in case of emergencies and usually managed to slot in one or two
planned operations during those sessions. If he had to be ready
for work, he'd always prefer to use his skill than hang about
waiting for a phone call to summon him to theatre.

The phone buzzed in Karen's pocket just as she was crossing
under the barrier into the car park.

'Karen Taylor.'

'Doctor Taylor, it's Sally here,' said a breathless voice, loaded
with distress. 'Sally Fane. You know, Lizzie's mother.'

'Of course I know.' Karen, who remembered giving the woman
one of her cards, spoke as gently as she could. 'Are you all right?
Is there something I can do for you?'

'Tell me where Charlie is.' Distress was now turning into
anger. 'You must. You have to.'

'But I don't *know* where he is.' Karen knew she mustn't let
Sally's anxiety heighten her own. 'I've been trying to phone him
too. Have you tried his office?'

'They won't talk to me there.' A hoarse laugh that ended in
a sob came down the phone, then: 'I used to ring them so often
they've stopped paying any attention to me, so even when I told
them, they wouldn't listen. Even when I shouted the news at
them, they didn't believe me.'

'What news? What did you tell them?' Karen admired Charlie's
patience with this woman more than ever.

'That I've seen Gyre. Randall Gyre – the devil who nearly
killed my Lizzie. For God's sake, you *know* who he is!'

'Where did you see him? When?'

'Just now. Well, half an hour ago. I've been phoning and

phoning, trying to get the police to take me seriously. He was walking about in Cowes, as bold as brass, with a young girl beside him.'

'Did he see you?'

'Yes, he bloody did. I wasn't going to have any other child risking what my Lizzie suffered.' Sally's voice and breathing were way out of control, spiralling off towards serious panic. She needed the so-supportive doctor to calm her down.

'This girl looked just like my Lizzie,' Sally went on, sobbing hard now, 'blonde and pretty and tall. At first I thought it was her. That's why I rushed over – I thought it was my Lizzie. Then I saw she was ten years too young. She was hanging on his arm and gazing at him. You could just see what was going to happen.'

'So what did you do?'

'Phoned Charlie, of course. They've got to get to Gyre before he does it. But no one's listening to me. Charlie's not answering. James is somewhere in the hospital and they won't page him unless it's a medical emergency. They didn't believe me when I said it was. I've left messages everywhere. That's why I'm phoning you. There isn't anyone else. You've *got* to tell me where Charlie is.'

'I can't because I don't know,' Karen said, professional satisfaction that she'd assessed Randall correctly fighting all her instinctive longing to get over to the Island to find and protect the young, slim, blonde woman who wouldn't have any idea of the risks she was taking. 'There's something you're not saying, Sally. After you couldn't get the police, what happened? What did you do?'

Karen was used to listening to everything that was not actually being said. And this gap in the narrative had been unmistakable.

'I told her,' Sally said, sniffing loudly. 'I went up to them and stood in front of them in a narrow bit of pavement, where they couldn't get away and I warned her what he was like. I told her he was a filthy brutal rapist and I'd take her home myself before she found out more than she wanted. She wouldn't listen. She said— Aaah, thank God. They're coming.'

The scream of a police car's siren drilled through the last of Sally's words, and the connection was cut. Karen hoped passionately that they'd find the young woman before Randall set about her body with a broken bottle.

Chapter 14

Friday, 10 October, 2.30–3 p.m.

'It's my friend,' Bella said, taking two steps backwards and waving the phone. 'She's waiting for me. I've got to go.'

Randall grabbed the phone, twisting it out of her hand so it really hurt, and threw it up into one of the tall bins. Then he scooped her legs out from under her so she went crashing backwards on to the filthy paving. Her head hit one of the old mattresses, so it didn't hurt, but she could feel wet rising all round where she had landed.

She thought of the mad woman in the street, yelling about how dangerous Randall was. Why hadn't she listened? She could have been safe now if she'd listened.

Randall plumped down on top of her, beating all the air out of her body.

'Let me go,' Bella shouted, but it came out hoarse and choked because of having no breath. And she kicked hard, but her feet couldn't reach him because he was sitting on her stomach.

One of her shoes came off as she kicked and she felt her heel splash into a puddle. Something ran by her foot, something hairy and warm. His hand was clamped round her mouth so she couldn't scream. She got her teeth apart and tried to bite, but he was holding her so tight she couldn't get any of his skin into her mouth. He was pulling at her clothes with his free hand. She *kicked again. He straddled her, pinning her down, sitting on her, with his knees held tight round her ribs.*

She thought her bones would break. He wrenched up her shirt and tied it round her mouth. Like a gag. She couldn't tell him she had a Tampax in.

A shadow came round the edge of the building. Bella screamed behind the gag. The noise came out like a kind of gurgle that hurt her throat. Her head felt like it was exploding. And then she saw the broken bottle. Hope made her eyes work properly, and her mind too. She reached out.

Blood was everywhere – in her eyes, sliding down her cheeks into her ears, clogging her nose. Drowning her.

Lisa stood on the afterdeck of the ferry, feeling as though the wind that blasted her face was cleaning all the stench and memories from her brain. But it didn't banish Lee, which was great. She still needed to be Lee. Sometimes.

At her feet were the trainers and the old jacket of her father's that she'd been wearing. The few lone drinkers in the pub didn't seem to have noticed how scuzzy they were, but once the first shock had been soothed by the vodka, she'd had to get them off her.

She hadn't wanted to use a credit card or a cash machine that would betray her presence on the Island, but she'd had just enough cash with her to buy a sweater and some cheap knock-off trainers to take their place. These would go into the sea, as soon as she felt inconspicuous enough to kick them over the edge. She'd put stones in each of the trainers and tied the jacket tightly round them, so the whole bundle would sink and no one else would have to smell the vomit she'd spewed over them.

The jacket was no longer important. Now she'd come back here and faced the demons and beaten them back, she could get in touch with her father without being afraid of letting him look after her. She could see him again as a free, independent, power-ful woman, so she didn't need his old jacket to hug round her any more.

Her back itched, as though someone was staring at her. Had someone followed her all day? Was it the same person who hovered around her house, leaving his footprints in the damp grass of her garden and the fields round about?

She couldn't turn round without drawing attention to herself. Maybe it was just her conscience, tricking her into feeling watched. After all, the only real evidence she'd ever seen was the footprints, and anyone could have made those.

Lisa swung her left foot casually up to rest it on the bottom railing and leaned forwards, staring back towards the Island. In a minute, she'd change legs and just tip the bundle over.

Later, risking a quick look behind her, she caught sight of a movement at the very limit of her vision, but when she turned her head to look more carefully, no one was showing any inter-est in her. There must be a hundred people on the boat. She told herself it was mad to think the movement had anything to do with her. Then she wished she could believe herself.

When she turned to lean against the rail, she let her right foot edge slyly backwards. A second later, a splash told her she'd got the bundle into the water. Making no sign of anything, she leaned against the rail for another five minutes, staring up at the wheeling seagulls and the racing clouds. Only when the loudspeaker announced the imminent arrival at Lymington did she obey the instruction for all drivers to go down to their cars.

Karen was away and picking her route through the maze of streets that led out of Southampton towards the M27, cursing the traffic. Why wasn't everybody working? It was only just after half past three but every junction was clogged. Just because it was a Friday!

Only when she was safely on to the motorway and cruising at a steady 73mph did she lean forwards to flick on the radio, expecting the *PM* programme. Instead she heard the voice of Radio Solent's afternoon *Drivetime* presenter, giving details of traffic problems on the Island and promising weather reports and news. She'd forgotten she'd switched channels last time she was in the car.

A vast lorry swerved into the middle lane, just ahead of her. The driver clearly hadn't bothered to look in his mirrors. Karen had to brake because a big BMW was overtaking her in the fast lane and a lumbering bus, belching dark smoke out of its exhaust, blocked the other. The smell of the exhaust rose through her car's ventilators, making her choke.

Through the spasms in her throat, she became aware of the radio presenter's voice again.

'The body of a man has been found behind the Eagle and Dumpling pub in Cowes.'

Karen fought the impulse to jam her foot hard on the brake, instead peering ahead for a sign warning of an exit. All she wanted to do was get off the motorway so that she could phone the police station for news. She leaned forwards over the steering wheel, as though she could move the car more quickly that way.

Commonsense returned, as she remembered that her route would keep her on this road for only just over twelve miles. She must have done at least ten of them. Sure enough, the familiar large blue sign at the side of the road told her the exit for Chichester and Brighton would be on her within a mile.

Her bottom lip was clamped between her teeth and her breathing was high and fast, but she was remembering to drive more or less within the speed limit and looking in all her mirrors at the appropriate moments. She signalled left and pulled off on to the slip road, more impatient than ever. Another four miles had flashed by before she found a lay-by where she could stop, switch off the engine and the radio and grab her phone.

The first number she rang was Charlie's. Her heart almost stopped again as she heard his voice.

'Karen? You OK?'

'I heard on the radio. A man's been killed.' She bent forwards again, to lie against the steering wheel, not telling him any of the fears that were eating into her.

'No time to talk unless you've got information,' he snapped. 'We're up to our necks and waiting for more manpower from the mainland.'

'Whose body is it?'

'Gyre's.'

'*Randall*'s been killed?' Karen said. 'How?'

'Throat cut. Got to go,' Charlie said and cut off the call.

Karen felt a visceral, mindless kind of satisfaction that Randall couldn't hurt anyone else, but it wasn't enough to stop her brain insisting that he hadn't killed Tod and Dr Franklin. She didn't want to deal with her suspicions of Annie – or decide how many of them Charlie shared but couldn't admit – and fumbled blindly among the CDs in the glove compartment. Some were modern and wouldn't do at all, but there should be the Mozart Concerto for Flute and Harp. If she'd ever needed her brain rinsing it was now.

She found she couldn't read the labels, but she was looking for a mainly white cover with sepia writing and she did spot it eventually. Her fingers felt thick and clumsy as she tried to open the cover.

A traffic cop zoomed past her on a large motorbike, which he braked hard. Moments later, he came striding towards her with the bike propped up behind him. Karen tried to pull herself together.

He stripped off his gauntlets and bent down to peer in through the window beside her. She let the CD fall into her lap and opened the window.

'Are you feeling all right?' he asked, not exactly sympathetic but as though prepared to show sensitivity with someone ill.

'I've had a bit of a shock, but I'm fine,' Karen said, smiling with all the nervous pacification of the stopped-but-innocent driver. 'I'm not doing anything wrong, am I? We're still allowed to park in lay-bys, aren't we?'

All hints of sympathy disappeared from his expression. She hadn't meant to mock.

'We had reports of you driving erratically on the motorway and veering off it at speed. Can I see your licence and insurance documents?'

Karen thought of refusing. She didn't see why she should show anyone anything unless she'd committed some kind of offence, but this was all too trivial to bother about in a world where some-one had slashed Randall's throat – and Tod's and Dr Franklin's. Karen got the documents out of the glove compartment.

The officer took an age to read his way through everything, clearly keen now to find something for which he could nail her. Karen thought of telling him that when your husband had died in a violent crash after a high-speed police chase you didn't take risks with cars, traffic, documents, or the law.

At last, the policeman flipped her licence back into its plastic folder and handed all the papers back through the window.

'That's fine. When did you last have a drink?'

'What? I can't remember. Yesterday probably. A glass of wine. Why? You don't think I'm drunk, do you?'

She'd allowed some petulance into her voice and swore silently as she saw it register with him.

'You were driving erratically. I have to check that it wasn't down to alcohol. I'd just like you to blow into this bag,' he said, producing a breathalyser.

Karen sighed. She'd had enough. She thought of Will, waiting for her in Lewes, worrying about whether she was driving safely enough to arrive in one piece.

'OK,' she said, still just about polite but obviously impatient. 'But please get on with it. I have to be somewhere.'

He slowed down even more, taking an infinity of time to explain the procedure and exactly how he wanted her to blow into his bag.

Wanting to strangle him, she nevertheless waited, forcing herself to smile, and then did precisely what he'd asked. She took a great deal of private satisfaction from the disappointment in his eyes.

'That's fine. But take care. Whatever the rush, don't take risks. And watch your speed. You were over the limit once or twice on the motorway.'

Not by enough to make anyone think of stopping me for it, she thought, but there was no future in making the protest aloud, so she nodded and thanked him and wondered why she felt quite so tired. She thought she'd wait until he'd left the lay-by, and take the time to phone Will to tell him why she was going to be late.

Even when the cop had straddled the bike, he merely sat there, occasionally looking over his shoulder, apparently determined to intimidate her. And when she left, making a U-turn to get back to the right road, he followed her, keeping a steady twenty yards behind her.

With her head and neck aching, she was tempted to jam on her brakes in an emergency stop and hope to see him crash his bike into her and catapult himself over her car. Instead, she stuffed the CD into the player under the dashboard and prepared to let go of horror and suspicion and fear.

Once again Mozart failed her. By the time she reached Will's flat in Lewes, at twenty past five, her mind was still jangling. And she'd heard nothing more from Charlie. When she'd parked, she phoned him yet again.

'I know you're busy,' she said as soon as he answered and before he could cut her off, 'but I want you to tell me as soon as you need me to do anything. Phone my mobile and if you can't get through, you'll probably get me on Will's landline. Have you got his number?'

'No time to look. Text me,' he said briefly. 'How long'll you be there?'

'Just till tomorrow morning. I should be back at the flat by . . . oh, by noon.'

'Bye.'

Will had emerged on the front step of the building in which he had the top two floors. He must have been watching for her, which wasn't like him. Karen got out of the car, pulled out her rucksack and locked up.

In spite of the way he'd been hanging about, watching for her, he looked so like himself she couldn't help smiling. Dressed in his favourite well-washed blue denim jeans and a pristine pink shirt made of heavy cotton tucked into the low waistband, he had made one concession to her style: he had no shoes or socks on.

Gesturing to his bare feet, he called out, 'I can't come any further. The streets are filthy.'

'I'm impressed by the relaxation,' she said, climbing the four wide steps to meet him. 'But it won't be complete till you don't care about treading in muck. Sorry it took longer than I expected.'

'Thanks for phoning. I was beginning to worry,' he said. 'I had the radio on and heard about an accident on the M27. A lorry swerved into the wrong lane and crushed the two cars overtaking it, before creating a massive pile-up. When you didn't get here . . .' He broke off and rubbed his face with both hands, before achieving a small smile, as though to show he wouldn't descend to pointless drama.

She thought she'd enjoy evidence of a drama different from the one playing out on the Island.

'I missed the accident,' she said, leading the way into his building. 'I came off the motorway early to phone the Isle of Wight police because—'

He took the rucksack from her with more of a jerk than she thought was absolutely necessary. She was so surprised she stopped talking.

'D'you think we could forget the Isle of Wight police?' Will's voice was so cold it set off an alarm in her mind.

'Of course,' she said at once. 'Whatever.'

Looking around the main room of the flat, not as large as hers in Southampton but much more recherché, with its few important ancient Chinese hangings and carefully chosen ceramics, she suddenly longed to break through Will's self-control, to find out what he really *felt* about something. Anything.

'But why? I mean, why should we forget about the Isle of Wight police?' she asked.

Will faced her. His skin was much paler than usual and his eyes were full of accusation. 'Because I don't like being told just how much you've been seeing of that thuggish cop over there.'

'What?' Karen was outraged at his attempt to control what she did and who she saw when she wasn't with him, then horrified to think she might be screwing up her life with him for the mess and danger that would always surround Charlie.

'The one you introduced me to last year.' Will's angry voice helped control her bad conscience. 'I don't believe you're having an affair – it's not your style. You'd have dumped me first. But it's humiliating to be faced with the idea that everyone else thinks you are and wonders why I let it go on.'

Everyone? Karen thought. Stella?

She couldn't believe it. Stella was a friend, and far too intelligent to think making this kind of trouble either amusing or clever. But there wasn't anyone else. Only to Stella had Karen so much as hinted that she found Charlie attractive.

'The only relationships I have with anyone on the Island are professional,' she said now. 'Who's been making mischief?'

'No one.' Will turned away to look out of one of the two long windows towards the stolid splendour of Lewes Castle. 'But I had dinner with Max when he was in Brighton the other day and he entertained me with a Jungian explanation of our relationship.'

'Max is . . .' Karen began, but she didn't get any further, as Will swung back to face her and spoke in a bitingly formal tone.

'You and I, he thinks, are together only because we see in each other's superficial presentation the persona we want – controlled, professionally successful, personally stylish and all that – while at the same time you have this, apparently very public, involvement with DCI Trench. Max says it's because Trench exemplifies the dark, dangerous masculine in your subconscious that you both long for and fear.'

'Oh, yes?' Karen knew her voice was sharp with exasperation. This was typical of the Prof, so intrigued by his latest application of classic psychoanalytical theory that he forgot there were human beings with real feelings involved. It was her bad luck he'd landed on such a hot and sore topic. 'You shouldn't take him so seriously. You know what he's like.'

Will didn't respond.

'Oh, come on,' Karen said, softening and leaning across the space between them to put her hands on his shoulders. 'You *do* know what he's like. You knew him even before I did. What did he say about you and your anima?'

'I don't know what you're talking about.' Now Will was very much on his dignity.

'If Max was telling you Charlie represents the unacknowledged masculine in me – full, no doubt, of violence and thrust and all that kind of provocative stuff – he must have picked the female equivalent in your life. He wouldn't be able to resist. Who is she?'

Will's deceptively youthful face took on even more hardness as he tightened every muscle. His colour was better but his expression was still rebarbative.

'Come on, Will darling!' Karen was laughing now, genuinely amused and feeling a lot less worried. 'Confession time: who's your anima?'

A small spurt of answering laughter made him look much more human and raised her hopes of a good evening.

'He did come up with a fantasy about some imaginary theatre nurse,' Will said, even his voice lightening now. 'I mean, he's never met any of the staff at Brighton, and I have no interest in any nurse beyond her professional competence.'

Karen leaned against him, tucking her chin over his shoulder. After a moment she felt his arms closing around her back and his lips brushing her hair. She let herself sag a little against his strength.

'The thing is,' Will said, holding on to her, 'that I saw you with Trench last year and watched him wanting you. Now, whenever I hear you talk about him when we're on the phone, your voice lifts. And in the flesh, you smile a whole different smile when his name's mentioned.'

Karen said nothing, thinking of the moment in the car when she thought he was dead.

'None of it's enough in itself.' For once Will was oblivious to her. 'But with Max banging on and on, telling me how much you've been seeing of Trench recently . . .'

'Only because of the case,' she said, glad to hear how casual she sounded. 'The man I've been advising the Ministry of Justice about was murdered today. Charlie's involved.'

'Murdered on the Island?' Will said.

'Yes.'

'And DCI Trench is involved?' Will sounded almost excited.

'In the investigation,' Karen said repressively. 'Will, don't let's—'

He wasn't listening to her and interrupted without shame. 'Did you know he barely escaped being thrown out of the Newcastle police force when he was in his early twenties, after beating up a drunk in the street?'

Karen shook her head in silence.

'Which is why he left the north,' Will went on. 'Did you know he had a run-in with a woman only about three years ago, when he was at the Met? A fellow officer. He'd date-raped her, apparently.'

'Was he charged?' Karen asked, hating what Will was doing.

'No evidence, but enough doubt for his bosses to ask him to move on again.'

'I've been told by an ex-colleague of his,' she said, hanging on to hope because that was all she had, 'that he hates seeing a woman hurt.'

Will produced a short sharp crack of bitter laughter, which Karen tried to ignore.

'I'll bet you'd find each of his so-called victims had previously damaged someone vulnerable,' she said. 'But don't let's think about Charlie now, Will. I'm much more worried about you. You didn't take Max so seriously that you went and looked Charlie up, did you? That's what this sounds like.'

His clear skin reddened.

'Oh, Will! That's bonkers. For God's sake ... Look here, Charlie's not the deep, dark secret of my unconscious, whatever Max says. He's really not – OK?'

'If you say so.' Will looked at her. 'But he is dangerous, Karen.'

Chapter 15

Friday evening, 10 Oct–Saturday morning, 11 October

Will was busy in the kitchen, which left Karen free to make a call in privacy.

Charlie's line was busy and she was diverted to his voicemail. There was no message she could possibly leave, so she clicked off without saying anything and took the risk of ringing Annie instead.

'Hi, it's me, Karen,' she said. 'Sorry to bother you, but there's something I need to know.'

'Whassat?' Annie's voice was slurred.

Karen thought of the way Annie had put her face in her huge wineglass in the Southampton bar, to emerge with those two little horned wine stains on either side of her mouth.

'You talked about the time when Charlie was having trouble with Eve's sister,' Karen said. 'Can you tell me more? I . . . kind of need to know.'

'Charlie wou'n't like me saying. Ask *him*.' Annie paused, breathing heavily, then added, 'Why d'you need t'know?'

Karen couldn't say, Because my boyfriend is jealous of him and trying to turn me against him, and I need to know how much of what he's just said about Charlie being dangerous is true.

Hoping Annie wouldn't pick up her lie, she said instead, 'Because he's displaying some odd reactions to the Gyre case. If it's because he was once accused of raping Eve's sister, I'll be able to discount it. If not, I'll have to find out why.'

Annie hissed like a short-circuiting electric cable. 'Daisy Clarke's stupid. M'licious too. Shou'n't've been in the Job. Ever. Community S'port Officer's more her level. Silly cow.'

'But what happened?' Karen said, assessing Annie's likely intake at a good deal more than a bottle so far this evening.

'*And* n'rotic with it,' Annie went on. 'So deprived of sex sh'ad to invent some. Charlie's not the first bloke she stalked. B't he felt sorry for her. Not like th'others. His mistake was listening: sad stories of men who'd hurt her. Huh! Nothing she di'n d'serve. But Charlie di'n see it. Then she said he raped her. Bollocks. Least she didn't steal condoms from his rubbish and plant 'em in her flat like in that other case. Few years back.'

'Didn't anyone warn him what she was like when they heard he was seeing her?' Karen had never liked the pinched and patronizing Eve, but she found it hard to believe any sister of hers would behave so irresponsibly.

'People think Charlie's too tough for warnings. Only on th'outside. Sad pussy cat inside. Sad. Sad. His dad hit him and his mum. D'n you know?'

'No,' Karen began, thinking of the ebullient woman she'd briefly glimpsed last year when Charlie had been in hospital after an accidental explosion.

'His mother seemed fine when I—'

'Got over it, hasn't she? Once the old bastard snuffed it, she got 'self OK, di'n she? Not Charlie. He's not f'gotten. Never will. Never can. His old man broke both his arms once when he was trying to d'fend his mum. Only eight then. Maybe nine. Too small anyway. Both arms broken.'

Karen thought of everything this news might explain.

'Fuck!' Annie suddenly shouted down the phone, as though her brain had slowly woken up to what she'd just done. 'Don't say I told you. He doesn't like people knowing.'

Her voice was tightening and getting crisper at the edges, as though having betrayed Charlie's secrets had sobered her.

'That's why Daisy hurt him so. He'd tried to help her and she turned on him.'

'If she was known as a fantasist and a stalker, why was Charlie sacked?' Karen said, determined to get the full story while she had the chance.

'Happened at a bad time for the Met.' Now Annie sounded as though she hadn't touched alcohol for weeks. 'Do you remember those two big sexism cases a few years back?'

'Vaguely,' Karen said.

'They came at the same time as some women who *had* been raped took action against co-workers. So no one dared call Daisy's bluff. They were afraid she'd turn round and scream sexism or something. Poor Charlie.'

'Sacrificed to political correctness. No wonder he doesn't want to go back to London,' Karen said. 'Thanks, Annie. That helps.'

'He's a good bloke is Charlie.' Annie sounded urgent, as though she had to make Karen believe her. 'A bit hotter under the collar than is good for him. And he can lose it when he's really riled. But there's nothing slimy about him.'

'Slimy's the worst thing, is it?'

'In my book?' Annie said. 'Yeah. Got to go.' She banged down the phone before Karen could get on to any of the questions that really mattered, such as where Annie had been at the moment when Randall died in the alley behind the pub.

'Karen!' Will's voice broke her concentration.

She turned at once. He was smiling at her with such wary hopefulness that she wondered what she'd been thinking of. Hadn't she had enough of the dark, damaging, damaged kind of man during her short marriage? Hadn't she fallen for Will partly because he was the absolute opposite of Peter: uncomplicated and disciplined, instead of threatening and difficult? She smiled back. Will held out his arms and she walked into them and hugged him.

'I'm sorry,' he said into her hair.

'Why?' She kissed his neck, feeling the tiniest prickles of barely escaping stubble just below his chin. 'I often let Max get to me too. It's hard not to when he's such a persuasive bugger. Let's forget his fantasies and start this evening again.'

'OK.' Will stood back, holding her by her upper arms so that he could look straight into her eyes. After a moment he sighed and smiled properly. 'Yes. OK. Come and tell me about your plans for the transformation of the chalet while I finish cooking. It's a kind of savoury bread-and-butter pudding, by the way.'

In the kitchen she leaned against the worktop as Will carried on with his preparations, setting roughly chopped ham, sunblush tomatoes and pieces of fine dry pecorino among the torn chunks of soft herb-flavoured bread, all soaked in a rich sauce of eggs, cream and more cheese. She told him about Stella and what the two of them hoped the competition would produce.

'We'll need a sharp salad to go with this,' he said, glancing over his shoulder after about ten minutes' solid talk from her. 'Watercress and endive, I think. I've got some in the fridge. I am listening, you know. How does Aidan feel about the competition? Will you be able to send him pdfs of the shortlisted entries?'

'Probably. Although he says he'll be happy to trust our judgement. He's pining to meet you, you know.'

'Me, too,' Will said, breaking a spare piece of pecorino in two and handing her one. 'Have you any idea when he's likely to come over?'

The cheese was very pungent. Karen swallowed, wondering whether it was the taste making her eyes water.

'I wish I knew. I used to think he was waiting till he could wave his success in front of our parents' eyes, but he's been doing really well for years and shows no sign of coming home.' She sighed. 'I miss him.'

'I know you do,' said Will, with real sympathy. 'You've never managed to describe him to me. I just have this feeling that no one will ever quite measure up to him for you – so I need to know what he's like.'

He tidied up the few implements he'd been using, carried them to the sink and washed them under a running hot tap, before returning with a clean, dampened cloth to wipe up the minute number of crumbs he'd left.

'You've seen photographs of him,' Karen said, surprised. 'He looks like me.'

'Tall, blond and handsome: I know. That's not what I meant. I suppose I've been wondering what his character's like.'

'Hard to know where to begin.' Karen knew she was beaming at all the memories surging up into her mind. 'I hadn't thought of it before, but in fact, he's a bit like you. Brilliant and self-controlled and . . . Well, you know. But his work's not as important as yours. He's only a lawyer. He doesn't save lives.'

Will looked at her, as though trying to assess her truthfulness.

'OK,' he said. 'Now, this pudding will take about forty minutes to cook. Shall we walk up to the castle? It's such amazing weather, we shouldn't waste it before the first frosts come. They can't be long now.'

Outside Lisa's studio the garden looked its perfect, informal self in the bright morning light. Apples hung from the trees, so full and heavy they pulled the branches nearly to the ground. Over the bridge and beyond her orchard, she could see Jed already working away in his nearest field.

He straightened up, as though he could feel the strength of her attention, saw her watching at the window and waved. She beckoned. He must have been surprised because he pointed to his chest, as though asking whether she really meant to summon him.

Laughing in the sudden release of knowing she could still paint and find Lee's persona whenever she needed it, Lisa pushed open the double glass doors of the lean-to building that provided her working space, and stepped out.

'Jed, hi! How's it going?'

'Fine,' he said, rubbing his hands together to get the soil off them, then rubbing them again down his trousers. 'I thought you were still away. When did you get back?'

'Yesterday evening, and I've been working more or less ever since.'

'You mustn't do it, you know,' he said, coming towards her across the bridge. 'You'll kill yourself.'

'You're a worker, too. I've seen you at it before now, long after most of the light has gone. I need a shower. Must wash the paint smell out of my hair. D'you want to come over then? We could eat. I've got some food in the fridge.'

'You ought to get some sleep if you've been working all night until now.' Jed looked at his watch. 'It's nigh on eleven. You must be nearly dead.'

'Wired, though. I couldn't sleep. I'll shower, then we can eat. I can have a siesta after that.'

A long lazy smile drew his lips apart. For a moment she thought he was going to say something, but he didn't. So she said it for both of them.

'If you're not busy, you could join me.'

He grabbed her and held on tight. Over his shoulder she could see the river – and the prow of a long grey canoe nosing out from under the willow. Clutching Jed's strong stocky body helped, but not quite enough.

Who *was* it in the canoe?

Karen didn't ask to piggyback on Will's Broadband and she didn't check her mobile until they'd parted outside the building on Saturday morning: he to go back to the hospital in Brighton; she, to Southampton. But as soon as he'd driven off, she leaned against the side of her car again and turned on her phone.

There were five missed calls from yesterday. She listened to the messages one by one.

'Well done for getting Ian back on side,' said Max's gravelly voice, making her grimace. It would be a long time before she'd forgive him for winding up Will. 'Don't let that triumph encourage you to neglect your undergraduates.'

'Al Marks here, Karen,' said the cool, unemotional voice of her Ministry of Justice contact. 'You'll have had the news about Gyre's death by now. His mother's creating. Apparently we – *you* – put him under too much pressure. All our fault he's dead, and so on. I need to see you. Can you come to London on Monday? I'm fending off flak on all sides, and we need to sort out a damage-limitation strategy. Phone me.'

'Karen.' Unmistakably Charlie, this one. 'You boasted last year that you're good at tricky interviews. I've got the worst one here, OK? Why the fuck've you got your phone off? Get in touch.'

'Doctor Taylor? This is Mollie Gyre. I don't know how much you know, but I imagine you will have been informed of my son's death. I should like to talk to you. In fact, I *need* to talk to you. Please could you ring me back, as soon as possible. Please.'

'Darling! Dillie here. Just wanted to check that the money really will be in our bank account by midday on Monday. I know how busy you are, but the hut on the Pile of Shite should be transferring from us to you then, and the money will have to be there. I know it doesn't sound very motherly . . .'

When were you ever motherly? Karen wondered. The money ought to go through without any more chasing from her. She'd signed enough bits of paper. Maybe she'd better check. The last thing she'd need on Monday, with all this going on, would be a raging call from Dillie.

The phone rang again before she'd found the number of her bank, which had made a great thing recently of being open for business on Saturdays.

'Karen?' said the beloved Americanized voice of her brother. He must have got up very early today. 'Just phoning to check my telegraphed transfer has reached your bank account. Monday's the great day, isn't it?'

'Aidan. Yes. Thanks. And I've had a message from Dillie this morning, wanting to make sure she gets her pound of flesh. You *are* kind to be going halves on the place like this. I'd have been stretched doing it on my own.'

'We couldn't let it go out of the family,' he said lightly, then added so casually she almost didn't take it in, 'and I owe you.'

'You do?'

'As you've so often reminded me, I abandoned you to our mad parents when I fled.' He still sounded casual, but it was a difficult subject for both of them, even now.

'True. But you were hardly more than a child yourself,' she said, as she'd said to herself so often in the past that she almost believed it. 'And there was no reason why you should be responsible for your little sister.'

'Worse though,' he added, as though he hadn't been listening to her reassurance, 'I didn't even try to stop you marrying that shit.'

'You couldn't have known what he was like,' Karen said, surprised that Aidan was opening these long-sealed wounds. Maybe it was the thought of the chalet, and the childhood they'd shared there, that had set him off.

'No,' Aidan agreed, 'but I was so angry you were dropping out of school and everything, I – I washed my hands of you. It wasn't fair.'

Karen thought of Aidan's silence after she'd written to say she was engaged to Peter. In spite of all her subsequent letters, Aidan hadn't responded until after Peter's death. That had hurt. But it was a long time ago, and there was no point going over it again.

'Water under the bridge,' she said. 'We've both got too much to do to worry about such ancient history.'

'And you a shrink!' He laughed.

'Are you really sure you don't want to be a judge for the competition?' she said into the phone, wanting to move them both on into the exciting future instead of the sometimes grim past. 'What if you hate the result?'

'I won't. You've got good judgement. And this Stella of yours seems great. I looked her up. I'd like to meet her.'

'You shall. As soon as you set foot on this hated shore again, you'll meet them all.'

'Even Max and Will and Charlie?' he said. Karen could hear he was still smiling. 'Reading your emails, I sometimes think I can see them. I can't wait to find out if I've got them right.'

'You'll meet them. I promise. So when are you coming?'

'How about Christmas?'

'Fantastic! Come and stay. I've got a great spare room, with an amazing view of the Island.'

'Sounds perfect. Who could resist it!'

'Really?'

'Yes,' Aidan said, sounding surprised that she could doubt him.

'Terrific. I mean, great, See you then. Right. Bye.'

On the rare occasions Aidan actually initiated contact, Karen was never the one to end the call, but today she had no time to spare.

Now the bank first, she thought, then Charlie. Al will have to wait till Monday. And Randall's mother too. I can't talk to her till I know more.

A tune ran through Karen's head, skipping and thundering. It was a long moment before she traced the connection to an old English folk song her grandmother had sung to her and Aidan when she'd bathed and put them to bed more than thirty years ago:

What will you leave your sweetheart, Randall my son?
What will you leave your sweetheart, my pretty one?
A rope to hang her, Mother,
A rope to hang her. Mother,
Make my bed soon for I'm sick to my heart
And I fain would lie down.

The phone buzzed again in Karen's hand. She could feel the vibration all the way up her wrist.

'Karen Taylor,' she said into the phone.

'Karen – at last. Where the fuck've you been? Why didn't you text me your boyfriend's landline number like I said? I've been trying to get it from all over, but that ice-man of yours is ex-bloody-directory, and his hospital refused to pass on anything.'

'Charlie. Hi. Sorry it's been a while, but I've had a lot of calls to deal with this morning. Who is it you want me to interview for you?'

'The schoolgirl rape victim who was struggling between Gyre's knees as his killer slit his throat from behind. She got a faceful of his blood.' Charlie sighed, then added in a much more gentle voice, 'She's only fourteen.'

'Christ! Poor girl.'

'So I need you, Karen. Will you do it?'

'Of course,' Karen said, her mind so full of all the implications of that kind of experience for such a child that she couldn't even think about his motives for involving her like this. 'I'll come straight over to the Island. I'll ring you when I get to Southampton to give you my ETA.'

'See you.' He cut off the call abruptly. No time to waste.

Karen flung everything on to the back seat of her car and turned on the ignition. It fired as faithfully as usual, but she saw she had only enough petrol to get her out of the town. She'd have to find a garage fast.

Ten minutes later, she was drawing up by a pump in a modern garage with every kind of unleaded and diesel fuel. There was even a recharging point for electric cars. She filled up with standard unleaded, paid, bought a couple of chunky KitKats to help control her unthinkable thoughts, and was on her way.

Nothing else impeded her and the traffic all behaved impeccably. As she drove, she ate both the KitKats in the first twenty miles.

Suddenly she felt sick. If the Major Crimes team from the mainland were involved in Sonia's murder, they must be in charge of this one too. They would have plenty of their own specialist interviewers and psychologists. How had Charlie persuaded them to let him send for her? And why?

Lisa stirred and wondered why her bed felt so different, so strange. Then she remembered and opened her eyes. Jed was lying with his head turned towards her and resting on the pillows. His eyes were shut and his breathing was deep and regular enough to suggest he wasn't merely faking sleep.

He wasn't touching her. She'd explained that she hated being touched while she slept and he had both hands tucked between his bent-up knees, as though to ensure that he didn't reach out to her in his own unconsciousness and invade the space she needed if she was to feel safe.

She thought back to the long gentle moments of tenderness they'd shared and her anxiety that he'd want more than she could give him, and the straightforward easy open words he'd used to tell her that this was enough for him, too.

One of her hands was lying against her breast. She moved it a little, cupping the slashed flesh, feeling the harder, raised edges of the scars under her soft, warm palm. How did anyone look at something like this, touch it, without feeling sick?

Jed's eyes opened and he smiled a slow, warm smile that was so like him she found herself leaning forwards so that she could kiss him full on his lips. He kept his hands clamped between his hairy knees, which made for a clumsy embrace, but she found the awkwardness more touching than the most skilled and sinuous lover could possibly be.

'You stay there, Jed,' she said, backing away and out from under the duvet. 'I'll get us a drink. Are you hungry?'

'I'm always hungry.' He yawned hugely and rolled over to look at her clock. 'Not surprised; it's half-past nine.'

'Bread and cheese?'

'Great. See you downstairs.'

She wrapped her kimono around her scrawny scarred body and padded downstairs in her bare feet. As she moved about the shabby kitchen, she could hear him walking to and fro in the bedroom above her head. She wondered why he was making such a meal of getting dressed, then realized he was changing her sheets, tidying up for her.

Not sure whether to be grateful or offended, she settled for the first. It was easier. But later, when she went back upstairs after he'd gone and she saw that he had indeed tidied up absolutely everything, all her bits and pieces of loose paper slapped into neat piles, each lying under one of her carefully collected dark-blue pebbles, she did feel invaded.

Had he read all her bills and letters, too? Would she have any privacy left now?

Shivering a little, she pushed the thought aside and picked up the phone to ring her father for the first time since she'd left the Island. She found herself smiling as she punched in the familiar number of his phone. Clicks followed and she practised the first words she'd be saying to him in four years.

A metallic voice sounded: *This number is no longer in use.*

Chapter 16

Monday, 13 October, noon

The rape suite at the police station was decorated in quiet yet cheerful colours, with pale yellow walls and a polished wooden floor, covered with a flat dhurrie rug woven in yellows, turquoises and pale greens. All the same colours were used in the cushions and other soft furnishings. There was even a blue glass jug of white roses, mixed with short branches of round crinkly grey-green leaves.

Eve, unnaturally subdued and gentle, sat in one easy chair, with Karen in the other. Charlie was nowhere to be seen. When Karen had asked Eve if he'd be coming, Eve had put on her most irritatingly superior smile and said he'd be working all day with Major Crimes on the Franklin murder, adding: '*If* he wants to talk to you, he knows how to find you.'

Opposite the two women was a big, squashy sofa, where Bella Shenley perched beside her mother. The older woman, who couldn't have been much more than Karen's age of thirty-five, looked as though she had to fight to stop herself touching her daughter all the time.

Bella had her legs crossed and her hands tightly clasped around the top knee. Every so often deep shudders ran through her body, and she was clenching her jaw so hard the skin around her mouth was tight and very pale. Her blonde hair looked greasy and unkempt and her big blue eyes were reddened and kept filling with tears.

Karen knew Bella had been through the customary post-rape processing on Friday afternoon. Even though her attacker was dead, all the usual swabs had been taken, along with scrapings from under her nails. She'd given Eve a clear account of everything Randall had said and done from the moment he had asked for her help in the street in Cowes to the second his blood had spurted all over her face.

The statement, which Karen had already read, was full and uncompromisingly convincing. But Bella had been adamant that she'd seen nothing of his killer. Karen's job was to get past whatever block was holding back her memory and so help her to reveal what they all needed to know. She'd dressed to reassure today, in a sober knee-length shift made of fine grey linen, cheered up by scarlet ballet flats, and she wore her shoulder-length blonde hair loose, hoping it would make her round button of a face look young enough to help Bella talk.

'In your statement, Bella,' she said, using her easiest, calmest voice, 'you said something about a bottle that I couldn't quite follow. Can you tell me more about it?'

Bella's hands tightened around her knee and her foot jiggled, as though her hands had sent an electric charge down her leg. She didn't speak.

'What kind of bottle was it?' Karen asked.

'Champagne,' Bella said in a dull voice. 'He went, "Let's go and have a bottle of fizz in the garden" and I was like, "Yeah. OK. Whatever". But . . .'

'Then what happened,' Karen asked, smiling. Bella wouldn't see the smile because she was staring at the floor, but Karen hoped it would make her voice sound warmer.

'We never got there.' For a second Bella's eyes flicked upwards and her gaze met Karen's. 'He pulled me into the passageway by the pub, and I . . . I couldn't . . .' She put a hand over her mouth, as though even saying the words would be unbearable. 'That's when I knew.'

'Knew what?'

'The mad woman in the street was, like, right. He was a rapist. Sadist. All the things she said. But I didn't run away. Even when I could of. But I, like, didn't. So it was my fault.'

Her mother couldn't suppress a gasp, and her hands twitched, but she caught Karen's eye and nodded to show her obedience to the instruction not to interfere in the interview in any way, unless Bella asked her for something.

'I didn't even *try* to run away.' Bella's eyes overflowed with tears and she bent forwards over her knee, her back heaving with the weight of her sobs.

'It's not your fault,' Karen said, looking at her with profound sympathy. 'None of us ever knows what we'll do in a moment of extreme terror.'

Bella raised her head again. Karen thought her expression might look the same if she were drowning.

'You have *nothing* to feel guilty about, Bella,' Karen told her.

Bella looked away, glanced at her mother for a second, then shuddered again and went back to staring at her feet.

'I bunked off school,' she said in the dreariest possible voice. 'I let him pick me up. If I hadn't I'd be, like, OK now.'

'Guilt isn't helpful, Bella. And sometimes it's a way of hiding from things we don't want to see, can't deal with. If we tell ourselves – and everyone else – that we feel guilty, then we don't have to face up to all the real stuff, the hate and anger that it's quite all right to feel when you've been assaulted like this. Sometimes it's easier just to feel guilty and leave it at that.'

'What d'you mean?' Bella sounded exhausted now.

Eve moved her forefinger in a series of fast circles, gesturing to Karen to hurry up.

'Never mind now,' Karen said. 'We can talk about that later. Tell me about the other bottle. Not the champagne bottle.'

'You mean the broken one that . . . that cut Randall?'

Karen carefully didn't look at Eve, or at Bella's mother. She didn't want either of them showing any triumph, or even satisfaction at this first hint of a breakthrough.

'That's right. The broken one,' Karen said calmly. 'Tell me about it, Bella.'

'It was brown. Like a beer bottle. Just the neck. No label. Broken off. Jagged.' The girl drew in a huge, sobbing breath.

'OK.' Karen wrote a note on her big lined pad, not because she needed a record of this interview – everything was being filmed and taped – but to make the process seem ordinary and official, a little dull even. 'Where did you see it?'

'In his hand.'

His, Karen wrote.

'What did his hand look like?' she said aloud.

'I don't understand.'

'Did it have a glove on it, maybe? Or could you see his nails? What did they look like?'

'Creamy white,' said Bella quickly, as though this was much easier than the earlier questions. 'No nails. It was rubber gloves. Thin ones.'

'Were there any cuts in the rubber? Any holes? Any other kind of marks?'

Bella frowned, closing her eyes, as though in an effort to force her memory. Karen could feel Eve looking at her, but she'd have to wait.

'I don't think so,' Bella said, sniffing. 'I think they were new.'

'And what about the sleeve above the glove? What colour was the sleeve?'

There was a long silence, then Bella said: 'Grey. Like your dress. But soft. Like in a sweatshirt. But only a little of it. Something different above it. Like green. Harder, too.'

'And above that, what could you see of his head?'

'A hood. Like on an anorak, with the strings tight, so it came up over his face.'

'What colour was it?'

'Dark browny green. The anorak was dark browny green. Like the Army.'

'And the skin of the face?'

'White.'

'And the eyes?'

Bella sobbed. 'I don't know. I didn't see. I don't know.'

'It's fine. You've done really really, well. Over Randall's shoulder, you saw a white person, wearing a grey sweatshirt under a dark brownish-green cagoule, with white rubber gloves on his hands, holding the neck of a broken brown beer bottle. Is that right?'

'I think so.'

Karen made her voice very warm. 'You've said "him" and "his". Are you sure it was a man?'

'I don't know,' Bella whispered, in amongst a series of small sudden intakes of breath, like a baby recovering from a crying fit. 'I couldn't see. I had blood in my eyes. I saw the bottle and I reached out for help 'cos I thought he was giving it to me and I saw the hand and the arm, and then the bottle went under Randall's head and across his neck and all I could see was blood. Only blood. I couldn't see anything.'

She started to rub her eyes so hard Karen worried about the damage she might be doing to her corneas. Against all the rules, Karen got up from her chair and went to kneel on the floor in front of Bella and placed her hands around the girl's wrists, without asking permission to touch her first. Then, very gently, she pulled Bella's tight hands down, away from her face.

'I can understand how horrible it was,' Karen said. 'But you must try not to rub so hard. Your eyes are clean now. Your whole face and body are clean and there is no more blood in your hair. Try not to wipe away what isn't there any more. Every time you do that, you will trick your brain into believing there is still blood left there. The more you do it, the harder it'll be for you to get over what's happened. Do you understand, Bella?'

'Who was he?' she whispered. 'Who *was* he?'

'We don't know yet.' Karen kept all her own ideas about Annie right out of her mind, knowing they could only ruin everything she was trying to do for Bella. 'That's why I have to ask you these questions. He saved you and we have to find him. Can you remember anything else?'

'I heard him run away. When I had the face full of blood and Randall fell on me, gurgling and kind of, like, jerking, I heard him running away down the alley.'

'Did he sound heavy?'

Bella's eyes flew open again and she looked up into Karen's face. 'No. You're right. He was very light. You think it wasn't a man, don't you? Was it another girl? Someone like me? Or the mad woman? Did she follow us?'

'I don't know. Can you remember anything else?'

Tears flooded out of Bella's eyes again, and she shook her head. At last she subsided against her mother, whose arms came around her and rocked her again and again.

Karen glanced at Eve, who nodded. Together they walked out of the room.

'Charlie's not going to be pleased. That wasn't much help,' Eve said with her usual lack of tact.

'Except to confirm that Bella didn't do it herself.'

'Charlie never thought she did. The shape of the cut, the pattern of the blood, all show it was done from behind, left to right by a right-handed assailant, who held up Gyre's head by his hair. Must've been so he could get a clean cut.'

'Where was Sally when it happened?'

Eve didn't answer. Karen's phone vibrated against her thigh. She dragged it out of her pocket to see Al's number on the screen. She stuffed the little rectangle back in her pocket.

'Not Charlie then?' said Eve, in a voice sharp with spite.

'No.' Karen wished it had been. She hated being shut out like this, and having to think about why he was doing it. Putting up with Eve's digs about her own superior access to him was a doddle in comparison. 'I *need* to see him, then I've got to go to London.'

'He's out, interviewing suspects for the Major Crimes SIO. I told you – he hasn't time for you.'

'Tell him I've had to go to London. I'll phone this evening.' Karen didn't wait for Eve's next crack. She had too much to do.

The meeting room in the Ministry of Justice felt cooler than the rape suite, in spite of the sun that poured in through the big windows. It was decorated in the same white, mid-blue and grey Karen remembered from the times she'd visited Al in his much smaller office. A single chair was positioned on the near side of the table with six people already seated opposite it, like some kind of board of enquiry.

Seeing how they'd set her up to feel like a prisoner in the dock, Karen paused for a moment to collect her thoughts, then nodded to the only two people she recognized in the line-up: Al himself and Dave, the probation officer, who gave her an ironic salute that seemed to underline her status as the accused. He was wearing a suit today, presumably in honour of being in the ministry building, but it did no more favours to his rounded gut than the tight striped shirt he'd worn last time.

Al got to his feet and introduced the rest. There was his line manager, Sarah Blake, looking hostile and efficient in a black suit and crisp white shirt. Beside her sat a press officer called Mandy Green, who had an anxious expression in her big grey eyes and was fiddling with her curly blonde hair as though she had nits. Next came DCI Richard Kent, stocky and powerful in plain clothes. The last to be introduced was a political adviser, Marty Jecks, who looked like a teenage trainee estate agent, with bad skin, an unnecessarily tight grey suit and a very slick haircut.

Karen sat down and only then noticed that her chair's position meant the sun was shining directly in her eyes. She shifted a little to the side, but it didn't make any difference.

'Al, will you kick off?' said Sarah, her voice hard and her eyes cold.

'Why not? Karen, we've asked you to come today because we need to manage this news with great care,' he said with a formality that reinforced the impression that she was on trial here.

'Oh, yes?' she said, remembering his refusal to take her warnings about Randall seriously. 'Why?'

'There are two potential problems,' he said in his usual detached manner. 'One, the press will pick up on the fact that Gyre successfully completed both anger-management and sex-offender's awareness courses in prison and was judged to be of no danger to anyone any longer, before his encounters with you triggered the old violence in him again, and two—'

'Hold it there,' Karen said, putting up her right hand like a traffic cop stopping a careering truck. 'Nothing in my encounters with Randall could have any bearing on what he did to Bella.'

'I've already fielded several calls from the media about the way he's been hounded since he came out of prison,' Mandy said, chipping in brightly like an interfering cuckoo, with the fingers of both hands twiddling her curls. 'They all think it's why he went back to his old haunts on the Isle of Wight – *and* his old habits.'

'*Hounded*?' Karen repeated with deliberately puzzled emphasis. 'Not by me.'

'I did warn you, Sarah,' Dave said, making his own pitch with a smug smile, 'about bringing in outsiders without direct experience of offender management. It's been a serious mistake. Next time, perhaps you'll listen to me.'

Karen saw how satisfaction was plumping up Dave's already fleshy face. Maybe the dislike he'd shown at their first meeting had nothing personal in it, after all. He could have simply resented any theoretical psychologist being brought in over his head. So had it been he who'd gone spouting malicious disinformation to a pack of journalists?

Anger rose through Karen's mind. She fought off the urge to wipe her forehead and breathed so deeply she made herself dizzy.

'All that happened when I met Randall,' she said when she'd controlled herself, 'was that I asked him to fill out sheets of straightforward multiple-choice questions. A week later, I conducted a filmed interview with him, which lasted about an hour. There was no aggression involved on my side. I didn't accuse him of anything or suggest I thought he could be a risk to anyone. Nor have I had any other form of contact with him.'

'Great,' said Mandy, looking perkier and leaving her hair alone for a moment. 'So there shouldn't be any problem. Can I offer journalists a sight of the questions and the films? That way, we could pre-empt any trouble.'

'Of course not.' Karen knew she shouldn't let her impatience show, but she couldn't help it. The whole tone of the meeting was ridiculous. And a shocking waste of time when there'd been such carnage on the Island. 'If my questions are published I'll never be able to use them again.'

'Why not?' Mandy was frowning now and had three fingers of her left hand wound into her curls.

'Think!' Karen said, forgetting for a second that the woman wasn't one of her students. 'If people taking psychometric tests get an idea of the questions they'll be asked, they can work out what their answers should be in advance, so the results can never be real – or worth a toss.'

Mandy blushed. No one came to her rescue.

'In any case,' Karen said more kindly, 'my work has nothing to do with what's happened on the Island. That's down to this department's refusal to accept my warning that Randall was highly dangerous. If he'd been under MAPPA control, or even more basic surveillance, we wouldn't be in this situation.'

Looking at their resentful faces, Karen could see they'd wanted her to crumple at the first sign of criticism. Even if she had been at fault, she wouldn't have given them the satisfaction.

'Now that's settled,' she said firmly, 'you said you had two problems, Al. What's the second?'

'Ah yes.' He put his hands together at the fingertips, leaving a triangular space below, and tapped his lips with the two first fingers. He looked like a child acting the part of an old-style mandarin. 'This is potentially even more problematic. Your study – and your conclusions – are highly confidential, as you know?'

He made his voice rise, turning the last three words into a question.

'Indeed,' Karen said. 'I mean, I know it is. So?'

'Obviously there's been a leak, which has – most unfortunately – resulted in vigilantes realizing what Gyre was doing and lying in wait to kill him.'

'Is anyone going to weep hot and salty tears over his death?' Karen said. 'He was raping a *fourteen*-year-old schoolgirl when he was killed. What journalist is going to use a man like that as a popular martyr?'

'Powerful people are interested in this case, and vigilantism is very unpopular just now,' Sarah said, ignoring the real issue in a way that made Karen curious.

'Powerful people like who?'

Marty, the political adviser, pursed his flaky lips, but didn't say anything. Karen looked along the row of uncompromising faces beside his.

'Come on,' she said. 'I know his mother is – or was – a hotshot fund manager, but that doesn't carry this kind of weight, even if she has made millions. His father doesn't sound like a man with any political pull. So who's behind this? An uncle? Godparent?'

Someone in the row opposite her twitched, but she couldn't be sure who it was.

'A godparent in the government?' she said, looking from one to the next and back again.

'That's an outrageous suggestion.' Marty's nasal voice suited his appearance.

'And that's as good as an acknowledgement,' Karen said, smiling at him. 'Thanks, Marty.'

'So, who have you treated to your opinion of Randall's potential violence?' Sarah said, her voice spiky with dislike.

'*I* haven't spoken to a single member of the press,' Karen said firmly, looking straight at Dave. For a second she thought he blushed, but with the light behind him and shining in her eyes she couldn't be sure.

'Maybe not a member of the press,' Sarah said, looking as eager as a cat leaping on to an unprotected fledgling. 'But you have told someone, haven't you?'

Sensing danger for Charlie, Karen crossed her legs and offered Al a non-committal smile, before facing Sarah.

'When Randall disappeared,' Karen said, speaking as formally as any lecturer now to hide all her anxiety, 'I was asked by this office to advise on his possible whereabouts. That commission took me to the Isle of Wight, where I was sure he'd go – as indeed it turns out he did – and so I contacted the police there.'

'Wasn't that outside your brief?' Sarah said, glaring furiously at Al, who nodded to her before offering Karen a tiny shrug, which might have been supposed to express apology.

'I did tell you, Karen,' he said, still managing to sound cool enough to suggest he had nothing to worry about for himself, 'that I wanted you to advise on Gyre's likely whereabouts so that *we* could offer your ideas to the relevant police force.'

Karen hoped her expression would convey all her contempt for what he was doing, then she turned back to Sarah and continued her list.

'I also spoke to DCS Stokes, in this building, when DS Tod Williams was killed in Winchester. Superintendent Stokes subsequently introduced me to a DS Colvin, who had useful information to offer about Randall, after her experience with one of his earlier victims. Other than those officers, the only person outside this room with whom I have discussed any aspect of Randall or his case is his mother.'

'Mrs Gyre could still go to the media,' Sarah said, glancing at Mandy, the press officer, and it was a moment before Karen realized how skilfully she'd shifted ground. 'She's horribly well connected.'

'Why exactly am I here?' Karen said, not bothering to hide her suspicion.

'So we can agree a formula to give the press,' Sarah said, as innocent as though she'd never thought of shifting any blame in Karen's direction. 'Mandy's drafted a statement.'

The press officer pushed a sheet of white paper towards Karen, who picked it up and read the eight lines printed on it:

Randall Gyre, who was found dead on the Isle of Wight last week, had been released from prison as part of the accelerated parole programme because he had successfully completed courses in anger management and understanding of his offending behaviour. He was participating in a study of re-offending, conducted by Dr Karen Taylor under the auspices of the Ministry of Justice. Dr Taylor is not due to complete her research for another eighteen months. No further details will be available until then. The police are investigating Randall Gyre's death and expect to make an arrest in the near future.

'So, there we are,' Sarah smiled. 'I think that covers it. We need everyone to sign up to this form of words and agree to say nothing more to anyone. So long as no one goes off-message there should be no problems for anyone involved.'

'No,' Karen said.

Six pairs of eyes glared at her from across the table. All of them were hostile now.

'If you use my name,' Karen added with even more deliberation, 'you must also say that I both phoned and emailed to report my serious misgivings about Randall being allowed to live in the community. I warned you that he would try to rape again – as he has done – and also that he was likely to kill. It's possible he killed two people before he himself died.'

'This is a most unhelpful attitude, Doctor Taylor,' said Sarah. 'There's no evidence that Gyre killed either DS Williams or the consultant on the Island.'

'No evidence *yet*.' Karen kept her gaze steady. She was glad she'd put up her hair today, in a tight chignon that gave her face a bit of authority. 'But I don't believe enquiries have been completed.'

She looked all along the line of her accusers. None of them responded.

'I must repeat that I've done nothing wrong,' she said, 'and I'm not prepared to sign up to this document that suggests I did. If anything is passed to the press about my involvement with Randall, I want it on record that I warned Al and told him what would happen.' She hated her stilted delivery, but she didn't think anything less would get through to this bunch of bureaucrats.

'No way,' Sarah said, picking at a rough patch on one of her fingers. She looked up again. '*No* way.'

'We've got to give them something, Sarah,' Mandy said, suddenly breathless and fiddling with her curls again. 'I've promised we'll issue a press release before the end of today. If we don't, they'll start to dig, sure we've got something to hide. That always causes trouble. We have to give them a statement.'

'And one that'll cool their interest,' said Marty, the political adviser.

'Or divert it,' Karen said casually. She didn't see why she should help them, but the solution was too obvious to ignore.

'That'd be great,' said Mandy, 'but how?'

'Put them on to one of Randall's earlier victims.' Karen wondered why it hadn't occurred to any of them already. 'That way they'd have a human-interest story, full of stuff that'll titillate half their readers and give the other half a warm wallow in outrage. It'll also remind anyone hoping to make Randall a victim of anyone or anything just how vicious he was.'

'Of course,' Mandy said, pulling her fingers out of her hair again. 'It'd be, like, a great idea. But his victim disappeared. No one can find her now. So we're stuffed.'

'Lizzie Fane isn't Randall's only victim,' Karen said, letting the impatience sound in her voice again. 'And you may well find one who'd want to talk to the press, if only to get some kind of acknowledgment of what he put her through. You must know he's been doing this for years. Make that the story, and this department is off the hook.'

DCI Kent had said absolutely nothing throughout the meeting. Now he exchanged glances with Sarah, obviously sending her some secret message the rest of them weren't supposed to decode. More than happy to take the hint and make her escape, Karen pushed back her chair.

'D'you need me any longer? If not, I've a lot to do.'

'Let Al take you to his office,' Sarah said, making it clear Karen had no option to disagree, 'and sort out how you're going to continue the study now.'

Karen had to listen to a lecture from Al about how the civil service would never manipulate the press in the way she was suggesting, nor betray the identity and whereabouts of any of Randall's earlier victims.

'No, no, I'm sure you wouldn't,' she said, with many mentally crossed fingers.

Al himself might work within the traditional strict standards of his service, but that didn't mean all his colleagues would do the same, still less the political appointees.

'Now, can I assume that I continue my testing and complete the study as originally devised?' Karen said, wanting to get back to Southampton and her real life.

'For the moment, yes,' Al said. 'We'll expect the finished report by the original deadline.'

'Unless there's some very disturbing fallout from the press interest in it,' Karen said, 'in which case you will presumably pull it.'

She tried to remember whether there was anything in their contract that dealt with how she would be paid if the ministry cut her off halfway through her work. With the extra mortgage she'd taken on to pay for her share of the chalet, she couldn't risk losing any budgeted income. As it was, she wouldn't be buying any new clothes for a long time.

'It would have to be very bad for that to happen.' Al talked as though he was twice her age instead of several years younger. 'Let's hope all goes well. Keep me informed, won't you?'

'Of course. Though telling you everything didn't do any of us much good last time, did it?' she said, unable to resist rubbing it in. 'Bye, Al.'

'Hang on a moment,' he said, reaching for the phone on his desk. 'DCI Kent wanted a private word with you after the meeting.'

Karen got to her feet and walked over to the window to stare out at London, ten storeys below her. From this height, the people looked very far away, scurrying about on unimportant journeys, going nowhere that mattered. Maybe it was seeing them as so insignificant that allowed Al and his colleagues to be so detached.

'OK. Great,' he said, before putting down his phone. 'He'll meet us by the lifts.'

DCI Kent was waiting for them, looking taller and more impressive than he had at the conference table. He held out a large, square hand for Karen to shake.

'Doctor Taylor,' he said as the lift doors opened. 'Shall we go? Thanks, Al. I'll be in touch.'

The doors closed on Al before he could comment. DCI Kent pressed the button for the ground floor and the lift lurched downwards. He leaned against the brushed stainless-steel wall, watching her.

'You've been cleared to work with the Isle of Wight police on this enquiry,' he said, giving no clue about what was to come.

'So I've been told,' she said, careful to sound as neutral as he had.

'At the special request of Charlie Trench?'

'Apparently.' All Karen's danger-warning instincts were alive and prodding her.

'How well do you know him?'

'Reasonably, although to say we're friends would be putting it a little high.' She was still feeling her way, determined not to drop Charlie in it until she knew what this man wanted. 'I met him last year, while I was doing some research on the Island. When family business took me back there a few days ago, I thought I'd get in touch.'

'With what end in mind?'

'The pleasure of Charlie's company,' Karen said and felt the dryness in her throat that always came as a response to threat. 'Why?'

'I *am* a friend of his, and I'm worried.'

Karen shot a quick glance at DCI Kent and thought she'd never seen a stonier expression on anyone's face. What was he hiding?

'As a psychologist, you could help.'

Karen's guard did not drop. 'Oh yes?'

'Why is Charlie so *personally* involved in this case?'

'I don't know what you mean,' Karen said at once.

'A team from the Major Crimes Unit on the mainland has been sent in to clear up both the Franklin and Gyre murders, but

Charlie won't stop interfering. He's causing trouble. Harassing the woman doing the photofit. Phoning the lab. Diverting the junior officers. Getting in everyone's hair. He's never obstructed an enquiry like this before.'

Karen didn't speak, but she didn't shift her gaze away from Kent's hard brown eyes either. Now she knew exactly what he was after. Someone, somewhere, had told Will that Charlie was dangerously violent. This man obviously had the same idea. Both of them had to learn how wrong they were.

'As a friend of his,' he said, settling his shoulders more comfortably against the metal wall, 'I was asked why he's causing trouble. I've no idea. Then I hear you're involved in the Gyre case and I know you're close to Charlie. So I'm asking *you*: what's going on?'

'I'll ask you the same question, DCI Kent,' Karen said, feeling queasy as she thought of Annie's surprisingly intimate knowledge of Charlie's background, and of his obvious affection for her, and of his hatred of seeing women hurt.

Could that hatred be strong enough to make him try to divert the investigators so they didn't discover that she had been the vigilante, killing not only Randall but also everyone who'd added to his victims' suffering?

Both Annie and Charlie had independently talked to Karen about the way Tod had bullied Lizzie when she'd been lying half-dead in hospital after the rape. And Charlie was convinced that Dr Franklin's negligence meant the septicaemia had gone undiagnosed until it had nearly killed Lizzie.

Could Annie have confessed during the meeting in the Goose Inn when Charlie had suddenly stopped answering his phone? Could a man like him try to protect a killer, even one motivated only by fury at the lack of justice for victims? A fury, of course, that he himself shared.

Fighting to keep any of the ideas from showing in her face, Karen added coldly: 'What is there about a bog-standard

provincial cop that brings a DCI to a meeting at the Ministry of
Justice in London?'

Kent shifted uncomfortably and stood up straight, looking at
the illuminated numbers on the fascia, which showed they were
almost at the ground floor. Karen felt even queasier.

'How much do you know about the Daisy Clarke affair?' he
said at last.

'Not a great deal,' Karen said, holding both hands tightly
together behind her back. 'There's gossip, and I've heard a bit.
Why?'

'Some people in the hierarchy think Charlie's owed. He swallowed what happened without making a public fuss and got us
all off the hook. If he's gone off the rails now, we'd like to get
him back on before he screws his career for ever. OK?'

'Why can't you ask him direct? If you *are* friends.' Karen didn't
trust any of the people who'd been at today's meeting. They were
all so clearly far more interested in protecting their own arses
than in finding Randall's killer.

Kent laughed as the lift jolted to a stop. It didn't sound like
genuine amusement to Karen.

'Hasn't your work shown you that blokes don't share confi-
dences?' he said. 'Especially when they're friends.'

The lift doors opened. Karen strode out ahead of him, making
for the plate-glass doors that led on to the bustle of Victoria
Street. Outside, she breathed in the mixture of petrol fumes, dust
and human sweat and longed to be back on the Island, with the
clean taste of salt from the sea in every mouthful of air she took.

'Give me a break,' Kent said as he caught up with her.

'I can't help you,' Karen said stiffly.

Kent glared at her, then produced a slight smile, which was
more a minute relaxation of his lips than an expression of real
pleasure or affection.

'There are moves to get Charlie taken off this enquiry altogether,' he said, no longer looking at her. 'I want to stop that

if I can. The gossip I've heard made me think you'd want it too.'

Karen didn't answer. Somewhere in the depths of her mind was an impulse to put DCI Kent and Will together in a stout sack and throw it into the nearest river. She wanted to be back on the Island, helping Charlie in any way she could, whatever he might have done to protect Annie. Glad she was wearing loose clothes and flats today, Karen turned and walked fast towards the nearest tube station, only to hear Kent's voice pulling at her.

'He told me you had the best legs of any currant bun he'd ever met.'

Karen stopped, and whirled round. 'So you really do know him,' she said, surprised.

'I do.' Kent was sauntering towards her over the uneven paving stones. A taxi lurched towards the kerb beside him, and he didn't even flinch. 'He told me all about you last year and the way you divide the human race into horses and currant buns, according to the shape of their faces. So *can* you help me help him? He's going to need every bit of support he can get now.'

Karen shook her head.

'I don't know what you're suggesting,' she said, lying because she had to, 'but I don't think he'd ever obstruct an investigation. If it looks like that it's only because he's trying to stop someone else fucking up.'

'Sure about that?' He didn't seem surprised by her language. Maybe Charlie had told him it always degenerated when she was stressed.

'It's certainly not because he killed Randall himself.' She laughed to show how ludicrous she found the idea. 'He wouldn't, whatever he felt about a rapist who targets vulnerable schoolgirls. He's no vigilante.'

Kent watched her face, a slightly more real smile playing about his lips.

'Clearly Charlie's views of you haven't gone unappreciated, whatever he thinks. But you'd do him more good by telling me what you know, instead of burying it in this kind of blind loyalty. He's going to need all his friends to get him out of this mess now.'

Chapter 17

Two days later Karen had to go back to London to deal with Randall's mother. It would have been much easier to see her after the uncomfortable encounters at the Ministry of Justice, but Mollie Gyre hadn't been free then. Not wanting to waste any more time, Karen took the 7.30 train on Wednesday morning. A woman in a short navy-blue cleaner's overall opened the door to the rich, hushed flat in Campden Hill Court. She was about fifty, of medium height, with sparse dyed auburn hair and an anxious expression on her rounded face.

'Doctor Taylor? Mrs Gyre expecting. She has papers. Not good. Very not good. You help her? You understand me?'

'I'll do my best,' Karen said, looking at the closed mahogany door to the study/dining room, where she'd had sandwiches the last time she'd been here. She pushed the door open.

Randall's mother was sitting at the table, as stiffly upright as a broom handle. Spread across the shining glass surface were the newspapers Karen had already read on the train. Randall's photograph appeared on the front pages of all of them, and the accompanying articles ranged from sober feminist analyses of rape and rapists, via the allegations of many women who claimed to have been his victims but had never reported what he'd done to them, to the shrieking, hysterical misogyny of the most upmarket of the tabloids, convinced he'd been murdered by a party of virago vigilantes.

Karen didn't feel any pride in this result of her idle suggestion to a group of officials worried about how the press might criticize the work of their department.

Mollie turned her head so that she was looking directly at Karen. Her skin was nearly as grey as Annie's had been at their first meeting, as though someone had rubbed cigarette ash into it.

The faint creases that had been only just visible under her perfect make-up were now deep, dark lines. Her fierce eyes were filmed with tears. There was a large raised red lump at the left of her lower lip, as though she'd been biting it all night. And she'd forgotten to pluck the whiskers from her chin. Her hair was unbrushed and hung in dried-out clumps on either side of her face.

'Is it true?' she said without offering any kind of greeting.

Karen felt pulled in two. Half of her longed to comfort the woman who had loved and protected the milky baby who'd been born innocent, then grown up to do all this, and the other half wanted to yell that it *had* to be all her fault. 'Yes.'

'*Why*?' Mollie's voice was anguished.

'I don't know,' Karen said, feeling more helpless than usual.

'Was it me? Something I did?'

'It's always the parents' fault', ran one mantra Karen had heard throughout her professional life. Underlining it was the bitter, ironic protest she'd once quoted to Charlie: 'a mother's place is in the wrong'.

'No one'll ever know now,' Karen said. 'The only person who could have explained why he did those things was Randall himself. And maybe even he didn't know *why* he did it. Just that he wanted to.'

'Was it because I divorced his father?' Mrs Gyre was clearly in that state in which nothing anyone else said could assuage the pain or stop the endless round of internal guilt and ever-crueller self-questioning.

'That rather depends on the circumstances,' Karen said. She thought of fourteen-year-old Bella, broken and guilty and in pain because of Randall, and tried to put all her feelings in a separate part of her brain so that they wouldn't affect what she had to do here.

'When Randall was born,' Mollie said, staring up at the ceiling as though to make gravity pull the tears back into her eyes, 'his father was having an affair. Should I have put up with it? Swallowed the lies and treachery? Would that've stopped Randall turning into a sexual sadist?'

She looked up towards Karen, who was still standing in the doorway. 'I can't answer that, Mrs Gyre. I just don't know.'

'He was too young to know anything about it. So how could it've turned him into this monster?' Mollie laid one shaking hand on the nastiest of the tabloids, then covered her face with the other hand and broke down. From behind her hand, her voice, muffled and soggy, went on: 'It has to be me. It has to be something I did to him when he was growing up. And because of that, these girls – all these poor young girls . . .'

Karen watched her with pity surging up again. With great care, she began to offer every conceivable explanation.

'Mrs Gyre, it is possible that a boy living with a woman angry and humiliated by what her husband had done might grow up to want all women punished.'

'I don't understand.' Mollie's force of character brought her fully upright again. She wiped her eyes. 'Why would he want *women* punished?'

Karen spoke as though to a seminar because that was the only way she could think of to protect the other woman: 'Every child who's got a grievance with the parent he knows, is likely to think he'd be happier with the absent parent – and it could be absent through divorce, or death, or merely through being away from home at the office. It's possible Randall identified with his father whenever he was told off or forbidden to do something or deprived of something he wanted.'

There was a long, uncomfortable pause before Mollie said painfully, 'I worked so hard to teach him how to be a decent man.'

Pity squeezed Karen's guts; pity for Mollie, for the women her son had raped and tortured, and even somewhere just a little for him.

'It's also possible,' Karen said more easily and with equal truth, 'that some kind of chemical pollution messed up his genes. We don't know enough yet about what genes make us do or how they work. You mustn't assume it was your fault.'

Karen thought of the way she'd always blamed her own parents, particularly her mother, for everything that had been hard about her childhood, and wished she'd been more tolerant.

'What am I supposed to do now?' Mollie said, pleading as she'd probably never pleaded in her life before. 'I need to make up . . . Somehow I've got to do something to help his victim.'

At last Karen had got the opportunity she needed. She moved forwards and pulled out a chair at the opposite side of the table and sat down.

'You can help the police find his killer by being franker than you were when I was last here.'

Mollie said nothing.

'I need to know where Randall went after I'd interviewed him,' Karen went on.

His mother played with a magnificent diamond she wore on her wedding finger, a square-cut stone about a centimetre across, twisting the ring round and round the finger.

'He said he was going to Winchester,' she admitted at last. 'He wanted to look up an old friend there before going back to the Island.'

'To do what?' Karen waited in curiosity, knowing Mollie would never say, to find out where his last victim was hiding so he could kill her, as he'd always promised he would.

'He wanted to see Dinny – Diana Hemming.' Mollie sniffed and tried to smile, but it was a poor effort. 'They were tremendous muckers as children, and Dinny visited him when he was in prison. She was his best friend, really. That's why I phoned Chloe to find out if they'd seen him when he went missing.'

She looked straight at Karen. 'I told you I'd done that, didn't I?'

'You did. So when was he in Winchester?'

'I don't know. I don't even know if that's where he was really planning to go. It's just what he said to me. I—'

'Why didn't you tell me *that* when I was here last?'

Tears dripped down Mollie's thin grey cheeks. 'Because I didn't believe it. Why would he have told me? In his place, at his age, I wouldn't have told my parents where I was going. And even if it had been true, I didn't want you hounding him.'

The repetition of that word 'hounding' sent Karen right back to the exasperating meeting she'd had at the Ministry of Justice two days ago.

'Did he say I hounded him?'

Mollie shook her head, obviously shocked by the suggestion. 'No! As you know, you were the first person to treat him with decency and respect.'

'So why did you complain about me to the press?'

'What? I don't understand. Why would I complain?'

'I must have got my wires crossed,' Karen said quickly. The sneak must have been Dave, as she'd originally thought, punishing her for getting a project he'd wanted for himself.

'In that case,' she went on, 'what is it that you want to tell me now? You said you had something that couldn't be passed on over the phone.'

Mollie swallowed, then breathed carefully, before saying, 'Doctor Taylor, please tell me there's some doubt about what they've all said about Randall.'

'I can't. I'm sorry.' Karen thought of Bella getting a faceful of Randall's blood. 'There's no doubt of any kind. What did you want to tell me?'

Mollie shuddered and suddenly clutched the arms of her chair, as though vertigo made her think she was about to fall.

'Nothing. I want *you* to tell me who killed him.'

Join the queue, Karen thought.

'I wish I knew,' she said aloud. 'Have you looked at the photofit picture the police produced?'

When Mollie said nothing, Karen shuffled through the newspapers until she found the one with the biggest photofit, which had been created with the aid of Bella's halting information. Mollie let her dull eyes look down at it.

'What could anyone tell from this?' she said, sounding tired to the point of passing out. 'It could be a man or a woman – or a child, come to that. Animal even. A pair of maddened dark eyes below an anorak hood — how could I recognize anyone?'

'What about the anorak itself?' Karen was determined to get at whatever Mollie was finding so hard to say. 'Is that familiar?'

'It's the kind of thing you could buy in any camping shop or army surplus.'

'Do you know anyone who might have wanted Randall dead?'

A hint of the old confidence seeped back into Mollie's expression. Her shoulders straightened too. She reached for the paper with hands that were no longer shaking.

'Vigilantes,' she said. 'It's the only thing that makes sense. Someone was tipped off. They must have followed my son and then . . .' Her voice trembled and tears began to leak out of her eyes again. 'Did you tell anyone what you thought of him after you met him that first time?'

'What about some of his old contacts on the Island?' Karen asked quickly, hoping to avoid having to answer the question. 'This Dinny. Could they have quarrelled?'

'That's ridiculous. They were friends. Whoever cut Randall's throat is a vigilante who hates rapists. I think you know who that is and I need you to tell me. It must be the same one who killed the man in Winchester. I know you thought that was Randall, but it wasn't, was it?'

Mollie picked up the newspaper with the photofit and tapped the anonymous face with her forefinger. Karen saw that the once-varnished nail was cracked and broken at the tip.

'It's this person. It has to be,' Mollie said. 'Did the man in Winchester ever rape anyone?'

Karen stared at the sketch. It didn't look much like Annie, but then it didn't look much like anyone else either.

The painting of the chasm was full of power. Finished and done with. Lisa stared at it, thinking, I can move on now. Draw a line under Randall and everything he did, and move on.

She looked longingly at her phone, aching to talk to her father. It seemed cruelly ironic that now she was ready to be with him once more, knowing she could cope on her own, he'd disappeared.

When she'd failed to get a number for any new mobile registered in his name, she'd phoned his office. They'd told her he'd left the Island three years ago 'after his divorce' and they didn't know where he was working now. His name wasn't in any of the internet phone directories, and when she'd Googled him, there'd been no hits at all.

She thought of his voice when he'd told her all she had to do was call and he'd come to John o' Groats or Land's End to find her.

Had he been lying then? Or had something happened to him?

Her mother would know. Lisa tried to imagine herself phoning the boutique to ask about him, and knew that even now she couldn't cope with the fallout. She'd have to fake a voice and pretend to be someone else.

She thought of the way Jed and his brother talked, and she practised their long vowels and soft consonants. Eventually she was satisfied, picked up the phoned and dialled.

'Sally Fane?' said the all-too recognizable voice, rising at the end to imply the question: how may I help?

'I'd like to talk to Robert Fane.' Lisa sounded pleasantly West Country to her own ears.

'He has no connection with this number.' Sally's voice had hardened and no longer invited anything.

'He's won a prize,' Lisa said, remembering all the dozens of unsolicited selling phone calls she'd had before she'd registered with the Phone Preference Service. 'But the mobile phone number given on his raffle ticket has been disconnected.'

'His bad luck then. What kind of prize?' Sally sounded marginally more interested.

'A holiday in the West Indies. All expenses paid. There's a voucher.'

'Send the voucher here,' Sally said, with a whole new eagerness. 'I'll do my best to forward it.'

'We're not allowed.' Lisa was thinking as she spoke. 'So if you give me the address you'd send it on to, I can do it from here and you won't be troubled.'

Sally banged down the phone, leaving her daughter staring out into the garden, wondering how her parents had ever got together in the first place. By the time she'd been old enough to notice anything, she'd seen how much they loathed each other, how they'd carried on a kind of war all the time.

If she wanted him, she was going to have to go back to the Island.

All her sketches for the transformation of the chalet there were spread over the work table in the window. The teardrop shape she'd planned for the whole site worked on paper, but she would need to see the ground again for herself.

She shook out the large map of the Island and pinned it to the cork board beside the table, adding more red-topped pins to show where she'd want the trees felled. Then she looked around for her digital camera, which still held all the photographs she'd taken of the site.

The camera wasn't anywhere in the studio. She couldn't remember where she'd put it, but it had to be somewhere in the house. She locked up and set off across the garden.

The unseasonable sun had failed her today and a slow warm drizzle fell on her as she left the studio for the short walk back to the house. Already it had made muddy puddles in the bald patches in the grass, where the ancient mower had got stuck and ground its blade deeper and deeper into the roots. And in one of the bald patches was a large male footprint. Beyond it were fainter marks in the grass. This time, someone had actually been in the garden.

Lisa stared at the line of prints, shuddering and feeling a lurch in her gut that made her think she might throw up again.

Slugs were oozing their way over the ragged stone edgings. And the sky was like lead. She didn't know what to do, where to turn, who could help. Except Jed.

She hoped he would come round tonight. She looked over her shoulder towards his fields, but she couldn't see anything moving there, except for the usual birds, pecking at whatever was left after the harvest. Maybe she should phone and ask him if he'd been in the garden.

The idea got her moving again. She kicked off her shoes by the kitchen door, padding inside in her socks to dial his number on the landline. His phone rang and rang. But then it often did when he was out of the house. After ten rings, she heard his voice in the familiar message. She waited till it was over, then said: 'Hi, Jed, it's me, about five o'clock. I'm thinking of cooking this evening. D'you want to come and share it with me? Should be ready seven-ish. Let me know.'

Sometimes he cut in while she was leaving a message, sounding breathless from his run to the phone, but today she got to finish without interruption. He never left a phone ringing where he could hear it. She put down the receiver, feeling lonely for the first time since she'd come here.

She couldn't remember why she'd left the studio and wandered round the kitchen, touching things, picking them up, only to put them down. She filled the kettle and switched it on, even though she knew it wasn't tea that had brought her indoors. All the makings for that were available in the studio as well.

'Camera,' she said aloud, remembering at last.

Normally it lived on the narrow shelf across the old chimney breast. But it wasn't there. Was it in one of her pockets? She shoved open the kitchen door, intending to feel in all her coats and jackets, which hung on pegs by the front door, but she was brought up short by the sight of an envelope, lying on the mat, addressed to her in Jed's childish writing.

For nearly a minute she stood, only realizing that she'd stopped breathing when her head began to swim. Forcing the breath back into her lungs, feeling her brain steady only a few moments later, she bent down to pick up the envelope. Even then she couldn't make herself open it. The sense of heaviness got worse. She knew trouble was coming.

In the old days, before Randall, she'd been up for anything. Now she knew better. She tried to think of the worst thing Jed could have written so that she'd be able to deal with it. As soon as she was sure she could manage the news that he'd decided she and her mashed-up body were more than he could cope with, she tore open the envelope.

A single card slipped out of it with two lines of straggly, badly formed writing:

Lisa, I've got to deal with something. If you need anything phone my brother at the pub. I love you. Jed.

She slumped into the nearest chair and re-read the card, trying to see in it far more than was there.

What was he doing?

Chapter 18

'All's well, Karen!' Al's voice was light and bouncy with triumph.

'What do you mean?' she said, her mind still stuck in the turgid undergraduate essay she was supposed to be marking. She'd got through a pile on the train back from London, but there were still five to go.

'They've got someone for Gyre's murder,' Al said.

Karen's focus snapped back. Her mind speeded up and her eyes saw more clearly. She tried not to imagine Charlie giving up his secrets to the head of Major Crimes.

'Who?' Her voice didn't shake, but it did catch in her throat. She coughed to clear it and asked her question again.

'God knows,' Al said, puzzled. 'Does it matter?'

'Of course it matters!' Karen suppressed the insult that was so vivid in her mind she couldn't believe he wouldn't sense it.

'Hold on,' Al, said, then: 'I've got the email here. He's called Gerald Boulting, known as Jed. Visitor to the Island. Tourist.'

Thank God! Karen thought, without any irreverence at all. A stranger with no connection to any of us. Thank *God*.

'Has he said why he did it?' she asked, wondering if the news was just too good to be true.

'He was passing the alleyway beside the pub when he heard a girl scream,' Al said jerkily, as though he was reading from the report as he spoke. 'Ran into the alley. Saw what was happening. Tried to pull the man off. Couldn't. Grabbed the only weapon he could find, which was a broken bottle, and dragged the guy's head up by his hair and slashed his throat. Hold on a minute. I've got a quote somewhere.'

The rustling of papers came clearly down the line. Then Al's voice again: 'Yeah. Great. Here it is: "'It was all I could think of to do,' Boulting said." What more could we possibly want, Karen?'

'What does he say about the other killings? Tod and Doctor Franklin?' She needed to know there was something that would shut up DCI Kent and all the other wankers behind him who must have decided Charlie had turned killer to get the revenge the courts were incapable of offering.

'Nothing,' Al said. 'When the question arose . . . hold on, it's here somewhere . . . Yeah. Right. When they asked Boulting, he said he'd never heard of either of them, and the interviewing officers believed him.'

'Bummer,' Karen said.

'Tiresome,' Al agreed. 'But Gyre has to be a credible suspect for both Tod and the doctor.'

'Why? You were so keen to make sure he wasn't in the frame before,' Karen said, hating the way Al and his colleagues shifted their ground whenever it was convenient.

'He's dead now.'

'So that makes it all right, does it?'

'No need to be like that, Karen,' Al said, sounding much younger and more human than usual. 'He probably did kill them. And now, in perfect serendipity, we've had a passing Good Samaritan putting a stop to his violence for ever. Let's count our blessings.'

'But . . .' Karen didn't get a chance to make her protest.

'We'll make sure the Good Samaritan gets a decent Legal Aid team. At best he'll get off altogether; at worst he'll do a short stretch in prison for manslaughter and come out a hero.'

'The stretch would be a lot shorter if he'd gone straight to the police.' Karen knew there was no point trying to force Al to forget his responsibility for the management of bad news. 'What does he say about that?'

'Panicked at the sight of all the blood,' Al said, rustling his papers again as he read from his notes. 'Didn't think about anything except getting away from the scene. Now realizes he should've stayed around to help the girl. Troubled about her. And so on. Sounds like a basically good bloke, and just exactly what we want. With this confession, no one could say you'd incited vigilantes. So you're off the hook.'

'I was never on it, whatever you all tried to suggest.' Karen thought of the only other member of her study who could still cause her real trouble. 'By the way, I assume John Clarence hasn't committed any new violent crime while I've been working on this. I know Dave's sure he will, but you'd have told me, wouldn't you, Al?'

'You can be sure of it.' A hint of self-consciousness in his voice suggested guilt. 'If I'm told anything else, I'll let you know at once. I can promise you that much. Bye.'

Karen got up from her desk and walked to the window, to stare out towards the Island, wondering why Charlie hadn't phoned her with the news of Boulting's confession. Wasn't that the first thing a friend would do? With the confession, the investigation must have slowed down, if not actually stopped. Charlie should have had plenty of time to phone. He knew how interested she was, professionally and, now, personally. *Why* hadn't he phoned?

She picked up her own mobile, ready to call him, then stopped. If he didn't want to talk, there had to be a reason. Hating every idea in her mind, she went back to her desk and reached for the next essay in her marking pile, tried to concentrate and found she couldn't.

Grabbing her keys instead, she locked up and went along the gloomy corridor to the corner of the building, where Max lurked.

As head of department, he got two windows and twice the office space she'd been allocated.

As soon as she knocked, she heard his growling, off-putting command to come in, then pushed open the door and looked round it, ready to back away if he had a student.

He was alone. At the sight of her, his expression lightened and he heaved himself out of his chair to welcome her.

'Perfect timing,' he said, leaning over to kiss her cheek. 'I'm all ready to wring necks.'

Karen put both hands round her throat. 'You're not having mine.'

'Clot,' he said. 'Come on in, sit down and tell me what's up. You look like a virgin being offered to the highest bidder.'

'What a disgusting simile, Max. You want to be careful or you'll be up on a sex discrimination charge.'

'You're far too sensible to take it like that. Or file it to use against me when we're competing for some plum job in the future.' He laughed again. 'Sit down and tell me what's scaring you so much.'

Karen perched on the edge of the chair opposite his laden desk, then made herself relax into it, stretching out her long legs in their skinny pink jeans.

'That's better.' Max looked a little kinder. 'Want some advice?'

'No. I mean, yes. Oh, fuck it.'

'This isn't like you, Karen. Your language is mostly purer than that, and you can usually fake confidence brilliantly. Is it Will? Or your students? No. You're not fretting over them. This Island house purchase?'

She said nothing.

'How's the competition going?' Max's big dark eyes were acute in their pouchy sockets. 'I ran into Stella the other day at the Vice Chancellor's drinks and she said she'd already had forty enquiries. Amazing.'

'Yes.' Karen could talk about this without any problem. 'She thinks if we get half that number of actual entries we'll be doing well. But she's had three already, which is fab in such a short time.'

'Any good?' Max didn't sound particularly interested, but Karen was so she answered.

'Two are dreary. But one's quite exciting, which may be because it doesn't come from an actual architect.'

'So it's not that,' Max said, much more interested now. 'Man trouble?'

Karen shifted in her chair. 'Did you *have* to tell Will I had the hots for my police mate on the Island?'

Max's eyebrows rose, which always made his dark face look positively satanic. And he laughed, which wasn't what she wanted at all.

'A bit near the knuckle, was it?' he said. 'I was only speculating. But I'm glad to see I haven't lost my touch.'

'You shouldn't speculate with laymen. They always take shrinks' ideas far too seriously. And personally. Will thought you were telling him I'm shagging Charlie.'

A hint of reddish colour seeped into Max's cheeks, but he wasn't going to admit to embarrassment. He never did.

'Aren't you?' he said, hitting back as usual.

Karen scowled at him. Why shouldn't she and Charlie be friends, just because she found him attractive and they enjoyed the same kind of jokes? If he'd been a woman friend – like Stella – would everyone assume Karen was about to leap into bed with her? Of course not! Could you never be ordinarily affectionate with someone of the opposite sex? Did gay couples feel jealous about each other's same-sex friends?

'Aren't you, Karen?' Max said again, looking even more sharply at her.

'No, I'm bloody not! I wish you'd all leave me alone.'

'All? Who else has been accusing you of infidelity to the brilliant Will?'

'Only you and Stella. Did you cook this up together at the Vice Chancellor's drinks party?' Karen detested the thought. They were her two closest friends at the university, and she'd trusted them both.

'Is that it then? If so, I'm busy,' he said, neither apologizing nor giving her any comfort.

Was that why she'd come? Had she wanted to lay out her anxieties about Charlie and hear Max tell her she was way off-beam? If so, she'd screwed up. He wasn't going to give her anything now.

'I suppose so.' She got to her feet, smoothing the well-fitting jeans down her long thin thighs. 'See you later.'

'Karen, wait.'

But she wouldn't wait. There was no help to be had here.

She needed to know that Charlie was going to emerge from the current crisis intact. If he had been screwing with the investigation on the Island in order to protect Annie, he could lose his job. Or, worse, face criminal charges.

With the unknown Boulting's confession accepted by everyone, she should be able to relax. But it was hard. She couldn't stop herself generating all sorts of questions. The worst two were: could anyone really believe that a passing stranger, however well-intentioned, would grab a rapist by his hair and slit his throat with a handily broken bottle? And would such a casual passer-by just happen to have by him the white rubber gloves Bella had described?

Neither question could be answered. But there was one thing she could do at once to make herself feel better. Leaning against the wall, she pulled out her phone and texted Will.

R U free this wkend? Cnt w8 2 c u.

Lisa turned over the flower pot outside Jed's front door. There were his keys, as usual. She picked them up and walked round to the back of the house. No one ever used the front door, which was bolted from the inside, top and bottom.

The mortice key turned easily in the oiled lock. She lifted the latch and pushed open the door, almost falling over his muddy boots. Had he come back?

'Jed?' she called, excited by the flood of relief she felt. 'Jed, when did you get in?'

Silence. She righted his boots, wiped her own feet and looked through the open door into the kitchen, calling his name again. Again she had no answer.

Everything in the shabby kitchen was tidy. She walked right inside the room and saw a small towel wedged between the ancient fridge and its chipped door. She pulled the door open to see clean, empty shelves. The motor didn't hum and the light didn't come on. He'd cleared it, washed it down and switched it off. She whirled round to look at the cooker, a second-hand electric one she'd helped him buy on eBay when he'd decided to stop using the fuel-hungry Rayburn. The cooker was turned off at the wall, too, and the burners looked scoured.

This kind of meticulous clearing-up was no spur-of-the-moment thing. This had been planned.

She tried the cold tap at the sink and found he'd turned off the water, too. Walking through the connecting door into the living room, she found everything tidy. No dust marked any of the surfaces. Nothing offered any hint of where he could be or what he was doing.

The ground floor had one more room, which he'd never shown her. Feeling like Bluebeard's last wife, Lisa tried the door handle. The spindle turned easily and the door yielded to her push. Inside, she found a study, with a desk piled with papers and folders. A thick red hard-backed book turned out to be a record of all his business purchases written up in the same straggly letters that could have been made by a six-year-old. Another file had copies of old tax returns in it, more professionally written up by Fred, who acted as his brother's accountant. Lisa didn't look closely at any of the figures; she wasn't a spy. The phone had an integral answering machine, and the light was winking. But the only message was the one she'd just left.

Upstairs, Jed's bedroom and bathroom were again spookily tidy. He'd even stripped the bed and folded the duvet flat beneath the bedspread. The bath was clean. In the spare room the bed was covered with newspapers.

She had never seen him read a paper in all the time she'd been in the village. His lack of interest in what went on in the world beyond it was one of the things that had made him feel so safe.

Lisa had to make an almost physical effort to force her eyes downwards so that she could read the headlines.

Randall Gyre. Randall Gyre. Every single one spelled out his name. And every front page showed his face.

Randall Gyre murdered.

Rapist dead.

Vigilante killing.

Lisa's hand was round her throat, holding down the pain. She read every single word of the first newspaper Jed had saved, her mind churning and ripping up one idea after another, like a massive wood-chipper, and her body reliving every moment she'd spent in the alley behind the pub: four years ago and last week.

Rapist's throat slit in flagrante. Last victim traumatized.

Her mind rebelling at last, she subsided on to the floor, closing her eyes in a pathetic attempt to block out everything else.

Rapist's throat slit in flagrante. Last victim traumatized.

She longed to faint, but consciousness had her in the toughest grip and wouldn't let her go. She got to her feet at last and stood, pressing her back against the wall, staring at the papers now strewn untidily all over Jed's spare bed.

'What have you done?' she whispered into the empty silence all round her.

When she'd got some control of herself, she picked up another paper and for the first time learned that there had been other victims. One was a doctor, who wanted to stay as anonymous as she had been throughout Randall's pointless trial for assaulting her.

I was a student when I met Gyre. He was fun, charming. I thought he liked me, so I went for a drink with him. Then he raped me. When it was over, he said he'd kill me if I ever told.

Even so, I tried to tell. No one believed me. The jury accepted his story and let him off to do it again and again. I don't sleep well when I think of all those other women.

Tears bloomed in Lisa's eyes, hot and sharp. They spilled over to burn trails down her face. Her chest heaved and from the depths of her gut she howled and howled. All these years she hadn't been alone after all. Other people out there knew what she knew, had felt what she'd felt, and tried to deal with it the same way. If only they'd known each other, she and this doctor. They could have talked. Everything would have been different then.

Fighting the tears, Lisa tried to get past everything she was feeling to work out what Jed must be doing now. It was impossible not to see a link between these papers and his letter.

Had he guessed what she wanted to do to Randall once he was out of prison? Or had she said something in her sleep?

Her knees folded at the thought and she hunkered down, rocking slightly, thinking back to the evening when she'd woken to find Jed in her bed, his hands clamped between his thighs so that he couldn't reach out in his sleep to touch and trouble her. Nothing in the way he'd looked or spoken when he'd been awake suggested that she could have said anything that night.

He'd even traced the scars on her breasts with one steady finger, telling her that nothing about her could ever disgust him, whatever she believed, that he loved her and would never hurt her. That he would do anything in the world to protect her and make her feel safe.

Was that what he was doing now? Trying to make her safe?

She couldn't leave all these papers for someone else to see. Anyone could find his keys and get into the house, just as she had. And, if they did, they mustn't find these. No one must know he had any interest in Randall.

Grabbing all the tear-soaked sheets of paper, she scrumpled them into a ball she shoved up under her shirt. Then she saw the bottom ones, photocopies of much, much older versions of the same papers, published at the time of her own ordeal in court. Jed must have gone to the local reference library to look them up. Who would have guessed he'd even think of that?

She looked down at the headlines:

Lizzie Fane gives up anonymity.

Lizzie Fane.

Lizzie Fane victim.

Lizzie Fane bottled and left for dead.

Lizzie Fane.

She'd never told him she'd changed her name, that she'd invented the identity of Lisa Raithe so she could start life again as a new person. What exactly had the discovery made him do?

'This is Doctor Karen Taylor,' Charlie said to the suspect in the interview room, as the friendly custody sergeant left them alone with him. 'Doctor Taylor, this is Jed Boulting.'

Karen looked at the tall man and liked his kindly, guileless face. His eyes were hazel, his skin clear, with the reddish look that came from spending large amounts of time in the wind and rain out of doors, and his roughly cut hair was mid-brown with a slight curl. He was dressed like a countryman who had tidied himself up for a day in the city, in an ancient, over-large suit of sludge-green tweed and a cream flannel shirt with a faint green and grey check. In spite of the kindness of his expression, he didn't look comfortable.

He had not yet been formally charged, but Charlie had said it was only a matter of time and the tidying up of one or two trivial loose ends.

'She is a forensic psychologist,' he went on, 'and she'd like to ask you a few questions. Is that OK? You don't have to answer any of them.'

'I don't mind,' the suspect said in a slow voice with a strong West Country accent. 'What do you want to know, Miss?'

'It's the gloves that worry me,' Karen said pleasantly. 'I just don't understand where they came from.'

'My pocket, of course.' Boulting was frowning a little, as though trying to understand a worryingly hard mathematical problem.

'So they're a pair you often used, are they?' Karen understood now why Charlie's voice was so gentle. This man exuded both simplicity and a sense of decency that would have made any aggression an outrage.

'Sometimes. I usually work in my bare hands, but sometimes I have to use gloves.' He showed them his hands. 'With big thorns and that.'

The broad hands looked very strong with swollen knuckles and callused skin that was covered with scars. He'd cut and scraped himself often; burned himself too, Karen thought. But she couldn't be sure whether the burns were from fires or chemicals.

'Where are the gloves now?' she asked.

He smiled, looking no less innocent. 'I threw them in the sea. Put a stone in each and threw them over the side of the ferry. Disgusting they were. Blood all over.'

'Where did you buy them originally?' Karen asked.

'I don't remember. Mole Valley probably. I get most of my stuff there. Farmers do.'

'Can you describe the gloves?'

'I don't think much about clothes. Just wear what comes to hand. They could've been green. Like the jacket,' he added, gesturing to his lumpy suit. 'Most things I get from Mole Valley are green.'

'Were the gloves leather?'

'No. Cloth. I don't have leather gloves. Brown rubber ones for spraying. Otherwise thermal.' His delivery was speeding up. Karen couldn't decide whether that was because he was telling the truth or getting excited by lies. 'I get chillblains when it's cold. Makes everyone at home laugh at me.'

'That seems unfair,' she said with absent-minded warmth. 'Can I ask what you were doing on the Island?'

'Having a holiday.' He beamed at her as though she were a charming baby in a pram. 'A bit late for that, I know, but we farmers can't go away when everyone else does. I've done my harvest, so I've some spare time. My village – the one where I live – well, it feels a bit stuffy sometimes. I like to get away. Day trips and that. Thought I'd try the Isle of Wight this time. Sunniest place in the UK, they say.'

'So they do,' Karen said. 'How well did you know Randall Gyre?'

'Never met him or seen him in my life. I didn't know who he was, nor anything about him. It was the girl. She sounded so scared when she screamed.'

Karen glanced at Charlie, who was looking at his feet, clearly unhappy.

'When she screamed,' Boulting repeated, 'I had to go and see what was wrong. Anyone would have.'

You're wrong there, Karen thought, remembering Charlie's story of the two delinquent constables who'd ignored the original report of Lizzie's screaming. But she could see how any jury would swallow this account of what had happened when Randall died. They'd love it – and they'd love Boulting too.

'Then why didn't you stay and help her after you'd cut the man's throat?' she asked, as though she was trying to tease out the meaning in a convoluted lecture.

'Shock,' Boulting said, with a pleading note in his voice, as though he longed for her to believe him. 'I never meant to kill him, just wanted to make him stop hurting her. Like I told the other officers before. When I saw all that blood, I panicked and went home.'

'And you a farmer! You must be used to blood,' Karen said.

He laughed, a slow, gentle rumble of amusement. 'Not that kind. I grow vegetables. Never birthed a calf or killed a pig in my life. I wouldn't know how.'

'Thank you, Mr Boulting. You've been helpful.'

'Is that it, miss?'

'Yes. Thank you.'

'Do you know what'll happen to me now?' He sounded only a little concerned, not afraid or anxious; just interested to know.

Karen looked at Charlie, who gave her no help. Surely Boulting was exactly the kind of man who'd get bail, even for murder, and this would have to be manslaughter at the very worst. No one could imagine he would go on to kill again or flee – or even harm himself. And his attack on Randall had saved Bella.

'It's not my decision,' Karen said. 'But I can't see why they'd want to keep you here for very much longer.'

His face creased for a second, then smoothed out as though it had been ironed. His smile returned too.

'Goodbye,' she said, before sweeping out of the interview room ahead of Charlie.

'Your colleagues are mad,' she said as soon as they were out of earshot of everyone else. 'That man never killed anyone. And his attempt to describe the gloves was hopeless. He couldn't have been anywhere near the scene of Randall's death. What are they thinking of?'

'Getting an embarrassing case out of the way as quickly as possible,' Charlie said. 'All Major Crimes teams like doing that. Good for targets and box-ticking.'

'Is an uncorroborated confession enough for a conviction these days?' Karen said.

'Technically. Though you can run into problems if they decide to retract it and you haven't got anything else to give the jury. The CPS like a bit more, just in case. That must be why Boulting hasn't been charged yet.'

'So can't you just let things take their course? If he didn't do it, Major Crimes aren't going to find any evidence. If they do, then maybe you and I are both wrong and he's not as innocent as he seems.'

Charlie frowned. 'Evidence isn't always what it looks like. You know that. Boulting was here on the Island that day. He's still got his day-return ferry tickets; paid with a credit card. He even had a lunchtime drink in the Eagle and Dumpling. He's on the CCTV. That's probably enough. And he must've had a good reason to go there – his muddle over the gloves could be shock. Maybe he really doesn't think about clothes or remember what he's wearing. He's not the sharpest pin in the box.'

'Any of his DNA found in the alleyway? That would settle it.'

'The lab's got the crime-scene samples.' Charlie was beginning to sound impatient. 'Hasn't been time to get results yet.'

'You'll get your answer when they come through. Let's go and eat,' Karen said, tucking one hand into the crook of his elbow, 'and we can talk about it. The Goose Inn?'

He looked at her in silence, a long analytical examination of her face. She tried to keep her expression bland, to show him nothing of what had been worrying her so much about him and Annie.

'Why not?' he said at last.

Chapter 19

Wednesday, 15 October, 8 p.m.

The evening wasn't quite warm enough to make outdoor eating comfortable, so they took a table in the window of the Goose Inn, as far as possible from the cheerful drinkers at the bar. After a short consultation, they both ordered Peg's latest special – a pancake filled with wild rabbit and mushrooms – and salad, with a pint of her home-brew for Charlie and a glass of Sauvignon Blanc for Karen. Peg poured their drinks, then brought the food and left them alone, as though she could tell they needed space and time for something private.

'What'll happen to Boulting?' Karen said, picking up the conversation they had broken off as they left the police station. 'I'm right, aren't I, that even if they believe his story and the CPS decide to go to trial, they'll have to let him go home in the meantime?'

'Yeah.'

'I still can't see them getting a conviction,' she added, frowning. 'Even if the prosecution persuade the jury he did it, any halfway decent defence counsel should be able to make them see he had no intent to kill. Randall was vicious, and Boulting saved the girl.'

Karen watched Charlie's immobile face, wishing she could see some of the old wickedness in his eyes, even a twitch of his lips, to show they were on the same side and he wasn't hiding something big from her.

'*Whoever* killed him,' she said with deliberate warmth, 'saved a terribly vulnerable victim. Anyone can see that. Anyone would understand.'

'Can't trust juries,' he said with difficulty. 'Or lawyers. They can twist any word to mean its opposite. I hope to Christ Boulting *doesn't* go down.'

Why? Karen thought. Because you liked him or because you know that Annie killed Randall in a way that would leave no evidence, and you don't want an innocent like Boulting taking the rap for her?

'He certainly convinced your Major Crimes colleagues that he did it,' she said aloud, watching Charlie with close attention. 'But there wasn't anything in his confession that hadn't been in the papers, was there?'

'Nope.' Charlie looked unhappier still.

'Which means he could have read about everything he's claimed to have done. And Major Crimes wanted to be convinced, didn't they?'

Charlie nodded, not looking at her.

'So why aren't you going along with them?' Karen asked as casually as she could. 'You always used to be so keen on increasing your figures for serious crimes solved.'

'That's crap.' For a second he did meet her gaze. She flinched. His jaw muscles were pumping at the base of his cheeks in a way she'd once known well.

'And you should know better than to try to make me swallow it,' he went on fiercely.

'*Why*, Charlie?'

'Because I don't give a shit about getting a case through the courts if it's a dodgy one. I don't give a shit about the crime figures.'

Karen looked at the condensation forming on the outside of

her wine glass and trickling down its stem, to puddle around the base. After a moment, she looked up again to meet his round dark eyes. They quickly shifted to the side so that he didn't have to see her watching him so closely.

'So you *want* the truth to come out?' Karen was hesitating because she couldn't see how to preserve their friendship, a friendship that mattered more and more to her, the nearer she got to smashing it for good.

If her fears about what he'd been doing for Annie were real, she'd always worry about his motives for anything he did and said to her. And if she was wrong and he ever realized what she'd thought, he'd hate her.

'Doesn't everyone with a brain want the truth?' he said, still not looking at her. His voice was more tentative than usual, as though he was hoping she'd disagree.

'Not always,' Karen said painfully. 'After all . . .'

'Oh, don't give me any more shrinky crap. I've had it up to fucking here.'

'I wasn't going to, Charlie. I was going to say there were obviously people involved in what Daisy Clarke did to you who didn't want the truth coming out. You must have been very angry about that.'

His hand tightened around the beer glass as he hissed, 'What the fuck's Daisy got to do with this? And who the fuck's been talking to you about *her*?' His eyes narrowed and for an instant they flickered towards Karen. 'Not Annie?' He paused for at least two beats, then said even more painfully, 'She wouldn't. Not now.'

Karen licked her lips, wishing she'd never started this.

'I bounced her into it,' she admitted. 'Didn't mean to. I had to ask her something completely different and I phoned late-ish, when she'd . . .'

'Downed a bottle or three? Stupid cow. And you took advantage. Fuck!' Charlie glugged down some beer, put down the glass and wiped his hands over his furious eyes. When he faced Karen again, some of the ferocity had left his expression. 'I wish she'd kept her fucking mouth shut.'

'But why? There's no shame in what happened, Charlie. You tried to help Daisy and she turned on you. Then you were sacrificed to save the Met from yet another embarrassing sex-related internal case. She's still safely at the heart of things in London, while you're stuck in a backwater here. *Anyone* would be angry.'

'I told you, I could've gone back. They asked me. But I like the Island now.' His voice was angry all over again. 'Why're you doing this, Karen? Why now? What the fuck're you trying to make me say?'

'Nothing,' she said, faster than her mind could work. Then she tried to retract it but couldn't choose words that would ask the right questions.

Suspicion was spreading through his expression; suspicion and something else that was even more worrying. She'd blown it now. All of it.

'Oh, I see.' Charlie sounded more bitter than cyanide. 'You think I'm capable of slitting a man's throat to punish him for carrying out for real the kind of rape *I* was accused of by a mad stalker. That it?'

'No, of course it isn't.' Karen felt as though she never wanted to probe anyone's mind ever again, however important the cause.

'It's worse then?' Charlie thought for a moment, staring at her with such hatred that Stella's fantasies seemed completely absurd.

'What could be worse?' Karen said, and got a harsh crack of laughter in return. She barely recognized his voice when he started to talk again.

'You think I *did* rape Daisy and feel so guilty I killed Gyre to punish him in the way my sub-whatsit, inner-fucking child, thinks *I* should be punished. Fucking shrinks.'

He pushed back his chair, with an ear-torturing noise as the rough wooden legs scraped along the stone floor, and grabbed his glass. Draining it as he strode to the bar, he called out to Peg from halfway across the room.

'Refill, please, pet. Ta.'

He stayed at the bar to pour half the drink straight down his throat. Then he came back to their table, walking as though through a heavy bog.

'Right. So what does your sneaky shrinky brain really want to ask?' Charlie's voice was loaded with dislike. 'Or say to me? We've got this far – you may as well go all the way.'

Karen wished she could tape his voice for Will. The sound should console him if he ever succumbed to another fit of point-less jealousy and suspicion.

'I couldn't understand why you'd give Lizzie's mother the time of day,' she said, feeling her way towards the important stuff about Annie. 'She's everything I'd have expected to drive you nuts: melodramatic, whiny, dependent on that emotional cripple of a doctor, and—'

'Christ! You're hard, Karen. You know, sometimes when you look at me with eyes like . . . oh, I don't know, pricey jewels, and a mouth like . . . I think I like you. Fuck that! You're only in any of this for curiosity, aren't you?'

Funny how anger and fear and sex can get so muddled up together, Karen thought, as all her instincts screamed at her to touch Charlie.

She heard Stella's voice in her head, urging her to encourage him, and she thought. This is how it starts – an indulgence, like a single cigarette for an ex-smoker. And the ending is almost certainly the emotional equivalent of some filthy lung disease. Don't go there. You so do not want to go there.

'Tell me about Daisy,' she said, more or less in control once more.

'I already did. Last time we worked together.'

He scratched his left ear hard enough to draw blood. Karen was about to ask a question when he added, 'Wasn't only me, you know. She'd done it to other blokes before. They weren't in the Job, though. My bad luck she did her thing when the top floor had to pretend to believe her.'

'But that doesn't explain—'

'Aren't you *ever* fucking satisfied?' Charlie's voice was raw, as though all his feelings had been scraped of their polite skin with a rasp. 'The past is past. Use that shrinky brain for something useful for once and tell me why Boulting's made a false confession.'

'The only explanation is that he's taking the rap for someone else.' Karen longed to say: 'Do you know of any connection between Boulting and Annie?' But she'd have to wait for that to emerge.

'Now you're talking,' Charlie said, looking a little happier. 'Who's the someone else?'

'One of Randall's victims?' Karen held up her left hand, ready to tick off each possibility on a different finger.

Charlie nodded.

'Or a friend – protector, maybe – of one of the victims?' she went on, bending the second finger and not looking at him. 'Or someone who just wanted Randall stopped and had given up hoping the police and courts would ever do it?'

'Any names to put to these theories?' Charlie's question sounded aggressive enough to stop Karen going any further.

'Not yet.' She shoved her fork into the pancake and ate another mouthful. It was cold and its stuffing had congealed, which made it hard to swallow. When she'd got it down, she looked at him and said: 'You know, I'm almost sure there's only one killer, or maybe a pair working together, who did Tod and Doctor Franklin and now Randall himself. When we've found the motive that explains all three, we'll know who it is.'

Charlie didn't answer. Light footsteps sounded beside them. Karen dragged her gaze away from his unreadable face and looked up to see Peg bending towards her, a long soft hand on Charlie's shoulder.

'Everything all right?' she asked, glaring at Karen as though warning her to treat him kindly.

'Perfect,' Karen said with a smile that took a lot of hard work to produce.

'No.' Charlie's grin was like a skull's. 'She's killing me.'

Peg's lovely face creased into an uncomprehending frown.

'Only joking, pet,' Charlie said after a moment.

'Fine.' Peg looked a little embarrassed. 'Shout if you want more drinks.' She hurried back to the bar and the easy company of her gently soaking regulars.

Karen looked at her watch. She couldn't take much more of this. Standing up, she said, 'I ought to think about getting back. I'll ask Peg to call me a cab. D'you want one too?'

'You saying I'm too drunk to drive? After two pints?' Charlie's voice wasn't remotely slurred and his eyes were still bright, and restless. He got to his feet, too.

'Two pints of something as strong as Peg's home brew must represent some vast number of units these days.' Karen hated this and wanted to get away from him fast. 'Six or something? But I've no idea what your capacity is, and it's none of my business anyway.'

Charlie shrugged and turned away. But after a moment he looked back at her with a ghost of his familiar wicked smile.

'I could always share your cab back to Cowes and get a colleague to drive me here tomorrow to pick up the car.'

Karen needed to get home before she did or said something that would ruin it all for ever. She hurried out of the pub and Charlie followed her.

'Or you could stay with me tonight, Karen . . .' He paused, but only to screw up the tension another notch. 'That way, you'd be around if they do charge that poor bastard Boulting. You can tell them they're wrong. They'll believe *you*.'

'No, they wouldn't. In any case, I have no standing. And I have to get back to Southampton tonight.' She moved towards the bar.

'Why? Can't trust yourself?' He laughed, and the sound was singularly unpleasant. Then he grabbed her arm and swung her round to face him. 'You could look on it as a test of your feelings for Will.'

She pulled her arm to get away from him. He held on, and she realized that if he didn't choose to let her go, her strength was not enough to free herself. It was a horrible discovery. Unless she called on Peg for help, all she had to use in her own defence were words. She did her best, manufacturing a light amusement: 'I don't need to test them. But I *am* going home.'

'So, Will's won again, has he?'

'Not Will,' she said, keeping her voice steady even though the blood rushed into her cheeks. 'It's my students. I have a seminar first thing in the morning, and I haven't done nearly enough work to prepare.'

'No excuse,' he said, but his voice carried a little less derision. 'You must've covered the same topic every year since you've been at Southampton. What is it about?'

'Guilt.'

He laughed, then put his hands either side of her face and kissed her before she realized what he was doing.

His lips felt warm but rougher than hers. She meant to stand absolutely still until he pulled back, not offering any encouragement or excitement-inducing resistance, but she discovered she had muscles and nerve endings she couldn't control. He took his hands from her face so that he could wrap both arms around her body and still use one hand to hold the back of her head.

How had he known that her greatest pleasure was having her head held?

When he withdrew a little way, she saw that he was smiling, closed her eyes and let her head rest, just for a moment, on his shoulder.

Chapter 20

Lisa was standing outside the pub, nerving herself to go in and face Fred. Opening time at the Old Sheep's Head during the week was six-thirty and there were still ten minutes to go, but she could hear him moving around the bar, and all the lights were on. What she had to ask him had to be private. But she didn't want him teasing her about it, or leering at her.

Still, it had to be done. She gripped the cold iron ring to bang it down hard.

'We're not open yet.' Fred's voice was unmistakable.

'It's me, Fred. Jed told me to come.'

She heard bolts being drawn back, then saw Fred standing in the open doorway, a blue-and-white-striped butcher's apron stretched across his ample gut.

'Come on in, girl. He asked me to look after you but not to crowd you – which is why I haven't come knocking on your door. Yet. Come on in. What can I get you? On the house.'

'Nothing, thanks.'

'You look like you need something. You're all white and shivery. Have a drop of ginger wine with some whisky in it – warm you up.'

She shuddered. 'Sorry,' she said quickly. 'I hate ginger. I'll have a glass of wine please. Anything that's open and red.'

'Come on, then. Sit by the fire. I know it's not cold yet, but you can feel the nip in the air. Autumn's on the way. Soon have the mists back to hide in.'

He walked behind the bar and started fiddling with bottle and glasses.

'I need to talk to you, Fred – in private,' Lisa said from the fire. 'Can we leave the drinks till later?'

'No one's going to come till near seven,' he said. 'We'll have a drink and that'll settle you and make it easier.'

'Make what easier?' said Lisa. How much did he know?

'I don't know, do I? Jed didn't tell me anything except he had to go away. Worried about you, he was, so he left you to me. Brave man, trusting me with his girlfriend. Ha!'

'When did he say all this?' Lisa ignored the innuendo and Fred's crack of laughter. Her heart felt as though it was shrivelling.

'Yesterday, just before he went off.' Fred hesitated, his hand still wiping the top of a newly uncorked bottle of wine. 'First thing in the morning, with him looking just like he did that day you both went wherever it was last week. Thursday, was it? No, Friday.'

'Jed went off somewhere last Friday?' she said, thinking, The day I was on the Island and Randall died. 'Where did he go?'

'Wouldn't tell me.' A hint of the familiar leer distorted Fred's unusually friendly expression. 'But you know, don't you? I saw you got home first, but I thought it was, like, discretion. Coming separately like that. Not that you need it here any more. Everyone knows about the two of you these days.'

'What *are* you talking about? I was on my own last Friday. Whatever Jed was doing had nothing to do with me.'

'That's what I thought when I saw your car passing early that morning. But I was wrong, wasn't I?'

'No.' She hated the way Fred kept grinning at her.

'Jed's old van clattered past half an hour or so later, so I knew he was following you.' This time Fred winked. 'I watched for the pair of you coming back. Six o'clock and you went past my windows. Hour or so later and it's Jed.'

Lisa remembered how she'd felt watched on the ferry when she'd been kicking her stained shoes and jacket into the sea. Had it been *Jed* who'd followed her and not the mysterious watcher who seemed to be hovering at the very limits of her peripheral vision wherever she went? If it had been Jed, what else had he seen? What else had he done?

'Too much of a coincidence, my girl.' Laughter erupted from Fred's huge belly and emerged in a mocking bellow. 'Why make such a fuss? Most of the village is really chuffed the two of you've got it together, even though you're a baby still. They all like Jed, simple though the poor sap can be.'

Lisa frowned, hating the idea that her every movement was monitored by her neighbours. How much would they tell the police if they came here asking about Jed? How much would Fred tell them?

'Don't look at me like that, girl. I'm chuffed too, like all the rest. Dead chuffed. You know,' he added, as though he thought she didn't understand him, 'pleased. I never see Jed so cock-a-hoop as when he looked in here that day. Tuesday, you know, when he'd been with you 'stead of working like he should've.'

With what Lisa recognized as real heroism, Fred refrained from winking at her this time. But she hated the thought that Jed might have come here straight from her bed to share the experience, even if Fred was his brother.

'I could see he'd do anything for you then,' he said, with a quiet kind of earnestness that convinced her. 'Anything.'

Her heart now felt the size of a pea and the temperature of her blood was dropping by the second.

'Like I say, girl, I'm dead chuffed. He's happy at last, poor sod. It's down to you. So you're welcome here whenever you want. You can ask me for anything.'

'Where is he now, Fred? I need to know. Where was he going when he put me in your charge?'

Fred shrugged his massive shoulders. 'Wouldn't say. Just told me there was something he had to do, and couldn't say when he'd be back.' Looking at her over his foaming tankard, he added more seriously, 'I was a bit shirty with him. He's never held out on me before. Then I saw it was to do with you and that was OK. I never seen him like this in his life before, you know, even when he was first in love with that bitch he married.'

Lisa fought to keep all her feelings hidden.

'I have to get in touch with him,' she said. 'He's never given me his mobile number because he said he hated using the thing, could never answer before it switched to voicemail so it panicked him. But I know he's got one. Have you got the number? Please give it to me, Fred. I need to talk to him.'

'Won't do you any good. Left the phone here with me. Don't ask me why. I told him he was mad, that whatever he was doing he'd need his phone. He said he wouldn't. What could I do? Drink up now, and I'll pour you another one. Like I say, he made me promise to look after you, so I'm thinking I'd better keep you here and feed you up. You look like the first gust of winter wind will blow you over.'

'Thanks, Fred,' she said, putting down her glass. It still had at least two-thirds of the wine in it. 'But I'd better get back. He may be trying to ring me.'

'Don't bet on it, love. Blokes don't like checking in with their women. Even if Jed was thinking of doing it, he couldn't. Left his phone with me, didn't he?'

Lisa abandoned him. Outside the pub, the air felt peculiarly clean. The first bite of cold was welcome on her flushed cheeks.

'Evening, Lisa!'

She whipped round at the sound of a deep friendly local voice, but it wasn't Jed standing behind her.

'Hi, Tommy,' she said, recognizing the local dairy farmer, standing beside his huge Rottweiler. The dog was growling deep in his throat, but for once Tommy had him on a lead so Lisa could relax. 'How are you?'

'Not so bad. Coming in for a drink?'

'Can't, I'm afraid. Got to get back. Bye.'

She almost ran back to her house, desperate for someone to trust, someone who could tell her what on earth to do now.

Karen looked around the bright, lively faces of her undergraduate students on Thursday morning and felt relieved at the sight of their mostly friendly expressions. They'd forgiven her. Today a pair of them were to give a ten-minute presentation on 'The Dangers in a Forensic Psychologist Coming to a Conclusion on the Guilt or Innocence of the Defendant'.

'Is it true you once knew this rapist who was killed on the Island last week?' asked Jules, a Scot from Dunblane, who was always ready to distract the group into byways she found more interesting than the advertised topic of the day.

The shuffling of bottoms on chairs and the increase in general alertness told Karen that they'd been discussing this among themselves. She decided to put their curiosity to some good use.

'Only in a professional way,' she assured them. 'I did meet him a couple of times.'

'What was he like?' Jules was a lot more interested than she should have been.

'Charming, and with all his destructive drives well-hidden. Since you're all more interested in him than in the subject of today's seminar, do you want to give me some reasons why he might have been killed?'

'Yeah, great.' This was Melvin, a sharp-faced Londoner with an ambition to work within the prison service. 'Actually, the obvious is revenge.'

'Revenge by one of his victims?' Karen said, well in control this morning, after a long session with Mozart's *Requiem* when she got back from the Island last night. 'Or do you share the press's idea of a vigilante, determined to stop him raping anyone else?'

Melvin gave the proposition its due, then shook his head. 'What do the press know? Specially the tabloids. I don't think any stranger's actually going to kill someone to protect women who're nothing to do with him.'

'Or her,' cut in Jules, who could never ignore any hint of what she could possibly interpret as misogyny.

'Or her,' he said with an exaggerated bow in her direction. 'Killing's always more self-interested than that.'

'Not always,' Karen said, looking from one to the other. They were her two most vocal students and she liked them both for it, even though some of their contributions were too wild to take seriously. 'There have been cases in which the preservation of the greater good has been the motive for murder. But what other ones could there be?'

'Greed. Lust. Money,' said Di, one of the quietest students. 'They're the classics. Then there are all the odd ones, like in that case – you know, from the thirties.'

'Which case is that, Di?' Karen asked, hoping she sounded as patient as she wanted to be. Di was perfectly clever and a lot more imaginative than many of the others, but she hadn't enough confidence, which meant her ideas would always be less well-received than theirs. And she hadn't yet learned to make a persuasive, detail-rich case without a lot of help.

'Not that one in which a man killed his wife over a bridge game because she made a stupid mistake?' Melvin said. 'He actually got off, you know, because the judge thought her stupidity was a reasonable excuse for any man to kill his wife.'

'*Actually*,' said Jules, using Melvin's favourite word with heavy sarcasm, 'the bridge-game killer was the wife; and the stupid victim, the husband. But she got off because her husband died after the "accidental" discharge of her firearm after he'd threatened to leave her. Nothing to do with the judge's views of over-ambitious bridge players.'

'Know-all,' said Melvin, laughing at her.

Jules's sense of humour often let her down, and Karen could see today was going to be one of those days.

'Never mind that now,' Karen said quickly, holding up a hand to keep Jules quiet. 'Di, which case *did* you mean?'

'I read about it after I'd looked up guilt on the internet,' she said breathily, looking at Karen with a pleading expression, as though she didn't expect to be believed. 'When I was getting ready for today. There's a book about it too. An insurance man in Liverpool killed his wife because he kind of felt so guilty for making her miserable.'

'Which leads us back towards the idea of guilt, the true and proper subject of this seminar,' Karen said with genuine approval. 'Great, Di. What had he done to her?'

'The website didn't give any details, just that he'd made her so unhappy he couldn't live with it, and so—'

'And so he killed *her*?' Jules's outrage was immense. 'He should have killed himself, like in *The Master Builder*.'

'It was only one of many theories.' This was the cool voice of Adam Palewski, who rarely contributed to any discussion but always made sense when he did.

Karen sometimes felt that he considered his brains and ideas rather too important to waste in discussions with people who were so far beneath him in terms of intellect, physical attributes, and class.

'The book Di's talking about was written in the 1950s,' Adam went on. 'In fact, Wallace – that's the insurance man's name – was so struck by Ibsen's play when he saw it that he wrote it up in his diary. But it doesn't have to mean what Di thinks. There've been other studies – more recent ones – showing that the killer was probably a neighbour. It'll never be sorted for sure now, so why waste time speculating?'

'Cold-case reviews are doing amazing work,' Karen said, to put him in his place and keep Di encouraged. 'The 1930s is a little out of range so far, but I can imagine – if the crime-scene evidence has been kept – there could be a chance in due course.'

'Actually, you're always reminding us that DNA evidence isn't fireproof,' Melvin said, taking his usual pleasure in pointing out a weakness in one of Karen's arguments. 'Which is why forensic psychology's so important.'

'True enough.' She longed for the hour to be over, but she owed them concentration. 'Now, after that interesting digression, let's get to the meat of today's business: the pitfalls for a psychologist about to give evidence in court. *Can* you do your work without forming an opinion about the guilt or innocence of the defendant? And why does it matter? Who wants to start? Di?'

When they'd all gone at last, Karen could let her own thoughts flood into the front of her mind again. She wished she hadn't been so quick to assume that Charlie could have been protecting Annie from the Major Crimes Unit, knowing she was a killer.

There had to be other suspects. Annie wasn't the only person outraged by the way Randall had never been properly punished for his crimes. The most obvious had to be the victims.

After a few minutes' careful analysis of the others, Karen picked up her phone to call Annie.

'Hi,' she said, sounding entirely sober for once. 'How's it going?'

'Not very positively. So I need some help.'

'Like what?'

'Don't sound so suspicious,' Karen said, having rehearsed this bit of disinformation in her head. 'I need to know more about Randall's m.o. The only person who could give me a truly accurate description is your friend, the surgeon.'

'No.' Annie didn't waste any energy being angry.

'All I want is her name and an introduction. You don't have to do anything or be there when I talk to her.'

'I told you, Karen – no, I won't do it. She's had enough. Leave her the fuck alone.'

'Come on,' Karen said, trying not to wheedle. 'Don't you want to know for sure whether Randall killed Tod?'

'Forensics'll show that in the end. When the lab reports, we'll know. You meeting Ca— *her* won't help. You'll just make it worse for her. And me.'

'You called her Ca . . . Catherine?' Karen suggested. 'Caroline?'

The phone was silent. Karen summoned up all her forces of persuasion.

'Annie, you must know I'll be tactful. I'm not going to wade in and torment her. But I need to talk to her. If you won't introduce me, just give me her name.'

'Catriona,' Annie said at last, the reluctance in her voice dragging out the syllables. 'Catriona Derby. Don't force yourself on her. And don't tell her I gave you her name. She's hurting, still.'

'I won't.' Karen could promise that. It was easy.

Half an hour later, biting into a magnificently chewy ciabatta filled with provolone, prosciutto and grilled red peppers, Karen speed-dialled Will's phone.

'Hi,' she said, through her mouthful. 'It's me.'

'I'd recommend swallowing gently and then talking,' he said, with enough amusement to show he'd got over his jitters – for the moment anyway. 'Otherwise you'll choke. I'm in no hurry. I can wait.'

Karen swallowed the inadequately chewed lump and felt it bump against the sides of her throat as it went down.

'Sorry,' she said. 'You answered more quickly than I expected. Have you ever come across a surgeon called Catriona Derby?'

'Don't think so. Should I have?'

'It'd be helpful if she was your friend.' Karen hesitated for a few seconds, then added, 'I need to ask her some tricky questions and I don't want to go in cold.'

'I won't ask why,' Will said. 'I know that voice of yours, and I don't want to make you lie to protect my feelings. I'll ask around and find a way to be pleased I'm doing something to help the police. I don't suppose you know her speciality, do you?'

'General surgery, I think,' Karen said, refusing to be embarrassed.

One down, she thought as she clicked off her phone. Well, nearly down. Now I've just got to find Lizzie.

Just, she repeated to herself with a healthy dose of self-mockery. Sally had failed to uncover her daughter's hiding place and so had Charlie. Clearly it wasn't going to be easy. But someone had to know where Lizzie had gone. The trick was to work out who – and then ask the question that would allow him to break whatever promises he'd made her.

Chapter 21

Dr James Fullwell, Sally's champion, lived at the top of a thin five-storey Victorian house on the edge of Newport, with views of farms and woods to the south and allotments to the west. Karen was breathless by the time she reached the door of his flat.

No wonder he's so thin, she thought. Anyone would be fit if they did this climb several times a day.

Karen took a moment to control her heavy breathing and thudding heart, looking around to see a row of neat plastic sacks of recycling, presumably awaiting his next trip downstairs. As soon as she'd got her breath back, she banged on the knocker.

Footsteps sounded behind the door, then there was a pause. She noticed he had a spyhole just under the knocker and smiled, in case he was using it even though he'd just buzzed her in through the building's street door. Metallic rasping sounds followed, as though he was fiddling with a door chain. The door opened by about six inches and he looked round.

'Ah,' he said, his grey eyes brightening under their thick brows and his sensitive mouth widening in welcome. 'It *is* you. Hang on a minute.'

He shut the door, unhooked the chain then opened it properly and shook her hand. His own was warm, if a little damp. For a moment Karen thought he was sweating with anxiety, then she saw his hair was damp too and he had swimming trunks in his hand. Following her gaze, he nodded and raised the dripping handful.

'I've just got back from the pool and was washing these out. Go on through. I'll hang them up, then join you. Straight ahead,' he said, waving to a white flush door at the other side of the small hall.

As Karen walked into the long narrow living room, she heard him fiddling about and double-locking the front door, which seemed odd for a strong young man living at the very top of a tall house. A pensioner on the ground floor, maybe, but this?

Holding the question for later, she looked around the bare room, which contained nothing but a black Ikea sofa-bed, two beige chairs, a glass and steel coffee table and a jute rug. The only picture was an anodyne grey-and-black print of a power station over the empty fireplace.

'Sorry about that,' he said when he came back at last. 'If I don't do it at once I forget, and then the chlorine makes the trunks smell. Now, you said on the phone that you wanted to talk to me about Lizzie.'

'Yes.' Karen smiled. 'But first tell me why you're so ... well, scrupulous about locking your front door in the middle of an ordinary day when you'll only have to unlock it again to let me out.'

He shivered and looked like *The Little Boy Lost* from the illustration in one of her grandmother's dog-eared children's books.

'All these murders of people who dealt with Lizzie,' he said with a gasp that was barely controlled. 'Even my old boss, Doctor Franklin. I can't ...'

'*You* don't need to worry,' Karen said, eyeing him with care. 'The people who've died are the ones who damaged Lizzie in one way or another; *you* saved her.'

'Whoever's doing this won't know that. The hospital let her down. And I worked there, and I ...' He rubbed one bony hand across his thin face, then let it slide over his throat, cupping his protruding Adam's apple. 'I'm not sleeping too well.' He forced a smile. 'Every creak and groan of the house makes me wonder who's out there and if my throat's going to be— Sorry. You don't need to hear all this. Coffee?'

'Love some. I'm a terrible addict, I'm afraid. Caffeine keeps me sane,' Karen said, wondering whether he'd ever had treatment for what looked like a severe anxiety disorder.

His gaze met hers for a second: rueful, self-aware, and more attractive than usual. 'I wish it worked for me,' he said.

'What does?' she asked, more frankly than she'd have dared without his encouragement.

'Drink. Single malt. But I have to restrict myself to the days when I'm not on call.' He smiled again, revealing the hint of something stronger in his character, and looking a bit more relaxed. 'I must say it's wonderful then: lying on that sofa, with some Glenmorangie or Macallan in my hand. In that moment, postponing pleasure for minutes, knowing what it'll do ... There's no drug like it.'

'Right.' Karen was surprised by his honesty.

'But you need coffee now. I haven't any Blue Mountain or anything like that. Would ordinary Lavazza do?'

'Perfect.' Karen always enjoyed the rich bitter-toffee taste of Italian espresso coffee.

'Come on through to the kitchen then and tell me what you want to know about Lizzie,' James said.

The kitchen must have been intended to be the flat's sitting room because it was much bigger and lighter than the depressing passage-like one they'd just left. This had a wide low dormer window overlooking the fields. A broad built-in seat filled the embrasure and was upholstered in deckchair canvas, striped in blue and yellow. The free-standing cupboards were made of stripped pine, and the floor was tiled in an aquamarine colour that went surprisingly well with both the yellow and the blue of the stripes.

Karen saw that the chairs round the long pine table had cushions of the same canvas, and the shelves of a big dresser were filled with pottery striped, checked and spotted in similar colours. It was a most unexpected room for such an anxious bachelor, even if he did have a taste for expensive single malts.

'This is comforting,' she said. 'Did you design it?'

'No. A friend did. She's got more imagination than me.' He gestured towards the dresser. 'She's a potter. These are all hers.'

'Girlfriend?' Karen asked, and watched his expression change back to anxious tension.

'I thought so, for a while – but it didn't work out. We met at the hospital.' He drew in a huge breath and hurried to explain: 'She wasn't a patient or anything. I haven't been – you know. She's Thea Morton, who does art therapy with some of the children. Teaching them to pot. That's how we met. But it turned out she's already involved with someone on the mainland.'

'Did she ever know Lizzie?' Karen asked. 'She was an art student, wasn't she, before the attack?'

'Yes, but in London. Thea comes from Birmingham. She didn't get to the Island till just before we met, long after Lizzie ran away. White or black?'

'Black, please. Lizzie running away is what I wanted to ask you about,' Karen said, taking the mug he offered her. 'Lovely, thanks. That smells great. She obviously trusted you.'

He flinched, which interested Karen.

'She *did* trust you, didn't she?' she said.

With eyes filling, he tried to speak, failed, and merely nodded. Then he wiped the back of his hand over his eyes and managed to find some words. 'Let me show you what she gave me just before she went away.'

Karen waited, sipping her strong, fragrant coffee and pitying him for not being able to find the buzz she got from it.

'Here.' He'd come back and was offering her a framed drawing, about two feet by eighteen inches.

Karen put down her mug so she could take it from him and carry it over to the window, where the light fell on it. The image was more representational than abstract, but there was nothing photographic about it. After a moment or two, she looked up at him.

'It's remarkable. I'd no idea she was this good.'

Lizzie had drawn her doctor in full regalia of white coat and stethoscope. He was looking down, as though at a patient lying in bed, so that the immediate impression was of prominent cheekbones, two sharp diagonal lines almost meeting at the base of the nose. His much softer chin was concealed, tucked in towards his neck. His forehead looked even broader than it was in real life and his big worried eyes were shielded by the drooping lids. He looked attentive. Kind, too. None of his anxiety showed, which suggested he'd managed to give his desperately ill patient a sense of security. And yet Lizzie had caught some essence of him that Karen could recognize.

'You're right,' she said, smiling at him. 'She did trust you.'

As she handed him back the picture, something fell from a gap between the backing and the frame, where the brown tape had come away. Karen looked down and saw a slip of paper, apologized and bent to pick it up.

'That's OK,' he said, examining the damage. 'It keeps happening. Do read it.'

Reluctant to break into his privacy, in spite of the invitation, but too curious to resist, Karen unfolded the small slip of paper.

Dear James, this is for you. An inadequate thank you. You saved me. I don't think I could have gone on without you. Love, Lizzie.

Karen knew she'd come to the right place. She refolded the note and handed it back to him. 'That's a great tribute. So, trusting you as she did, I think she must have given you a clue about where she was planning to go.'

She paused but he didn't offer her anything.

'James, I have a feeling that you – and you alone – know where she is. I can understand why you'd keep that knowledge from Sally if Lizzie'd asked you to. But she's in danger now.' Karen very carefully avoided specifying exactly what kind of danger she meant. It wasn't going to help James to open up if she made him see that his protegée was an important suspect, who'd have to be interviewed by the police as soon as someone could lay hands on her. 'We have to find her, talk to her. I *know* you could help. Will you?'

His face closed down. It was as though a Victorian shopkeeper had put up the shutters so that no one could see what was on offer inside.

'James,' Karen said, 'I need to find her. I wouldn't hurt her, you know.'

He poured cold milk into his coffee. Karen winced. What a waste!

'I'm sure you wouldn't,' he said, not sounding at all as though he meant it. 'But I've got nothing to tell you. Do you think I'd have left Sally in this state if I could've changed it? She needs Lizzie more than anyone.'

'Does she?' Karen didn't try to keep her lack of sympathy from showing. If James had been in Lizzie's confidence, he couldn't be quite as much on Sally's side as he'd seemed. And if he was completely on Sally's side, then he must know less of Lizzie than Karen had hoped.

'That's not fair. Of course she does,' James said, like a teacher telling off a lazy pupil. 'She adored Lizzie and she's breaking up now. All the time she's like: "Where *is* Lizzie? Are people hurting her? Is she eating enough? Has she any money?" It's driving Sally over the edge.'

'I can imagine,' Karen said, softening a little.

'God knows what'll happen if she loses it completely.' James's voice was shaking now. 'Did you hear how she saw Randall in the street and started yelling at him?'

Karen nodded.

'I never thought she'd lose it. Or take such risks when she . . .' His voice died.

Karen made a mental note to ask Sally more about her encounter with Randall. 'But Lizzie: come clean, James. You must have some idea where she is.'

He paused with the striped mug halfway to his mouth, his eyes blank. At last he shook his head with all the vigour of a killer whale with a still-living seal in its mouth.

'I haven't. Honestly. It's four years ago now. For most of the time I saw her, she wasn't conscious, and she certainly never discussed her plans with me. I'd do anything to help. She was . . . so vulnerable, and we all failed her for so long. We only just caught the septicaemia in time. For a while, I thought she might die. Look I can't help you. Sorry.'

'I'm sure you would if you could,' Karen began, wishing she could like him, in spite of the twittering anxiety that kept her on edge and must be half-killing him. He had to be a seriously good doctor to have kept his job.

Suddenly he jerked to his feet.

'Can you smell burning?' he said urgently, sniffing hard.

'No.' Karen sniffed, too. And then again, catching a whiff of warm smoke from somewhere. 'Did you leave a fag burning in an ashtray? That's what this smells like.'

'I don't smoke.' He was already moving to the cooker, checking all the knobs and laying his hands over the burners as though he thought one might be invisibly alight.

Anxiety disorder hardly covers this kind of excess, Karen thought.

'Could be one of the plugs.' James was breathless, as though he'd run up and down the stairs twice. 'Electrical fires smell fishy. Does this? I can't tell. Can you smell fish?'

'No,' Karen said, sniffing again. 'It's straight smoke. And not much of that. But we do need to find it and put it out, whatever it is.'

To Karen's surprise, he bent down to floor level, once again laying his hands on each of the plastic plugs in turn. Standing, he inhaled again, and his eyes flicked from side to side as he searched the room for signs of danger.

'It's getting worse,' he said, his voice higher and faster than it had been. '*Where's* it coming from?

He ran out of the room. Karen followed him more slowly into the small hall, then across to the living room. While he searched under and behind every piece of furniture and, again, tested all the electric plugs, she pushed open the first of the other two doors and found a tiny pristine bathroom, with no sign of any burning. Here the air smelled of nothing but soap, a wet flannel, and bleach.

She retreated to the hall and caught a whiff of hotter smoke. Feeling her own heart-rate speed up, she pushed open the last door, to find herself in his bedroom. The double bed was made up with plain white poly-cotton, the wardrobes were built-in with white melamine doors, and the only other furniture was a black-ash table on steel trestles, containing a desk-top computer, which was humming companionably. The smell was less here. She turned away to see James looking at her as if she was mad.

'There's a *fire*!' he shouted. 'And it's getting worse. Listen – can't you hear crackling? We've got to find it. Put it *out*!'

Karen heard the sound of flames at last. Real fear touched her, like a cold sharp finger pressing into her cheek.

'No, we don't,' she said. 'We need to phone 999 and get out of here. Fast.'

She couldn't remember where she'd left her bag and therefore her phone. Her mind screamed at her that she'd been stupid to hang about. She held on to the impulse to scream back and forced herself to speak aloud but quietly: 'Where's your phone, James?'

He didn't answer, just seized her arm and pulled her out into the hall. Smoke was curling inside from under the front door.

He let go of her arm and ran to the door. As he put his hand on the keys he'd hung beside it, Karen shouted, '*Stop*!'

James looked round, his eyes rolling like those of a terrified horse. She calmed her voice again. 'If there's fire out there, opening the door will just make it rush in. And if it is out there, we can't use the stairs to get out. Where's your fire escape?'

'What?'

'You must have one, living this high up. It's in the building regs – and landlord's rules. Come on, where is it? Think!'

'I don't know. God! What? Where?' He was hyperventilating now.

Karen didn't waste any more time. Once more she told him to phone 999, saw him reach for the landline and herself ran into the living room to peer out of the windows, looking first one way then the other. There was no sign of a fire escape in either direction. On her way out again, she saw her saggy shoulder bag on the sofa and grabbed it. As she pulled it up, she saw the phone underneath. It must have fallen out. She stuffed it into the bag.

Back in the small lobby, she glanced upwards and saw a hatch in the ceiling. Memories of climbing out through the roof of her parents' chalet made her point to it.

'We may be able to get out that way,' she called. 'Is there a ladder?'

'I don't know.' He was putting the receiver back on to the phone. 'The Fire Brigade's coming. I've never been up there. I'll get a chair.'

'It's too high for that. You need a ladder.'

'I haven't got one.' His breathing was a little more controlled than it had been, but his eyes were still wild. 'Let's wait for the firemen to get us out.'

'But—'

'No. You could fall and break your back. They said on the phone we shouldn't take risks. If you fell, you could be a quadriplegic. I couldn't cope knowing it was because of me that you'd got hurt.'

'We must get out, James. The biggest danger of fire is the smoke – and fumes from paint and stuff. We haven't got time to wait.'

He clutched her again, this time grabbing her left forearm with both hands and squeezing with painful strength.

'I've remembered,' he said, panting heavily. 'There *is* a way. Through the bedroom window. Come on.'

Karen could feel the chemical bite of burning varnish in her throat now. She took a second to lay her palm on the inside of the front door. The wood was so hot she had to whisk her hand away.

'Come *on*,' he said, sounding tougher.

Karen followed him into the bedroom and watched while he upended a pencil pot to retrieve a bunch of window keys. Then she had to control every instinct to grab them from him and undo the locks herself. He fumbled through the bunch until he found the one he thought was right, but it didn't fit. The smell of burning varnish and charring wood was stronger all the time, and the noise was rising from a crackle to a roar.

Her throat was hurting now, and she had to fight to breathe. She longed for Will and his neat, careful fingers. He'd have had the windows open long ago. He'd have known where the fire escape was too. And he'd never have taken the risk of waiting so long.

At last James got the right key, then dropped the whole bunch on the floor. Karen swore silently.

'Oh, God! I'm sorry,' he whispered. 'I'm so, so sorry. It's all my fault.'

The window opened at last and sweet clean air rushed in. The roaring from outside the front door intensified. Through it, Karen heard the blessed sound of a fire engine's siren.

'Listen, James.' Her whole body was relaxing, and breathing was much easier. 'They're coming for us. All we've got to do is climb out, shut the window after us and wait for them. No scary abseiling down the walls or anything. No risk of falling. They'll get us down now.'

Outside on the tiny balcony, she pushed the casements shut behind them as well as she could, then turned to see him hanging over the decorative iron rail, fighting to control his breathing.

Laying a hand on his heaving, pulsating back, she said, 'They're coming. Listen, you can hear the siren getting louder. It's all going to be all right, James. You haven't done anything wrong.'

He straightened up and turned to face her. Despite the choking, his skin was very pale. 'But you understand what this says, don't you?'

She knew exactly what he meant, but she waited for his explanation. It might help him to articulate his worst fears.

'I *am* a target. Whoever's doing the killing thinks I hurt Lizzie.' He turned away, biting his lip. Karen thought she'd seen tears on his face. 'Whoever it is, they're blaming me too. I'll *never* be safe.'

'Yes, you will. The police will find the killer and deal with him. Or her. Where was Sally planning to be this afternoon?'

The look he sent Karen then was the kind offered to someone who had admitted sympathy for a paedophile, or worse.

'It's *not* Sally. I know it isn't. She'd never hurt anyone. Least of all me.'

'Then who, James? Who do *you* think it is?'

He looked ahead towards the empty countryside, in the direction of Carisbrooke, where Dr Franklin had had her perfect house and died in it. He bit his lips. Karen saw more tears gathering in his eyes.

'Could it be Lizzie herself?' she said quietly, hoping that by making it a question like this she wouldn't choke off the information she was still sure he had, in spite of everything.

He turned away, clinging to the rail. The sound of the siren was louder. Over his bowed head, Karen saw the fire engine, red and silver, promising safety. It pulled up below them. The blue lights continued to flash but the siren was silenced.

'No,' James whispered, as though to say the word more loudly would bring terrible danger on him. 'No. No. No. No. Never.'

'Hey there,' called a fire officer, tipping back his yellow safety helmet. 'Well done for getting out. We're coming up. We'll have you down in no time.'

'Thanks.' Karen thought it the most pathetic word she'd ever used for something that mattered so much.

The fireman didn't seem to mind. He gave her a thumbs-up as his colleagues began to raise the fire-engine's platform towards them.

'Why would Lizzie start now?' James said, sounding a little tougher. 'If it was her, why would she have waited? Why not do it right after the trial?'

'Lots of reasons,' Karen said, pleased not to have to think about the fire behind her now that there were flames as well as smoke visible in his bedroom, only feet away. She could feel the heat on her back, and hated the bitter, choking smells that surrounded them, even here in the open air.

The platform came to a gentle rest against the side of the balcony. The fireman inside it stretched out an arm towards them. He smelled of rubber and soap, and the mixture was the most delicious Karen had ever inhaled. She breathed even more deeply just to get a second blast.

'You go first,' said James, with a chivalry she wouldn't have expected from one so nervous.

Karen grasped the dark-blue clothed arm and put one leg over the balcony's rail, willing herself not to look down.

'You're doing great,' said the fire officer in the comforting Island accent that reminded her of her grandmother. 'You're doing fine.'

Her back leg had got stuck. She couldn't move it. Straddling the rail, she did look down and swayed.

'One more heave,' said the fire officer in the same comfortable voice.

The sound liberated Karen and her leg moved.

'There you go,' he said, patting her.

Karen moved to the other side of the platform so that James could take her place.

Below them, there was the sound of applause. Karen looked down again, without any dizziness now, and saw a small crowd of clapping people, standing beyond the engine. The platform began to move smoothly downwards.

'Why?' James said. 'Why now?'

The fire officer said: 'No saying how a fire starts till we can investigate. But we will. Don't you worry.'

'Thanks,' Karen said. Turning her face towards James, she answered his real question, which had nothing to do with the danger they'd been in: 'Sometimes people can only deal with their anger once they've begun to recover from a trauma.'

'But—'

'At first they feel too fragile, too powerless. It's like suicidal depressives. You must have come across it at work. They don't kill themselves in the depths; only when they're halfway back to health. Or perhaps it was news of Randall's release that tipped her over.'

James shook his head, but his lips were clamped together. And he was rolling his eyes in the direction of the fire officer. Karen waited until they were safely on the ground.

'What?' she said. 'What were you going to tell me?'

'The killer didn't wait till Randall was out.' James's expression had changed to something Karen found hard to read. He looked as though he was trying to see through a mist to something terrifying beyond it.

'What do you mean?' Karen kept her voice gentle enough to avoid making whatever it was worse for him. 'Randall was free well before Tod Williams was killed.'

'Tod wasn't the first. I've never thought about it like this before, but now I can see . . .'

Karen frowned, wondering why Charlie hadn't told her this. 'Who? Who are you talking about?'

'There were two useless cops.' James's voice sounded as though he was dazed by the enormity of what he'd only just understood. 'They were rescuing a trapped squirrel when they should've saved Lizzie.'

'How do you know?' Karen asked, remembering Charlie's first account of what had happened to Lizzie. She felt as though her stomach had been grabbed and squeezed.

'Sally told me,' James said. 'She tells me everything. She found out they died too. In a fire. Like this, but last year. Before anyone knew Gyre was getting out.'

'*Both* of them?' Karen said.

'That's what Sally said.' James sounded exhausted. Karen wasn't surprised. Anyone who put himself through such emotional storms would be worn out most of the time.

'They were together,' he went on. 'Married when they left the force, and bought a B and B on the mainland. It burned down. They were trapped, like we could've been. *They* died.'

Karen said nothing as she tried to work the news into the various theories in her mind.

'The police'll need to take statements,' said a voice from behind them.

Karen whirled round, to see the firefighter.

'Arson,' he said. 'No doubt about it. Got any enemies, mate?'

Chapter 22

'So here we are again, Karen.' Eve sounded tired and bored. She looked as though she hadn't slept much, with deep dark patches under her eyes. Karen would have been tempted to use a bit of concealer, but Eve's sharp-boned face was stripped bare.

'But this time you're a victim,' she went on, looking as though Karen was the worst kind of interruption in her busy day. 'I've been told to take a statement from you about this fire. So we'd better start. When did you first notice something was wrong?'

As Eve led her through everything that had happened, Karen tried to make sense of it all, her early refusal to take James's panic seriously, which now seemed so irresponsible, then the belated fear that had left her with a kind of hangover. Her head ached and she felt nauseous and hollow and stupid. When she'd answered all the questions and given Eve the pitifully small amount of information she had, Karen asked a question of her own.

'How bad was it? I mean, how bad could it have been?'

'The fire?'

'Yes.' Karen hated asking Eve for favours, but she needed to know. 'It seemed scary at the time, but the firefighters had it out quite fast. Were we ever at any real risk?'

Eve shrugged. 'Fire's always dangerous. But I don't think you need to have nightmares about narrow escapes. Once you'd phoned 999, you were always going to be OK.'

'How did it start?' Karen was surprised Eve was being so helpful and she wasn't going to waste her chance.

'In a bag of paper items for recycling.'

'So that's why you asked me if I'd seen any rubbish.' Karen could picture the bags easily, including a huge orange plastic one, thin enough to have been torn by the blunt corner of a muesli packet and gripped at the neck with a wire tie. 'Did anyone else in the building see anything?'

Eve shrugged again. 'No idea. This kind of arson's fairly common. Mostly boys – eleven to fifteen, usually. They like fire. Setting rubbish alight is one of their things.'

'But not five floors up, surely,' Karen said.

Eve wagged her head to and fro. 'Not usually. It's a street thing.'

'How could they have got into the building?'

'It's hardly difficult, Karen.' Eve was talking in the exaggeratedly kind voice of someone dealing with a dementia patient. 'And now if you've got nothing more to tell me, I must get on.'

Lisa walked up and down outside her mother's shop, still not sure whether she wanted to be recognized or not. Through the plate-glass windows, she'd been watching Sally for ages. Sometimes she was alone and preening in front of one of the long mirrors; sometimes putting on the charm to talk to a customer.

She hadn't changed: still the same over-the-top gestures; still the same fatness and vanity. Lisa thought of all the awful Saturdays she'd spent working in the shop, embarrassed to death. Bored and resentful, too. But in those days she'd never felt anything to match the fury that exploded in her when she watched her mother on the CCTV film snuggling up to Randall after the rape.

Randall's dead, Lisa told herself. Punished and dead at last. Doesn't that make it OK now? Sally can't have known who he was and what he'd done when she was slobbering all over him. She probably thought he was a doctor, too. Why can't I forget the sight of the two of them together and try for a truce now?

If she did, she'd be able to track down her father. If she didn't, she might be without him for ever. No one she'd spoken to so far during this trip had any idea where he was. Wasn't finding him worth making peace with her mother?

Trying to gather up the courage to face Sally, Lisa waited for the current customer to leave the shop, then set off to cross the road, ready at last to push open the door. Halfway across, panic grabbed her and she stopped. A motorcycle skidded as the driver braked hard to miss her.

'Stupid bitch!' he shouted.

Sally moved towards the front of her shop, as though to find out what the commotion was. Lisa scuttled back to the other side of the road, the safe side, with every nerve shrieking at her to stay away. She wasn't ready to deal with Sally. Not yet. Not even to find her father.

Charlie was passing through the foyer of the police station as Karen emerged from her session with Eve. He saw the two women and hesitated.

Eve smiled and walked over to ask him a question, laying a possessive hand on his arm. Karen remembered how she and Charlie had parted the other day and decided to leave him to Eve for the moment.

As Karen left the building, her phone beeped. Surprised because she thought she'd turned it off when she went in to the interview with Eve, she thrust her hand into her bag to dig it out, couldn't find it and had to reach right to the bottom, where it had got stuck under her wallet. Bringing it out into the air, she looked at the screen and saw she had a text from Will.

R U OK? Phone me.

She stopped in the street, with streams of people dividing around her, barely conscious that she wasn't alone. She called him and put the phone to her ear.

'Will? How did you know?'

'Know what?'

Words wouldn't come. She opened her mouth but couldn't make any sound.

'Karen, what's happened?' Will said with a strange but warming mixture of gentleness and urgency.

'Nothing much,' she said at last, managing to sound relatively relaxed. 'But I was scared. I was involved in a not-very-serious fire. No harm done. But I want to know what made you text.'

'I was worried. I came out of theatre, knowing there was something wrong.' Will laughed. Karen recognized the sound as a tension-reliever rather than an expression of amusement. 'In all my nightmares about you, I've never thought of fire.'

She was surprised he had nightmares, and that he'd admitted to them. Something had changed in him as well as in her.

'You sure you're OK?' he said. 'Have you been checked out by a medic?'

'No need. I've been giving a statement to the police.' Karen fought for normality so she could reassure them both. 'They're not too fussed. They think it was probably young hoodies after excitement. Some kind of accelerant dropped in a bag of paper for recycling.'

'At your flat?'

'No.' Karen tightened her grip on the mobile. He'd have no idea where she was. She could tell him anything. She chose the truth. 'I was talking to a doctor on the Island. We were in his flat.'

'So *you* weren't the target? That's something.'

A hand pressed down on her shoulder and she jerked her head round to see Charlie's dark face. Close-up like this, she couldn't see his expression properly, but she didn't think he was angry any more. As usual, he smelled of toothpaste and Pears soap.

'I'm fine, Will, honestly,' she said, saying his name clearly.

Charlie took his hand away at once, stood back. But he didn't go away.

'I'd better go,' Karen said. 'They want to ask me more questions.'

She waited for Will to say goodbye. He didn't utter anything for several seconds, then in a voice as dry as sand, he added a casual, 'Give him my regards.'

'Fine,' Karen said, pretending there was nothing to worry about. She clicked off and put the phone in her pocket to make it easier to find next time. 'He sends his love.'

'I bet he doesn't,' Charlie said. 'You OK?'

'James smelled the fire and called for help long before it became serious,' Karen said, without answering the real question.

'Who set it?' Charlie asked, speaking as though to a colleague rather than a victim. She liked that. 'Any ideas?'

'I didn't see anyone. Or hear anything. There was no one around when I arrived. But listen: I've got a question for you, Charlie.'

'OK. Shoot.'

'Did you know your two derelict officers died in a fire on the mainland?' Karen asked, trying not to sound as though she were accusing him.

'What? Who?'

'James told me the two constables who rescued a red squirrel instead of Lizzie died in a burning B and B last year.'

'Oh, them. Yes, I did know.' Charlie sounded grim. Something about the set of his lips made him look as though he had a mouthful of thorns.

'Why didn't you tell me? Their deaths happened *before* Randall got out.'

'So?'

'So that makes it even less likely that he killed Tod.' Karen watched Charlie consider the idea and quickly dismiss it. 'It matters. You should've told me.'

'What's your point here?'

'You're not being very helpful.' Karen wished she had access to scopolamine or some other more modern truth drug she could have dropped into his drink.

'I don't see what you're getting at,' he said, stubborn as a rubber wall.

'Come on, Charlie! All three were involved in making what happened to Lizzie worse. As was Doctor Franklin. *And* James – in a way. Isn't someone targeting everybody who hurt her and possibly Randall's earlier victims, too?'

Annie's name seemed to Karen to be hovering in the air. She could hardly believe that Charlie didn't know what she was thinking.

'The fire that killed the two PCs was an accident,' he said with exaggerated patience, not looking at her. 'No arson involved.'

'How do you know? It happened on the mainland. Would you be told?'

'Karen, they'd worked for me.' Now he was exaggeratedly reasonable. He glanced at her for a second. She tried not to see the desperation in his eyes. 'They still had friends here. Friends talk. I heard it all.'

'How did it happen?' she asked, still not convinced that anyone involved with Lizzie in any way whatsoever could have died by accident.

Charlie sighed. 'You're fucking relentless, aren't you? OK, so the two of them bought a run-down guest house. They were DIY-ing it. No less sloppy than when they'd been working here. She was undercoating upstairs; he was burning off paint downstairs. He tripped over something, knocked himself out, set fire to the woodwork with his blowtorch. Upstairs, plugged into her MP3 player, and breathing in paint fumes, she hadn't a clue.'

'I suppose that's feasible,' Karen said, wondering whether the accident had given someone ideas.

'Yeah. Anyway, she tried to get out in the end. Fell out of a window. Died. Nothing suspicious.'

'Right.'

'Her falling like that's what made me ...' Charlie leaned forwards so that his forehead was resting on Karen's head. 'I had to check you were really OK. Your hair smells of smoke.'

Karen stepped backwards. 'I'm fine. I didn't jump; I didn't inhale any toxic fumes. I wasn't in any danger. Look, I must get back. I've got work piling up and my report to write – *and* another meeting with the Ministry of Justice people. How's Boulting by the way?'

'No idea.' Charlie looked vague, which was so unlike him that Karen's anxiety level zoomed even further upwards. 'Not my problem.'

'Charlie, concentrate! You know he didn't kill Randall. You were worried about him taking the rap for someone else. We need to know who's pulling his strings.'

He scowled, then turned his head to one side so that he didn't have to meet her eyes.

'Like I say: not my problem. Or yours. Now I know you're OK, I must go. See you later.' He strode off.

Karen was gripping the phone in her pocket. She couldn't let him go like this, still not knowing. 'Charlie!'

'Can't wait.' He had his back to her and he didn't look round.

Karen watched his retreating back view, almost more afraid than in the moment when she'd realized the fire could be serious. Would Will pick up this too?

After a while there was nothing more to see. And she had to get back to Southampton. As she walked up Shooter's Hill towards the High Street and Fountain Quay, gulls screamed overhead. Even through their noise she could hear her phone ring. She saw Annie's name on the screen and thought of everything she wanted to ask.

'Hi, Annie,' she said, hoping none of the suspicion sounded in her voice. 'What can I do for you?'

'You know how you wanted to meet Cat?'

Having shared the fire with James, Karen was sure it would be safer to stay away from everyone who'd ever had anything to do with Randall or his victims. Major Crimes were looking for the killer. Surely she could leave it to them. It was their job and they had all the resources – as well as the training.

'Have you changed your mind about introducing us?' She tried to sound enthusiastic.

'Not exactly,' Annie said, even more unhappy than usual. 'But she's been on to me because she keeps getting these calls from Mollie Gyre – Randall's mother. Cat says it's creeping her out.'

'What can *I* do? Can't she get an injunction if the calls upset her that much?'

'It's not so easy. Here's this calm-sounding woman who's like "now my son's dead, I would be grateful for ever if you'd see me". Cat says it's hard not to respond.'

'I can see that, but—' Karen began.

'But she doesn't want to meet the woman on her own.' Annie's voice was too strong to fight against. 'A police officer's not appropriate, so I thought of you. Cat'll go along with it, if you will.'

'You mean you want me to chaperone one of Randall's victims while his mother . . . what? Apologizes for him?'

'No idea. You wanted to talk to Cat,' Annie said, sounding even tougher. 'She wants someone to defend her. You both get what you want. If you're not interested . . .'

'No. No.' Karen said quickly. 'You're right. Of course I'll do it. Give me Cat's phone number.'

'She'll call you.'

'OK. But, Annie, how did Mollie identify your Cat? She didn't forego anonymity at the trial like Lizzie did. Or in all those press reports after Randall died. She was just "a doctor".'

Annie sighed. 'God knows! Mollie must've leaned on someone. Unless she knew all along. Maybe Randall told her about them all.'

'But—' Karen began, but Annie had gone and the phone was dead.

Was Mollie making the same investigative journey as Karen? Did she think Randall had been killed by one of his victims, or one of their supporters? Did she know about the other deaths, realize they all *had* to be connected? Was she hunting his killer now?

They were to meet in the coffee shop at St Thomas's Hospital in Lambeth, on the south side of the Thames in London, just opposite the Houses of Parliament. Cat had said it would have to be there because she was too busy to take time away from work. Karen thought it more likely she wanted to be able to leave the meeting quickly.

When Karen arrived, the lunchtime rush had ended. A few tables were full, some with patients in dressing-gowns and others with visitors in street clothes, but there were plenty that were free and had been cleaned as well as cleared. Mollie was sitting at one, dressed once again in an impeccable dark business suit and with one long leg crossed over the other. Her back was absolutely straight, as usual, and her face was once more perfectly plucked, tidied and made up. She had a cup of black coffee in front of her and she was reading the *Financial Times*.

'Hi,' Karen said, pulling out the chair opposite hers.

'Doctor Taylor.' Mollie folded the pink broadsheet and tucked it neatly in the outside pocket of the briefcase she had at her feet. 'I wasn't expecting you.'

'Cat Derby wanted some support. Friends thought I could provide it.'

'What is she expecting me to do to her?'

'Frankly,' Karen said with her most confidence-boosting smile, 'I can't imagine. I am sorry, you know.'

'Sorry? About what?'

'About the death of your son. I can't imagine anything harder.'

Mollie's face barely twitched. But her voice was stiff when she said: 'Then your imagination is defective. Harder is to discover that he *was* capable of imposing intolerable suffering on blameless young women, not just once but again and again for nearly two decades, and that I never believed their stories.'

Karen sat rebuked.

'May I ask why you want to meet Cat?' she said, after an uncomfortable silence.

'I think this must be she.' Mollie stood up as a tall, slender young woman threaded her way between the tables.

The newcomer had rough blonde hair scraped tightly back from her face, and she was wearing a white coat hanging open over her loose grey and black clothes. But her likeness to Lizzie – and to Karen herself – was obvious. A stethoscope hung around her neck like a badge of office, even though she was a surgeon, and a blue plastic badge on her left shoulder announced her as *Miss Catriona Derby*.

'May I get you some coffee?' Mollie said, when she'd introduced herself. 'Tea?'

Cat's hands were folded inside each other. She shook her head. 'I'm fine, thanks.'

'Then do sit down.' Mollie could have been chairing a City meeting for all the emotion she showed, but Cat was trembling.

'Hi,' Karen said, remembering how very closely Mollie's dead son had resembled her. 'I'm Karen Taylor.'

'I thought you must be. Thanks for coming. Annie gave you a good write-up.' Cat shook Karen's hand, then let it go and turned to Mollie. 'This is hard for me, and probably for you too, so may we get on with it? What is it you need to say to me?'

Mollie crossed her legs again and breathed carefully, before putting both hands on the table, almost as though to show off her perfect manicure. She stared down at her buffed, blunt-cut nails, then raised her head and looked directly at her son's victim.

'I spent many years telling myself, and anyone else who wanted to know, that Randall was a victim of fantasizing women, police harassment and miscarriages of justice,' she said, with no apparent emotion, as though she was making a speech to the board. 'I have come to believe – since his death – that I might have been wrong. And I wanted . . .'

For the first time she showed hesitation. Cat didn't offer any help at all.

'I wanted first of all to be certain,' Mollie went on eventually, 'so I hoped you'd be able to put my mind at rest.'

Cat swallowed, then spoke in a tone that sounded almost as detached as Mollie's.

'If you mean you want to know if he really was a violently sadistic rapist, then I *can* help you. Everything printed in those newspaper articles was true.'

Mollie bent her head. Her shoulders rose and fell. At last she looked up again. Her face showed nothing but polite attention.

'You're an intelligent woman, Miss Derby. Can you tell me *why*?'

'Why I became a victim? Or he a rapist? Of course not. How could I? Doctor Taylor's much more likely to be able to do that. She's the psychologist here.'

Mollie looked at Karen, then back at Cat. 'She's already told me she can't help me. Haven't you ever wondered why he chose you?'

Cat pushed back her chair, but she didn't get up. The fingers with which she was gripping the table edge were white with the effort of holding on. 'If I'd known this was what you wanted, I'd have refused. If you're trying to make me say I provoked him, I can't. I won't. I didn't.'

'Did you flirt with him?' Mollie asked.

Karen glared at her, but Mollie didn't even notice. All her concentration was on Cat.

'OK, so I flirted,' Cat said. 'So? That doesn't make it my fault. It *doesn't*.'

Mollie seemed to be arguing about something with herself. After a few seconds, she offered Cat a small smile, the first she'd produced at this meeting.

'Would it help to know why *I* think he chose you?'

'*Do* you know?' A dull red flush was covering Cat's face, making it almost ugly. 'Did he *tell* you about the things he did?'

'He never told me anything, but I can guess. And I have come to understand that some of you, some of his victims, do blame yourselves, even though nothing that happened was your fault.'

Cat's flush was dying back and Karen sat more easily in her chair, realizing that she was not going to have to intervene. She was fairly sure Cat was no killer. But she still didn't understand why Mollie had insisted on this meeting.

'That's why I wanted to talk to you,' Mollie went on. 'All of you. Or all of you that I can find.'

Karen watched Mollie's face and thought that if it were the victims who were being picked off, one by one, then this woman would have to be a suspect. She was so disciplined, so determined, so ruthless. But Karen could not fit Mollie's story into those of Tod and Dr Franklin in any way that worked.

'All right,' Cat said at last. 'Hit me with it.' She looked as though she'd had to brace herself for the blow she'd just invited.

'When I saw the photographs of some of you in the papers, I saw how alike you all are.' Mollie's voice was not as hard as it had been when she'd talked to Karen, but it sounded as though it hurt her to talk about her son's crimes, as if she got a drop of acid on her tongue. Listening to the pain without trying to offer comfort was difficult.

'And how like one of Randall's childhood playmates,' Mollie went on. 'She was two years older and very beautiful.'

Cat didn't react.

'When Randall was fourteen, he and all the other boys were besotted with her. At first she favoured Randall. I watched her excited by him and was amused. They were so young, I thought;

it's just a charming play thing, a kind of practising for real life. Let him learn about girls in such a good protected situation.'

Mollie drank some of her coffee, which must have been foul by now, Karen thought: stewed and cold.

'Then he wanted more and got pushier. Too pushy for her. She turned away, fixed all her attentions on his best friend and would barely speak to Randall again.'

Cat sat stony-faced. Mollie might not have reached the end of her story, but it looked as though she couldn't go on with it now. Karen had to intervene to get the meeting moving again.

'Did he ever talk about it?' she said.

Mollie dragged her gaze away from Cat's face, saying: 'No, but I think he chose other women as vehicles for the punishment he wanted to visit on her and could not, either because he was afraid or because he knew he would be found out.'

Mollie turned her lips inwards, sucking them, which seemed astonishing in so controlled a woman. When she relaxed again, Karen could see lipstick on her teeth. Mollie turned back to Cat.

'You look so like her,' she said, sounding much less certain than usual. 'All of you do. I wish I could do something to change what happened, to repair what he did. This small truth is all I have to offer.'

Cat covered her face with both hands. Karen's mobile rang. Mollie looked at her with the cold, determined ferocity of a guard dog. Karen silenced the phone and stuffed it back in her bag. The interval had given Cat time to get herself in order. She took her hands from her face, stood up and leaned heavily on the back of the chair.

'It's not such a small thing,' Cat said. 'It can't have been easy to face what you've had to face and try to help me – us. We won't meet again. Goodbye.'

And she walked away without looking back.

Karen pushed back her chair, ready to follow, then glanced at Mollie.

'I have to say something to her. Can you wait?'

'For a little while,' Mollie said.

Karen ran after the doctor and caught her just outside the lifts.

'Miss Derby,' she said. 'Can I talk to you for a second?'

Cat looked round. 'If you must. But I wasn't faking it. I do have to get back.'

'I'm sure.' The lift doors opened. 'Maybe I could come up with you.'

Cat shrugged. Luckily there was no one else in the lift.

'If you think I killed Randall, you're wrong. I've already given the police my alibi. I was here. It's all on record.'

'That's not quite what I wanted,' Karen said, glad to hear that the Major Crimes team had been taking all the obvious steps to eliminate possible suspects.

'Then what?' Cat's voice was sharp now.

'It's not just Randall who's been killed, you know, but also other people who've made the life of at least one of his victims worse even than he did,' Karen said, watching Cat closely. She did not react. 'I've met several people who are angry enough to want them all dead,' Karen went on, 'but not many who seem capable of killing him – and without leaving a lot of clear evidence behind.'

'So?' Cat wasn't looking at her.

'So can you think who could be capable?'

'Why are you asking me?' Still Cat wouldn't look at Karen. 'I heard about Randall dying, but I know nothing of any other victim.'

'But you know . . .' Karen stopped to give herself time to pick the right words. 'I mean, you do know people who are right at the heart of this.'

At last Cat swung round to face her.

'If you are asking me whether Annie Colvin is capable of killing, then you're mad. She's a police officer.'

'Why pick her of all the people who might come under suspicion?' Karen asked, interested that she wasn't the only person to wonder about Annie.

'Because she's the most obvious.' Cat sounded confident and certain. 'She's tough. She knows how investigations work so she could take evasive action. And she drinks too much; when drunk, she can say all sorts of stuff. She's often said she wanted to kill Randall.' The confidence in Cat's voice had dwindled a little. Then she gathered herself to finish: 'But she *didn't* kill him or anyone else.'

'That sounds like blind faith to me,' Karen said. 'It's not enough.'

'It's more than that.' The lift reached the tenth floor and the doors opened. Cat stepped out, then looked back. 'I *know* Annie. I know her better than you could possibly imagine. She might want people dead, but she would never kill them. *Never.*'

The stainless-steel doors closed, cutting them off from one another. Karen's hand went to the 'open doors' button, but she resisted. If Cat had an alibi for Annie, she'd have given it. If she hadn't, there was no point inviting more simple statements of faith.

Mollie was standing by the table, holding briefcase and gloves, when Karen returned.

'Did you get what you wanted?' Mollie asked.

'No. So I have to ask you: what did Randall do to his childhood friend to scare her off like that?'

Mollie let her briefcase drop a little to rest on the edge of the table, saying, 'Dinny won't tell me what happened, says she can't remember the episode at all.'

'Dinny?' Karen said. 'She's a Hemming, isn't she? Part of his godmother's family? You sound as though you've talked to her recently. Since Randall's death?'

'I suppose it's your job to ask questions,' Mollie said, looking even more like her son than usual. 'But I don't know that I have to answer them.'

'Did you go to the Island to talk to her?'

'They say people enjoy some kind of catharsis after confession.' Mollie stared out of the great plate-glass windows overlooking the River Thames. 'It hasn't come to me yet. Maybe it will this time. Dinny lives in Winchester now, but she was staying with her mother on the Island. Yes, I went there last week to ask her what he did to her. She can't remember any cross words between them, or any kind of sexual approach, rejection or embarrassment.'

'Did you believe her?' Karen tried to suppress all the mental pictures of Mollie so enraged by what she'd discovered about her son's activities that she'd arranged to meet him behind the pub where he'd committed his last rape – and kill him. The images were vivid but not convincing. Karen opened her mouth to ask another question, but Mollie had left the table.

When she was out of sight, Karen sat down again and pulled out her offending phone to listen to her voicemail.

'Come back asap.' Charlie's voice was urgent. 'Boulting was given bail last night and he's left the Island.'

'Isn't that what you wanted?' Karen said, as soon as she'd got through to him. 'What's the problem, Charlie?'

'Sally's dead. Found in her stockroom by her assistant first thing this morning. Throat cut with a scalpel. Boulting was here and on the loose when it happened.'

Chapter 23

Tuesday, 21 October

Lisa sat with her right hand between both of Jed's as he talked. They were in his clean but primitive kitchen, with untasted mugs of strong tea on the table in front of them.

'I worked out who you are,' he said, stroking one of her knuckles with his big thumb, over and over again until she wanted to scream, 'and what your real name is, when you showed me your scars. I don't know why I remembered the case, except it happened when . . . when my wife and her lawyers were making me so angry I . . .'

His soft West Country voice died. Lisa wondered if he meant that he'd been so angry with his wife he'd sympathized with the rapist who'd ripped up his young victim. She hoped he didn't.

'So I looked up the records,' he said, with the usual patient, sweet smile, 'and I saw how he got off the main charge.'

'The rape charge,' Lisa said in a voice whose coldness was only a means of control.

The sound of it stopped his painful stroking, but he kept his hold on her hands.

'I had to know everything if I wasn't going to hurt you more. I couldn't ask you: you've been through too much already. So I went to the Island to find it all out. Where you lived and – and that.'

'The week before last?' she said, remembering Fred's certainty that his brother had been following her as she'd driven away from the village to Southampton and the ferry. 'You just happened to go there that Friday. Is that right?'

'That's right,' he said firmly. She didn't believe him. Even now. He *must* have been following her.

'What did you do on the Island? Where did you go?'

'I went to your mother's shop.'

'Why?'

'I wanted to meet her.'

'Did you talk to her?' Lisa heard her voice turning sharp and harsh and hated it.

'She was nice to me. Kind. Thoughtful. I liked her.'

Lisa stared at him. How was it possible?

'When I said I'd read about the case and thought it was the worst thing I'd ever heard and asked if she was your mother, she told me she'd lost you because she made a mistake. A terrible mistake,' Jed said. 'She told me that nothing she could do would ever make it better.'

Lisa felt her eyes heating up and tears forming. Jed let go one of her hands so he could run his thumb under each of her eyes in turn to collect the tears. She could feel the roughness of his skin catching on hers.

'Did she . . .?' She couldn't put the question into words, wasn't even sure what she wanted to know.

'She said she'd be lonely all her life now but she knew she'd deserved it because of the mistake she'd made.'

'Did she say anything about my father?'

Jed shook his head. His eyes were full of sympathy. 'I didn't ask her about him. But you can, Lisa, if you want to. I can take you back there any time.'

Lisa thought of her attempt to make herself go into the shop again. There had to be another way to find her father.

'What did you do then, Jed?'

'I went to the pub where it happened.'

'But why?'

His hands grabbed hers again so violently that she had to pull away and sat cradling one hand inside the other. She daren't try to drink any tea; she knew that trying to swallow anything would make her retch.

'Because I had to understand,' he said quietly. 'I don't understand much unless I see it for myself, Lisa. You know that. I'm not good at getting what people mean when they tell me stuff.'

'Yes,' she said, thinking. He must have missed me by minutes. 'I mean no. You understand everything. All those teachers who told you that you were dumb were just fools. You see more than anyone.'

'That's when I heard the girl scream.' Jed wasn't interested in anything she was saying. 'You understand, don't you, Lisa? I went to the pub and I heard the girl scream.'

'But—'

'And I ran in to the alleyway and had to save her. So when I saw him hurting her, I had to stop him.'

'Jed, I—'

'No, don't say anything. It's better if you don't say anything. That way I can manage.'

Lisa tried to work out what he was telling her, what he really meant.

'And it's what I told the police. They believe it. They let me out because they believe me and know I'll go back there for the trial when I'm sent for.'

'And you came straight home?'

'No, I went back to see your mother. I wanted to tell her that now he's dead, maybe she and you can . . . put things right.' His eyes were filmed with tears, but his voice was its usual kindly self. 'So I went back to the shop.'

'And?' Lisa said.

He looked very unhappy.

'She was different. She wouldn't talk to me. A customer was there, she said, looking through things in the back shop. Maybe she thought I'd cause a fuss.' Jed looked down at his father's old green tweed suit, baggy around the knees and arms. 'But I only wanted to put things right for you.'

He took Lisa's chin between his fingers and turned her face towards him.

'Even if I have to go to prison, it'll only be for a few months. The police understand I was only trying to save the girl, and they think the judge will too. Everyone will understand. It's sorted, Lisa. Now the man who raped you is dead, you'll be safe for ever. If I have to go to prison for a while, Fred'll look after you.'

A sound had been insinuating itself into her brain, getting in the way of the words he was saying and the ones she wanted to throw at him.

'Is that a police siren?' she said.

'Not here.' Jed smiled at her. 'The only ones who've been here since I can remember are the lot who came when Tom thought the travellers had stolen his calves.'

'It *is* a siren,' Lisa said. 'They're coming here. Jed, I mean, why are they coming?'

His eyes changed, narrowing as though he was working something out, making difficult plans.

'It'll be easier for me if they don't find you here,' he said. 'I can cope if I'm on my own, but if they're coming to take me away, I don't want them to see you. If they do, they may think twice about how it was just chance that I was there on the Island when that man was raping someone else. They'll think what I did was premeditated, so I could be in real trouble.'

Lisa had never heard Jed so articulate, so confident.

'You go on home across the fields,' he added. 'I'll deal with them. Go on now.'

He smiled, the same trustworthy, trusting smile he'd offered when she'd woken to find him still in her bed that day.

'I love you,' he said. 'But go. Now. And don't look back.'

The body had been removed from the stockroom at the back of the boutique long before Karen arrived. Even the police tapes had been taken down. But Charlie had photographs for her, showing the scene as it had been before Major Crimes and the CSI had done their stuff.

Karen tried not to breathe too deeply, hoping she wouldn't get the smell of old dried blood too deeply into her brain again.

The concrete box of a room was grim and comfortless. A bare light bulb swung from the ceiling, throwing a cold, brutal light on everything else. A fire door was blocked by piles of boxes and a heap of neatly folded plastic. Blood was everywhere, sprayed in great arcs and pooling on the rough, untreated concrete floor.

Once she'd examined everything, Karen looked at Charlie's face and saw in it nothing but anger. What could be more appropriate?

What could more easily hide emotions he didn't want her to see?

At last, she took the photographs he was offering and looked down at the pitiless representations of Sally's dead body.

As Charlie had told her, the killer had used a scalpel again, first cutting Sally's throat, then ripping her clothes apart and slashing the body with deep diagonal cuts. Karen had never met Dr Franklin, and her death had been horrific enough, but she'd had coffee with Sally, sitting opposite her in all her over-emphatic, overweight physicality.

Looking at the photographs of her stiffening body, Karen found it impossible not to imagine how she'd suffered, how she must have felt, screaming for help, getting none, knowing there was no end to the pain except death.

'It's hard to be sure from this,' Karen said, with a reasonable degree of self-control, 'but are these cuts worse – more savage – than the ones in Sonia Franklin's body?'

He nodded, looking ill now as well as angry, which made Karen even more suspicious.

'Sally could be a right pain, you know,' he said, 'but I liked her.'

'I know you did,' Karen said, still not sure why.

'She deserved better than dying in a windowless shithole like this. Left like a heap of leaking blubber all night.'

'Has the lab produced the DNA results from the earlier scenes yet?' Karen said, wanting to get away from the personal as soon as possible.

'DNA's nothing to do with you.' Charlie sounded impatient, angry with Karen now instead of with Sally's nameless killer. 'You're here as a psychology expert. So do your job. What does the scene tell you?'

'Very little,' she said steadily. Was he doing this as a way of making certain Annie had left no behavioural clues? Annie would be experienced enough to ensure that she had left no physical or scientific evidence, but she might not have thought of the other kind.

'I'd have said it was likely to be the same person who killed Doctor Franklin,' Karen went on, clinging to professionalism because it was all she had now. 'Probably Tod as well. I don't know about Randall because you never showed me that scene. The m.o. here is exactly the same as in the Franklin case. Once again the victim wasn't afraid. She allowed herself to be alone with whoever killed her, and turned her back on him without trying to defend herself. She trusted him. Or her.'

Charlie nodded, with a quick decisive movement. Karen looked away, peering all round the room as though checking her first impressions.

'Once again there was no struggle,' she said. 'Sally wasn't afraid – or not until the very last moment. Were there any defence wounds on her hands or arms?'

'Nope.'

'So, whoever it was asked her to look through the clothes or something like that, crept up behind her as she was sorting through them and slit her throat from behind.'

'Exactly.' Charlie wiped his face with his hand again in a gesture that was coming to look horribly like Lady Macbeth's endless longing to wash the blood off her hands. 'Another reason why it can't be Boulting.'

'What do Major Crimes think?'

'They're interviewing him now.'

'Why?' Karen tried to make sense of the big, kindly – obviously innocent – man she'd met in the interview room at Charlie's nick. 'Have they got any evidence this time, or is he confessing again?'

'No confession this time. He's even asking for a brief.'

'So why have they got him back?'

'He's there on the CCTV going into the shop right after he was released on bail. The shop wasn't open, but he banged on the door. On the film, he looks violent. It wasn't just knocking. He really banged, with both hands, and Sally admitted him. He left ten minutes later. There's no sign on the film of her leaving at all. This morning she's found dead.'

'Oh, shit!' Karen's language always degenerated when she was under stress. Could she have got this all so wrong? Had Boulting outwitted her with his parade of slow decency? If he had, then all her fears about what Annie had been doing and Charlie helping her to hide could be binned.

'Charlie,' she said softly, 'if Major Crimes have evidence and a suspect, why am *I* here?'

'Worrying about whether you'll be paid or not?' His voice had taken on a nasty suspicious edge. Then he sagged a little and sounded less aggressive. 'You may not. Sorry. Look – it's all a bit personal.' He turned his head away.

She touched his shoulder, half-expecting him either to flinch or hit her. He did neither.

'I've been axed from the investigation,' he said. 'Officially told I'm in the way and causing trouble. But I can't just quit. Sally was a mate. I can't leave it to them.'

'You have to, Charlie.' Karen thought of DCI Kent and the official suspicions he'd passed on. Were they the reason Charlie had been pushed out? 'If it's gone that far, you must.'

'It's worse. Officially I'm on sick leave. I'm showing signs of stress, they say.' He laughed without humour. Then he looked at her for a second. 'I need you for that too.'

'What?' Karen felt as though she'd woken up in the middle of a motorway in a storm. 'What are you talking about?'

'I can't leave the Island till I know what's what, but I'll go nuts if I just hang out at home. Can I help at your chalet? Hack away at that jungle of a garden for you, maybe. You said it would need doing.'

'Charlie, you—'

'Don't,' he said, backing away. 'Don't go kind on me. I can't fucking cope with that. Let me clear the nettles out of your garden and I'll be fine.'

'If you want. Whatever. But it's a foul job, and you may be interrupted.'

'Who by?' Suspicion was bristling all over him.

'My mate Stella from the Architecture Department at the university. She's emailed me the best of the competition entries so far, and there's stuff she's got to check at the site itself.' Karen looked at her watch. 'I'm supposed to meet her there in an hour.'

'I'll drive you out. I don't want you running about the Island on your own.'

Karen stiffened. 'Why not?'

He looked at her as though weighing up how much she could take. 'There's a killer out there. You could be at risk.'

'Me? Why?'

'Because you know too much. That fire, Karen – it did start in the recycling. Which means you could've been the target, not James.'

'What?' It had been one thing for Dave to try to scare her into believing she could become one of Randall's victims, but this was different. Much more real.

'Someone who thinks you're on the right track could've followed you,' Charlie said, 'spotted all the inflammable paper and cardboard outside James's front door and seen an easy way to stop you finding out any more.'

Now's the time to ask the real questions, Karen thought with half her mind, while the other half was cowering at the idea of her narrow escape. He's opened up so much today, I have to try.

'Was Annie on the Island the day the fire broke out?' she said.

Charlie's face was bleak, and stubborn, but she could tell he understood exactly why she'd asked the question.

'I wish I knew,' he said.

The ramshackle wooden bungalow looked so unappealing in its gloomy setting that Karen thought Charlie would be better off anywhere else as he dealt with his fears and the humiliation of his suspension on sick leave. But now was not the time to say so.

She'd insisted on picking up a packet of PG Tips and a pint of milk on the way. She'd already had the electricity and water switched on and the accounts put in her name. While Charlie set about making two mugs of tea, Karen fired up her laptop so she could check out what Stella believed they should do with the chalet. If Charlie was going to start hacking at the garden, he ought to have some idea of the shape it was supposed to have in the end or else his work could land her with paying someone else to put it right. And she didn't have any spare money at all.

Karen had to fumble in her shoulder bag for the laptop's lead because the battery was so low. There was no Broadband or phone line here, but she'd already downloaded the email and now only needed to open it and the huge attachments that had come with it.

Stella's message, which Karen had already read, said:

Best of the five entries so far. We'll probably have to wait until
a few more come in, just in case there's something extraordi-
nary, but I don't myself see how anything could better this. It's
far more interesting than the other four, none of which seem
worth bothering you with because, although they're technically OK, they're pedestrian and derivative. This one's much
more original, fits the site beautifully, it's practical, likely to
get permission, shouldn't cost too much, and it's imaginative.
You and your brother may, of course, have other ideas. Let
me know if you want me to sound out the planning people and
so on.

If I were you, I'd take the screen tour first. Amazing what
computer graphics can do these days. It's almost photographic,
so you'll see exactly what you'd be getting if you went for this.
Click on the plans and elevations later because they're a bit
amateurish and won't tell you nearly so much. But she's done
a great job in the essentials, and I'd be happy to add the necessary technical input myself.

Incidentally, I was quite surprised to see it because after
I'd met her that day I looked up some of her paintings and
they're pretty enough but more greetings-card than art. I'll
paste in some of the websites below, so you can have a look
too.

Karen was much keener to see what the artist planned to do
for the chalet than what she painted, so she ignored the on-line
exhibition sites and opened the first of the attachments Stella had
forwarded.

Slowly the screen revealed an aerial view of an elongated oval
with a sharp tip at one end, bright clear green in the middle
of grey-brown leafless trees. At the broad end was a curl of a
structure with a roof that looked as though it must be sloping
rather than flat. At the other was a small pale strip, like a newly
designed punctuation mark.

A complicated sign invited Karen to click for a change of view and the graphic swung itself around so that she was looking at the curved structure from ground level, seeing a range of full-length windows, edged in silvery, unpainted timber. Clicking again, she watched the view swoop past the boundary of lawn and trees on round to an eye-shaped sculpture on a plain plinth. Both were made of unpolished white stone. In the centre of the eye, where the pupil should have been, was a circular hole, through which the sea showed, with two small white sails in the distance.

Clicking again, Karen was led back up the lawn and watched the two central windows part to allow her inside the main room. Its walls were plastered and painted a soft colour between dove grey and steel. Above it the ceiling soared into an asymmetric inverted v-shape, lined with the same silvery timber that edged the windows and provided the floor beneath some plain, beautiful rugs. The furniture was sparse and simple in line and colour: a pair of charcoal sofas, a few white Saarinen tulip chairs and a trestle table that looked as though it could serve for both eating and working, much as the ratty old table here in the kitchen-living room already had.

There were two bedrooms in the new plans, one on either side of the main room, each with its own small bathroom. On one side of the front door was a kitchen, mainly furnished with dull zinc-covered units, and on the other a study with a workmanlike desk carrying a desktop computer, printer and phone.

'Wow!' Karen said, looking up from the screen at the shabby reality that might one day be transformed into the elegant simplicity the unknown artist had designed for her.

Charlie had to see this, and not just to give him a guide for his gardening.

'Here's your tea.' He put one of the old cracked, stained mugs down beside Karen.

Her mind instantly replaced it with one of the austere matte porcelain ones she'd seen in Mollie's flat. Life in the transformed chalet unreeled in Karen's imagination, a life quite different from the playfulness she'd described to Will. This would be a scene of calm, quiet, scholarly productivity. With amazing coffee and Mozart pouring out from hidden speakers all over the house, she could work here and get to grips with all the big questions of how to be and think and engage and relate that were so difficult to answer in her ordinary life on the mainland.

'Look!' she said. 'What do you think, Charlie?'

'Seems OK to me,' he said, barely looking at the glory on the screen. 'D'you agree with your mate it could be a runner?'

'I think it's great,' she said, pushing the laptop round so that he could see its screen too. 'Click on those squares and you'll get the full picture. I'm going outside to see if I can imagine how it'll be if we do organize the site as she suggests.'

The air was distinctly cold on her face. Winter was coming and, with it, the prospect of Aidan's return to England for the first time in years. Karen wondered how he'd like the plans and what she'd do if he didn't. And how he'd get on with Will. And Charlie. And whether Boulting could really have killed Randall and Sally, and the others. And whether any of them, even Randall, had deserved to die. And whether his mother was right in her ideas about his need to punish the teenage girl who had humiliated him in his first attempt at a sexual relationship. And whether any of it was Karen's problem now that Randall was dead and she should have been concentrating on the other subjects of her Ministry of Justice project. And what she would do if Annie and Charlie . . .

'Looks a bit minimalist to me,' he said from behind her. 'But if you do go for it, you are definitely going to need the garden cleared. So can I spend my sick leave slashing and burning for you?'

Karen turned. 'If you really want. But aren't the isolation and gloominess here even more likely to drive you bonkers than hanging around at home waiting for news?'

He looked at her with hostility for a second, then, when she allowed herself a tentative smile, his full lips parted and he laughed, with a strained artificial note somewhere in the sound.

He sauntered towards her and slung an arm around her shoulders, kissing her ear. 'You know you need to lose the jargon. People like me don't understand tough professional shrinky terms like "bonkers".'

Karen withdrew, laughing to encourage him, then stumbled over a muddy tussock and had to use his shoulder to steady herself. She liked the sensation of him holding her up.

'Besides,' she said, trying to hide it, 'I think it would be much more use – to you as well as everyone else – if you spent your sick leave finding out more about Boulting.'

'Not my job.'

'Someone's got to do it,' Karen said.

'He's yelling for a brief. He'll have professional help now.'

'But you—'

'Oh, shut up, Karen. If Boulting came from the Island, I could maybe get in there. But he doesn't. I can't go digging around another force's area. In any case, I've been warned off the investigation.'

'Nothing to stop you being a tourist in a picturesque part of the West Country, sitting in the local pub and picking up gossip.' Karen was becoming more and more certain that Charlie's bosses could be right and he was under more stress than he could manage. In which case, he shouldn't be alone. This was as good a way as any of making sure of that for the rest of the day at least. And it would get him away from Annie and anything else she might be planning to do here on the Island.

Karen lightened her voice to add: 'I'm assuming it's picturesque, by the way, and that there is a pub. And that you know where he lives.'

'Farm on the edge of a village called Hoaxley, near Wells in Somerset. No idea what it looks like.'

'Aren't you curious?' Karen said. 'Here's this man who drops out of the sky into the middle of a longstanding and difficult case. Don't you want to know where he fits in? Why he came? Why he confessed? Who he's taking the rap for?'

'What's the fucking point?' Charlie said in a defeated, exhausted voice that screwed her anxiety even tighter.

'What about your search for the truth?' she said, trying to prick him into life again. 'You said you needed the truth. Don't let that go. It's part of who you are.'

He didn't move.

'Don't let the buggers do you over, Charlie. If you do, you'll be complicit in the cover-up, or whatever it is that's going on.'

'You don't understand.'

'I do,' Karen said, with passion. 'Believe me, I do. I understand all too well. And I know you need to go on fighting or you'll go down, Charlie. Now, think. What did Boulting do between his release on bail and his re-arrest for Sally's murder?'

Charlie didn't answer. Karen tried again. 'How long was he in her shop? *Could* he have killed her?'

'Yeah. Could've. But why? What's the connection between them?'

'Go to Hoaxley while he's being processed here and find out if he ever mentioned Sally or Randall or the Island. People in villages talk about each other all the time. If there is anything that links him to all this, someone will tell you. His arrest's probably the most exciting thing that's happened all year.'

Charlie scowled and said nothing.

'Come on!' Karen was almost shouting and saw him wince. She moderated her tone to add: 'Dig out your faith in yourself. We have to go to Somerset.'

'We?' His voice was a little brighter.

'Yes, "we",' she said. 'I'm coming too.'

Lisa sat on the river bank, ignoring the damp that was seeping through her jeans. She stared over the water towards Jed's carefully prepared fields and tried to press her mushy mind into deciding what to do next. Obviously her life here had to end, but she couldn't go without knowing that Jed was safe.

She wished she'd never taken the risk of going back to the Island, just to reclaim the sense of courage that acting the part of Lee Wills had given her. So stupid! So dangerous! Everything she'd done had been useless and it had led Jed into disaster.

Lisa was surrounded by the smell of burning. The surface of the river in front of her was pockmarked with dots of burned paper. Every scrap of evidence of Lee Wills's existence was disappearing into ash. Her solicitor had power of attorney, so he could pay all the taxes due on the money Lee's paintings had earned. And give any excess to charity. She didn't want it.

Randall was dead. There was justice of a kind in that, although not the lifeblood kind she'd wanted for so long. No judge would ever pronounce on his true guilt now.

Did it matter? After all, the whole world accepted that he was a rapist, that everything she and all the others said had happened was true.

Maybe it didn't matter. But his death hadn't brought her anything she'd wanted. And the cost of it had been awful.

She would never forget the sight of Jed's face as he'd forced her to run from his house before the police got there. He'd looked like he was in agony, as if someone was pulling him apart like that man in the myth who'd been ripped apart by four horses tied to his legs and arms.

Lisa had to face the fact that Jed would never have got involved without her. She was the one who'd tied the horses on.

Something brushed her hair. She put up a hand and found a piece of charred paper, a torn corner of newsprint from a review Anton had sent her of the first Lee Wills exhibition.

Power and anger combine in a work of ext

That was all that was left. She tore the scrap into even smaller pieces, then opened her hand to let the wind take them and fling them down on the surface of the river.

Her mother's death and her father's total disappearance lay over her like an iron blanket. The weight of it bent her head and shoulders right over her knees.

If Jed had been telling the truth, then her mother *had* understood. She had wanted to make it up, had wanted to be forgiven. And now she was slashed-up and dead. She'd died alone, cold, in pain and wanting to make it right with her daughter.

For only the second time since she'd run away from the Island, Lizzie allowed herself to cry.

Chapter 24

Tuesday, 21 October

'Whose is the car? Are we meeting someone else?'

The disembodied male voice floated towards them from the far side of the chalet. It had a strong Midlands accent. Karen didn't recognize it and looked questioningly at Charlie, who shrugged and shook his head.

'Not as far as I know,' said another voice, which she identified at once as her mother's at its airiest and most artificially cheerful. 'Did you tell anyone we'd be here?'

'Not me.'

'Well, we don't need to worry. It'll only be some local government official, inspecting the drains or foundations or something,' Dillie went on, sounding perky in the extreme. 'No one else'd have such a dreary little vehicle. But they won't get in our way. Come on in and see the place in all its full gruesomeness. Really it couldn't be better for our purposes. You'll see.'

Karen gestured to Charlie to stay where he was and herself walked round to the front of the chalet to see her mother, beautifully, if inappropriately, dressed in a black suit with a wide belt made of scarlet patent leather to match the soles of her vertiginously high Christian Louboutin shoes. She was smiling adoringly at a squat man in his late forties with a broad, good-humoured face. He was dressed in a rumpled grey suit and brown suede shoes. Behind them was a taxi, with the driver settling himself into his seat and shaking out a newspaper, as though he expected to be in for a long wait.

'Good heavens, Karen, darling,' Dillie said, flinging her arms wide in a gesture of extravagant affection. 'I didn't expect to see you here. It's not *your* ghastly suburban car, is it?'

'No, Dillie. It's not. What on earth are you doing here?'

'Darling! You must meet Derrick Parkin, who's come to us for a really stunning campaign for his whole new range of DIY tools and equipment. Derrick, this is my gorgeous daughter I was telling you about. Karen. She's a psychologist, mostly living on the mainland, but popping across at intervals to help transform this shit-heap into something we can all enjoy.'

He shook hands and smiled with an innocent pleasure that surprised Karen.

'Dillie didn't tell me you'd be here. What luck! I think it's a great idea. And she's right – you'll be a wonderful "face" for the campaign. I'm so pleased you've gone for it.'

Karen looked at her mother with deep suspicion. Dillie laughed musically.

'I was telling Derrick how *we're* planning to turn this into a luxury holiday home for *you*, darling,' she said with heavy emphasis, 'and he had the brilliant idea of letting us use all his products, so that—'

Karen grabbed her mother by the elbow, flashed a smile at Derrick and said, 'My mother and I just need to have a quick word. Won't be long. Please, have a look around – anywhere you like. We'll be back in a minute.'

She dragged her mother round to the back of the chalet, where Charlie was still sitting on the step, with his feet lost in the mess of nettles, ivy and brambles. He stood up, but Karen waved him off.

'No,' she said to her mother.

'But—'

'Listen to me,' Karen said, speaking very clearly. 'No. You have sold me this place. I have taken on a huge amount of debt I do not need, in order to get you out of a hole. Therefore this chalet is mine – and Aidan's – and it is *not* available for your business shenanigans. Go and tell that nice man that you made a mistake.'

'Darling, it's the opportunity of a lifetime. If I'd known we were going to pick him up as a client, I'd never have needed to flog you the hut in the first place, and all along I've been worrying about how I've put you in debt. So, you see, the least I can do is help you get it into decent shape for the smallest amount of money possible. Then you can sell it on, and reap a huge profit. And I won't feel guilty any more. It's not just the materials Derrick's going to offer you for free; he's going to provide labour too.' Dillie laughed again, the sound rising charmingly towards the greying sky.

'We will have to film you faking some of the work for the TV shows, but it'll only be a tiny proportion. Most of it will be done professionally by Derrick's team. And if this campaign goes global, *you*'ll be a star, and *we*'ll probably get the account for the whole of his group. It's not ICI exactly, but it's big enough.'

'No.'

'Karen.' Dillie's voice had changed into something steely. 'I *need* this account.'

'I have plans for the chalet's transformation and they do not include either DIY or being prostituted in some ad campaign of yours. That would hardly enhance my professional reputation, and it matters to me. I've worked bloody hard for it. Go and take him away.'

Dillie managed to make herself look as though she'd been stabbed. Karen, fighting hard against her natural instinct to help, reminded herself of all the times she had been in real need and Dillie had been too busy to listen. It didn't make any difference. She still felt guilty. Guilty, but determined.

'You are the most unnatural daughter, Karen.'

'That may be true. But the chalet is no longer under your control.'

'Karen, you have to—'

'Dillie.'

At the sound of Derrick's voice, she whirled round, her most charming smile forming on her reddened lips.

'Derrick. Come and look at the ghastly garden and let your imagination fly free. Just think what we can do with it, using your full range of faux-lead planters and that brilliant weatherproof plastic trellising you were telling me about. Isn't it *exciting*?'

'Dillie, I wasn't eavesdropping but you were both shouting. I heard everything. If I'd known your daughter wasn't happy with the plans, I'd never have let you bring me here.' He turned towards Karen, an expression of apology all over his crumpled face. 'I'm sorry. We'll be off now.'

'But Derrick!'

'Plenty of other semi-derelict properties on the mainland'll be far more accessible than this place. Come along, Dillie. There are things to discuss. And your daughter needs space.'

Dillie looked in the direction in which he was pointing and for the first time noticed Charlie, who waved. Then she glared over her shoulder at Karen again, with an expression that was easy to read in all its supercharged hostility: If you've lost me my latest account I will never forgive you.

Karen blew her a kiss.

'What was that all about?' Charlie said when Dillie had flounced away.

'My bloody mother hatching one of her specials. Don't ask. You *so* don't want to know. But she's gone now. I'm free.'

Karen thought about it for a moment, then realized that she really had got rid of something that had chained her to the past.

'Good. Did you mean it when you said you'd come to Somerset?' Charlie said.

'Of course. But I have to phone Stella quickly,' she said. 'Will you wait for me here, or drop me at Reception Point and wait for me to catch you up at the main road?'

'Reception Point?'

'Don't you remember?' Karen said, smiling at him as she understood the full measure of her new freedom. 'It's the bit about halfway up the lane, where you can get mobile reception again.'

'I'll drive you,' he said.

Charlie drove up the muddy lane so slowly Karen realized he didn't know where Reception Point was and expected her to make him pull up at no notice. After three turns in the lane, she said:

'It's about forty yards further up. There's a kind of lay-by. You can drop me there and carry on to the junction with the main road. There's room up there to wait. I'll find you when I've finished on the phone.'

'Sure?'

She nodded and got out of the car, knowing she didn't want him listening in to the call she had to make to Will. Not quite ready for it herself, she phoned Stella first to explain that she couldn't wait at the site any longer but would fix another date. Then she rang Max.

'Karen,' he said, sounding, as usual, as though someone was rattling gravel in a metal bucket. 'What's new? How're the men in your life?'

'I've got to be away this afternoon,' she said, without even thinking of answering his question, 'and I hoped you'd see Ian for me. I've a date to talk about his dissertation again, but I *have* to do this.'

'I've never heard you sound so emotional,' Max said. 'How interesting! OK. The deal is: if I see your masters student, you tell me all about it. OK?'

'Whatever.'

'Good. I'll leave a note on your door telling him to come to me. When will you be back?'

'Probably tonight. Maybe the morning. I'll phone you.'

'Good luck.'

She pressed in Will's number.

'This is Will Hawkins,' said his voice. 'I'm operating at the moment. Please leave me a message. If it's urgent, phone my secretary on . . .'

Karen didn't listen to the familiar number, concentrating instead on the surge of pleasure that rushed through her at the sound of his voice. With both of them working last weekend, she hadn't seen him for far too long. When the beep invited her to speak, she knew she would sound warm enough to reassure him.

'Will, it's me. Can you phone me when you've got time? I'll keep my mobile on. I miss you. Bye.'

Then she locked the keyboard and dropped the phone into her pocket, before setting off to trudge up the lane to the main road and Charlie.

Will phoned back an hour later, while she was in her flat, shoving some clean knickers and a T-shirt into her laptop bag in case she and Charlie had to stay the night in Somerset.

'Hi,' Will said. 'You recovered from the fire?'

'I'd almost forgotten it. How did the op go?'

'OK. I can't talk for long. Why did you ring? Is it urgent?'

'There's been another murder, which throws out all the earlier calculations.'

'How?'

'The police more or less decided Randall killed the policeman in Winchester and the doctor on the Island before grabbing another victim to rape, only to be killed himself by a good Samaritan, trying to protect her.'

'So I gathered from Max,' Will said crisply.

Karen had a moment's fury that the two of them kept in such close contact without involving her. Then she took herself to task. She didn't want anyone criticizing *her* friendships: that had to mean Will had every right to whatever mates he wanted.

'Now someone else has been killed in exactly the same way,' she went on aloud, 'so the police accept it can't have been Randall at all.'

'And . . . ?'

'They've fixed on the Good Samaritan – because he's available – but it's a nonsense. They're going to get into all sorts of trouble, and . . .' She tried not to hesitate on Charlie's name but couldn't help it.

'Trench,' Will supplied, sounding more or less relaxed.

'Exactly, Charlie wants to find out more about the Good Samaritan's background and wants me to sit in on the interviews to advise him on what questions to ask.'

'So? What's new? Why am I being treated to this bit of information?'

'Because the interviews will have to take place in Somerset.'

'So?' Will said again. 'It's hardly the Antipodes. Presumably it won't take much more than an hour or two to get there.'

'No, it won't.' Karen allowed herself to smile. Clearly all his suspicions were dealt with now. What a relief! 'But I didn't want to go without telling you.'

'You're not asking my permission, are you?' Will sounded almost as amused as Max would have been.

'I'm exercising my right to tell you – or not to tell you – where I'm going to be. That's all. OK?'

'Fine. And will you still be at home this weekend, if I appear on Saturday?'

'Absolutely.' She could feel her mind and her voice warming up at the prospect. 'It'll be heaven to see you, Will.'

'I'll bring breakfast.'

'I'll be waiting.'

'You'd better be.' Will laughed.

Karen managed to laugh too.

Her laptop bag bulged so much she couldn't stuff the black plastic teeth of one end of the buckle into the slot in the other. Sighing, well aware of Charlie sitting patiently in the car downstairs, she pulled out the scrumpled underwear and folded it more neatly.

The sight of the laptop reminded her of the competition entry and the need to get it across to Aidan before her mother started trying to entice him into her ghastly project with the DIY merchant.

Tugging the computer out of the bag, she fired it up and concentrated on sorting out her clothes and washbag while it went through all its time-consuming loading of the anti-virus software and inviting her to type in her password. Somewhere in her mind, she knew she was deliberately delaying the moment when she had to drive off with Charlie.

When at last her email inbox filled the screen, she clicked on Stella's email with the enormous attachments and forwarded it to Aidan with a quick email: 'Hi. Hope you like this as much as I do. Stella approves. If you hate it, let me know quickly.'

While it was going through, a car hooted below, three long angry blasts. Karen opened the sliding glass doors on to the balcony and craned over the steel-wire balustrade. She could see Charlie lounging against his car with an open newspaper in his hand, he and the car both looking like toys from this height.

Further down the road, another toy figure was leaning into his car. The hooting sounded again. Not Charlie. Good.

Karen turned back to the laptop and saw that both emails had cleared, so she quickly clicked on to Google and typed in *Lisa Raithe*. There were about one thousand entries, but she only needed the first. Clicking on that, she found a range of charming watercolours of a flat green landscape, punctuated by lines of pollarded willow trees, pools of water and small white farmhouses.

'Pretty but meaningless,' she muttered, clicking on to the bottom of the website in case there were any hidden surprises. 'Just like Stella said.'

Wave after wave of sunny, rainy, and snowy landscapes followed each other, charming, safe, unthreatening, unexciting. As Stella had warned Karen, the paintings gave no indication of the austere elegance of the artist's designs for the chalet.

Intrigued but not able to make herself waste any more time now, Karen shut down the system and put the laptop in its bag. Her knickers and shirt, now properly folded, slid neatly in on top of it. Her toothbrush went into one of the pen loops on the inside of the cover and all the rest went into her shoulder bag.

She locked the glass doors, flung a quick look around the flat, remembering James's panicky testing of all the plugs and switches. Seeing nothing wrong and no burners alight, she left, locking the door behind her.

As soon as they were free of Southampton, the traffic cleared and they roared up the A36 towards Frome almost unimpeded. Charlie's matronly car was not equipped with Sat Nav, which meant Karen had to sit with the map on her knee, following the junctions with her finger. She wasn't a bad mapreader, but she had a childish tendency to panic if she couldn't see where they were on the map. This way, she felt safely in control as they approached roundabout after roundabout in the gathering dusk.

In fact it was an easy route, and they bypassed most of the towns, skimming the edge of various estates of small boxy houses, and skirting Wells, the smallest city in the country. The cathedral's square stone tower was floodlit and raised to a modest height above the bowl effect created by the surrounding buildings.

Within a mile they had left all hints of suburbia behind and soon found the turning off the main road to Hoaxley and three other villages. Karen felt as though they were in a much older England. Charlie's headlights showed that all the fences had disappeared. Now the roads and fields were edged with straight, canal-like ditches, full of weedy water and huge birds. She'd never seen so many wild swans before, or so many stately grey-feathered herons, perching on the banks.

The road twisted and turned back on itself, revealing small farms and cottages and glimpses of a river, wider than the ditches but still on an almost nursery scale. Another signpost pointed the way to the village of Hoaxley and they turned right by a small row of pink and grey cottages.

The clouds drifted away from the moon, allowing enough of its light to show them eight poplar trees shading a clutch of cream-coloured farm buildings at the top of a small rise in the ground. They looked like something from a Dutch landscape painting, and to the right a wide expanse of absolutely flat land stretched to some far-off hills. Only the pylons and telegraph poles catching the moonlight defaced the scene.

'It's like the end of the world,' Karen said.

'I didn't see a pub, did you?' Charlie said, as they left the cottages behind and drove on with the river on their left, reflecting the thin grey light from the moon and stars.

'No. And we couldn't have missed it. Carry on. Some of these villages straggle on for miles. Yes, look – there are more houses up ahead.'

A pink building appeared on the left of the road, with neat hanging baskets overflowing with white flowers and silver-leaved plants. The flood-lit sign announced it as the Old Sheep's Head. Charlie swung left into the almost empty car park and they looked doubtfully at each other.

'I've never seen anything like it,' he said. 'Did you have any idea places like this still existed?'

'I've never thought about it,' Karen said. 'But if there is any information here about Gerald Boulting, someone in the pub will have it. This village is so small they must all practically live in each other's pockets. Come on. Let's see what we can get.'

She paused outside the green-painted door, pointing to the inscription that ran around the architrave: *Frederick Boulting: Licensed to sell by retail all intoxicating liquor for consumption on or off the premises.*

'Told you,' she said with glee. 'They're probably all related here.'

Chapter 25

Tuesday, 21 October, 6.35 p.m.

The man behind the bar was well over six foot tall, more or less bald, and looked as though he didn't stint on his food.

'Evening,' he said, beaming at them. 'What can I get you?'

'Glass of white wine for me,' Karen said, looking appreciatively from the deep leather sofa and chairs by the roaring fire to the well-stocked pristine bar. 'Charlie? Beer?'

'Why not? What have you got?'

'Bellringer Bitter from Abbey Ales in Bath, Theakston's Old Peculier – or there's cider. This is local.' He laid a hand on a tap. 'Or we've got bottles of Old Speckled Hen and Stella.'

'I'll try the Bellringer,' Charlie said. 'I've never come across it. Pint, please. You don't brew your own?'

'Nope. More than enough to do, with only a small staff, without that.'

'Nice pub.' Charlie took a good look round. 'Must be hard work. You been here long?'

'All my life in the village.' The barman put a large hand across the bar for Charlie to shake. 'Fred Boulting. I took over the pub nearly fifteen years back when my old man died and my brother got the farm. What brings you folk here?'

'We were in Wells, shopping, and felt a bit claustrophobic in amongst all those buildings. I don't suppose you get much passing trade,' Karen said, glad to find him so chatty. 'It must be beautiful round here in daylight, but it did feel like we were heading out into nowhere.'

Fred preened a little. 'You'd be surprised. In summer we're a bit of a destination, you know. In all the good pub guides.'

'Good for you,' Charlie said, settling himself more comfortably on his tall stool. 'D'you do food?'

'Sure.' The big man reached for a couple of leather-bound menus. 'We start serving at half-seven. All organic. OK for you?'

'Great. I was hearing about someone called Boulting, who grows organic veg. Any relation?'

Fred's professionally cheerful expression changed into an even wider beam. 'My big brother. Jed. Supplies most of my stuff and has a contract now for a restaurant in Wells to go with the box deliveries that are his bread and butter. He doesn't do any meat, so I get that from a farmer the other side of Glastonbury.'

'They were recommending his veg in Wells today. I'd love to meet him. Is he likely to be in tonight?' Karen said.

'He's not here just now.' Fred wasn't giving anything away. His voice didn't falter, nor did his smile. Either he didn't know Jed was with the police, or he was certain they'd have to let him go.

'That's sad,' Karen said. 'We'd hoped to meet him. Who's looking after the veg?'

Fred laughed easily. 'Sprouts aren't like livestock, you know; they can look after themselves for a day or two. He'll be back.'

'Maybe we could talk to his wife,' Karen suggested. 'We're looking for a supplier, you see.'

'He doesn't have a wife,' Fred said, twinkling. 'Yet. But from what I know of his girlfriend, I don't think it'll be long. In the meantime, he's left me in charge. I can deal with any enquiries. You looking for a quote for regular supply?'

'It's just for a one-off,' Karen said quickly, thinking on her feet and managing not to catch Charlie's sceptical eye. 'My mother's got a big birthday coming up. She's a veggie.'

'Sounds good, but you'd better wait for Jed for something like this. He'll be back any day now. Leave me a phone number or an email address and I'll get him to give you a call.'

Karen wrote a random name and imaginary phone number on a scrap of paper and handed it across the bar.

'His girlfriend might have some good ideas,' she said. 'Is she local?'

'Lives a few doors down. She'll probably be in later – comes most evenings – but I shouldn't think she'd be able to help you over the veg. She's an artist.' Fred waved towards the dining part of the pub, where a dozen or more tables had been laid with white paper cloths and stainless-steel cutlery. The walls were covered from waist height to the ceiling with framed pictures.

Karen slid off her stool. Carrying her glass, she wandered down the long room, past the roaring fire, towards the tables, just as Charlie's phone began to ring.

'Sorry,' he muttered, walking off in the opposite direction.

Karen stood in front of a large oil painting of the river with a willow that had been left unpollarded, to sweep down over the water. A pair of swans emerged from under its curtain of leaves on the far side. In spite of the different medium, this was so like the watercolours she'd seen on her screen only this afternoon she didn't think she needed a signature to identify it. But there were pearly letters in the bottom right-hand corner to give her confir-mation that it was one of Lisa Raithe's.

Karen felt a hand on her shoulder and turned to see Charlie, his dark face scrunched in a grimace of pain.

'What?' she said, distracted even from this.

'The DNA results are back. That was Eve. She "forgot" to tell me earlier. The vomit behind the pub . . .' He rubbed his eyes. 'It's Lizzie's.'

'Oh shit! D'you think she's been there on the Island all along?' Karen said, just as Fred called down from behind the bar.

'What d'you think of them? Great, aren't they?' he said. 'They're all for sale. I've got a price list. She wrote it out for me when she came round to hang them all. Here you are.'

Karen walked down the long room, forcing her reluctant muscles to move, and took the list from him. Studying it for a moment, she felt as though someone had opened heavy doors in her mind, allowing light and air to flood in at last.

'What?' Charlie said sharply.

Karen took his arm and pulled him away from the bar. 'Come and look at these paintings.'

'What're you doing? Didn't you hear what I told you? Lizzie *must* have killed Randall.'

'Maybe. Maybe not. She painted these.' Karen gestured to the pretty watercolours. 'She's Jed Boulting's girlfriend.'

Charlie stared at her. 'How the fuck do you know?'

'Because this is her handwriting.' Karen gave him the price list.

'I never saw Lizzie's writing. How do you know it's hers?'

'James has a note from her, tucked into a portrait sketch she did of him. It's identical. You wanted to know who could be pulling Boulting's strings . . .' Karen allowed her voice to dwindle. Charlie didn't need to have everything spelled out.

He wheeled round and strode back to the bar.

'You must see a lot of the painter,' he said to the gabby man behind it.

'Fair amount. Why?'

'Where was she the day before yesterday?' Charlie's voice was so tight with anxiety and frustration that Karen knew he wanted to bang the bartender's head on his own bar to make him hurry up.

Fred nodded his gleaming head. 'Working, all day. Saw her myself. Got a call from my brother midday-ish, asking me to look in and make sure she was OK, so I went by boat, along the river. Didn't want to disturb her by banging on her door if she was busy, which she was. You can see right into the studio from the water.'

'And you actually saw her, did you?' Charlie said, catching Karen's eye.

Now he had a disappointed expression in his own eyes, which she had no trouble interpreting: if the artist had been here in the village all of the day before yesterday, the day when Sally had been murdered, then either she was not Lizzie, or Lizzie was not the killer they were chasing.

'Large as life. Her studio's got one big window overlooking the river. You can't miss seeing the whole room from a boat. I wasn't the only one watching her either. There was a short-arse in a hat and sunglasses on the river too, hanging about half under a willow.'

'Do you like her?' Karen asked, ignoring the news of the short arse because it didn't seem important.

'What kind of question is that?' Fred said, looking insulted.

'Lots of people don't like their brother's girlfriend. Is she good for him?'

Fred pulled himself a half-pint, then left it on the bar to settle. 'I'd say so. He was lonely till they got together. Married for ten years to a bitch. Lisa's much better for him. Do anything for her, he would.'

Karen and Charlie exchanged glances, both of them thinking, Did he kill for her or just take the blame for the murders he knew she'd committed and then kill someone else while she was well away from the scene and so couldn't be implicated?

'So she lives in the village, does she?' Charlie said aloud. He drained his pint, before adding, 'Nearby?'

'Like I said, a few doors past the village hall. Little white house called Apple Tree Cottage. Usually drops in about seven, after she's finished working. But you don't need her. If you want to buy one of her things, you can do it through me. She trusts me; that's why she left me the price list. I sold one only half an hour ago.'

'I'm sure she trusts you,' Karen said, handing it back to him. 'Even so, I'd love to meet her – but we can't just walk in on her. Have you got a phone number?'

Fred looked at her for a few moments, as though to check her sincerity, then shrugged and scribbled a number on a piece of paper.

'Thanks.' Karen reached into her bag for her phone and had the usual fumble before she could find it.

Pulling it out, she was surprised to find it switched off and stared down at the small blank screen, as though it had deliberately thwarted her. She never turned it off. When she pressed the on button, all ready to enter her pin, she saw a completely unfamiliar screen-saving picture on it and no demand for a pin at all.

'This isn't mine,' she said to Charlie, just as her own familiar ring tone sounded from the depths of her bag. 'Oh, shit! I've picked up someone else's phone.'

Powering through her memories of the last few days to work out when it could have happened, she thought of the fire, and the way she'd been surprised to see what she'd thought was her phone under her bag on James's sofa. This must be his. How inconvenient that they had exactly the same make and model. He must be cursing the loss of his phone.

Embarrassed to have made such a stupid mistake, but curious too, she couldn't stop herself clicking on his messages and saw a stream of texts from 'Sally'. There were none from anyone else. She clicked into 'contacts' and found only Sally's number. Pressing 'call records' and 'missed calls', again she saw only Sally's number. James must know some other people; had he kept a special phone for dealing with her so that she wouldn't interfere with his real life?

In his place, Karen might well have been tempted to do just that, but it didn't fit with the saintly gentle man who would drop everything to run to help Sally whenever she called for him.

Karen thought back to the few times she'd met him and began to see how neatly he'd presented himself as the worried unthreatening protector of both Sally and her daughter. The more Karen looked at the idea, the odder it seemed. Charlie's surprising tolerance of Sally's dramatics had been more or less explained by Annie's account of his childhood experiences. But if the doctor had needed to protect himself against Sally's demands by keeping a separate phone solely for her calls, why had he allowed himself to stay so close? Lizzie had been a patient of his nearly five years ago. He must have had hundreds of others during those years.

Why was he still involved?

Karen looked at Charlie as the answer appeared in her mind, as though one of her students had chalked it up in red letters ten feet high. She grabbed his arm and dragged him out of the pub into the empty road outside.

'It's not Lizzie,' she said. 'Or Jed Boulting. Or Annie. *It's James.*'

Lisa stepped back from her sketch of Jed. Drawing him would have been much easier if he'd been sitting in front of her. Everything would have been easier if he'd been sitting in front of her, instead of in some police station somewhere miles away.

Nothing in the face she'd recreated on the thick drawing paper had anything in it of violence or even anger. However she'd drawn him, she couldn't find them anywhere. But if it hadn't been him, then who *had* killed her mother?

She thought of Jed's spare bed, covered with newspaper cuttings of her case and those of Randall's other victims.

Of them all, she was the only one who'd lived on the Island, the only one to have encountered DS Williams or Dr Franklin, the consultant, and she was the only one to have Sally as a mother. She was the only link between all the dead and Randall.

She knew she hadn't killed them. If Jed hadn't either, then who had?

Her pay-as-you-go phone rang.

'Lisa Raithe,' she said into it.

'Oh, Lizzie. You sound exactly the same,' said a gentle voice that seemed familiar but which she could not place. 'Thank God I've found you.'

'What the hell d'you mean – *James*, Karen?' Charlie's voice was urgent, making him sound much more like his usual self than he had this afternoon.

She managed to smile at him, even as she came to terms with the enormity of what she was just beginning to understand.

'Listen, Charlie. Please.'

'I'm listening,' he said grimly. 'Convince me.'

'We know Lizzie's the link to all the murders, don't we?' she began.

'I'll give you that.'

'But we now know – from what the landlord's just told us – that it can't be Lizzie herself who's been doing all the killing because she was here when Sally's throat was cut. OK?'

'Yeah. Right.'

'So it's either someone who's so angry with what Lizzie suffered that he's determined to punish everyone involved,' Karen said, 'or . . .'

'Like Jed, who we now know is her boyfriend.' Charlie had never minded interrupting her. 'And who actually confessed to Gyre's murder.'

'Except that both you and I doubt that Jed ever killed anyone.' Karen thought of all the murderers she'd encountered and knew how hard it would have been to guess what they'd done if she hadn't been told. Even so, she was still fairly sure of Jed's innocence.

'He lied, though, didn't he?' Charlie said. 'He said he'd never heard of Randall and was just passing the pub's alley when he heard Bella scream. But if he's Lizzie boyfriend, he must've known. Why did he lie if he's *not* guilty?'

Karen paused again. 'He must have thought she'd done it. We always suspected he could've been taking the rap to protect someone else. Yes, that must be it. He thought Lizzie was guilty so he came to confess, which explains why he knew nothing about the surgical gloves.'

'But why James? Why not her longlost father? I've wondered about him all along.'

This was an idea Karen hadn't considered. She looked down at the phone in her hand, then up again at Charlie's frowning face.

'OK, but I'm sure it's James.'

'Why the fuck?' Charlie looked as though he hated her.

Karen tried not to mind and held out the phone, explaining how she'd picked it up in James's flat, assuming it was hers, and adding, 'There's nothing on it from or to or about anyone except Sally. James kept it just for her. And look at these recent texts from her, which he never got because I'd grabbed the phone.' Karen handed it to Charlie, who read them out aloud:

Where are you, J? Y Rnt U talking 2 me? S

J. I need 2 C U. S

I'm afraid. I need U. S

J. I cant wait any more. I need U. I'm coming to the hosp. S.

Charlie's voice stopped. He stared down at the tiny screen for a moment longer, than looked up at Karen.

'But why would *he* kill Sally? He cared about her.'

A huge black crow flew just in front of Karen's face, making her flinch.

'He felt responsible for a lot of Lizzie's suffering,' she said, staring after it as it surged upwards again and disappeared. 'He thinks he should have diagnosed the septicaemia more quickly and he's been tormenting himself with guilt.'

'So? That doesn't explain it all.'

'It *does*.' Karen's voice was getting higher with the frustration of not being able to make Charlie believe her. 'He knew all about the deaths of your two delinquent cops. I think when he first heard about that, he had a deep sensation of release from his guilt.'

'*What?*'

'Think about it. He could tell himself that what they'd done to Lizzie was even worse than what he'd done, and now they'd been punished, so he could let himself off.'

Charlie shrugged and turned away as though he couldn't bear to interact with her any longer. But Karen wasn't going to let him ignore her.

'That kind of neurotic guilt doesn't go away, Charlie.' He looked back, but he wasn't remotely receptive. Karen ploughed on: 'I think it got worse and worse for James. The more he thought about his guilt and tried to get rid of it, the more deeply engrained it became. And there was no more release. So eventually he set about killing someone else who'd damaged her.'

'You mean Tod? Because he pushed his first questions when Lizzie was too weak to resist? Come off it, Karen. This is nuts.'

'I don't think so. I think it works. It explains everything, even the shortening intervals between the deaths. And the increasing violence. He's like an addict, needing a bigger and bigger fix at shorter and shorter intervals.'

'Bollocks. But even if you're right, why would James have waited so long to start killing?'

Karen repeated what she'd already said to James himself. 'Randall's release must have been the trigger.'

'I don't buy it. What about the fire at James's flat? Even if you *were* the intended target . . .' Charlie broke off. 'You're about to tell me he did it as a way of making you see him as a victim just in case you'd guessed the truth, aren't you?'

Karen nodded. At last he was beginning to see sense. 'The recycling bags were just outside the front door. He fiddled about for ages after he'd sent me into his sitting room. I think he was setting fire to the bag then, knowing perfectly well how to get out of the flat, and only acted being terrified and clumsy with the keys once we'd both smelled the smoke.'

'You're mad. Why Sally? He always took care of her.'

'Look at the texts,' Karen said. 'Each one sounds more desperate than the last. Then she threatens to turn up at the hospital. He never got the text because I had his phone, so she probably did turn up. She'd have made a scene. You know that.'

Charlie offered a grudging nod.

'Suddenly she was becoming a threat,' Karen went on, seeing that he was almost ready to believe her. 'And she hurt Lizzie, too. Remember what you told me about how the CCTV of her snuggling up to Randall made the jury refuse to believe he'd raped Lizzie?'

'Who is this?' Lizzie said into the phone.

'Don't you recognize *my* voice? Look out of your studio window and you'll see me. I'm in your orchard. I've been looking for you for so long. Come on out, Lizzie. We need to talk. Terrible things have been happening, but I can help you if you'll trust me now, as you did four years ago.'

She walked to the window and peered out, cupping her hands around her face to shut out the studio's light. A tall thin man was standing in the orchard, on the far side of her rickety bridge, waving to her. There was more than enough moonlight for her to recognize him easily.

'Doctor Fullwell,' she said into the phone, smiling. Maybe *he* could tell her where her dad was now. 'How did you find me?'

'James, Lizzie. Call me James like you did before. It's a long story. Can I come across and tell you all about it?'

'Like I once said.' Charlie's voice was harshly mocking now as he glared at Karen. 'I'd love to be an "expert". You can make it all up, manipulate every bit of evidence into a shape to suit your theory, and never have to justify any of it.'

Karen barely noticed his tone, and certainly didn't care about it, because she had to make him see what she saw.

'He'll come to hate Lizzie herself for putting him through all this. In the end he'll blame her for all of it – including the killings he's committed,' she said. 'And he'll go on needing his fix. So he'll twist it all round and tell himself the only way he'll ever manage to stop feeling guilty is if Lizzie herself is dead. She's going to be in real danger. Maybe even—'

Karen suddenly swung round to look back at the pub.

'Wait here,' she said to Charlie, running back in.

The publican grinned at her. Karen didn't waste time smiling back at him.

'You said you've just sold one of the paintings,' she gasped. 'Did the buyer ask where your brother's girlfriend lives?'

'Yeah, he did. Why?'

'What did he look like?' Karen said urgently.

'Tall bloke. Young. Thin and twitchy. Short brown hair, flaky skin.'

'When was he here?'

'Few minutes before you arrived. Quarter of an hour. No more.'

'Did he leave a cheque?' Karen asked, longing for the certainty of a signature on a piece of paper.

'No. Paid cash. I was surprised. Couple of hundred quid. Who carries that much? But I was pleased for her. No tax.' Fred winked.

Karen didn't wait any longer.

Lisa stepped on to the swaying bridge, looking across it into the orchard, where James stood, a half-eaten apple in his hand. In the thin, cool light, she could see he hadn't changed a scrap in four years. He was still thin as a rake and gentle-looking.

'How did you find me?' she said. 'And why?'

'Like I said, I've been looking for you for the last four years. I've been so afraid for you.' He smiled and kindness blazed from his eyes. 'It's wonderful to know you're safe and in such a lovely place as this. If only your poor mother could've seen it too. She lived in agony, you know, worrying about what could be happening to you.'

Lisa said nothing. She was fighting an absurd terror, which must have come from the way her mind linked him to the old days of pain and horror in hospital. He smiled at her again, even more kindly, and held out his right hand with a half-eaten dark-red apple in it.

'I raided your tree – hope you don't mind.'

'Of course not. Help yourself. There are more than I can ever eat myself.' Lisa took a step back and watched him take one pace forwards, as though they were tied together. '*How* did you find me?'

'I heard about the man who confessed to killing your rapist. I knew he couldn't have done it, so I realized he just might lead me to you.' James's smile shrank a little. 'I got his name and Googled him, saw he had a website for his veg, saw the illustrations you'd drawn for it, made a few enquiries and . . . and, well, here I am, Lizzie. It'll all come right now.'

'But—'

'I've been watching while you worked. At first I wasn't sure. You're so thin, Lizzie, and you've cut off all your lovely hair. But the way you walk is the same, and lick your lips and scratch your nose.'

Lisa felt as though insects were crawling all over her body and through her hair.

Karen and Charlie were running along the narrow road beyond the pub. The evening air smelled very sweet, and there was only the faintest breeze to make the trailing branches of the willows whisper against each other.

'I don't know why we're doing this,' he said, barely out of breath, even though Karen was already panting. He stopped.

Karen grabbed his hand and tried to pull him on.

'Lizzie's in danger,' she said. 'Come on!'

'No. Either we need back-up, or we're going to go crashing in there to find she's entertaining an eager fan. If she makes an official complaint I'll be—'

'Oh, for Christ's sake, Charlie!' Karen wrenched her own phone out of her bag, wheeled through the stored numbers and phoned the number for James's hospital on the Island.

'Hi,' she said, as soon as the call was answered. Her panting was going to help now. 'I need to talk to Doctor James Fullwell. It's an emergency. I must talk to him.'

She put the phone on speaker so Charlie could hear the pause, and then the reply: 'I'm sorry, but Doctor Fullwell's away on leave just now. What kind of emergency?'

'Don't worry,' Karen said. 'I'll try my GP.'

Charlie still didn't look convinced but he was already running on down the road. Karen caught him up and felt the taut strength of Charlie's hand under her arm. They ran side by side round a willow-shaded curve in the road until Karen saw a huge Rottweiler standing in the middle of the pot-holed tarmac, growling deep in its throat.

'Shit!' she said, a lifetime's terror of large strange black dogs making her afraid she was going to throw up.

'Keep calm,' Charlie said. 'And don't move. I'll deal with this.'

'But *why* did you want to find me?' Lizzie asked.

'Someone had to tell you that your mother's dead.' James's voice was gentle, but his eyes were hard and glittering. 'You need to know that she's not suffering any more. It was a mercy really. You see, it's over for her. She died thinking of you. The last thing she said was your name.'

Lizzie knew now what he was telling her. All her old rage and resentment at her mother had gone. If this man had heard the last thing Sally had said, then he had killed her.

The two of them were alone together. He was nearly twice

her size. There was no help any nearer than Fred in the pub and he'd never get here in time, even if she had some way of calling him.

James threw the apple core into the river and slipped his right hand into his pocket. Lizzie stepped even further backwards on the bridge, so that she was almost in the garden again. She could feel the trailing branches of the willow brushing her shoulder as she forced her freezing mind to think of every possible weapon that might be within reach.

In the studio she, too, had scalpels and knives of all sorts. Matches as well. Out here there were great chunks of old paving stones, but she could hardly lift them with both hands and he'd never give her time to get one and smash him down with it.

'And the others?' she said, proud of the way she kept her voice firm.

'Others?' he said in a completely new voice as he stepped towards her.

She felt the boards of the bridge's surface bounce under his step. Despite its flimsy rope sides, the bridge's main structure took the weight of the big mower she used to keep the orchard grass under control. There was no hope of its breaking under the load of James's narrow body.

'Yes,' she said, now standing her ground. She'd survived Randall: somehow she would survive this too. She *would*. 'Someone killed Randall, and that boss of yours, Doctor Franklin. You always hated her, didn't you?'

If she could keep him talking, then maybe – just maybe – someone would pass by and see she needed help.

James laughed. Now there was nothing gentle in any sound he made.

'You saw that, did you? Even when you were so ill yourself. Yes, I hated the fucking bitch! She was a bully, who loved humiliating her house officers. Whenever she made mistakes, she blamed us. She worked us nearly to death. Then shifted the blame on to us.'

'So you enjoyed killing her,' Lizzie said, more and more frightened but still determined to keep him talking.

There was very little to choose between this man, whom she'd always thought of as her greatest support, and Randall himself.

'I loved it,' he said, with a broad smile. 'Every time I put the knife in her I remembered something she'd said to me, something she'd done, and I tugged harder as I made the slashes in her flesh.'

He laughed, and Lizzie's skin tightened all over her body.

'You'd have loved it too, Lizzie,' he added. 'You nearly died because of her. She deserved everything I did for that alone.'

'And my poor mother? What did *she* do to deserve her death?'

James took another step. The bridge shuddered, as though he was ten times heavier than his real weight. A sharp wind sent all the willows thrashing about. And a clutch of moorhens scuttled along the surface of the water. It was as though the whole of nature knew what James was and found it as terrifying as Lizzie did.

Now she longed for her mystery stalker in his long grey canoe to appear. But today there was no sign of him.

'What did my mother do to you, James?' she said.

'Screwed your chance of seeing Randall convicted of rape,' he said in a bland, matter-of-fact voice that was almost creepier than his laughing. 'Quite apart from humiliating you, driving your father away, ruining your childhood, and making everyone laugh at you. I knew you'd find it easier to come home if she was dead,' he said, then added in a surprised kind of voice: 'And she kept coming to the hospital demanding to see me. People were beginning to talk. She had to go.'

'But—'

'And all the time you've been sitting pretty here, happy, rich, and loved.'

'You sound as if that makes you angry,' Lizzie said, clinging on to the idea that she might survive because not to hope would be to give in to him. She couldn't do that. 'Why?'

'I've been in hell, worrying about you. Just like your Jed's in hell now. He must love you very much, Lizzie, to give himself over to the police for you. That is what he's doing, isn't it?'

She thought of Jed, gallantly trying to take the blame because, having followed her to the Island and to the pub, he then later heard about Randall's murder there and thought she must have killed him herself.

'I think so. But don't you see what that means, James?'

'No.' He came closer, his right hand dangling behind his back so she couldn't see what he was holding.

'It means you can run away now, make a new life for yourself with a new name. It can be done. I know, as I did it myself. If you stop this insane killing now, you can go and be safe.'

He laughed. 'Oh, Lizzie. I'll be safe anyway.'

Karen fought the trembling she knew would only excite the dog, but she couldn't suppress a gasp as Charlie strolled forwards, ignoring the rising sound of the growls. Only a couple of feet in front of the Rottweiler, Charlie dropped slowly on to one knee and opened his arms, saying, 'Oh, puppy!' in the sweetest, friendliest, most cheerful voice Karen had ever heard from him.

She held her breath. The great brown and black animal stopped growling, stepped forwards into Charlie's embrace and allowed himself to be hugged.

Karen began to breathe again. 'Now what?' she said quite quietly.

'Hold him by his collar,' Charlie said. 'And don't let go. While I find Lizzie.'

'I'll go,' Karen said, already running past them both. She'd rather face any kind of murderer than stay with an unmuzzled, untethered dog like that.

'Karen!' Charlie's voice was urgent but she didn't look back.

*   *   *

Lizzie held James's gaze as he came towards her. She remembered the long hooked stick she used to fish rubbish out of the river. It was lying along the edge of the grass to the right of the bridge. Could she get to it in time?

A large dog started barking loudly somewhere behind her. She saw James's eyes flicker in the direction of the noise, bent double and ran under the tree for the rubbish pole, bringing it up in a great swinging arc that ripped through the rotten rope that had formed the bridge's only balustrade and crashed into the side of his knee. As he staggered and tripped over the tattered ropes into the shallow water, she saw something shiny falling from his hand. She straightened the pole, holding it above her head, like a trident. Smashing it down, she pinned him against the weedy, muddy bank, knowing she wouldn't be able to hold him there for long.

Behind her came the sound of running footsteps. James called out for help. Turning her head, Lizzie saw a woman racing towards her, long blonde hair flying in the wind. Behind her was a dark-haired man, running clumsily with his hand hooked in the collar of Tom's Rottweiler.

'I can't hold him,' Lizzie shouted over her shoulder.

'Get out of the way, Karen,' the dark-haired man yelled. 'Take the dog, Lizzie.'

She grabbed the collar from him, barely recognizing one of the police officers from the Island and watched him rush down the six stone steps that led into the river. As he slammed a punch into the side of James's face, the nose of the long grey canoe shot forwards from downriver.

The canoeist shouted, 'Lizzie! Are you all right? Lizzie. *Lizzie!* Where are you? Are you OK?' He grabbed one of the posts near the steps and fought his way out of the plastic canoe, took one look at her gaping at him and pulled off his glasses. She saw her father. He chucked the glasses on the bank and joined in the fight.

Moments later, all three men clambered up the steps, trailing weed, pulling gouts of mud off their skin. James stood still between the other two. His face was badly bruised and blood was pouring from a cut under one eye. His clothes were soaked. He looked shocked and scared. But Lizzie couldn't think about him now. There were other people here, far more important.

'Dad?' she said, still clinging to Tom's Rottweiler. '*Dad? You* were my stalker?'

He came towards her, bedraggled and stinking of river water.

'I couldn't think of any other way,' he said. 'I knew you didn't want me here, but I had to know you were OK.'

'But how? I mean, where . . .?'

'I've been working in Wells, keeping my head down, watching over you, making sure you were safe, that your Jed wasn't hurting you.'

Her knees gave way and she sagged onto the grass. Tom's dog was bored and pulled away, lolloping off across the grass, uninterested in any of them. Lizzie saw her father come towards her and felt his arms pulling her up. A second later, she was leaning against his chest, feeling his heart banging beneath her, while his arms tightened around her back.

Vaguely, in the distance, she heard a crisp female voice saying, 'That was brilliant, Charlie. I'm sorry about the dog. Do you want me to phone someone to take over?'

'Major Crimes on the Island,' he said. 'I can't let go of this scrote. The number's in my phone. Press nine. Then hold the phone up so I can speak.'

Postscript

Karen woke to a smell of coffee, mushrooms and bacon. Will must have let himself in and be cooking breakfast.

The only sounds she could hear were faint clatterings from the kitchen, far-off traffic noise and the scream of the gulls outside. She stretched her legs under the weight of the duvet, enjoying the warmth of the sunlight that lay across her face and the satisfaction that flooded through her mind as she thought of everything she and Charlie had achieved. Her happiness was tempered only by the knowledge that she'd been such a coward when faced with the Rottweiler. Balancing that was the memory of Lizzie leaning against her father, neither of them speaking at all, just holding each other. Karen didn't think she'd ever forget the sight.

The sharp sound of her phone ringing cut through the slow easy warmth that surrounded her, and she stretched out a hand to pick it up.

'Hello?' she said, before licking her dry lips.

'Karen? Charlie here. You recovered yet?'

She laughed. 'More than. But, not having fought anybody, I didn't have any cuts and bruises. What about you?'

'I'm good. Specially now that we've had the lab results back. James left DNA at all the murder scenes. We've got him, Karen. Well done! You will give evidence at the trial, won't you?'

'If I'm asked.' She saw her bedroom door opening and had a wide, wide smile ready for Will.

He looked so like himself, so tidy and clean and controlled and gorgeous that she used her free hand to fling back his side of the duvet and pat the mattress to encourage him to join her.

When he'd put the heavy tray neatly on the chest of drawers between the windows, he slipped off his loafers and stretched himself out on the bed beside her, taking her free hand in his and kissing her, in spite of the phone.

'Sorry, Charlie,' she said, having kissed Will back. 'What was that?'

'I just said "you will be asked",' he said. 'Have you got Will with you?'

'I have.' She rolled her head on the pillow to smile at Will again.

'If that's Charlie Trench,' he said cheerfully, 'ask him to join us for lunch here. Max'll be riveted to meet him and I haven't seen him for ages.'

Karen kissed Will's chin, then repeated the invitation into the phone.

'I heard,' Charlie said. 'But I've got Annie with me.'

'Bring her, too. That way we can all fill each other in.'

'Great. OK. One o'clock?'

'See you both then.'

Will had got off the bed again while she was talking and now brought the laden tray back. Karen saw he'd even laid her post between the cups and the coffee pot.

She reached for them and saw an official-looking envelope on top, with the Ministry of Justice logo on it. The sight of it drove a sudden chill into her mind. But she couldn't be a coward over something like this as well as facing the Rottweiler, so she grabbed the envelope and ripped it open. Inside was a short letter from Al.

Dear Karen,

I promised to keep you up to date with news of John Clarence. You ought to know that three days ago he killed himself. His body was found hanging in his flat. There's a note, blaming no one. It's quite clear he couldn't live with the memory of what he'd done.

So you were right. He was never going to attack anyone else. Congratulations.

Good luck with your remaining subjects. We look forward to the report next March.

Karen folded the single sheet of paper and put it back on the tray.

'What?' said Will.

'Today's not going to be quite such a celebration, after all,' she said, handing him the note.

He read it, then looked up.

'So you were right,' he said. 'You should be pleased.'

'Being right isn't enough.'